# SUNFALL

www.penguin.co.uk

# SUNFALL

## JIM AL-KHALILI

BANTAM PRESS

TRANSWORLD PUBLISHERS
61–63 Uxbridge Road, London W5 5SA
www.penguin.co.uk

Transworld is part of the Penguin Random House group of companies
whose addresses can be found at global.penguinrandomhouse.com

Penguin
Random House
UK

First published in Great Britain in 2019 by Bantam Press
an imprint of Transworld Publishers

A CIP catalogue record for this book
is available from the British Library.

ISBNs 9780593077429 (cased)
9780593077436 (tpb)

Typeset in 11.25/13.25pt Sabon by Jouve (UK), Milton Keynes.
Printed and bound in Great Britain by Clays Ltd, Elcograf S.p.A.

Penguin Random House is committed to a sustainable
future for our business, our readers and our planet. This book
is made from Forest Stewardship Council® certified paper.

To Julie

# Prologue

*40,000 BC – Neander Valley, east of modern-day Düsseldorf, Germany*

HE HAD BEEN STARING OUT AT THE RAGING STORM FOR DAYS, *hungrier than he could ever remember. The limestone cave was still warm thanks to the fire he had started as soon as he'd regained enough strength to collect wood. The flames were weaker now and his stockpile had run out. His skills with fire had always been a source of great pride, both for him and his mate. Now, his cave, his sanctuary, was also his prison.*

*He knew, with a deep and intuitive certainty, that he was the last of his kind. It made him sad. And angry. He stood at the cave entrance, his furs wrapped tightly around his shoulders, and screamed in defiant rage at the world outside as though he could drown out the howling wind.*

*During the night of the last full moon his mate had been angry that he was too sick to go out with the other hunters to find food, so she had gone instead. She hadn't come back. When he had eventually grown strong enough to leave the cave he had gone looking for her. He hadn't found her, but had instead stumbled across the bodies of several others of his tribe – not just the hunters, but their mates and a few of the young. They had been half-buried in the snow where the gorge opened into the wide river valley and he had puzzled over what had befallen them. Many of his people had already died, either from hunger or cold during the previous harsh winter – their already low numbers dwindling steadily as the winters became worse and powerful storms ravaged the landscape. They had found it difficult to adapt; familiar plants and animals had disappeared, and food supplies had become even scarcer.*

*None of the bodies he'd found showed any obvious signs of injury from attack by rival groups or wild animals and he attributed their red and blistered skin to frostbite, but was confused about why they had stayed out long enough to freeze to death, when they were so close to the shelter of their caves.*

*Overcome with grief he had struggled back to his cave. He had wanted to bury and mourn them properly but knew that would have to wait until his strength returned. His priority had been to find food and he'd been lucky to come across a skinny young deer lying dead against the base of a tree. He was so hungry and exhausted he didn't stop to question whether its death was related to those of his people.*

*He'd carried the carcass back to his cave high above the valley floor, where he cooked it over the fire and ate until he was fit to burst. Now, four days later, with the carcass cleaned to the bone, he used its hollowed-out skull to cook what little quantity of root vegetables and grasses he had been able to find before the storm set in. But his hunger was back again.*

*Two weeks later, with the storm showing no signs of abating, he too would die, but of starvation rather than the fatal radiation exposure from the powerful coronal mass ejection that had taken the lives of the rest of his tribe, the shelter of his cave offering him the cruel protection that had pointlessly prolonged his life.*

*He died oblivious to how special he would become. Many millennia later, when his remains were found, no one would know that he had indeed been the last of his kind to survive in northern Eurasia. And yet, by one of those rare twists of fate, he was also the first of his kind to be identified by the* Homo sapien *scholars who studied his bones. They named him Felhofer One, or Neanderthal One, and many of them would ponder what had caused so many of his species to disappear so suddenly.*

# PART I

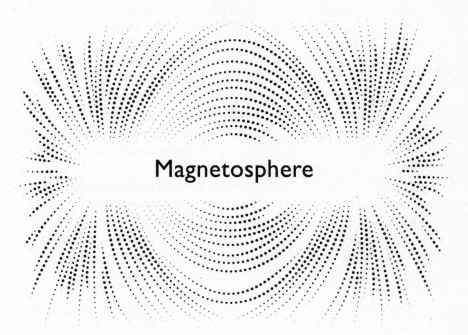

# Magnetosphere

# I

*Saturday, 22 October 2039 – outside Fairbanks, Alaska*

BRAD GROCHOWIAK WAS LOOKING FORWARD TO SPENDING some holiday time with Laura and the kids. First, though, he was looking forward to the end of this particular drive, to unloading and hitting the sack at the Holiday Inn Express. To be fair, the regular 350-mile route north from Anchorage to Fairbanks wasn't so bad, even in late October, as long as the weather stayed clear.

The night had been uneventful and he had less than an hour of his journey to go. Behind him, almost bumper to bumper, were six other giant trucks, identical to his own apart from their lack of a human occupant. Instead, all were linked via their autonomous AI systems. Although Brad had not had to do anything the entire journey, he knew the trucking company felt reassured having a human in the lead vehicle ready to take over manual control if necessary. After all, there was always the chance that severe weather could close in unexpectedly, particularly at this time of year. While this was an unnecessary regulation – the truck's AI system could see far better than he ever could in bad weather and poor light – Brad wasn't complaining. It kept him in work. In the twelve years he had been working for the company he had yet to intervene on any journey.

He stretched his arms out, arching his back to loosen the

stiffness, then, giving the stubble on his head a vigorous rub, he leaned forward and touched the windscreen where the movie he'd only half been paying attention to faded away and the glass reverted to its natural transparency, allowing him to take in the landscape outside. It was already late morning, but the sky was only just showing signs of changing colour, heralding the start of a new day. As the sky brightened, the blackness of the snowy landscape on either side of the road turned a deep blue, contrasting spectacularly with the fiery red band of light spreading across the peaks of the mountain range far to the west. Brad had witnessed this Alaskan alpenglow all his life and it never failed to take his breath away. This had always been his favourite time of day, just before the sun spilled its first rays over the opposite horizon.

It was only once the sun had dragged itself up into view, flooding the world with its winter light, that a tiny detail of colour caught his attention. Against the backdrop of dazzling white snow a smudge of orange and black stood out. At first Brad thought this was another vehicle far ahead on the road, or possibly a brightly coloured building in the distance, but then realized that it was a smear on the windscreen – most likely an insect that had, thanks to the unforgiving law of conservation of momentum, come off worse in its head-on collision with an object a hundred million times its mass.

In itself, the fate of one bug wouldn't have registered on Brad's consciousness, but he soon noticed there were marks of several more suicidal insects all over the windscreen. He surprised himself by recognizing what they were: monarch butterflies. Last spring he'd helped his daughter with a school project collecting butterflies in the garden. Grace had informed him, with the innocent sagacity that only a nine-year-old possesses, that they were called tiger swallowtails – even though, she explained seriously, they looked very similar in colouring to their more famous cousins the monarchs. Apparently, despite monarchs never venturing this far north, you could tell the two species apart by the shape of their wings. Leaning forward to examine one of the smudges decorating his windscreen more carefully, he decided that these ones were almost certainly monarchs. But Grace was a smart kid and if she said you didn't get monarchs in Alaska then you didn't. Besides, butterflies were pretty little things you saw fluttering about in summertime, not in late October and this far north where the temperature was well below freezing already.

With not much else to do with his time, he decided to investigate the matter further. His on-board computer was basic, but sufficient for his purposes. Brad didn't feel the need for the latest holographics or virtual reality surround displays – as long as he was online he was happy. And it was reassuring to know that, however isolated he might feel out in this desolate landscape, there were always dozens of solar-powered internet drones in the stratosphere miles above his head, instantly linking him to the rest of the world.

He cleared his throat, then spoke loudly enough to be heard above the hum of the truck's electric motor.

'Computer, show me a picture of a monarch butterfly.'

No sooner had he finished speaking than he was staring at an array of colourful images on one side of his windscreen.

Here is a selection of images of monarchs.

Yup, he had been right. The insects stuck to his windscreen were indeed monarchs. Grace would be proud of him.

'Tell me about monarch butterfly migrations.'

There was a brief pause before the computer answered. Brad knew this delay was deliberate. People didn't like the machines they communicated with responding instantly, which they were of course capable of, as though knowing in advance what they were going to be asked. Instead, all virtual-assistant AIs and chatbots these days had up to a second of built-in delay time to make them seem more humanlike in their interactions.

Monarchs undertake one of the world's great annual migratory journeys, when millions escape south-east Canada's harsh winters and fly south-west all the way to Mexico. Others, west of the Canadian Rockies, will migrate due south to California. Monarch butterflies are among the many species of animals, which include several migratory birds and marine creatures, that use an inner biological compass to find their way by following the Earth's magnetic field lines.

'When are Monarch butterflies found in Alaska?'

Monarchs cannot be found in Alaska. It is too far north for them.

Brad conjured up in his mind an image of the map of North America. Wherever these insects had flown from, they had most certainly not been heading towards warmer climes. Clearly this group must have been hopelessly lost. Did their squadron leader have such a bad sense of direction that it had led them north instead of south? And if so, how the hell had it landed such an important job? The thought amused him. No. Surely they obeyed some sort of collective swarm mentality. But was it possible that there had been some fault in their inner compasses, however the hell they worked? He would ask Grace when he got home. It would make for a good science project. He thought about sending her the AR footage of the butterflies he had recorded on his retinal display but decided it could wait. Anyway, it'd be more fun to chat to Grace about this face to face rather than just copying over an augmented reality clip of what he was seeing on his screen.

It never occurred to him that the fault might not lie with the butterflies at all. Absent-mindedly, he flicked on the wipers to clear the windscreen of the multi-coloured carnage.

# 2

*Monday, 28 January 2041 – Rio de Janeiro*

SARAH MAITLIN STARED AT HER DISPLAY AND TRIED TO CLEAR her head, her third cafezinho of the evening cold and forgotten on her desk. She had always found coffee more effective at clearing niggling headaches than pills. Running both hands through her hair, she absent-mindedly gathered it up, twisting and tucking it into a self-sustaining bun. The coolness of the air-conditioning on her exposed neck caused a chill to run through her, despite the climate-controlled environment in the lab. She retrieved the sweater that had been hanging over the back of her chair all day, slipping it over her T-shirt, and had a sudden vision of her mother rebuking her for not caring enough about her wardrobe. 'Why do you still wear that horrible old thing?' she'd no doubt say. 'You're a very attractive woman, if you'd only make the effort.' She smiled wryly at the thought. Her mother back in England was desperate for grandchildren and kept a close eye on Sarah's biological clock – more than ever now that she was in her late thirties – and her multiple failed relationships.

She dragged her attention back to the holographic display in front of her. Ordinarily, these images would have been of no more than academic interest, but this was different. As the physicist on duty at the Solar Science Institute in Rio, it was Sarah's responsibility to keep a close eye on the Sun's activity.

Although the Institute had been set up twenty years ago to carry out basic astrophysics research, its main function over the past couple of years had been to provide early warning of any abnormal solar activity that might be of concern – the current situation being a case in point.

The centre of the holo filling her field of vision was dominated by a high-resolution 3D video feed of the Sun, captured by a group of satellites in orbit around it – a detailed image that was both beautiful and terrifying. It was so realistic she could almost feel the heat on her face. Staring at the slowly spinning three-dimensional projection, she focused her attention on one region of the Sun's churning and fiery surface. What she was looking at was more than a little concerning.

She'd hoped to knock off for the day a couple of hours ago, but now knew she wouldn't be leaving her desk just yet. Her cats would be hungry, so she made a mental note to call her neighbour in a few minutes and ask her to feed them.

It suddenly occurred to her that she hadn't eaten anything herself since breakfast. Working this hard wasn't doing her any good; there'd been no gym in a fortnight and her social life was a disaster. She couldn't remember the last time she'd been out for a drink or dinner.

A decent break was what she needed, just as soon as this latest crisis was over. Maybe a day or two down on Copacabana. Although given the recent increasing size and number of ozone holes being punched through the atmosphere, the UV-shielded zones on the beach would be packed. These days not even the most dedicated sun-worshipper would risk lying out in the unprotected open for long. In many parts of the world it was becoming so bad that some people were reluctant to venture outside their own homes at all these days, even at night, so as not to risk unnecessary exposure to the increasingly powerful cosmic radiation. Many had micro sensors embedded under their skin to monitor the presence of high-energy particles and to alert them if it reached hazardous levels.

But when it came to dangerous radiation from space, nothing could compete with a well-aimed blast from a coronal mass ejection. Until a few years ago, these enormous bubbles of hot plasma spat out by the Sun were of interest only to solar physicists. Sarah recalled trying to explain to her father why she found the subject so fascinating.

'What's the worry?' he'd argued. 'After all, the Earth has survived just fine for the past however many gazillion years without the Sun frying us.' Ben Maitlin made no secret of his wish that his daughter had followed him into political journalism. 'That's how to change the world,' he'd told her, 'more effectively than any politician can.' But Sarah had chosen a career in science instead, dealing with concepts he often found difficult to get his head around. And yet she knew he was immensely proud of her, always insisting she send him a copy of each research paper she published. Her mother had told her how he would often pull out her most recent article at dinner parties when asked how his daughter was getting on, and proceed to read out its title with an extravagant flourish, without the faintest idea what it meant.

Ben Maitlin was an intelligent man who tried hard to keep abreast of scientific developments. Sarah sometimes found it frustrating that many other journalists, scientifically illiterate hacks, now regarded themselves as experts on coronal mass ejections. Their interest was certainly understandable given the very real threat CMEs were beginning to pose, and at least they were reporting on them. And that at least meant that the politicians might now finally do something.

Over the last two years, Sarah's work had taken on an urgency that was in stark contrast to the sedate, curiosity-driven research she had enjoyed ever since her PhD. The most recent measurement of the strength and distribution of the Earth's magnetic field was terrifying. It was now down to just half the strength it had been when she was born and the implications of this were only too clear to her.

Of course, governments around the world had avoided engendering widespread panic by simply downplaying the risks. This policy created its own problems for many scientists, who could see what was coming but found their warnings falling on deaf political ears, exactly as had happened a generation earlier with climate change. It was beyond short-sighted that there was *still* no coordinated international response to the crisis that was beginning to unfold. The science couldn't be any simpler: the Earth's magnetic field, which for billions of years had protected the planet's fragile biosphere from dangerous radiation from space, was now no longer up to the task. And that meant humanity had some serious problems.

She examined the images and streams of scrolling data hanging like ghosts in the air in front of her. Like the conductor of an orchestra, she manipulated the data, saving the information in a virtual folder. This coronal ejection would hit the Earth in less than forty-eight hours and it wasn't going to be pleasant.

'Hey, Miguel, come and take a look at this.'

Replacing the holo of the Sun with one of the Earth, she highlighted all the data collated on the CME – its energy, spread, and the all-important SAT, the Shock Arrival Time.

Miguel wandered across and peered over her shoulder. 'Well, that's going to knock out some power grids. Where will it hit?'

'Looks like the Indian Ocean mostly. Almost definitely central and south-east Asia too.'

'We might get lucky if it arrives a few hours early. Then most of the flux would hit—'

'—the South Pacific, yes. But, that's just wishful thinking. Anyway, I'm not sure it'd be much comfort. It's still going to knock out a stack of comm sats.'

Sarah closed her eyes and rubbed them with thumb and forefinger. She decided to run her simulations again. No need to panic the authorities in those countries unless she was sure. If she'd got her calculations wrong and the CME ended up missing the Earth entirely then she would be accused of crying wolf.

'Do me a quick favour, Miguel? Run a check on paths of all medium- and low-orbit sats above a five-thousand-kilometre radius centred on, um . . .' She stared at the slowly spinning globe. '. . . Centred on Nepal, I think.'

'Then correlate it with SAT, right?'

Sarah knew that the SAT was the big uncertainty. No one

could accurately predict the variation in the speed of an approaching CME, or the extension of the pulse. 'Yes, and assume the usual eight- to ten-hour window.'

Feeling stiff, she extended her legs and arched her back, lifting her body off the seat, stretching cramped muscles. Another late night beckoned. In mid-stretch, she suddenly became aware that she hadn't heard Miguel walking back to his desk and that he was still standing behind her. She swivelled round in her chair rather more quickly than she intended.

'Well?'

Miguel grinned and ambled back to his corner of the lab. Once seated, he pulled his display visor down over his eyes and started to hum tunelessly as his fingers danced across the virtual display hanging in the air in front of him, gathering and manipulating the data from the thousands of registered satellites. He would rule out the ones that would definitely not be crossing the path of the high-energy cascade of electrons, protons and atomic nuclei, then feed all the information on the rest into his simulation codes.

Despite his irritating humming, Sarah felt a sense of admiration for the bright young Brazilian. He was smart and passionate about his work. She wondered whether his outward cheerfulness was genuine or whether he was just trying to hide his own apprehension.

# 3

*Wednesday, 30 January – Waiheke Island,*
*New Zealand*

MARC BRUCKNER WAS ENJOYING THE PEACE AND QUIET OF
his favourite vineyard. When he'd arrived there late in the
afternoon there had been several other customers, mainly elderly couples. He'd nodded greetings and then found a secluded
table at the far end of the courtyard tucked under the shade of
a large kauri tree. Its thick brown trunk was full of carved
romantic graffiti from previous love-struck patrons. None of
this registered on Marc's consciousness, though; his own failed
marriage was still too raw. He'd initially felt self-conscious
about drinking alone while all around him people seemed to
be blissfully paired up. A few glasses of wine would soon dis-
pel any awkwardness. Alcohol seemed to be his only faithful
companion these days.

He remembered only too well the accusing look on his daughter Evie's face when he had told her he needed to move back to
New Zealand for a while. 'How is running away to the other
side of the world going to make things better?' she'd asked through
angry tears.

It was true that he had come back to New Zealand with the
genuine intention of 'getting his shit together' as his father had
been fond of saying. Well, it had only been two weeks – surely
he couldn't be expected to turn his life around as soon as he'd

landed. After all, he'd been fighting his demons for a long time; he'd been diagnosed with depression and anxiety several years ago, which meant he'd received all the clinical help he'd needed, but he still found it hard to shake the feeling that his problems were no more than a failure of moral fibre and will-power and that he could somehow talk himself better.

It had been a warm and sticky afternoon, with the westering sun bringing out the best in the colours of the surrounding flora. The vineyard sat on top of a hill and afforded Marc a beautiful panoramic view of the island – from the well-manicured bushes and shrubs of the garden itself to the surrounding apricot, lime and plum trees further down the hill. Beyond was a lush rolling landscape, with more vineyards and farms dotted on adjacent hilltops. In fact, if he strained his neck up over the nearest bush he could see all the way down to the westernmost point of the island and Matiatia Bay, where the ferries transported inhabit-ants and the tourists to and from Auckland twenty kilometres across the water.

Marc had sat pondering the mess of a life he'd left behind in America: his failed marriage, the broken relationship with his daughter, the car crash that his academic career had turned into, despite his success as one of the world's foremost physi-cists . . . The only intrusion on his thoughts this afternoon had been the soft, competing sounds of insects and birds. Although he had not seen them, he knew an entire ecosystem existed hidden beneath the foliage, with grey warblers and fantails hopping from branch to twig searching for bugs, beetles and caterpillars.

That had been a few hours ago. Now that darkness had closed in, with the lights of the Auckland skyline sparkling in the dis-tance, he decided that Waiheke Island had to be just about the most beautiful spot on Earth. Why hadn't he thought of spend-ing more time here before? He recalled summer holidays on the island as a boy, swimming, fishing or messing around on his father's boat. But his parents had only bought their retire-ment home on the south side long after he had moved to the States. Now that they were gone, their home was his. But he refused to accept that he was ready to settle down here just yet. There was still a flickering hope that he could put his life and research career back on track.

Well into his second bottle of Syrah, he leaned carefully back in his chair to gaze up at the night sky, deciding to count shooting stars. He guessed he was probably the last customer still left at the vineyard. Faint music drifted across the courtyard from inside the building and he kept catching snatches of it, deciding it was Frank Sinatra, crooning about flying off to Jupiter and Mars – rather appropriately, thought Marc, as he tried to locate those two planets among the hundreds of twinkling stars.

Coming back to New Zealand had definitely been the right move. The stress of the divorce coinciding with the meltdown he'd suffered at Columbia University and the small-mindedness of academic colleagues he had thought he could count on as friends had all finally become too much to cope with.

Maybe he really should put his past behind him and settle down here. Was it really such a bad idea? There were plenty of projects he could think of that would occupy him. And if he got too stir-crazy he could always go back to New York and try to pick up where he'd left off. After all, he was still on the right side of fifty, so it wasn't like he was ready to retire any time soon.

He allowed his eyes to adjust to the dark so that he could pick out the very faintest dots of light. It was funny how people assumed that all physicists were familiar with every star, planet and constellation in the night sky. He'd lost count of the number of times he'd had to explain that he was not an astronomer and that his research involved looking down at mathematical equations, or getting buried in complex electronic kit, studying the world at the tiniest of scales, rather than looking up at the heavens. Thanks to his colour-blindness, he couldn't even tell Venus from Mars.

He'd taken out his augmented-reality lenses so as not to have the spectacle ruined by any unnecessary overlaid information. The night sky lost its aesthetic beauty and majesty when each bright dot had detailed statistics superimposed around it. Of course, it wasn't difficult to switch off his AR feed whenever he wanted, but there was something liberating about taking his contacts out – like walking barefoot on fresh grass.

And yet, like countless others, Marc found it hard to do without AR – its use had become so ubiquitous that it was now hard to remember a time when no one had access to instant information overlying their field of vision. He marvelled at humanity's ability to adapt to new technologies so quickly that it forgot how it had ever coped before. Born, as he was, just a few years after the dawn of the internet, and despite his scientific training, Marc was finding it increasingly hard to keep up with the pace of change, and when it came to the very latest fads he considered himself a bit of a dinosaur, preferring to wear the old-fashioned AR contact lenses rather than the liquid Nano-Gee retinal implants that had become all the rage in recent years.

The field had been revolutionized with breathtaking rapidity once it was discovered that AR no longer needed the user to wear glasses or contact lenses on which to superimpose text, images and video – a veil of data through which they could still see the physical world around them. Instead, if you chose to – and most people under the age of forty chose to – you could access everything you needed from the Cloud as an integrated part of your vision. In fact, if you closed your eyes to block out the external world, the AR world really came into its own.

It was a research team at Berkeley who had first discovered how to control the light-sensitive cryptochrome biomolecules covering the back of the retina. Several members of the team had quickly seen the potential of their breakthrough and within five years had become the world's first trillionaires. Once it was understood how these proteins could be switched on and off with tiny electromagnetic signals sent to the users' eyes from their Cloud-linked wristpads, rapid advances were made in the technology. Almost overnight, it seemed to Marc, everyone had access to double vision: reality and augmented reality, overlapping and yet, with a little practice, quite separate. So good had the AR projections onto the retina now become, that the technology's main teething problem came from the user confusing the projection with the physical universe beyond.

'Can I get you anything else, Professor Bruckner?'

The soft voice behind him that snapped him back from his reverie belonged to Melissa, the vineyard owners' daughter, who was waitressing at Stony Hill during the summer. She was doing a good job of hiding her impatience to knock off for the night.

'Thanks, Melissa, no. Just finishing this glass and I'm off.' Then he added, 'Sorry if you've been waiting to close.'

'That's all right,' she smiled. 'Dad pays by the hour.' She collected the small lamp from the adjacent table and pushed the four surrounding chairs in closer. Turning to go back inside she looked up at the night sky. 'It's so pretty up there, isn't it? All those swirling colours.'

Marc was puzzled and turned to look, following her gaze. 'Oh, my God, it's the aurora!' he gasped. 'It's so vivid!' The evening sky over the Pacific glowed majestically in green-white swirling patterns, constantly changing and stunningly beautiful.

Marc decided this was the perfect end to the evening. Together they gazed up at a curtain of light to the left of the vineyard roof that grew more intense, then spread slowly round behind them before fading, only to be replaced by an equally stunning pattern on the right side. He and Melissa watched in appreciative silence.

However, as the novelty of the spectacle began to wear off, Marc got a niggling feeling that he was missing something obvious. Something very important. The thought germinated and grew in his mind, despite the wine that was blunting his analytical skills. Then it suddenly hit him. He ran a quick mental check to make sure he'd got his bearings right. The impressive Aurora Australis he was looking at was in completely the wrong direction. It should have been in the southern sky, towards the Pole. But this display was to the north. How the hell was that even possible?

# 4

*Thursday, 31 January – 05:30, New Delhi*

FLIGHT AI-231 FROM STOCKHOLM WAS BEGINNING ITS DESCENT
into Delhi. Captain Joseph Rahman preferred these old-fashioned
subsonic journeys even though they took all night. He just
didn't feel comfortable doing too many hyperskips these days.
Thanks to the weakening magnetic field of the Earth, they carried an increasingly high radiation risk. While he could understand the attraction of getting from Europe to India in forty-five
minutes by skimming off the upper atmosphere at Mach 10,
like a stone on the surface of a pond, he was determined to
minimize his own exposure to the bombardment from cosmic
rays.

He switched on the cabin's exterior projection, so that the
feed from the hundreds of tiny cameras covering the outer surface of the plane mapped onto the interior of the windowless
fuselage, making it appear entirely transparent to the passengers. But it was a pointless exercise. Ordinarily, the panoramic
view this gave as the plane came in to land would have been a
quite dramatic experience, with the lights of the mostly still
sleeping megacity spread out below. Instead, they were greeted
by a wall of white thanks to the thick fog that often engulfed
Indira Gandhi Airport at this time of year. They'd been circling in a holding pattern at three thousand metres for forty
minutes now, waiting their turn to land.

Suddenly several of his displays went blank.

It looked like an issue with the satnav system. He waited a few minutes for the aircraft's AI to resolve the matter. With nothing for him to do he flicked on the intercom to update his crew and passengers. Like all pilots for the past hundred years, Captain Rahman's tone was deep and rich, and, with twenty-five years of flight experience under his belt, exuded calm confidence.

'Sorry for this slight delay, ladies and gentlemen, we're still waiting to be given a slot to land. There might also be a further short delay as we look into a problem with the plane's AI. We hope to fix this quickly and I'll keep you posted.' Then, to avoid any unnecessary panic, he added, 'There's absolutely nothing to be alarmed about.'

Still, he now had to keep an eye on the battery gauge. A strong headwind for most of the journey from Stockholm, then this long hold above Indira Gandhi Airport, meant that the charge was lower than he would have liked.

While his two young co-pilots busied themselves trying to find the source of the satnav problem, he radioed air traffic control.

'Delhi, this is Air India two-three-one. We've lost satlink, so I guess we're entirely in your hands now. We're running low on batteries too.'

The response from the control tower was reassuringly immediate:

'Copy that, two-three-one. You now have clearance to land. Sit back and we'll take it from here.'

Rahman allowed himself a small sigh of relief. Most airports now had AI systems that would take control of all incoming flights if necessary, particularly in poor visibility, manoeuvring the planes remotely to the correct approach angle. However, thanks to the ubiquity of artificial intelligence in all complex systems, aircraft were generally more than capable of doing the job themselves, and international regulations stipulated that airports' air traffic control should only step in when absolutely necessary. Captain Rahman was more than happy to hand over his plane on this occasion: his aircraft's AI system, more powerful than old-fashioned autopilots, could not function without GPS. Still, he promised himself he'd get to the bottom of the problem once he was on the ground. GPS had only ever failed him on one previous occasion; and that time he'd at least been able to see outside and watch as the invisible hands of the airport's AI system had guided the plane down safely.

Then, just as suddenly as the satellite signal had dropped out, so now did the aircraft's entire communication system. There was a sudden jolt as it was released from the hold of the control tower.

OK, *now* he would have something to do. Shit, this was getting serious. Still, no need to panic. He turned to his co-pilots, who were both watching him intensely. He smiled at them reassuringly and tried to keep his voice steady. 'Come on, guys, let's stay professional here. It'll be a story to dine out on, right?' Without waiting for a response from either of them he turned his attention back to the job at hand.

'Delhi, this is Air India two-three-one. What the hell just happened there?'

'Sorry, two-three-one, seems we have a major electronics issue down here too. We—'

The voice in Rahman's earpiece was suddenly drowned out by static.

'I didn't catch that, Delhi, say again?'

Still nothing but static.

Joseph Rahman took a deep breath and checked his fuel gauge again. He no longer had enough juice to pull up and climb above the fog and wait for the issue to be resolved. He thought back to his early days of flying twenty years ago when an airport's instrument landing system would have allowed him to conduct a textbook instrument approach – particularly in this thick fog, which would have been a definite CAT 3. But hardly any airports had ILS systems any more – a technology involving a localizer antenna and a glide slope system that would between them provide the aircraft's computer with all the information it needed to land safely without the pilot's intervention. Nowadays, everything was reliant on AI minds and GPS. And neither looked like being of any help to Flight AI-231 right now.

Landing a modern aircraft manually was something of a novelty that he would normally have relished, but this was going to require considerable skill and a bucket-load of luck. He was confident that before they'd lost contact they were on the precise bearing to come in on the south-east runway. He also knew that his air speed was right and the glide slope indicator was still showing that he was approaching the runway at the correct angle: three degrees to the horizontal. That meant trying to land was a far less dangerous option than circling through the fog in the hope that the problem got fixed. For all he knew, the other dozen or so aircraft in the vicinity were also flying blind.

'OK, here we go,' he said, more to himself than anyone else. 'We just have to keep this bearing steady and descend smoothly, then hope to God we see those runway lights in time to tweak our approach.'

He flicked the comms button. 'Can I have your attention again please, ladies and gentlemen? I am about to adjust your seats to cocoon mode as this might be a bumpy landing.'

He then quickly added, 'Cabin crew, please confirm all passengers secure then take your seats. Five minutes to landing.'

He could tell his co-pilots were now more than a little scared. They'd been chatting away in Hindi throughout the flight but were now silent. They were both sitting bolt upright in their seats looking out straight ahead, waiting to catch a glimpse of the runway lights through the fog. Rahman kept his eye on the altimeter, which now showed that they had dropped to four hundred metres and slowed to two-fifty knots. If he'd had more time to consider the situation he was in, as a detached observer, he might have remembered something he had been taught all those years ago in training – information that he'd never needed to consider or act upon. So, it never occurred to him that an altimeter can give a false reading of altitude in thick fog because pockets of cold air screw with the pressure reading.

He shot his two co-pilots a quick glance and winked. 'We've got this. Two minutes to landing, guys. Let's just hope we see those lights s—'

Captain Joseph Rahman wasn't used to being confronted with his own mortality so unexpectedly.

'What the *fuck*?'

Flight AI-231 slammed down into the airport carpark two kilometres short of the runway at a little over three hundred kilometres per hour.

Captain Rahman had just enough time to wonder why the ground had come up to greet his plane so early and to feel the searing heat of the explosion before everything went black.

# 5

*Friday, 1 February – Waiheke Island, New Zealand*

THE SUN HAD BEEN STREAMING IN THROUGH THE GAPS IN the blinds for hours and Marc had been trying, unsuccessfully, to block it out by draping one arm over his eyes. Reluctantly, he rolled over in bed to check the time, squinting and trying to raise his head as little as necessary off the pillow. It was already ten-thirty. He'd not got to bed till just before dawn but knew the way he was feeling had little to do with the lack of sleep. It had been two days since the strange aurora and it had bugged him all day yesterday while he was out on a fishing trip. By early evening, he'd been famished, so he'd returned, moored the boat and headed up to the house. Of course he tried to convince himself that the quickness in his step was nothing more than a combination of hunger and a keen scientific urge to investigate the aurora, but he knew the deeper need was to get back to the unopened bottle of Scotch calling out to him.

The most popular opinion on the various news feeds regarded the strangely displaced aurora as just another crazy consequence of the increasing influence of cosmic rays on an ever more vulnerable planet. However, the beautiful magnetic display in the upper atmosphere above south-east Asia was a sideline to the big news: a plane crash-landing in Delhi and the loss of three hundred and twenty lives. Air disasters were extremely rare these days and this one appeared to have been caused by several communication satellites being fried. By the time he'd dragged himself off the sofa and stumbled to the kitchen to find something to eat it was past midnight and the bottle of Scotch was already more than half empty.

Well, he was most certainly paying the price this morning for his over-indulgence. Not that it bothered him so much any more. The dull ache above his eyes first thing in the morning had become such a familiar friend these past few months that he hardly gave it a second thought; he even welcomed the groggy feeling that did such a good job of numbing the ever-present wretchedness. He rolled out of bed and plodded unsteadily downstairs. Shuffling into the living room, he voice-activated the blinds across the French windows to open, then decided against it and closed them again. Instead, he activated the wall display and headed for the kitchen. But the news report he caught as he was leaving made him turn back to the large screen.

All the networks were reporting the same story: that at least six communication satellites had been damaged by a burst of high-energy particles from space. Authorities in India, China and Malaysia were saying how lucky they were to have escaped so lightly. Apart from the Air India passengers, the only other casualties being reported were three hospital patients on life-support machines in a remote Indian village, where the emergency generator had failed to kick in after a power-grid failure in the region, and a Bangladeshi construction worker who had been electrocuted while replacing components at the top of a transmission tower. It saddened Marc to think that the economies of countries like Bangladesh, still counting the cost of climate change, continued to use humans rather than bots to carry out such dangerous work.

He checked what was currently trending on both the surface and dark web social media. But while most of the chatter was about whether this direct hit from a coronal ejection was just a one-off event or a warning that the Sun would be belching out more of its contents in the Earth's direction, the cacophony of noise made it hard to pick out anything sensible. Viewpoints ranging from enraged libertarians and conspiracy theorists disputing that anything had happened at all, to the even more vociferous end-of-the-world fanatics convinced this was finally the sign they had been waiting for, all competed for attention. The virtual-assistant system installed in the house, even running its highly sophisticated sorting algorithm, was proving unable to weed out the spam from the ham to build any reliable picture.

Marc sighed. As usual, you had to do a little digging to get to the truth. 'Select favourites only. Past twenty-four hours. Keywords: magnetic storm, solar flare, threat level.'

One thing he hadn't done yet was change the VA's settings, so it still spoke in the voice of the old British natural-history broadcaster Sir David Attenborough, a favourite of his mother's:

> The top hit discussion is whether the current event was due directly to the weakening of the Earth's magnetosphere – consensus rating 95.2 per cent – and how soon the Flip will happen and restore the planet's protective magnetic shield – consensus on when this will occur is in the range of six months to five years from now.

None of this was new. For several years now, many scientists had been debating the expected reversal of the Earth's field, when the north and south magnetic poles would switch over. But unless this was going to have a clear impact on their daily lives, most people were not interested. Now, it seemed, they were finally sitting up and taking notice.

At least he had an answer on the impressive aurora he'd witnessed at the vineyard last night, because this had to be more than coincidence. The solar ejection must have caused an impressive geomagnetic storm, screwing with what was left of the magnetic field and producing the colourful northern sky. Marc grunted and turned away from the wall screen. He wondered whether he should be more concerned about this latest crisis – indeed whether he should be showing more of an interest in the state of the planet generally. But he just found it too difficult to care much about anything these days.

A cool shower and two coffees later and his head began to clear. He popped a couple of painkillers anyway. He knew he could have avoided this hangover entirely if he'd taken an enzypill last night. He knew there was a supply in the house somewhere – and sure, they'd have guaranteed he woke up bright and fresh, thanks to their anti-diuretic hormones, ADH and ALDH enzyme enhancers and sugar-level controllers, but that defeated the object; why bother drinking in the first place if you were going to stop the alcohol from fucking up your brain's neurotransmitters? Marc sometimes wondered whether a wholesome hangover was penance for his over-indulgence.

Needing something to eat to settle his stomach, he padded barefoot into the kitchen in his boxer shorts and an old CERN T-shirt with its *Particle physics gives me a hadron* slogan now barely legible. Charlotte, his ex-wife, had always hated that T-shirt. But then, towards the end, it seemed there wasn't much about Marc that Charlotte *hadn't* hated. Not caring about the outside world was, he knew deep down, just another symptom of his illness, but he also knew that she was partly right when she would accuse him of just being selfish. In the Marc-centric universe, stuff happened elsewhere to other people and they would just have to deal with it. If it didn't impact on him then he preferred to mind his own business. Shaking his head, he wondered when that had started. Did it really coincide with the onset of his depression? He hadn't always felt like this; there had been a time when, as an idealist and brilliant young scientist, he'd thought he could change the world.

Ah, what the hell. What difference would it make anyway what he thought? Twenty-four hours from now the global media would have moved on to some other story. It had taken the world decades to acknowledge that anthropogenic climate change was a real threat to humanity, so why should this rare threat from space be anything more than a temporary distraction from the constant backdrop of terrorism and global cyber wars?

He took a bowl down from the cupboard – almost everything

in the house was just as it was when his parents had died, within four months of each other three years ago, and he'd not got round to having a good clear-out.

He sat down at the breakfast bar with a bowl of cereal and forced himself to think more positively. Yesterday had been a good day out on the boat, with the sea breeze taking the edge off the warm sun. He'd felt physically lighter and the future didn't seem so dark. Today, he decided, he would be more productive. He'd get started on a few DIY projects around the house. There was plenty to do. He'd spent the past fortnight generally loafing about, but now it was time to get his arse in gear.

He'd just finished eating his breakfast when his wristpad buzzed. It was Charlotte. He did a quick mental calculation. It would be early evening now in New York and she would be just getting home from work. No doubt she would exaggerate how frazzled and tired she was feeling. And to be honest, who could blame her – considering that she was holding down a stressful job that she didn't particularly enjoy and was bringing up a teenage daughter singlehandedly, while he wallowed in his lazy self-indulgence on the other side of the world? He knew only too well that, like Evie, Charlotte was convinced he'd taken the coward's way out by escaping to New Zealand instead of continuing to get the professional help he needed in New York.

He tapped his wristpad and Charlotte's face appeared on the kitchen screen in front of him.

'You look like shit.'

He ran his fingers absent-mindedly through his drying hair in an attempt to tame it. He immediately regretted not sticking her on audio only. 'And hello to you too, Charlie. To what do I owe this honour?' He tried to sound as cheerful as he could manage.

Charlotte sighed. 'Hard as this might be for you to believe, I genuinely wanted to see how you're doing.' She looked tired, but to Marc it was still the same face he'd fallen in love with all those years ago. In fact, she looked more attractive than ever now – now that he'd lost her to someone else. And he had long since come to terms with the fact that he had no one to blame but himself.

'. . . and I see from the bags under your eyes that you're still not sleeping well.'

He chose to ignore the comment. The last thing he wanted was another cycle of pointless argument: *No, this time I really will quit / I've heard that a thousand times before.* They'd been down that road too many times. Anyway, when he did drag himself back from the brink, and he would, it would be on his own terms and for Evie's sake.

'So, how're things? How's Evie?' Marc asked. If there was one light that had continued to shine throughout even his very darkest days, it was his daughter. 'Still mad with me? I've tried contacting her every day, but she won't respond.'

'What did you expect, Marc? She's fifteen; she's had to live with her father struggling with depression since she was ten, then watch her parents tearing their marriage apart; and finally, without any warning or explanation, her father disappears from her life.'

Marc didn't protest. His mood swings had driven a wedge between him and those he loved. After being kicked out of his faculty position because of the drinking, he knew he'd had to 'get away', just when Evie was getting used to the routine of spending weekends with him. He'd hoped she'd be able to understand that he needed, temporarily, to put some distance between himself and his old life. His relationship with his daughter had always been close. Sometimes it felt like she was the only human on Earth who understood his struggle with his inner demons. And despite the hormonal changes she was going through at the moment, it would still melt his heart when she gave him one of her tight, unconditional, almost urgent hugs.

He nodded slowly. 'I guess I had that coming. And it's not like I've ever had any illusions of winning Father of the Year, right? Anyway, and I was going to let you know, there's a conference in Princeton on dark-matter physics next week, which I plan to attend. Qiang is going and it would be good to catch up with him too. As soon as it's over I'll head up to see Evie. I'll stay at George Palmer's place.'

Charlotte raised an eyebrow and gave a wry smile. 'You mean

you were going to let me know once you'd got here. Well, I'm sure Evie will be pleased to see you, I promise. She's just hurting and needs a bit of time. Try to spend more than a few hours with her, though. It would be good for both of you to try and mend some bridges.'

Marc heard the sound of a door slamming in the background behind Charlotte and detected a sudden stiffening of her features. She turned round and called out, 'Hi, honey, I'm in here, chatting to Marc.' Her boyfriend Jeremy had just got in. Jeremy Giles, the successful politician, was in so many ways the exact opposite of Marc. And OK, so 'boyfriend' was no longer the right term to use since he'd moved in with Charlie as soon as the ink had dried on the divorce settlement papers. Still, Marc didn't want to have to face his smarmy smile again any time soon.

Luckily, Charlotte didn't want to prolong their chat any more than he did. 'OK. Well, let me know your travel plans as soon as they're firmed up. And, believe it or not, it would still be good to see you.'

'You too. Love to Evie.'

The screen blinked off.

Maybe it was the thought of a fit and virile Jeremy Giles screwing his ex-wife; or maybe it was just the urge to blow off some of his pent-up frustration, but Marc decided he would go out for a long run – as if an hour's jog on the beach was all that was needed to put his life back together. For a man of forty-seven, he was in remarkably good health and had at least avoided the expanding waistline of so many of his contemporaries.

Before he went upstairs to change, he decided to take one final look for any serious reporting on the geomagnetic storm and what had caused it. He thought about searching for any announcements from NASA, ESA or CNSA, but he knew the space agencies of America, Europe and China could no longer be relied on to give the whole story – the old secrecy and rivalries of the space race of the 1960s and '70s were back stronger than ever as the competition for resources on the Moon and Mars became ever fiercer. He sat down in front of his kitchen screen. If anyone knew, it would be the team at the Rio Solar

Science Institute. Last year, he'd sat on a US grant-funding committee and reviewed a research proposal from the SSI. His conclusion was that they did solid science and that it would be crazy not to support them in the current climate.

'Search past twenty-four hours. Filter. Coronal mass ejection. Solar Science Institute. Statement.' The results came back quickly. There were over two million internet sites reporting on an interview given by a Dr Sarah Maitlin from the SSI on a morning show on Globo in Brazil. A further search on the name returned forty-eight million hits, all in the past ten hours. It seemed that Dr Maitlin was something of a news sensation. Marc was intrigued enough to watch the Globo interview in full, then did a quick search on Maitlin's scientific work. She was a British solar physicist in her late thirties whose most cited research papers had been over ten years ago, on sunspots. He started watching another interview she'd given, this time with a BBC journalist whom she appeared to know. Her slightly more relaxed demeanour, compared with her somewhat nervous Globo performance, meant that she smiled when he introduced her, revealing just how attractive she was – no wonder the shallow news networks all wanted a piece of her – although in this particular instance her academic credentials spoke for themselves.

Despite the potential levels of radiation that, according to Sarah Maitlin, were now getting through more easily than ever, especially here in New Zealand, which was sitting under a massive hole in the ozone layer, Marc decided to go out for his run anyway. As it was, the midday sun was going to make it unpleasantly warm, and he hadn't yet acclimatized since arriving from a freezing New York. His headache now receding, he bounded up the stairs two at a time to grab his running shoes.

Whatever Dr Maitlin had to say about the fate of the world could wait.

# 6

HER HEAD WAS BUZZING. SARAH SAT ALONE IN THE BACK OF the Manhattan taxi as it raced across town. She could have got a drone cab, but the street traffic this time of the evening was no busier than the air above it.

So much had happened to her since first detecting the coronal ejection back at the Institute that she really hadn't had time to take stock. It felt as though she had talked herself dry to the press; surely there wasn't any more she could possibly say about solar cycles, solar storms, solar flares, sunspots, solar wind or coronal mass ejections. The media attention was finally waning now after a whirlwind few days and she felt drained, but she was still a long way from being able to get back to her research at the SSI, or any semblance of normality.

Sitting back, she closed her eyes, overcome by an unexpected feeling of loneliness. There was no one she felt close enough to and on whom she could offload, or simply unwind with – and not just here in New York, but anywhere. Sure, there were plenty of academic colleagues around the world she knew well enough to socialize with when their paths crossed, but none were close friends. And, as her mother would all too often point out, many women her age had found partners to share their lives with and even settled down to start families.

She smiled to herself. Much as she loved her mother and

enjoyed spending time with her back in England when she could, she had long since stopped taking advice from her. In any case, she enjoyed her own company . . . most of the time. And, heaven knows, she certainly didn't need a man in her life right now. After two mistakes, there was no way she was prepared to get involved in another relationship just yet. She would readily admit that both failures had partly been her fault. She had been accused by Simon during a big row in Rio last summer of being too preoccupied with her work, which was true. But she certainly didn't regret that. The truth was she really loved her research, and Simon just hadn't been important enough for her to be prepared to make the room for him in her life that he had expected.

But now her work was being put on temporary hold. First had come the phone calls from the local media in Rio; within an hour of the Delhi plane crash, still late Wednesday evening, Rio local time, reports were emerging that the accident had not been due to any fault with the aircraft, pilot error or even extreme weather conditions. It had been a severe and catastrophic comms failure. Once the Indian news agencies had pinned the accident on the exotic explanation of particles from space knocking out the communications, the hunt had been on for someone to explain the science.

It began when a local TV news researcher had called, sounding overly cheerful given the graveness of the news. Like many news networks around the world, he had traced the sequence of events back and found a report of Sarah having warned the authorities of the arrival of a serious cosmic-ray storm. The Globo News journalist had struck lucky by being the first to get hold of Sarah's private contact details. It was gone 11 p.m. when she'd taken that first call just as she was getting ready for bed. By one in the morning, she had given seven other online interviews to various news agencies.

Following three hours' sleep and a quick shower, she had been driven to a nearby helipad where a team from Globo had been waiting to fly her to the downtown media hub for a live slot on the morning news.

After the interview, an excited young analyst working for the station told her that the regular twenty million Brazilian viewers of the programme had been joined by hundreds of millions watching online around the world. The interview had started smoothly, and Sarah had felt surprisingly calm. The TV anchor who interviewed her was absurdly glamorous and immaculately dressed, making Sarah feel self-consciously scruffy alongside her. But the woman was a consummate professional and seemed to show a genuine interest in what Sarah had to say. She had explained in very careful, non-technical terms how the weakening magnetic field of the Earth could no longer deflect the high-energy particles from space, and that while this particular energetic solar burst would normally have been treated as an isolated and freak incident, the world could expect more violent events in the future as the planet's defence weakened further. She'd felt on safe ground explaining this and was confident with the science. Most people knew about the growing number of holes in the ozone layer in the upper atmosphere and the general heightened levels of radiation exposure, but a direct hit from coronal mass ejections was something new to many, and the fact that this one seemed to have been directly responsible for bringing down Flight AI-231 had captured the world's attention.

But just when she thought the interview was winding up, the woman began asking questions she felt she couldn't offer a confident opinion on. She knew that being a scientist meant she was expected to be an expert on everything, but what had annoyed her was that the woman could clearly see her discomfort and yet carried on pressing for answers. She had wanted to know when Sarah expected the Flip to happen and how quickly the strength of the field would be restored once magnetic north and south had switched over. She then asked how satellites or electricity grids could be protected before this happened and things settled down, and even what could be done to protect people from the harm cosmic rays could cause them directly. Had Sarah been lulled into a false sense of security by being first asked about the stuff she knew? Was this a trap? Did the network or the producers of this particular news

programme have any political agenda? She had forced herself
to remain calm.

She explained how, once the poles had flipped and the field
had regained its strength, everything would slowly return to
normal, but until it did, and that could take decades, the surface of the planet was highly exposed.

But her reluctance to be drawn in to speculating about these
issues and her mumbled protests about not being qualified to
comment were all instantly dubbed into fifty languages by
software that even picked up, and mimicked, the frustrated
tone of her voice.

By the time the interview was over she felt drained. The syr-
upy smile and exaggerated fake gratitude of her interviewer
had only made her more resentful of the woman. She'd been
eager to get back to her apartment. Maybe if she'd had the
chance to discuss all this with her boss, Philipe Santos, he
could have advised her on what she should and shouldn't comment on. But, as director of the SSI, he had been just as inundated
as her with media enquiries and had brushed off her concerns,
saying he had full confidence in her. He had then flown to
Brasília to talk politics. No doubt he would be looking for
ways of turning his institute's early detection of the CME to
his advantage by talking up the role the SSI could play in providing an advance-warning system which could help avert any
future such tragedies, naturally only by securing significantly
larger funding.

The following day she'd received a message from Santos telling her to set up a VR meeting with the SSI's counterpart
research organization in London, the Helios Institute, to see
if there was any mileage in collaborating more closely on a CME
early-warning system. Although she knew it was a long shot,
she asked him if it would be possible for her to fly to London to
speak to them in person. These days, the convenience of a VR
visor meant no one had to travel to conferences any more. Sarah
knew full well that her avatar could meet up with the avatars
of the Helios Institute scientists at a computer-simulated location of their choice, but she was also aware that she hadn't

visited her parents in almost a year. So she had argued the case for needing to be physically in London in order to properly discuss the latest solar data face to face. Santos was no fool and knew her real reason for wanting to go, but he was also a reasonable man.

By early Thursday evening she was flying across the Atlantic to the country of her birth and the chance for some brief respite, and maybe even a relaxing weekend at her parents' house on the south coast of England.

In fact, visiting them had highlighted just how long it had been since she'd last been over. She had been sensible enough not to try and adjust her body clock for the three short days of her trip, knowing she'd be flying back across the Atlantic soon enough.

Her parents had both been following her Globo interview. 'You sounded very confident and self-assured, darling,' remarked her mother, 'and, do you know, for the first time I think I now understand what your work is about. I know you've tried explaining it many times to me but, well, you know me.'

Her father had suggested they go out for a pub lunch at one of their old haunts; one that held fond memories for Sarah too, from what seemed like many lifetimes ago.

During the relatively short drive along the coastal road from her parents' home in Southsea, she had only half listened to her mother's animated monologue updating her on the latest news of family friends and relatives she hadn't seen or spoken to in years. She stared out at the soggy world outside through the rivulets of rain running down the window. She recalled vividly, as though it were just yesterday, the childhood frustration both she and her brother would feel during the family's regular summer drive to the sandy expanse of West Wittering beach; frustration at losing valuable beach time before the tide came in as the car crawled slowly along with the rest of the summer traffic towards the popular resort. But on this particular Sunday three decades later, the roads were nearly empty. With the pitter-patter of the rain on the car roof making more noise than the hum of its electric engine, her father had informed her in his typical matter-of-fact way that these days this coast road wasn't much busier even during the height of the summer season. West Wittering beach and much of the surrounding low-lying marshlands were now permanently underwater, part of the changing coastline of the British Isles thanks to the rising sea levels.

But the dismal weather notwithstanding, the day had been wonderful. After eating Brazilian cuisine for so long, a proper English Sunday roast with 'all the trimmings' had really hit the spot. The Lamb Inn down by the seafront in the Witterings was a family favourite and they were lucky to have got a table when booking so late. The entire day had felt soaked in nostalgia, just as it did every time she came back to visit her parents. As she always did on such visits, it made her question why she had moved so far away from all these childhood memories.

That day now seemed like a parallel reality in which time ran at a different pace – a temporary haven of sanity in the eye of a storm. But there had been yet more surprises in store. On Sunday evening, she'd received a message from the prime minister's office and a summons to attend Whitehall first thing on Monday morning to brief the UK government's crisis response committee, COBRA.

Sarah was intrigued as to why they would feel it necessary, or even useful, to speak to her. After all, if they had just wanted reliable scientific advice, then surely any number of solar physicists at the Helios Institute in London could have briefed them. She figured that political aides and civil servants were no less lazy than many in the media when it came to looking for expert opinion. You just checked to see who everyone else had been talking to.

Her meeting with the PM, along with several ministers and aides, had been a somewhat surreal experience. The British government had been debating recently whether to fund a joint Sino-British ten-year project to build a new early-warning satellite system and couldn't decide whether it would be worth the multi-billion-pound outlay, given the nature of the new threat posed by solar particles. The prime minister and several faceless civil servants had all been pleasant enough – in fact,

the PM had positively oozed an obsequious charm that was
mildly unsettling. Having been out of the country for so long,
she didn't really have a strong opinion on his true political
views. Like the previous few populist governments, these people
seemed keen, and short-sighted enough, to insist on knowing
the views of any British scientists who they felt could give them
technological insider knowledge that they could use to negotiate a deal with China.

But what on earth she could tell them that they didn't already
know, she had no idea. Maybe they were crediting her with
deeper insights than she could offer. She had simply repeated
what she had said already countless times about the uncertain-
ties of even the most sophisticated solar model. Why couldn't
they understand that space weather was just as unpredictable
as terrestrial weather?

But if Sarah had thought she'd now be able to head home
and get back to her research, then she had underestimated the
impact of her sudden fame. The day after her Whitehall meeting, and while immersed in discussions at Helios in London,
she'd received a further unexpected message. This time her
presence was requested in New York, by the UN Secretary-
General Abelli herself. She had made her excuses to the Helios
scientists and looked around for somewhere she could make a
call in private. In the end she decided to play it safe and headed
for a rear exit from the building. Although she had not been
told that her invitation to the UN was a secret, she still thought
it prudent to have some privacy.

She'd stepped out into the chilly late afternoon air and the
deserted backstreet and immediately wished she'd remembered
her coat. The steady hum of hundreds of drones in the air above
her head filled her ears: delivery drones, window-cleaning drones,
surveillance and monitoring drones, all going about their business, choreographed by the London Transport AI so that they
zipped past each other in every possible direction in three dimensions, never colliding or getting in the way of the much larger
taxi drones that buzzed through the swarm.

Sarah tapped her wristpad and called her father. As a retired political correspondent, he would have as good an idea as anyone what this all meant.

For all the justifiable criticism of the UN's ineffectiveness, especially since the epicentre of global power had shifted to east Asia, it still had considerable influence. And in any case, it remained the only body that even came close to being neutral on the world stage.

His smiling face filled the screen on her wrist, although she could see that he was speaking to her from his study.

'Hi, Dad. Listen, I'm afraid I'm flying out again tomorrow so I'm not going to get the chance to get back down to see you and Mum after all. I'm really sorry.'

'What? Already? But sweetheart, you've only been in the country a few days.'

'Yeah, I know. I'm sorry. And I need some advice.'

'That's what dads are for, right?' His features took on a more serious look, which amused her. Sometimes he acted as though she was still eight years old rather than thirty-eight. She smiled. 'Well, you know I had my Downing Street meeting yesterday? The PM seemed a nice enough guy. Wouldn't trust him as far as I could spit, of course.' This was exactly the sort of thing her father would say, for she knew full well what he thought of the current government.

True to form, he grunted his disapproval. 'Well, yes, I could have told you that for nothing. So, how did it go? Assuming you're allowed to tell me anything.'

'Well, we'll probably both get shot for treason if we're caught,' she said in mock trepidation. Her father had retired seven years ago, but still wrote the odd stingingly critical article on the government's unpopular and draconian robot ethics and drone surveillance laws. She recounted her hour-long meeting the day before. 'Nothing much to report, really. I went over the usual science and the risks of a coronal ejection hitting the UK. It's all stuff they know already, Dad. They really didn't need to hear it from me. Anyway, I called because of something else that's just come up that's even more important and I wanted to pick your brains.'

His eyebrows shot up and he sat back in his chair in mock astonishment. 'Really? Even more important than explaining basic science to a philistine like our prime minister? What could possibly be more pressing?'

Sarah chuckled. Then, without thinking, she quickly glanced up and down the street to make sure she was still alone. 'I've been invited to join some crack UN committee looking into the solar threat. To be honest, the whole thing is nuts. The committee seems to be full of government ministers, ambassadors and other high-profile characters. I mean, people with real power. I keep wondering why they suddenly want the advice of a mid-career scientist like me who has not had any real experience in science policy or politics.'

'Don't knock it. You're an excellent solar physicist and they would do well to listen to what you have to say. And as for this committee, it sounds like another one of those intergovernmental panels to me – you know, like the IPCC. What bloody good this new one would do I don't know, but I guess it's about time some action, any action, was taken.'

Sarah knew only too well that it was largely thanks to the efforts of the IPCC over the past forty years that the worst effects of climate change had been averted. And the same was true for the panel on antimicrobial resistance. The controversy these days was with the Intergovernmental Panel on Population Displacement, which had its work cut out and was hugely unpopular. But then the mass migrations forced by sea-level rises were still going on.

'Well, anyway, I hope I'm not the only scientist on this panel and it's not just a bunch of megalomaniac politicians with their own vested interests. I mean, how do these things work?'

'I'm happy that you think I'm the fount of all knowledge and wisdom. But I'm just a retired hack keeping his head down while watching others try to sort out the planet. But since you ask, I'm not catching any whiff of conspiracy theories here.'

Sarah had wondered whether those who held the reins of power really did have the planet's interests at heart, or if that was an outdated and naively optimistic view. In any case, did her father still have his finger on the pulse of world politics any longer? Well, she'd find out soon enough.

'OK, Dad, I'll try to keep you posted. Give my love to Mum.'

'I will. And try to get some sleep, you look tired.'

'Don't worry, Dad, I'll get a decent night's sleep before I head out.'

'Good. Saving the world can be exhausting, you know. And remember, your mother and I are very proud of you.'

That had been twenty-four hours ago. Here she was now on the other side of the Atlantic, in a driverless cab weaving its way across a vibrant Manhattan on a bitterly cold evening. She still wasn't sure what she felt about having been thrust into the limelight like this.

The truth was that she wasn't cut out for this world of politics and public relations. In fact, rather than feeling flattered by all the attention, she'd felt a growing insecurity – a nagging anxiety that her shortcomings and the many gaps in her knowledge would, sooner or later, be exposed. She kept telling herself this was classic imposter syndrome. She was easily as highly qualified and knowledgeable as anyone else in her field, and she'd worked hard to get to the position she was in. Still, returning home briefly had meant she could hide away for a couple of days and hope that everyone forgot about her as the world moved on to another story.

As the taxi pulled up outside her hotel, a cheerful electronic voice said, 'Have a nice day, Dr Maitlin. Thank you for using New York Autocabs,' and the door of the car slid open as her fare registered. The place she was staying at was a small but comfortable hotel ideally situated in downtown Manhattan between 5th and Park Avenues. There was a welcoming aroma of coffee in the lobby. Nodding a hello in the direction of the bored-looking receptionist, she poured herself a mug and headed up to her room.

She felt relieved to finally have some time to recuperate, catch up on some work and maybe look up an old friend from university days who now lived and worked in New York, before her Saturday morning meeting at the UN. Walking into her room, she was greeted by a gust of warm air and absent-mindedly commanded the heating to be turned down a few degrees. As she turned to close the door she spotted an envelope on the floor.

Who delivered paper notes any more? And who slipped them under hotel-room doors, for Christ's sake? Intrigued, she picked it up and pulled out a neatly folded sheet of paper. The words were quaintly hand-written on UN headed notepaper.

*Dear Dr Maitlin*

*My name is Professor Gabriel Aguda, a geologist at the University of Lagos, but mostly these days I act as an Advisor on Earth Sciences to the UN here in New York. Like you, I have been recruited onto the new UN committee. I must say it's a relief to have another scientist on board and as you can imagine I'm looking forward to meeting you. If possible, would you like to get together for breakfast first? I can try to bring you up to speed on what this is all about. If so, I can meet you in your hotel lobby at 7.30 on Saturday morning.*

*If I don't hear from you, then I'll assume this is the plan. But if for any reason we cannot touch base before the meeting itself then do ping me at any time in the coming days.*

*Yours truly,*
*Gabriel Aguda*

The note had a charm to it. Presumably, Aguda was someone who didn't trust cybersecurity systems enough to leave her a message online. She blinked to activate her augmented reality and her field of vision was filled with her favourite 3D search engine intervening semi-transparently in front of her view of the hotel-room surroundings. She said, 'Search Gabriel Aguda United Nations.'

It seemed the geologist had been a powerful mover and shaker in the academic world and had written a number of influential and highly cited papers on earthquake prediction early in his career. Recently, though, he seemed to have operated more as a politician than a scientist, although he still spent part of his time back in his home country of Nigeria as well as teaching as an adjunct professor at the University of Rochester.

Since she had no UN allies yet, breakfast with Gabriel Aguda sounded like a good place to start.

# 7

*Thursday, 7 February – Tehran*

TWENTY-YEAR-OLD COMPUTER SCIENCE STUDENT SHIREEN Darvish was certain her mother cooked the very best *fesenjoon* in the world and she would take on anyone who claimed otherwise. When the rich aroma of the pomegranate stew wafted up to her bedroom, seeping beneath her closed door, she realized how hungry she was.

Although she was physically in her room, which was so crammed with electronic equipment it resembled a space mission control centre, Shireen's mind was somewhere else entirely. Inside her virtual reality helmet was a universe of data and lines of machine code – an electronic landscape of pure information. And it was a world Shireen had always found more familiar and reassuring than the real one.

She'd been working hard for several hours but was still reluctant to leave her computer even for a moment. She was at last closing in on something big. The last few months had been spent testing and re-testing her Trojan horse hacking software; she'd almost been badly burned on a couple of occasions when she'd been sure the authorities were on to her, but finally she felt that all the bases were covered.

Which was just as well, because she had important end-of-year examinations in the summer and didn't want to fall behind in her classes. She justified the time spent on her extracurricular interests because they were so closely aligned with the courses she was taking at Tehran University. Still, she found that her thoughts were increasingly drifting towards her secret project, even during lectures. The only person who knew that her mind was elsewhere was her close friend Majid. And even he didn't know the half of it.

Shireen was well aware she was far from alone, for there were millions like her around the world – though few were as smart – all obsessed with finding ways of cracking uncrackable codes, infiltrating the most secret recesses of cyberspace, whether by stealth or in the open. She hated the generic term 'cyberterrorism', which was used by the authorities to include anyone who preferred the anonymity of the dark web. At least it meant that cybersecurity remained a lucrative career of choice for many young computer science graduates around the world. But while Shireen acknowledged that there were people who wished to use cyberattacks to harm humanity because of some ideology they had bought into, she felt she was part of a more benign and altruistic movement of cyberhackers. She was a cyb, and she was proud of it. She saw the aim of the cyb movement as exposing injustices committed in the very name of global cybersecurity. Not that the authorities would see it that way if she were ever caught. She smiled to herself. *I'm too clever to be caught.*

Born in the early 2020s, Shireen had not known a time when quantum key distribution was not the standard means of securing online data. She knew from her cryptography classes at university that until the mid-twenties data had been protected online using public key cryptosystems like RSA. Several months ago, while staying with her elderly great-aunt Pirween in Isfahan, she had tried explaining encryption to her. 'If I asked you to multiply two big numbers together, Auntie, say one hundred and ninety-three times five hundred and sixty-nine, could you give me the answer?'

'Not in my head, dear, but I can do it easily enough on my tablet,' her aunt had replied, holding up the old-fashioned device close to her mouth. It amused Shireen that the elderly woman, like many of her generation, still didn't trust the technology of augmented reality, preferring archaic handheld tablets – there was even still a market for early-twenties smartphones.

Her aunt began speaking into her device. 'Tablet, multiply one hundred and—'

'—you'll find it's a hundred and nine thousand, eight hundred and seventeen.'

'Did you just do that in your head? If so, I'm very impressed.'

'Actually, no, Auntie, I've used this example before, so I just remember the answer. Now, what if I asked you to work out the only two numbers which, when multiplied together, give a hundred and nine thousand, eight hundred and seventeen? Could you do that?'

'Isn't that what you just asked me?' said her aunt, looking genuinely puzzled.

'No!' said Shireen, feeling a little exasperated. 'The first time I gave you two numbers to multiply and asked for the answer, which is straightforward. But now I've given you the answer and I'm asking you to do it in reverse.'

'Well, it's five hundred and something-something times . . . I mean, if I had a pen and paper—'

'Please, Auntie, I meant if I'd started the conversation just with the big number . . .'

The old woman had laughed. 'I know, dear, I'm teasing.'

'OK, bear with me. You see, the first problem: multiplying two numbers together, however big they are, can be done on any calculator. Lots of people can even multiply two three-digit numbers in their heads easily enough. But the reverse used to be an almost impossible task. It's called finding the prime factors of a number. When you were young, that would have been how your credit-card details were stored securely online.'

'Public key encryption. I remember it well. And I remember the panic when the first quantum computers came along, and nothing was secure online any more.'

'Yup, they could do what no other computer had been able to do before, however powerful, and crack the problem of factorizing big numbers. So, quantum key distribution came along and was much more secure because—'

'Because,' her aunt chipped in '. . . because . . . wait, I know this. It's because of quantum entanglement. If you try to spy on something you disturb it, however careful you are, and you set off the quantum alarm.'

This time it was Shireen's turn to laugh. 'That's a pretty good summary, yes. The "observer effect".'

Having grown up with it, Shireen felt completely at home immersed in the world of fuzzy quantum bits of information, a strange digital reality in which the binary certainty of zeros or ones is replaced by a ghostly existence of both at the same time.

Hers was a world within a world, the vast cyberspace – a universe made up not of physical particles, but of pure information, flowing, interacting and constantly evolving within its own dimensions. Shireen's talents of course ran in the family. She was very proud of the fact that both her parents had been among the early whizz-kids of the Invisible Internet Project, the underground network that sat below the surface of the web and which had originally been used for secret surfing and information exchange. Her father had even worked on the anonymous communication software project, Tor, at MIT before returning to Iran to join the underground dark web movement of the early 2020s that toppled the Islamic regime. This meant he knew more than most about cybersecurity, anonymized communication, multi-layer encryption and so-called onion routing. Her mother had pioneered techniques for hacking public key cryptosystems with home-made quantum computers running codes that made use of Shor's algorithm to factorize large numbers.

But Shireen was a child of the new world order, which was dominated by the code war. When pervasive computing took off in the early twenties, when she was a young child, it still had a name: it was referred to as the Internet of Things; but it was soon clear that it no longer needed to be called anything. In a world where everything was connected to everything else, only her grandparents' generation still used phrases like 'look online' instead of just 'look'. It had begun with home and office appliances linked wirelessly to handheld devices, but eventually everything was networked; sensors, cameras, embedded nano servers and energy harvesters were all ubiquitous and built into the infrastructure of the modern world, from buildings and transport to clothing and household items.

Eventually world governments and multinationals woke up to the desperate need for advanced cybersecurity systems, but not before the anonymous hacking of international crypto-currency banking had brought the world markets crashing down in 2028, followed by the devastating cyberattack six months later on the AI system controlling London, one of the world's first 'smart cities'. That onslaught had infected many of the algorithms controlling the city's transport, commerce and environmental infrastructures, sending ten million people back into the Stone Age for three weeks.

These events prompted action and led to the development of the Sentinels, cybersecurity artificial intelligences that would continuously patrol the Cloud, hunting for anomalies, viruses and leaks. They became the guardians of the larger AIs, or Minds, that ran everything from air traffic control and defence systems to power plants and financial institutions. And despite the cyberattack on London in '28, most large cities were now run entirely by Minds. Since the mid 2030s, a constant battle had been raging between the Sentinels and the rogue AIs developed by cyberterrorist groups, sent into the Cloud to test them.

Shireen didn't feel she truly belonged in either camp, but the code war fascinated her nevertheless. She rated her talents high, far exceeding those of her parents, which was why she had avoided any mention of her latest project – not because they wouldn't understand the technical details, but because she knew they would have warned her off. In any case, she was now playing in the big league and it wasn't just her own safety she had to think about; her parents would also be in jeopardy if the authorities ever tracked her down.

There was a knock on her bedroom door. 'Come on down and eat, darling; it's time you took a break from your studies.'

Wearing her VR visor, Shireen couldn't see her mother, but knew she wouldn't set foot in the room for fear of disturbing her daughter's concentration.

'It's OK, Mum, you *can* come in, you know.' Shireen had to smile. Her mother was the sweetest person in the world but could be so naive. She felt a pang of guilt, as she always did, that her mother had mistakenly assumed she was hard at work behind her visor. She blinked several times in rapid succession to turn down the volume of the music she was listening to. She was everything her mother wasn't: brash, self-confident and subversive. On the walls around the house there were old hard-copy photos in picture frames, of her mother when she was a young student, around Shireen's age, showing her still wearing a headscarf – the strict Islamic dress code that had been enforced in Iran for half a century. And here was Shireen in her shorts and T-shirt, with VR headset wrapped around her bright-pink cropped hair, and tattoos covering more than half her body. This played to her advantage: the more her parents focused on their daughter's rebellious fashion sense the less they were likely to notice her cyberhacking projects. Of course, they knew she wasn't spending all that time in her room on her studies, but they would have been mortified to discover what she was really working on.

She waved her haptic-gloved hands elegantly in front of her face and wiggled her fingers, touch-typing in a 3D virtual-reality space that only she could see, to iconize the multitude of windows and applications. She then removed her visor and stretched. Her mother was still standing smiling in the doorway. She cut an elegant figure – slim and considerably taller than her daughter. Shireen wondered if she herself would look that good thirty years from now. Her life was so much more comfortable than her mother's had been at her age. The pace of cultural change in Persian society during Shireen's lifetime had been nothing short of remarkable. In the space of less than twenty years, their country had gone from a conservative religious state to a liberal democracy with all the excesses and corruptions of any mid-twenty-first-century capitalist state. Many older

Persians could even remember the time under the Shah seventy years ago and so had seen the country come full circle. Did being able to dye her hair, dress outrageously and be open about her sexuality mean that life was really any better now? But then she hadn't lived through the Iran of her parents.

Even though they were only three, her mother always insisted on laying the table as though for a banquet. Even the large dish of rice at the centre of the table was a work of art, with saffron-coloured grains piled in a neat spiral over plain white rice, and raisins and almonds sprinkled on top. Then there was the *fesenjoon*. She was again suddenly conscious of how hungry she felt. But, as usual, she knew that by the end of the meal she'd be so full she'd struggle to get up.

Her father, already seated at the table, looked up when she came in. 'Ah, she's back in the real world. Still busy trying to hack through the great firewall of China?'

To an outsider, Reza Darvish's casual attitude towards his daughter's hobby might have appeared at best cavalier and at worst shockingly reckless. But Shireen had gone to considerable lengths to ensure that, as far as her parents were concerned, she was indulging in nothing more than an innocent pastime.

'*Trying* to hack through? I'm unstoppable, Dad,' she replied light-heartedly as she shovelled a large portion of rice onto her plate. The smile disappeared from her father's face and his voice took on a more sombre tone.

'It's a dangerous game, Reenie. A lot of cybs who get too close to secrets simply go missing. I'd hate to think you're mixing with that crowd.' He sighed. 'And I should know,' he added for good measure.

She hoped the meal wasn't going to be accompanied by one of her father's well-rehearsed lectures on cybersecurity. He could sometimes be infuriatingly old-fashioned in his views.

Her mother walked into the dining room with a large bowl of salad and caught the last few words. 'Come on, Reza, Shireen's smarter than that.' She ruffled her daughter's spiky hair affectionately as she sat down next to her. Shireen waved her mother's hand away in mock annoyance.

'Well, as long as you're keeping on top of your studies, I suppose,' said her father, his voice softening again. 'I just wish you had other interests beyond your bedroom walls. You do know there's a big world out there, full of art and music and literature and science?'

'Plenty of time for all that, Dad,' she said through a mouthful of food. 'I'm only twenty and I have cyberspace at my feet. Once I've conquered that, I'll explore the real world.'

Her mother laughed, tilting her head back as she did so. The sound had a purity about it that made her look even more beautiful. Shireen caught her father looking over, smiling. It was clear in his eyes just how deeply he still loved his wife. Her mother turned to her. 'If this were twenty years ago we'd have been looking for a husband for you by now,' she joked.

For all their middle-class, left-leaning liberal secularism, her parents still identified with their Muslim culture. Shireen found this poignant and somehow comforting. Persians were stubbornly proud of their rich history, sometimes infuriatingly so. But then they did have five thousand years of history to call upon. Anyway, Shireen had not found the right time to tell them that they should give up any hope of having a son-in-law. One day, Iran would truly catch up with the rest of the twenty-first century and then her parents might get themselves a daughter-in-law.

'If it's OK with you, I'd like to pop out later. I need to talk to Majid about a coursework assignment for next week.' The part about meeting Majid, at least, was true.

'What time is your first lecture tomorrow?' her father asked. 'It'd do you good to have an early night for a change.'

'I don't have a class until my advanced algorithms at eleven.' The new maglev meant her daily commute from Ray on the outskirts of Tehran to the campus in the centre of the city took less than twenty minutes. She could afford a lie-in tomorrow.

She saw her parents exchange exasperated looks and decided it was best to change the subject. For the rest of the meal they discussed the growing concerns about the threat from the Sun and whether governments were keeping any information back.

After dinner, Shireen helped her mother carry the dishes through to the kitchen, stepping over the cleaner bots heading in the opposite direction to suck up any stray grains of rice on the floor underneath the table. Her mother could see she was eager to escape and waved her away. 'Go, go. Say hello to Majid for us.'

Majid had been Shireen's friend since childhood, and since they were now both studying on the same course, he was one of the very few people – no, wait, scratch that: the only person – whom she could trust entirely. And even then, she didn't feel able to share her latest project with him completely – mostly for his own safety. Plus, he'd probably tell her not to be so foolish. So, she would have to be careful how she elicited his help. Majid didn't have her intuitive feel for navigating through the dark web, nor her brilliance in quantum information theory. He certainly lacked her sixth sense when it came to knowing how to probe for weaknesses in multi-layered encrypted data.

It was a clear, chilly evening when she left the house. She felt a thrill at the thought of how close she was getting to a real breakthrough. Her small car was parked in the drive. She jumped in and voice-activated the destination. 'Majid's house' was all it needed to know. Slumped back in her seat while it reversed itself onto the road, she wondered how much she could confide in Majid.

The car weaved its way silently and unerringly through the early-evening Tehran traffic and Shireen stared out of the window, impatient to get to her friend's apartment, not taking much notice of the familiar sights and sounds of the city rushing by outside. Soon, the car turned off the highway and travelled along quieter tree-lined avenues. Shireen ran through in her head how she should tackle Majid without alarming him, or insulting him. It wasn't his views or advice that she was interested in eliciting, but the use of the quantum computer he had recently acquired – or rather that his father had bought for him. Strictly speaking, she didn't actually need a quantum computer to hack into a quantum key distribution repeater system, but the firewalls around it were impregnable. There was no way they could be watching her watching them – whoever 'they' might be.

She felt confident that running her algorithm on his machine would be the final phase, when she would at last gain access to files that had been better protected than anything she had encountered before. She still had no idea what those files contained, but the way they had been encrypted and hidden bore all the hallmarks of ultra-sensitive government secrets, probably Chinese in origin – red rag to a bull for any self-respecting cyb. Now, after months of effort, she was approaching the endgame, even though she hadn't given any thought to what she would do with the information once she had it.

For Shireen, being a cyb was more than a hobby. She sometimes tried to convince herself that hacking was just an intellectual challenge, like solving a maths problem or completing a tough jigsaw puzzle. But the truth was that she was addicted to it – her desire to break an unbreakable code was no different to the obsession of an old-fashioned safe-cracker. And the dangers of getting caught were just as real.

With her thoughts already on abstract lines of coding, Shireen watched the world go by – couples wrapped up against the chilly evening air, out for an after-dinner stroll, and late office workers eager to get home after a long day, overtaken by joggers in colourful kit preferring the fresh evening air to their virtual-reality treadmills.

She didn't ping Majid until her car pulled up outside his apartment. That way he couldn't make any excuses about wanting an early night or being too busy.

'Hey, Hajji. I'm outside. Can I pop up for an hour? I need the use of your new toy . . . and you know how you just live to make me happy.' 'Hajji' was her term of endearment for her friend, who had been on a pilgrimage to Mecca with his grandfather when he was ten. He hated the nickname, which was why Shireen enjoyed using it.

'Yeah, OK. But not for long. I've got a class in the morning.' She heard the sigh of resignation in his voice. He buzzed her in. 'Thanks. I promise I won't outstay my welcome.'

When Shireen got to his floor, the door was already open. She breezed into the apartment to find her friend standing in the hallway. He had a slight frame and was no taller than Shireen. His carefully barbered goatee beard, which he was convinced added gravitas and compensated for what he lacked in physical stature, was a source of constant teasing by Shireen.

She gave him a tight hug. 'And don't you dare give me that "class in the morning" shit. You forget: I know our timetable.'

'Whatever. I could still do with an early night. What was it you wanted? Don't tell me it's to do with your Trojan horse attack algorithm, whatever the hell that is, because if it is, I really don't think I can help much.'

Shireen gave him a wink. 'Don't worry, it's not your acute intellectual powers I need right now; it's your hardware.' Majid's recently acquired solid-state giga-qubit quantum computer – a matt-black cube the size of a shoebox that now had pride of place in the middle of his desk by the large window overlooking the street – had, in theory at least, the processing capacity of a human brain, but until someone figured out how to write the software to get it to think for itself it was still just a dumb machine.

Majid's apartment unashamedly betrayed his family's wealth. It was an interesting mix of old and new, decorated with luxurious drapes and classic, almost gaudy furnishing. But to the expert eye, the trappings of mid-century technology were integrated everywhere, with sensors and microchips in every appliance and fixture, communicating with each other and ready to adjust or go into action on command. Shireen often joked that a man who even needed his socks to have their own IP address, so they could remind him when they needed washing, wouldn't last five minutes in a post-apocalyptic world. 'And don't expect me to be there to help you survive,' she would say. 'You know you'd only slow me down.'

Majid went over to his desk and placed the ball of his thumb on its black glass surface. There was a hum and ripple of light as a keyboard and colourful array of function keys appeared. Shireen stood behind him, rested her chin on his shoulder and murmured in his ear. 'Thank you, Hajji.'

Majid looked like he had resigned himself to letting her do

whatever she needed to because he walked away from the desk in silence and collapsed onto the sofa to watch. But no sooner had he sat down than he bounced back up again and said, 'OK, before you get too lost in code, would you like me to order pizza?'

'No thanks, I've eaten,' she replied without even turning to him. 'But you go ahead. I'm hoping this won't take too long anyway.' Her fingers darted around the smooth surface as she tapped the keys, then she spoke a few commands into her wristpad to allow the computer to identify her. When she was satisfied she was connected, she wandered over to a chair, picked up the hololens visor and haptic gloves she'd brought with her and put them on. Sitting down, she tucked her feet underneath her body like a meditating Buddha.

After the briefest of pauses while the computer connected with the new hardware, her vision was filled with a glowing display screen and her retinal AR was relegated to a tiny icon in the bottom left corner. Using her gloved hands to control the display, she quickly accessed her files and, within seconds, was floating in the reassuringly familiar three-dimensional vir-tual reality of her dark-web space.

*Right then, this is it.* She felt a surge of adrenalin as she con-templated what she was about to do. As she always did when she was concentrating, she began to talk through the steps she needed to follow, providing herself with a running commen-tary as she worked.

'You're mumbling again,' she heard Majid say.

'Hmm?' She was no longer really paying attention to the real world outside.

'I said you're doing that thing again . . . you know, where you talk to yourself.'

Then, after a brief pause, he added, 'Reenie, I don't *need* to know what you're up to, but can I just check that whatever it is won't be traced back here?'

It hadn't occurred to her just how much she was asking of her best friend, but something in his voice betrayed his ner-vousness and she suddenly realized that she wasn't the only one taking a risk. Of course, she would make sure all traces of having used Majid's computer would be thoroughly erased, but maybe she did owe him some explanation.

Her concentration broken, she paused to think about what she should do. How much could she afford to tell him? Wasn't it more sensible, and safe, to keep him as much in the dark as possible? No, that wasn't fair.

She tried to push away what she realized were her true motives for revealing what she was doing to Majid. If she was honest, it was really more about her. Opening up would be a mixture of a boast and a confession.

She felt full of nervous energy at the prospect of sharing her ideas with another person, even though she guessed he would struggle to follow all the details. She took off her visor, untucked her legs again and turned to face him. He was staring at her like an affectionate puppy. Under all her bravado and tattoos, Shireen was well aware, because she had been told so on many occasions, that she was elfishly attractive; and she also knew that Majid had feelings for her that went beyond friendship. But they had an understanding, and he knew those feelings would never be reciprocated.

'OK, Majid, I'm going to let you in on my little project.' She pulled off her gloves to signal that she was going to devote all her attention to him for the next few minutes. 'You know I've been trying for ages to find a way through those new encryption protocols I told you about?'

'Yes, but just last week you said—'

'I know . . .' interrupted Shireen eagerly. 'Last week I said that was impossible, right? Because the Chinese had increased the number of their Sentinels protecting the repeater stations.' She knew that Majid was familiar with the basic science, but unlike her he was less than comfortable with the whole subject of quantum key distribution. He sometimes confessed to her that he should never have chosen computer science as his major at university. Why couldn't he just have opted for a simpler subject – basically anything that didn't involve the counter-intuitive ideas of quantum physics.

'Well, that was last week. I think I may have found a back door,' Shireen continued. 'There's been some rather busy traffic recently between the Chinese authorities and other governments, and all the communications have been locked with unusually high levels of encryption, so I'm pretty sure there's something big going down that is being kept very hush-hush.'

' "*Something big*"?' Majid almost shouted. 'Are we talking international espionage? Or just your crazy conspiracy theory shit?' He chewed his top lip and ran both hands over the back of his shaven head. Two years ago, they had both been arrested during the student anti-corruption riots. Luckily his father had sufficient influence to get the charges against them dropped. But the incident meant they had needed to be more careful. Shireen tried to reassure her friend. 'Don't look so worried. You know that I know what I'm doing, right?'

'I know you *think* you know what you're doing. And OK, I don't know any cyb smarter than you. But how can you be so sure you're not biting off more than you can chew this time?'

'Because . . .' Shireen jumped out of her chair with renewed excitement and onto the sofa next to Majid. 'Because . . . I think I've found two weaknesses. The first, which I've suspected for a while, is a vulnerability in the repeater control system that allows me to hack in to it. The second – and this really is quite beautiful – is a weakness in the cloning algorithm in the repeater, which means I can make a copy of the quantum key without it affecting what's sent on to the genuine recipient.'

Majid was gaping at her.

'All I need is for a window to open up for a few seconds. I can get in, copy the key and get the hell out again.' She sat back and looked at Majid's reaction, then looked over at the black box on his desk containing the quantum computer. 'And that's why I need your new toy.'

However, Majid looked anything but reassured. He leaned forward and grabbed her by the shoulders. For a brief moment she wondered whether he was going to try and *shake* some sense into her. Instead, he said, 'But the whole point of quantum key distribution is that you *can't* eavesdrop without giving your-self away! I may not be as smart as you, Reenie, but I know enough from my quantum cryptography classes that this is the whole fucking point of the system. Any attempt to break the code disturbs the delicate quantum entangled state and sends an alert to the source, which then immediately switches to a different encryption key. Wasn't that the subject of last week's lecture – something about the Ekert 91 protocol?'

Shireen grinned, suddenly feeling even more pleased with herself. 'I know, foolproof, right? And you know as well as I do that every cyb in the world is looking for new attack strat-egies that target vulnerabilities in the system. And if you ask any of them they'll tell you that the obvious man-in-the-middle attacks and the photon number splitting attacks don't work. In fact, government and corporation sites don't even bother fol-lowing up on these cyber alerts any more. And that's the beauty of it; they're so cocksure their encryptions can't be broken that no one is watching me.'

'And that's what you think you've done, is it? You've found a way of getting hold of a quantum encryption key without detection . . . a window where the laws of physics are no longer in control?' Majid's curiosity had now seemingly got the better of his nerves. He leapt to his feet and paced around the room. 'OK, how?'

'This, my dear Hajji, is why I will one day rule the world, while you will simply exist to wait on me hand and foot and serve me *bastani* and *faloodeh* until I get so big I explode. You see, I've found the one weakness in the system that plays them at their own quantum game: my very own Trojan horse code. It's so quiet, so imperceptible, that no one will ever know I've been snooping.'

'OK, your majesty,' he said, placing both hands on his chest and bowing, 'but . . . surely if—'

Shireen interrupted him, realizing she would have to try harder to explain. 'OK, listen. Quantum Information Theory one-oh-one – well, more correctly, basic communications engineering – says it's not possible to completely eliminate errors in electronic communications because of factors like noise and signal degradation, right? Well, early quantum encryption systems allowed for key exchanges where the error rate could be as high as twenty per cent. They felt that was acceptable since any eavesdropper would be too loud and clumsy and so give themselves away. But then ten years ago those new phase-remapping "intercept and resend" attacks meant things had to tighten up.'

'OK, please stop patronizing me, Shireen.' She could tell by the impatient look on his face that he still hadn't heard anything he didn't know already. 'I know that when cyberattacks suddenly grew a few years ago it was because eavesdroppers got so good they could intercept a tiny fraction of the signal sent during a quantum key exchange while never pushing the error rate over the twenty per cent threshold. So, their attacks were hidden in the noise. But once the authorities discovered this, they worked to bring that error threshold down.' He then added for good measure, 'Correct me if I'm being too slow-witted for you.'

Shireen ignored her friend's indignation. 'Exactly. So now only error rates below three per cent are accepted as noise and ignored. Anything above that and you're screwed. The problem has been that no one can eavesdrop quietly enough not to trigger much higher error rates than three per cent.'

Shireen left a dramatic pause to maximize the impact of what she was about to say. 'Well, no one, that is, until it was figured out by yours truly.' She grinned broadly. 'You see, I've found a crucial chink in the armour. It's a weakness in the quantum cloning algorithm. If it wasn't so cool, I'd be thinking of writing a paper on it. But why tell the rest of the world when I can have a bit of fun first?'

But instead of the unadulterated admiration she had expected, he just stared at her.

'How can you possibly call this fun? Who else knows about it?'

'Just you and me, of course, you idiot. And it's going to stay that way.' *For now*, she thought to herself. It all depended what the files contained.

'Well, now I really wish you hadn't shared any of this with me, Reenie. It's too much of a responsibility. I mean, if this works then you've most likely just put both our lives in danger.'

'Oh, don't be such a drama queen, Hajji. When I'm finished, I'll make sure I erase every last qubit of data and code from your system. I'll be out of your hair – if you had any – and you can go get your beauty sleep.' She pulled down the visor again and put on the gloves. 'Now, this should only take a few minutes.' She compiled the cloning code and, after a quick run through her checklist, set it running.

Five minutes later she sat bolt upright and let out a whoop of triumph. She couldn't quite believe she'd done it. She now had stored deep in her dark-web file system the passwords that would unlock data no human other than a chosen few was meant to see. She recognized that whatever was in those files was so sensitive that she dreaded to think what might happen to her if she was ever found out. For the time being she had no intention of accessing the files. So, she spent the next few minutes covering her tracks and deleting all trace of her evening's activities.

Finally satisfied, she ripped off her visor and gloves and stretched her legs out. She glanced over at Majid. He looked like he was still sulking. 'I have a really bad feeling about this,' he muttered.

She stood up, suddenly feeling exhausted. 'Thanks for this, Hajji. I'll see you tomorrow morning, OK?' And then she added, 'It's going to be fine, I promise.' She leaned over and kissed her friend on the top of his head. He looked up at her and smiled weakly.

She walked out of the apartment without waiting for a reply and closed the door behind her.

Stepping out into the late-evening air, she felt elated and full of nervous excitement. She would open the files as soon as she got home. She just hoped that whatever they contained wouldn't stop her getting to sleep. Tomorrow, she would have to go to her classes as normal, as though nothing was any different.

She got in her car, told it to take her home, then began humming to herself.

Within minutes of Shireen's departure, a black van pulled up outside Majid's apartment. Oblivious to the chain of events that were already unfolding, Shireen could not know that her life, and her friend's, were about to be turned upside down.

# 8

FRANK PEDERSEN HAD BEEN CHECKING THE WEATHER UPDATES since he'd woken at six. He'd been following the news of the storm that was building in the Atlantic and which was heading his way. It certainly didn't look very pretty out there. After half an hour working up a sweat in his gym, he'd eaten a large bowl of muesli and had a cold shower. It was such a warm and muggy morning he was soon sweating again through his T-shirt. He now prowled from room to room like a caged cat, not able to settle or take his mind off the approaching storm.

Frank Pedersen wasn't the sort of man to feel anxious. He'd pretty much always got what he'd wanted in life, and on those few occasions when there was worrying to be done, he'd left it to others. In fact, it could be said that one of his skills was to surround himself with professional worry absorbers. Over the years, people had debated whether his success was due to ser-endipity, brilliance or sheer perseverance – the truth being a combination of all three. He'd made his first million by the age of nineteen and his first billion by twenty-six. He hadn't achieved this by being particularly ruthless either; just by being . . . well . . . lucky, brilliant and hard-working. Even before he went to California, his entrepreneurial skills, combined with his keen eye for the next big thing in computing, had attracted lucrative job offers from several up-and-coming tech companies.

That was at the turn of the millennium when a lot of smart, computer-savvy young people were beginning to shape the course of history. But even though he was eager to get over to Silicon Valley to be part of the IT revolution, Frank wanted to do things his way, which he duly did. Much to his parents' initial disappointment, he'd left Aarhus for San Francisco and never looked back. Throughout his career, he never deliberately courted or achieved the fame or star quality of others of his generation, such as Zuckerberg, Dorsey, Page and Brin, but then his self-belief meant he had only ever needed to impress one person: himself.

Now, with two marriages behind him, a business empire that pretty much ran itself and no more mountains left to climb, he had taken early semi-retirement to enjoy the quiet solitude of his own company and his two German shepherds in a secluded villa on top of a hill on a remote Caribbean island. The villa had originally been a hermitage, built by a Roman Catholic priest just before the Second World War, which he had instantly fallen in love with. Although he had spent millions converting the old building into a twenty-first-century fortress, he had refused to invest in a decent road up from the small town of New Bight, a few kilometres away on the west coast of the island, deciding that he preferred the isolation afforded by the steep rocky climb to reach him. Not that Frank Pedersen thought of himself as a recluse – forty-five years of keeping his finger on the technological pulse of the planet wasn't an addiction he wished to be cured of. Anyway, who was ever truly alone these days?

But he was feeling pretty cut off and alone this morning. This storm was looking increasingly ugly. Truth be told, it had been a pretty unremarkable hurricane season, with fewer than the average number of tropical cyclones being promoted to hurricane status. One of the consequences of the changes to the Earth's climate over the previous two decades had been the extension of the traditional autumn Atlantic hurricane season well into December, and even January. However, this new one, quickly dubbed Hurricane Jerome, was late by any standards.

Not only that, but it had skipped several stages in the usual life-cycle of such storms, which would typically build up from depression, through tropical storm, to full-blown hurricane within a matter of several days. Instead, it had jumped from nothing to a category five in just a few hours.

Yesterday evening, when he first heard the news of the storm, he'd been advised by friends and associates back in California to get the hell out. After all, it was their job to worry about him. His heli had been flown over to the island and sat waiting on the tarmac six kilometres away. A quick call from him and it could have been at the Hermitage in a matter of minutes to whisk him away to safety. However, he insisted this was an unnecessary precaution and had instead ordered it to fly back to Florida, five hundred kilometres away, without him. He'd experienced six hurricane seasons on Cat Island and had never seen the need to flee, preferring to stick it out here just like he always did. After all, the Hermitage was designed to with-stand anything nature might throw at it, particularly since he'd had its walls reinforced with criss-cross beams of a steel–graphene alloy, making it no more likely to blow over than the hill itself. And its situation at the top of Como Hill meant that, unlike the town below, it was safely above the high-point of even the most formidable tsunami. Nevertheless, this morning he was starting to feel that his decision to stay might have been somewhat imprudent. And Frank Pedersen never made impru-dent decisions.

The dogs were showing signs of anxiety too. It might have been something they could smell in the air or just that they were feeding off Frank's unease. Unusually for her, Beth was curled up quietly beneath the living-room table with her nose tucked under her tail and just one brown eye following Frank around the room. Sheba paced around after him wanting to be made a fuss of all the time.

He turned around to look at them and, hands on hips in mock exasperation, spoke in a stern voice. 'You're being such babies. Go on outside and run around a bit while the weather's still OK.' Christ knows how long they were all going to be cooped indoors once the storm hit. He opened the door for them, but they just sat where they were and looked at him suspiciously. 'Suit yourselves.' Before closing the door, he stepped outside himself. The world seemed so quiet, but not in a peaceful way. Unusually for his hilltop, he noticed there was no wind at all, nor, rather more surreally, any of the usual chirping of birds or buzzing of insects in the bushes around the Hermitage. The thick grey cloud above him seemed almost solid in texture, and so low he could almost jump up and touch it. The air felt heavy and suspenseful. It was as if the world was full of pent-up energy, like a compressed spring waiting to be released.

He wandered back in, closed the door and went to the kitchen for a beer. Ten o'clock in the morning wasn't too early, was it? Of course it wasn't. And it might help cure him of his stupid jitters.

He'd bought the Hermitage eleven years ago and it had taken him five years to renovate it – essentially to transform it from a crumbling stone shell to a high-tech luxury villa. For years before he'd bought it, it had served as no more than a tourist destination, mainly on account of it being situated at the highest point in all of the Bahamas – or rather, of what was left of the Bahamas, since the rising sea level had consumed almost three quarters of the islands' land. Frank had always enjoyed his holidays in the Caribbean and had happily donated hundreds of millions of dollars of his personal wealth to relief funds over the years. In fact, Cat Island, where he had decided to settle, had emerged remarkably unscathed by virtue of protruding a few tens of metres higher above the water than the other islands.

He took out a bottle of Kalik from the fridge and twisted off the cap, then wandered back to check yet again for a weather update. The centre of the living room was taken up with a real-time, high-resolution, three-dimensional hologram of Hurricane Jerome. Frank stood in front of it and took a deep swig from the bottle. The swirling mass of cloud was spinning slowly and dragging its spiral arms like tentacles around its edges. It certainly looked like one mean motherfucker. There were interspersed flashes of light at the bottom where lightning discharged the storm's huge electrical energy into the sea. He found it interesting that the hurricane's name was the same as that of the priest who'd built his hermitage; the Right Reverend Monsignor John Hawes had also been known locally on the island as Father Jerome.

Meteorologists were already claiming that Jerome should be designated a category seven. When he'd first settled on Cat Island, Frank had taken a serious interest in hurricane classification and was aware that a new category six had recently been added beyond the previous highest five, which had been deemed insufficient to describe hurricanes with wind speeds over 280 kilometres per hour, as had been recorded with increasing regularity in recent years. This morning, drones and satellites tracking Jerome had recorded sustained wind speeds of well over 350 kilometres per hour.

He flicked through the different networks on his holo display and stopped at the BBC News Channel. Frank stood and watched as a young meteorologist explained in a very excited voice what was so special about this particular superhurricane:

*'Scientists have known for over a century that galactic cosmic rays – subatomic particles reaching us from deep space – could adversely affect the weather on Earth, but they were mostly of academic interest only. After all, the Earth's magnetic field has always done its job of deflecting most of these particles before they got too close to the Earth's surface.*

*'The only other group of people they had been of any concern to were satellite manufacturers who had to build in appropriate shielding to avoid their sensitive electronics being fried. But now, the conjunction of two occurrences is having a dramatic effect never experienced before by humankind.'*

Frank was well aware that his own business empire relied critically on the reliability of communication satellites, and while none of his own had been affected by the CME that had struck over India last week, he was becoming increasingly worried about the potential risks of the weakened magnetic field. The meteorologist meanwhile was now in full explainer mode.

'Firstly, the Sun happens to be going through its solar minimum right now, the low-activity stage of its eleven-year cycle, which means that its own magnetic field, the Heliosphere, is much weaker, so the number of galactic cosmic rays that can now reach the Earth is higher.

'Secondly, the dramatic weakening of the Earth's field itself, which we have been hearing a lot about of late, means that these cosmic rays can penetrate to much lower levels of the atmosphere, ionizing the air, which in turn seeds thick, giant clouds.

'This increased ionization also causes the electrical conduction of the lower atmosphere to increase dramatically, creating exceptional temperature and pressure gradients over heights of just a few kilometres. Our models predict that already violent storms are able to feed off this electrical energy. To make matters worse, over this past week astronomers have observed a sharp spike in the intensity of cosmic rays hitting the Earth, and are busy trying to locate the source. I'm told, and this is of course not my area, that a powerful supernova, an exploding star in a nearby galaxy, may be responsible.'

Frank was beginning to feel a little incredulous. Having to cope with higher levels of radiation, even hurricanes, was one thing, but 'exploding stars in nearby galaxies'? Come on. Seriously?

'In any case, this sudden surge in cosmic ray intensity is giving us some interesting, to say the least, weather conditions. And this is now evident over the mid-Atlantic, where dramatic changes in atmospheric conditions are having a profound effect on the hurricane season. The warming ocean has already resulted in more severe, and frequent, storms, but it appears that Hurricane Jerome is the first true superstorm to draw on this vast new source of energy from space. It's basically plugging into the power source of distant exploding stars. And as we can see, the results are quite stunning.'

'Stunning' might be an adjective appropriate for someone

safely watching from the other side of the world, but when you were in the hurricane's path . . .

*'If anything, Hurricane Jerome is just getting started. Thousands of metres above the sea, more and more storm clouds are now coalescing and joining its giant swirling vortex. The winds in its outer wall are at this moment sweeping across the ocean in a circle twelve hundred kilometres in diameter, at well over a hundred and sixty kilometres per hour, whipping it up; and this is combined with exceptionally low atmospheric pressure just above the surface of the water. This means . . .'*

Frank had heard enough. He turned away, commanding the holo off as he did so. Normally so rational and logical, he decided that discretion was the better part of valour and that it was probably time to head for the safety of the wine cellar. He wandered around the villa collecting together the few essential supplies he'd need for a day or two underground: bedding, food and water for him and the dogs, several LED lamps, the portable holo, an induction charger and a couple of e-pads. He hadn't been confident that his net drones would be safe enough above the storm and had already commanded them back to the mainland. This, of course, meant that his connectivity to the outside world was going to be patchy, particularly underneath several metres of rock.

So confident had he been in the past about the solidity of the Hermitage that he had never felt the need for a dedicated storm shelter. In any case, unlike the stone buildings above it, the wine cellar was carved out of the rock of the hill itself. But he had also never felt it necessary to stock the cellar up with emergency supplies on the off-chance he ever had to use it. Well, now he did.

What he missed right now was Maisie, his assistant, on whom he relied increasingly these days to organize his life and ensure that the 'little things' were taken care of. During the lengthy periods that he now spent out here at the Hermitage, Maisie would come over for a full day every week to make sure he wasn't entirely neglecting his businesses and that he wasn't in need of anything. Now, she was hundreds of kilometres away and Frank was having to think for himself. But he felt confident that he had everything he needed for what might be a couple of days. The wine cellar, true to its primary purpose, was as perfect a place as anywhere to spend some time.

It had originally been a crypt, though Frank had no idea whether anyone had been entombed there, nor what had become of the bodies if they had – although it still had the words 'Blessed are the Dead Who Die in the Lord' carved on a large block of granite above the entrance. To reach it involved going outside, crossing the courtyard and descending several roughly chiselled steps to approach from the side of the rocky outcrop on which the Hermitage was built. Frank had had a thick oak door put in to replace the metal gate that had previously blocked the entrance. So, his wine collection, last valued at well over a million dollars, was safe within the crypt's cool and dry conditions.

The dogs had initially been reluctant to abandon the safety of the house and had taken some coaxing. Then, when he had left them in the cellar to return to the house for a few more bits and pieces, they had started howling, clearly spooked by the approaching storm.

Finally secure, with vault door safely closed, Frank could hear that it had started raining heavily. The wind had suddenly picked up too and was now howling around the building above his head. He mentally ran through his checklist to make sure he'd not forgotten any crucial items he might need. Although if he had, it was too late anyway – there was no way he would be going back up now.

He decided it was as good a time as any to sample one of his prize wines and he strolled down the dimly lit passageways past arrays of dusty wine bottles stacked from floor to ceiling – which was only one and a half metres high at the sides, but arched up to three metres down the middle of the passages. The place had a strange smell. It was more than just a dry, stale mustiness and Frank had always found it slightly unnerving. It was an imperceptibly faint, sweet stench of rot, as though the place wanted to cling to its original role as a resting place for the decaying flesh of long-dead inhabitants of the island, and that Frank and his precious wine collection were merely temporary intruders.

He settled on a modest Malbec and, wrapping it in the bottom of his T-shirt, he twisted it round to wipe it clean, transferring its filthy film of dust to his clothes. He then wandered back to the deeper end of the cellar, where the lighting was better and the noise from outside fainter.

The dogs, sitting side by side a few feet away, were watching him intensely. 'You two girls OK? Come on, this is fun.'

They both jumped up eagerly and trotted over to him to be made a fuss of, reassured that, despite his earlier tension, their master now appeared more relaxed and calm. Frank knew they would hate not being able to go outside to do their business. Come to think of it, he wasn't particularly delighted by the prospect of shitting in a bucket either. He hoped it wouldn't come to that. Fuck. Toilet paper! Oh, well, too late now.

The storm raged outside. The noise was now deafening. Suddenly, without any warning flicker, the lights went out. The solar-powered generator must have been knocked out. He reached down in the pitch black to the floor by his feet where he remembered he'd left the LED lamps and felt around for the nearest one. He picked it up and switched it on. He left the others off but still within reach – no need to use up their charge unnecessarily.

Beth and Sheba settled down again, now that they knew Frank wasn't abandoning them, and both curled up on the filthy floor under the old wooden bench. He opened the bottle of red, feeling pleased with himself for remembering to bring down a wine glass. Making himself as comfortable as possible on the bench, he tried to distract himself with a book. For the first time that day he started to feel less tense. Let the storm do its worst. Frank Pedersen was going nowhere.

After several hours during which the storm raged with increasing ferocity, he must have fallen asleep, because he was slowly dragged back to wakefulness by the sound of Beth whining by the cellar door at the far end, scratching it to go out. It took several seconds of disorientation before it struck him what had changed. He could only hear the dog whining because there was no competing noise from the other side of the oak door. After the deafening racket of the storm outside, the contrast was eerie. He checked his watch. It was late afternoon, and his first thought was that the hurricane had passed, allowing himself a moment of self-congratulatory triumph. But his relief was short-lived; a quick mental calculation told him this was impossible. When he'd last checked, just before coming down to the cellar, the storm had been over a thousand kilometres across. At the speed the forecasters had said it was moving, it could not have covered a distance equal to its entire diameter in the time that had elapsed. In fact, by his reckoning, it should only be halfway across. The silence must mean that the eye of the hurricane was now directly overhead.

He went over to the door and released the catch. Something outside was stopping it from swinging open, but with a firmer push he managed to dislodge the tree branch that had been blown across it. Before he could stop them, the dogs scampered out from behind him. Sheba came to a halt just outside the door and sniffed the air, while Beth trotted down the steps and disappeared into a bush. Frank stood and stared. *'Jesus Christ!'*

The scene that greeted him was astonishing. The villa above him was blocked from view at this angle, but he could see out right across the island. There was a very light breeze and the sky overhead was clear, but a few kilometres out to sea was a sight he knew he would never forget: a wall of dark churning clouds that extended all the way around him, stretching up into the sky. That the sun was peeking through the hole in the roof of the hurricane only added to the dreamlike scenario. He looked down towards the coast – or rather, where he expected the coast to be. The sea now extended almost a kilometre further inland than it had done yesterday, only stopping where the land began to rise. New Bight had disappeared. All that remained of the town above water was the church steeple.

Venturing further out, Frank walked down a few steps to

get a better view of his home behind him. The first thing that struck him was the missing Hermitage tower. The thirty-foot bell tower had been the only part of the old building not re-inforced along with the rest of the property. The storm had brought it down, reducing it to a mound of rubble – large chunks of brickwork and stone were now strewn across the courtyard. He needed to have a quick scout around to assess any further damage.

He walked briskly up the path that led round to the top of the hill. A wave of relief washed over him as he saw that, apart from the bell tower, the rest of the Hermitage was relatively undamaged. Luckily, it appeared that the back of the building had taken the brunt of, and survived, the full force of the winds. He scrambled over the scattered bricks knowing he didn't have long before he had to get back to the cellar. Looking back the way he'd come he caught a glimpse of both dogs trotting back inside.

Relieved at his animals' good sense, he started back across the courtyard himself. It occurred to him that if the first half of the hurricane had battered the back of his home then it would now be the turn of the front to bear the brunt. Oh well, if he had to rebuild the place, then so be it.

Zigzagging his way across the courtyard around the ruins of the collapsed tower, he was about ten metres from the steps when he felt the winds suddenly pick up. Puzzled, he turned round. The approaching wall of the storm had been over to his right and so he hadn't seen how close it was. Now, it was patently obvious that he had utterly misjudged how fast it was moving towards him. With a renewed sense of urgency, he hurried on, his progress slowed by the large chunks of masonry.

In the space of those few seconds it took him to cover the short distance to safety, the winds sweeping across Como Hill picked up from a gentle breeze to the full force of Hurricane Jerome: over three hundred and eighty kilometres an hour. Frank Pedersen was running now.

Or at least he went through the motions of running, for he was suddenly plucked up off the ground, as though he were no more than a dry leaf caught in an autumn breeze, along with pieces of the Hermitage roof and an assortment of tree branches and bushes. Tumbling through the air like a rag-doll, Frank didn't have time to feel afraid or to make sense of what was happening to him, because the logic circuits in his brain that had served him so well all his life now simply ceased to function. Instead of terror, he felt a strange sense of exhilaration, as a child might when tossed into the air by a parent. But unlike the child's relief as it fell back down to the safety of strong adult arms, Frank had no such reprieve. Hurricane Jerome was no respecter of Newtonian gravity.

Any feelings of anxiety or exhilaration he might have had ended the moment a passing oak tree slammed into him, snapping his neck instantly.

# 9

*Thursday, 7 February – off Grand Turk Island,*
*northern West Indies*

SIX HUNDRED KILOMETRES SOUTH-EAST OF CAT ISLAND, AND
while a still alive but edgy Frank Pedersen was about to open
a bottle of beer, the rain had been steadily falling all morning
and was getting heavier. The sea was becoming choppier too –
more irritable than tempestuous, but it was clear to anyone
who knew the sea that nothing but raw rage lay ahead. Joseph
Smith knew the sea. He'd been a fisherman all his life and had
a pretty good idea what was coming, but for the time being his
small fishing trawler trudged along happily enough. Given the
recent meagre hauls, Joseph knew that he couldn't afford not
to go out these days, whatever the weather. So, against the
wishes of his wife, he had left the village with his son Zain
before dawn to ensure a good few hours for a semi-decent
catch before they had to turn back. Joseph figured that if there
was a sudden change, then they'd need fifteen minutes to reel
in the nets, then another hour to get back to shore, if he opened
the engine all the way up.

On the other hand, why take any unnecessary risks? Maybe
it had been foolish to come out at all. Joseph had always trusted
his instincts, and his instincts were now telling him to call it a
day, albeit a very short one, and head back. It was still only
ten-thirty in the morning and they had been out for just over

three hours. But then no other fool was even out on the water today.

'Start the winches, boy, I'm calling it,' he shouted across the deck to his son.

'Why, Pa? It don't look too bad to me yet,' laughed Zain with the bravado of youth.

'Just do it. I'm not in your mother's good books as it is, so it's best we get back before things get too interesting out here.'

Joseph ducked inside the wheelhouse to work out the most efficient bearing to take if the wind suddenly started picking up in the next hour or so.

Zain was sixteen and, Joseph was sure, would be happy enough to get back home as soon as possible too. The boy had recently developed a serious crush on their neighbour's daughter, Aliya. A year younger than him, he'd known her all his life, but this past year she had blossomed into a beautiful young woman. The two had been spending a lot of time together.

Joseph stared at the screen in front of him and tried to make sense of the live weather map it was showing, when it struck him why it had looked so odd. A sudden chill ran through him. When he'd last checked the satellite data, just under half an hour ago, the centre of Hurricane Jerome had been seven hundred and twenty kilometres to the east and heading towards them at about twenty knots. Given its size, this meant that the outer edges, where the wind and rain really picked up and the sea turned brutal, would not reach them for another couple of hours – plenty of time to get back to shore. But that had changed. His mouth suddenly felt dry. He licked his lips. The storm had just doubled in size in the space of thirty minutes. It was such a ridiculous notion that Joseph assumed it had to be a mistake in the readings. But if the current data were correct then the outer wall of the hurricane was far closer than he'd thought.

He rushed back out on deck. It seemed to him that even in these few minutes conditions had worsened, and the rain was now pouring down. His son was standing at the stern, his legs braced against the roll of the boat, next to the boom holding the power block that fed the nets out behind. Joseph shouted out to Zain, but the boy couldn't hear him. Holding on to the rail, he made his way to the stern and grabbed his son by the shoulders. 'Zain,' he yelled into the storm, 'we're going to have to cut the nets free and get the hell out of here.'

Joseph tried his best to appear calm and relaxed, but Zain read the nervousness in his eyes. 'Cut the nets? Why don't we reel them in?' his son shouted.

Joseph didn't want to lose his nets, but he knew it would take at least twenty minutes for the hydraulic pump to winch them in – time he now calculated he didn't have. In any case the pump ran off the main engines and he needed all the power he could get if he was going to outrun the approaching hurricane.

'The storm's a lot closer than I thought. We really don't have a choice,' he shouted above the increasing roar of the rain and wind.

Zain didn't question him any further and instead hurried back to the wheelhouse where they kept the tools. Joseph tried to rationalize that this wasn't a decision he was taking lightly. They would struggle to afford new nets to replace these ones. He watched as his son came back with the large cable cutters and Joseph left him to it, struggling against the driving rain back to the wheelhouse. They were twenty-two kilometres away from the coast. At full throttle, in this weather, they would get back to port in about forty minutes. Although the hurricane to their east was moving in the same direction, the circling winds at its outer edges, if it caught up with them, would be slamming into the port side of the boat.

Joseph wrestled the boat around against the angry sea and began the race for home. A few minutes later, the door slammed open as Zain stumbled in accompanied by an angry gust of salty spray. He leaned his weight against the door and forced it shut. 'The nets are gone,' he said breathlessly and reached for an old towel to dry his face. Joseph cursed himself for thinking that coming out this morning was ever a good idea. There would most definitely be all hell to pay when he got back home and had to admit his folly. Still, he would worry about that later.

Joseph Smith knew the sea and still felt confident. With the nets cut and the boat heading home, he had done all he could. It was now a straight race between him and the storm.

The wipers skidded ineffectively back and forth across the windshield as the rain lashed down. Joseph couldn't see much beyond the bow of the boat through the curtain of rain, just the deep charcoal-grey hue of the stormy sky. It seemed to him as though the thunder clouds extended all the way down to the sea.

Then a sudden flash of lightning briefly lit up the world outside, and Joseph froze.

'Oh, dear God, no.'

The dark sky he'd been staring at wasn't sky at all, but a giant wall of water bearing down on his small boat.

His knuckles whitened as he gripped the wheel with a futile intensity. Had he been able to articulate any semblance of rational thought at that moment he might have admitted that this was no longer a fair struggle between man and nature – that his puny little fishing boat was but an insignificant toy at the mercy of the rolling mountainous waves.

'Forgive me, Elsa,' he sobbed, thinking of his wife back home. He could hear his son screaming somewhere behind him.

For a second or two, the world outside went quiet as the wind dropped, as though in respectful anticipation, and the boat began to tilt up.

# 10

*Thursday, 7 February – San Juan, Puerto Rico*

CAMILA HAD LIVED THROUGH HER FAIR SHARE OF HURRICANES during her eighty-five years in San Juan and knew the drill. She'd spent the morning calling family and friends, making them promise that they would stay safely indoors with sufficient supplies to keep them going for a few days until the storm had passed. She'd been busy baking and cooking since hearing the weather forecasts two days ago. Wiping her hands on her apron she took out several Tupperware boxes from the cupboard. The rich aroma of chorizo and shellfish in her large pot of *asopao* permeated the whole of her ground-floor apartment. She'd now cooked enough food to feed a platoon for a week and began portioning up the thick soup. She'd keep most of it in her fridge but decided to take a couple of portions up to Grace Morales on the fifth floor.

Camila was feeling rejuvenated after the recent stem-cell injections had cleared up the arthritis in her knees, and was keen to impress her friend with her newfound vigour. Besides, she wanted to have a better view out to sea than she had from her own flat on the ground floor.

It had been an exceptionally warm and sticky week, and now the rain had started. The wind had been building all morning and was currently strong enough to blow the lids off garbage bins, sending them rolling down the street with an assortment of autumn leaves, paper, plastic and anything else not firmly secured. Counting the cost of the damage wrought by storms was a fact of life for Camila, and she was sure it would be much worse than just a bin lid that needed replacing. Last year her two sons had clubbed together to replace her old windows with graphene-toughened glass that could withstand the brute force of the far stronger winds – something she was even more grateful for today.

Picking up the soup, she left her apartment. She thought about getting in the lift, but then decided she'd like to see the look on Grace's face after telling her she'd climbed five flights of stairs.

Grace was indeed impressed by her old friend's regained mobility, though at first she'd been startled by Camila's breathlessness.

'Well, there's no need to show off on my account, my dear,' she scolded. 'What's the use of healthy knees if your heart gives out?'

Camila still managed to chuckle as she caught her breath. 'I can see how jealous you are, Grace. No point trying to hide it. Now put the kettle on.' She barged past her friend into the apartment.

To Camila's relief, Grace seemed just as unconcerned as she was by the approaching storm. They would keep each other calm.

After catching up on family gossip the two women settled down by the front window with a coffee and a piece of cake. It was a beautiful view to the north, overlooking the Laguna to the picturesque district of Condado, an affluent tree-lined neighbourhood with hotels and apartment blocks that, in turn, overlooked the Atlantic. To the west was the hundred-and-thirty-year-old Dos Hermanos bridge that linked Condado with the entrance to old San Juan.

That is, it would have been a beautiful view. But not today.

Over the next hour, they watched as the storm continued to build outside. From their vantage point they could see the palm trees below them swaying ever more dramatically in the strengthening winds. And as the hurricane approached, their unease began to build. Camila had lived through hundreds of storms in her life, but there was something different about this one that she didn't like. And yet she couldn't quite put her finger on why she felt a growing sense of foreboding.

Had visibility been better they would have seen the first of the storm surges approaching from out at sea. As it was, Camila could just make out the other side of the lagoon. Through the driving rain she saw a few foolish motorists still out on the roads, despite the tsunami warnings that had been broadcast all morning, including several cars crossing the Dos Hermanos bridge spanning the lagoon, trying to reach safety as quickly as they could.

Arriving about a minute apart, it seemed that each tidal surge was bigger than the previous one.

Then, as though tiring of playing games, Hurricane Jerome decided to show Camila what it was truly capable of. She sat transfixed, her coffee cup slipping, unnoticed, from her fingers onto the floor. She watched as first the roads and then the bridge itself disappeared underneath the giant wave. Her heart began pounding in her chest, this time with terror rather than physical exertion. She could just about make out a few cars being carried along by the water as it advanced across the lagoon towards them. The scene looked like something from one of those badly made disaster movies she remembered watching as a young girl.

'Oh, sweet Lord. Those poor souls,' cried Grace.

An almost forgotten memory from Camila's childhood rose unbidden, of a summer's day on the beach with her two sisters when they had built an elaborate sand castle. After hours of painstaking work, sculpting turrets, battlements, walls and moat, they had then watched as the tide came in, quickly washing away their creation until the sand was flat and featureless once more.

As the wall of water continued across the lagoon towards them, looming ever larger, she instinctively reached across and grabbed hold of Grace's hand. Their apartment window was thankfully higher than the top of the wave, so they were able to watch from their prime location as it slammed into their building, causing it to shudder. She heard screams from downstairs followed by what sounded like several explosions. Maybe those newly reinforced windows weren't a match for a million-ton tsunami.

The wave had reached as high as the floor below them when it hit but had now subsided so that only the first two floors of the building were underwater. The realization that her trip upstairs had most likely saved her life left Camila shaken. How many hundreds of lives were, at this very moment, coming to an end, trapped in their homes underneath the water? She looked across at her friend. Tears were running down Grace's cheeks as she let out an anguished whimpering sound.

Camila felt too numb to speak. She still hadn't moved when, less than a minute later, the next, even larger surge hit land. This time, the wave seemed to have one purpose only. Reluctant to give up its immense store of energy until the final moment, it came for Camila.

## II

*Saturday, 9 February – New York*

SARAH HAD SPENT THE HOUR SINCE WAKING UP IN HER HOTEL room following the awful news of the devastation wreaked by Hurricane Jerome. The casualty count already stood at well over thirty thousand, and would no doubt rise further. Now, two days after it had reached maximum strength, it had been downscaled to a category four, but was still strong enough to pose a threat to life. It had switched direction and was moving north, still out at sea, which meant it would miss the US eastern seaboard. Sarah had been brooding over whether its extraordinary strength was indeed correlated with the weakened magnetic field, as many commentators were now claiming.

She showered, dressed and headed down to meet Gabriel Aguda. She found him sitting on a sofa in the hotel lobby. He smiled and stood up to greet her. He was a giant of a man, in his mid-sixties, and clearly carrying more weight than even his almost two-metre-tall frame justified. What also struck her was the garishly coloured cotton shirt he was wearing under a faded brown corduroy jacket. He might move in high-powered political circles, but he nevertheless maintained a typical academic dress sense.

'Dr Maitlin . . . Sarah, if I may, it's good to meet you at last.' He extended an enormous hand.

Sarah shook it. There was something else about him that

didn't fit the mental image she'd formed from his profile and the photos she'd found online. But she couldn't put her finger on it. 'Well, it's kind of you to come and meet me like this, but I wasn't sure—'

'I hope you haven't had breakfast,' Aguda interrupted. 'There's a nice pancake place just across the road. And we have a lot to discuss before this morning's meeting. And do please call me Gabriel.'

They stepped outside.

The cold air stung her face and she yanked her woolly hat from a coat pocket, quickly pulling it over her head. All around her were signs that the normally stoical New Yorkers were nervous and preoccupied. Most of the people she passed wore the familiar glazed look of attention being focused on retinal displays, presumably following reports on Hurricane Jerome and its progress. Her own attention was snapped rudely back by Aguda's booming voice alongside her. And she wasn't the only one, as several passing pedestrians were startled out of their reverie and gave him a wide berth.

'I hope you don't mind if we start talking shop right away . . .' he said, as he stepped off the kerb and strode across the busy street without a moment's hesitation. He appeared oblivious to the dozen or more driverless cabs that had to brake suddenly, jolting their passengers. Sarah rushed to keep up with him. 'It's just that you and I are the only two scientists on the committee, and there are certainly others on there who don't quite appreciate the magnitude of the danger our planet is facing.'

On the other side of the road, she quickened her pace to draw level with the giant Nigerian. 'These people are politicians, Sarah,' he continued. 'They only listen to us when they think they have to, and they cherry-pick evidence if it suits their purposes and ambitions.'

Where was he going with this? Was he about to reveal something important to her? Was there some conflict of interest on the committee such that he needed friends?

Aguda seemed unconcerned that anyone else might overhear him as he continued in his loud, deep voice. 'At the moment, governments are in panic mode,' he thundered. 'Despite the months of warnings that something like the Air India incident was bound to happen it's only now that they're taking it seriously; of course, you and I know the situation is only going to get worse. We've seen the destruction that Hurricane Jerome has caused. You know as well as I do that these events are connected.'

Sarah made a mental note to get him to explain this connection further. But a more immediate question popped into her head.

'OK, so if governments are now finally listening to the scientists and putting contingency plans into place, why is this committee necessary at all?'

Aguda gave her an indulgent smile. 'You have a lot to learn, Sarah. It's not so much *having* contingency plans, but rather who chooses *which* ones to put in place, and then who pays for them. Oh, and even more crucially of course, who pays to replace all the communication satellites that get damaged in any future event like the recent CME. We have to have a solid international consensus. As for us, well, I guess you and I are there to give the committee scientific legitimacy.

'Don't get me wrong, I'd like to think we still have a vital role to play. But the fact is, Sarah, while the UN is pretty toothless, and not exactly untouched by corruption, it is still the only organization that can claim to stand up to China. And if we – you and I, that is – don't press home the seriousness of the current threat facing the world, then China will just act in its own interests, as it always does.' He gave a rueful grunt.

They had reached a busy intersection and Sarah lost Aguda for a few seconds as they fought their way through a crowd waiting at a crossing. She hoped this breakfast was worth all the effort and wondered whether it wouldn't have been more sensible just to grab a snack at the hotel before heading to the meeting. She drew up alongside him again.

None of what he'd said so far was news. Sarah knew full well that the UN had struggled for many years to ensure that its voice was heard on the world stage. But she had detected an urgency in Aguda's voice that hinted at something more – something he wasn't telling her. It felt as though he was rather too keen to win her over to his side. But if so, what or who were the opposition? Before she could quiz him further, they arrived at the diner.

The place was packed, but the warmth provided a welcome respite from the sharp cold outside. The smell of coffee and baked pastries pervading the air was enticing, and the general hubbub of conversation was so loud that Sarah almost had to shout to be heard.

'OK, so my next question is: why me? Why would a committee as high-powered as you say it is recruit someone like me, with no experience of dealing with politicians, and all just because I made it onto some news networks?' She wasn't quite sure what she wanted to hear. 'I hope they're not just looking for someone to be the scientific spokesperson for the committee, wheeled out to face the media every time there's a crisis.' She had no intention of acting as a mouthpiece for governments wishing to tell the world that everything would be fine.

Aguda's guffaw coincided with a lull in the buzz of the diner, startling a passing waitress, who dropped the handful of cutlery she'd been carrying. Sarah watched as two bots glided over and helped the girl pick it up.

Aguda didn't seem to have even noticed and simply carried on where he'd left off. 'On the contrary, my dear, your credentials as a researcher have been thoroughly vetted and, believe me, you come with the very highest recommendations.'

Sarah bit her lip and let his patronizing tone pass. Aguda had clearly mistaken her misgivings for insecurity. She certainly didn't need his approbation.

He continued, 'We needed someone to tell us, not only just how bad things are likely to get in the coming months, but how reliably and how far in advance we can predict these sorts of geomagnetic storms. Of course, just as importantly, we did indeed want someone without the baggage of vested interest or political ambitions.'

Aguda's lecture – because that was what it was beginning to feel like to her – was interrupted by one of the bots that had been helping the waitress. Gliding up to them, it informed them in its singsong voice that a table was now available. Sarah noted absent-mindedly that it was a model popular these days, both in homes and in the service industry, mainly for its versatility. It didn't have the processing ability and machine-learning skills of the new companion bots, which were able to react to human emotions almost as well as dogs, but then there really wasn't much call for empathy in a New York diner. In fact, dispassionate and efficient service was ideal.

She followed Aguda and the bot to a corner table near the back of the diner. After a moment checking the menu screen, they each tapped out their orders of coffee and pancakes. Sarah checked the time on her retinal clock; they had less than an hour before they had to report at the UN building across town.

Luckily, Gabriel also appeared mindful of their limited time and his demeanour suddenly became more serious. He leaned forward across the table towards her. 'OK, Sarah, how much do you know about geomagnetism?' His breath smelled of peppermint and stale cigars.

Was this going to be an interview, or was he just gauging her level of knowledge before he continued his lecture? 'Well, I'm a solar physicist – my expertise is in the magnetic field of the Sun, not the Earth. So, if you're asking me how much I know about the weakening strength of the magnetosphere and the approaching Flip then, no, it's not really my area.'

'Good, because it is *my* area.' Gabriel smiled. 'Please stop me if I'm telling you anything that's too basic, OK?'

'OK.' Sarah nodded. The shoe was on the other foot for a change, she thought wryly to herself – she'd spent the past few days saying the same thing to journalists and politicians.

'Well, as I'm sure you know,' began Aguda, 'the location of the Earth's magnetic north has been on the move for the past few centuries, but in recent years it's been speeding up. It used to be in North America; now it's in Asia.' Sarah was shocked by this revelation, and equally by the fact that she hadn't known about it before. She was aware the pole had been shifting, but she clearly hadn't been keeping up to date.

'That in itself, of course, is not the issue,' continued Aguda. 'Unlike the Sun's magnetic polarity, which reverses every decade or so, the Earth's magnetic field only flips over a few times in a million years, but each geomagnetic reversal takes thousands of years to complete. And in any case, the next one is now long overdue – by about half a million years, in fact.

'But a long-standing problem is that we don't fully understand what triggers such a reversal. I mean, we know that the Earth's molten core is disrupted in some way, but—'

'—But what's happening now isn't one of those slow reversals, right?'

'No, the speed at which the field is changing suggests a quite different mechanism. And it's one that we geologists have seen before, in the relatively recent geological history.'

Gabriel paused theatrically just as their coffee and pancakes arrived and he lowered his voice to a conspiratorial whisper.

'Have you ever come across something called the Laschamp excursion?'

'Can't say that I have, no,' she replied, unwrapping her knife and fork from their napkin and immediately tucking in to her breakfast. 'Tell me.'

Gabriel grew animated, his own pancakes forgotten. 'Well, in the 1960s, geologists found strong evidence in the ancient lava near the village of Laschamp in central France showing that there'd been a temporary, and geologically very brief, reversal of the Earth's magnetic field. This happened about forty thousand years ago. In fact, the magnetic poles switched over for such a short time before flipping back again that we call it an "excursion", rather than a "reversal".'

Again, Sarah was surprised she hadn't come across this information before. The scientist in her was intrigued and she looked up from her plate, fork with skewered piece of pancake frozen halfway to her mouth. 'Forty thousand years ago; that would put it during the last ice age, right?'

'Correct. And guess what else is of significance forty thousand years ago.'

Sarah took an educated guess. 'Um, isn't that round about the time that modern humans arrived in Europe?'

'Yes, that's partly correct.' Aguda was clearly getting into his stride now, his own pancakes still untouched. '*Homo sapiens* migrated to Europe from both Africa and Asia in several waves, many tens of thousands of years ago. But forty thousand years ago was also when Neanderthals disappeared from Europe.'

'Wait a minute. Isn't that the same thing? Didn't *Homo sapiens* replace Neanderthals in Europe? And where they overlapped, they even interbred, but Neanderthals gradually became extinct because they couldn't compete . . .' Sarah recalled a lecture by a highly regarded palaeontologist in which he'd argued that Neanderthals hadn't gone extinct at all but were simply lost in the noise as they interbred with the much larger *Homo sapien* numbers.

Aguda smiled. 'Your knowledge of palaeontology isn't bad for a physicist.' Not for the first time, Sarah wondered where this was all going. She checked the time. They would need to be on their way soon if they were to make the start of the meeting, and she still wasn't sure what point Gabriel was trying to make. But the geologist continued with his lecture.

'Certainly, there were pockets of Neanderthals hanging around southern Europe for another ten thousand years, but the majority disappeared rather suddenly – we think this is because of some cataclysmic event. And most geologists now believe it was the Laschamp excursion.'

Sarah felt a growing sense of foreboding as the implications of what she was hearing began to sink in. 'Hang on – you're saying that what's happening with the Earth's magnetic field *now* is like an event that happened forty thousand years ago – and that it was so awful it caused the near extinction of an entire species of humans? Fuck! And this was all down to a weakening of the magnetic field?'

'That's exactly what I am saying. The geological data suggest that during those few hundred years that the field was temporarily reversed it had just one tenth of its normal strength.'

'So, considerably weaker than now.'

Aguda nodded. 'But that's not even the most interesting thing. During the few months of actual transition, while the field was doing the flipping, it disappeared almost entirely. So, you can imagine what that would have meant. The potential disintegration of the ozone layer in the atmosphere leading to lethal levels of radiation streaming in from space as well as a serious and very sudden disruption of the Earth's climate.'

Sarah had by now lost her appetite. She thought about Hurricane Jerome, a thousand kilometres out to sea from where she was sitting, with a trail of death and destruction in its wake. Maybe it was just her imagination, but the diner seemed a lot quieter now – perhaps her senses were just blocking out the surrounding sights and sounds as she focused on processing all the new information. She turned back to Aguda. 'I guess it makes sense that the reason Jerome was so powerful may be because the high cosmic ray flux is playing havoc with atmospheric conditions . . .'

Aguda finished her train of logic. '. . . And the reason that radiation is so high? Because the weakened magnetic field can't block it. So, the energy of the cosmic rays that are already getting through the atmosphere is being absorbed to transform hurricanes into deadly superhurricanes.'

Sarah had spent the past two weeks concerned about geomagnetic storms wiping out telecommunication systems. But this was all far more terrifying.

She ran her fingers through her hair and tried to clear her head, her half-eaten plate of pancakes forgotten. She needed to remain rational. And, yes, maybe this was all getting a little far-fetched. 'But this Laschamp event . . . you're talking about climatic conditions that brought about the end of an entire species . . . and if they were that severe why didn't they cause a mass extinction of lots of other life on Earth at the same time?'

'You have to remember that the climate in northern Europe during the ice age was already harsh enough. So, any further disruption would have tipped the balance from unforgiving to intolerable as far as the Neanderthals and many other animals and plants were concerned.'

'Okaay . . . I'll buy that,' she said, still not entirely persuaded. 'But why would it be the Neanderthals who were affected and not *Homo sapiens*? I thought the Neanderthals were a hardy species.'

Aguda leaned back in his chair and spoke through a mouthful of pancake – the end of the world seemingly not affecting his appetite. 'It's simple geography, Sarah. The further north you go, the harsher the climate and the narrower the margin for comfort if things get worse. So, southern Europe and Africa, where most modern humans had settled, didn't fare so badly. Also, Neanderthals tended to be fair-skinned and redheaded, which suggests that, in the almost complete absence of an ozone layer, they would have been especially susceptible to ultraviolet B damage.'

Well, that certainly seemed to make sense, thought Sarah. The ozone layer was already depleted dramatically in several regions around the globe and presumably with further weakening of the field it would be one of the first casualties under the bombardment of solar particles. Still, was Gabriel Aguda pushing a controversial theory that the rest of the scientific community wasn't ready to accept, one based on an overly dramatic interpretation of meagre data? It was one thing to be speculating about an event that took place in the last ice age, quite another to suggest it might be happening again.

Gabriel must have sensed her scepticism because his demeanour changed, and he leaned forward again. 'All the evidence we have points to it: the dramatic cosmic ray activity getting through the ionosphere and the resulting increased concentration of long-lived cosmogenic isotopes like beryllium-10 and chlorine-36 in the atmosphere, the sudden changing weather patterns. What we've got to hope for is a quick transition to the Flip so that the field can pick up strength again in a few months.'

'And in the meantime?'

'In the meantime, we have to do what we can to minimize

its impact. After all, we should surely be better placed to protect ourselves than those poor Neanderthals, right?'

Sarah wasn't so sure. It wasn't the continuous bombardment
of cosmic rays from deep space that worried her as much as the
sudden unpredictable bursts of activity from the Sun. The UN
committee weren't going to like what she would tell them about
the potential impact of any future large coronal ejections. Of
course, a lot depended on how much weaker the Earth's field
got. But there was something bugging her about all this and she
suddenly realized what it was. 'OK, tell me this. How can you
be confident the transition will be over quickly so the field can
recover its strength? I thought geologists only worked on time-
scales of millions of years. Surely, even the forty thousand years
since the Laschamp excursion is just a blink of an eye for you.'

Aguda went quiet for a few seconds, as though gathering his
thoughts. 'Well, in a sense you're right. But our computer simulations of the way the Earth's magnetic field evolves are pretty
sophisticated. A geomagnetic reversal isn't like a planet-sized bar
magnet swinging around a hundred and eighty degrees. Instead,
you tend to get a brief, messy stage when it's all over the place,
as though there are multiple magnets inside the liquid centre of
the planet all acting in different directions. These different fields
*should* then coalesce into just one, in which the magnetic north
pole ends up near the geographic south pole, in Antarctica.

'In fact, the satellites currently mapping the magnetic field
intensity have already picked up regions over the Pacific and
South America where the field strength is actually increasing.
All our computer simulations using these data predict that the
transition will be over before the end of the year, by which time
full recovery should be quick.'

The diner customers were beginning to thin out now and
Aguda, noticing that Sarah had put down her knife and fork and
wasn't making any attempt to finish her pancakes, tapped his
wristpad onto the interactive table display to pay the bill.

'But things are going to get worse before then, right? The
coming months are going to be tough.' Sarah tried to fight back
the strong sense of despair.

Aguda nodded. 'That's where you come in, Sarah. We need to know how bad things will get if the field intensity drops much further – maybe to just a few per cent of its full capacity. And if we get another direct hit from a coronal mass ejection.'

'And *if* we get through this?'

'Once the field has flipped, things should recover quickly, and everything will be business as usual. Of course, it'll be a huge boon for compass manufacturers, since all compass needles would then be pointing the wrong way!'

Sarah made a half-hearted attempt to smile. Deep in thought, she stood up and reached for her coat hanging on the back of her chair. She looked around the diner at the preoccupied New Yorkers getting on with their lives despite the growing threat from space. We take so much for granted in our thin biosphere, she thought, that we forget just how fragile it – and we – really are.

# 12

*Saturday, 9 February – New York*

SARAH FOLLOWED AGUDA THROUGH THE HUGE REVOLVING glass doors with their built-in biometric scanners, into the vast hallway of the United Nations building. The time on her retinal display showed 08:45. The Nigerian geologist towered over her as they waited at the reception desk. Like many others, she had often wondered why the United Nations still carried its old name. It barely made sense now that many multinational companies had seats at the table. Yet everyone knew that the UN, however ineffective it had become, still endeavoured to present itself as a benign global organization. She looked up at one of the huge black granite walls. Above the United Nations symbol of a circular world map between two olive branches, were emblazoned the words:

**Security Without Liberty is Oppression.**

**Liberty Without Security is Delusion.**

The motto had been adopted soon after the signing of the Geneva Convention on Privacy eleven years ago, in 2030, which had been required to cope with the rise in cyberterrorism, cyber espionage and the weaponization of code. Sarah contemplated how the twentieth-century 'cold war' had turned into the twenty-first-century 'code war'.

The desk bot directed them to a security gate on the far side of the hallway. There, she followed Gabriel through a sophisticated retinal scanner. Once through, she was asked by a disembodied voice to stand still with her arms outstretched. A robotic arm with an oval-shaped black pad extended itself and skimmed around her body. The process took seconds.

Once through, she turned to Aguda. 'Is that it? Don't we get issued with electronic passes?'

He grinned at her. 'Oh, but we have been. The retinal scan you just had has other functions beyond mere identification. Your normal AR capability has been temporarily deactivated and replaced with an internal one that'll allow you to identify committee members and access documentation. You've also been tagged with a retinal ID code that not only gives you access to those restricted areas you have clearance for, but tracks your movements all the time you're in the building.'

'And that body scanner?'

'Ah, that's a recent addition. It's a full-body B-Mouse scanner – sorry, a Blümich portable MRI scanner combined with an ultrasound transducer. Basically, nothing can be hidden from it.'

Aguda must have seen the blank look on her face and smiled. 'Been standard issue here for a few months now. I'm surprised you haven't come across one before.'

She shrugged. 'I guess I've never been this close to real political power and such high-level security.'

'Well, the UN now has a detailed 3D scan of your anatomy that even your doctor would envy. And if you happened to be carrying on, or in, your person any form of electronic or chemical device, right down to the nanoscale, they'd know about it.' Sarah wondered how long it would take for someone with the know-how and determination to beat this technology.

They were joined by a smartly dressed man in his mid-twenties, who escorted them across a large, bland hallway to the elevators and up to the fifteenth floor. When they emerged, she noted that the corridors here were brighter and the whole place buzzed with activity. They reached a frosted-glass door with a sign saying

HCR1. 'Here it is, sir, madam: Holographic Chamber Room One,' said their young guide. 'The senator and the rest of the committee are waiting for you.' Sarah guessed that sensors throughout the building would have been tracking their progress from the moment they passed security, constantly reconfirming their identity, because the sturdy aluminium oxynitride door swished open as they approached it. She noted the one-way mirrored windows of the room: opaque from the outside, but transparent when viewed from inside, so the occupants of the room had already witnessed their arrival.

The room was smaller than she had anticipated and dominated by a large white oval table covered by interactive display glass, with seating space for about twenty people around it. Only half that number were present. Apart from two empty chairs for the new arrivals, the remainder of the places were taken up with sleek black holotubes instead of chairs, each about two metres high. The cylinders' entire outer surfaces were covered with thousands of nano-devices, each of which in turn contained a tiny solid-state laser. When activated, these would beam out light in all directions to create a high-resolution holographic real-time image of any remote committee member not able to be physically present at the meeting. The result, always impressive, was an illusion so realistic it was easy to forget that the person wasn't actually in the room. For now, the eight tubes sat dormant.

A man with cropped light brown hair and an expensive-looking suit stood up as they came in. He was tall and athletic-looking, though still dwarfed by the Nigerian geologist. 'Ah, Gabriel. And Dr Maitlin. Good morning to you both.' He approached, hand outstretched.

'Sarah,' said Aguda, 'this is Senator Hogan, our committee chair.' The man's grip was firmer than it needed to be and his dark eyes pierced hers as though he were probing her soul more thoroughly than any retinal scanning device. It was unsettling. 'Pleased to meet you, Senator.' She managed to keep her voice steady and hold his gaze.

'We're all very pleased to have you on board.' His smile had all the warmth of a great white shark. Sarah knew very little about the senator from Indiana other than what she had read online: that he was a highly skilled and ambitious politician and one of the youngest on Capitol Hill. Aguda had briefed her during their cab ride, filling in some of the gaps about Hogan, as well as a few of the other committee members.

She saw her name glowing on a prism-shaped LED display on the table, adjacent to an empty seat, and walked over to it. Aguda's seat was to her left. To her right was a younger man she recognized as the president of AramcoSol, the world's largest company. His name was Jassim Othman, and he was a renowned playboy. It was widely known that his company, built by his father, had risen phoenix-like from the smouldering ashes of the dramatic collapse of the once wealthy Gulf States, whose economies had been destroyed by the twin catastrophes of climate change and the abandonment of fossil fuels as a resource. AramcoSol had seen this coming and had invested heavily in perovskite-crystal technology for solar power as soon as it became clear that this was the material of choice for cheap, efficient photovoltaic cells. At the same time, it had shaken off its historical allegiances to the Kingdom of Saudi Arabia. Jassim Othman saw that Sarah had recognized him and gave her what she presumed was his most alluring smile.

She suddenly became aware of a low hum from the holotubes around the table. Within a few seconds their black solidity faded and was replaced by full-sized holograms of the remaining committee members. Once they had all materialized there followed a brief buzz of conversation as the remote members exchanged pleasantries with those physically present and with each other. Everyone seemed to know everyone else, Sarah noted, and some exchanges were warmer than others. She looked round the table at each person in turn, scanning the rudimentary information provided on her AR feed. Several of them were not politicians but CEOs of multinational companies. She reflected on how world politics had been transformed during her lifetime. Even before the mass migrations forced by rising sea levels in the early thirties, physical country borders had been getting increasingly blurred. The world was now more noticeably split along economic rather than geographical boundaries and was defined as much by online firewalls set up by multinational companies operating in the Cloud and the movement of cryptocurrencies between them as it was by the old national borders.

The hubbub of conversation was cut short by Hogan, who called the meeting to order. 'Welcome, everybody,' he said, looking around the table. 'We will dispense with personal introductions; most of you know everyone already. But of course I want to extend a special welcome to our new member, Dr Sarah Maitlin, a scientist whose expertise is, I am sure, going to be invaluable to us.' A few looked at her and nodded. 'In any case,' continued Hogan, 'you all have AR info about each other. I'm sorry it's so sparse, but it seems some of you still don't trust the security measures here and are being somewhat reticent.' He looked across and smiled thinly at one of the holos. Sarah's AR informed her that this was Xu Furong, the Chinese ambassador to the US, and that he was speaking from his office in Washington.

Ambassador Xu responded sombrely – Sarah's universal translator implant converting his Cantonese into English while at the same time mimicking the deep, gravelly tone of his voice. 'That remains to be seen. Let us hope that the young English scientist can give us some encouraging news.'

The illusion that the man was physically in the room was made complete as he appeared to look straight at Sarah as he spoke.

'Indeed,' said Hogan. 'Well, you'll all be aware that our business for today centres around what Dr Maitlin can tell us about the recent solar activity.' Hogan turned to Sarah.

'So, "*young English scientist*" –' He said it in a tone obviously intended to be light-hearted, but which came across to Sarah as patronizing. She let the comment pass but decided she most certainly did not like Hogan. '– let me give you a brief summary of why our committee exists. You may recognize one or two of the people around this table, but others you will not. We come from a wide mix of backgrounds. As I'm sure you're aware, geopolitics has been on the rise again in recent years. And even though the movement of displaced populations has blurred state borders further, it has also led to a rise in the powers of governments as the world has experienced renewed competition for space and resources. And yet many multinationals –' He glanced over and smiled at Jassim Othman, who nodded curtly back. '– remain larger and more powerful than all but the richest countries.

'This, um, welcome desire for international cooperation means that there is still a need for an umbrella organization like the United Nations that can provide a forum for global decisionmaking. Now, you might argue that the UN is a beast that has long since lost its teeth, but it is once again being called upon to act as arbiter and overseer of humankind's affairs. And that's why you see seated around you representatives from several large multinational companies, which of course have as much right to have their say as any nation state.'

Sarah tried to give the impression that she was grateful for this tutorial. Did Hogan think she'd just woken up from a decade-long suspended animation? Thankfully, it sounded like he was finally getting round to business.

'And you will know that the reason you have been invited onto our committee is because of your unrivalled knowledge of these solar events and how to model and predict them. We're informed that the most recent model you've been working on in your institute in Brazil is the most advanced yet.'

'We believe it is, yes,' replied Sarah without trying to hide her sense of pride in the work, even though, if she were honest, it was mostly done by a powerful AI. The computer simulations of the Sun no longer existed as thousands of lines of code written by human programmers. Like almost everything in the modern world that required the analysis and processing of huge amounts of data, pattern recognition and predicting how those patterns would evolve in time, it was really the job of deep neural networks rather than humans.

She suddenly realized that Hogan and the other committee members were looking at her expectantly, waiting for her to say something more. Hogan broke the brief silence. 'Well . . . we need to know what it tells us about the predictability and impact of any future events like the one that caused the recent geomagnetic storm that brought that plane down and, more importantly in my view, fried a quarter of the commsats over the Indian Ocean. We also need to know what effect they may have on our weather systems and if we should expect more extreme events like Hurricane Jerome.'

It surprised Sarah that Hogan would be more concerned with damage to global communication systems than the loss of human life, and she wondered what political causes this committee had been set up to serve. She decided that full disclosure as soon as possible was the safest course of action and butted in. 'Can I make clear that, as a solar physicist, my expertise doesn't extend to geomagnetic storms and their effects on the climate.'

Hogan shot her a quick glance, suggesting he was not used to being interrupted. But his features softened almost immediately as though a switch controlling them had been flicked. 'I perfectly understand. So rather than detain our distinguished members, or indeed you, any longer than necessary, maybe you can give us an update on your work; in lay terms, of course.' He laughed and looked around the table. Several others laughed too.

What a bunch of patronizing fools, thought Sarah. While she couldn't assume that they knew much about her research, she wasn't naive enough to think that they wouldn't all have been thoroughly briefed by their science advisors.

'Thank you, Senator,' she said. 'Yes, of course, I'll try to keep this, ah, simple.' She placed her left hand on the table and tapped her wristpad, transferring the holographic presentation she'd prepared the day before to the room's system. Then, taking a deep breath, she began. 'I'm relieved to hear that you don't want me to comment on whether cosmic rays were linked to Hurricane Jerome – not until we've made further analyses. But hard though this might be for you to accept, I believe we have an even bigger problem to worry about.' She had rehearsed this part of her speech several times in her head and felt her confidence return.

'As most of you will probably know already, coronal ejections –
giant bubbles of electrified gas thrown out from the surface
of the Sun – take place on average several times a day. And since
they can be ejected at any angle in three dimensions, the chance
of one heading directly towards Earth is low, typically once every
fortnight.' As she spoke she activated the presentation. A holographic animation of the Solar System appeared hovering above
the centre of the conference table at head height. The Sun was a
football-sized, glowing and dynamic orange sphere, exquisite in
its detail, with Earth and the inner planets orbiting slowly around
it. Every now and then it spat out a tiny diffuse ball of fire that
travelled radially outwards, spreading and fading slowly as it did
so.

'A typical CME carries a total amount of energy *one hundred times greater* than that produced by the giant asteroid
impact that wiped out the dinosaurs sixty-five million years
ago.'

Several people stared at her incredulously as this statistic
sank in.

'So, how have we managed to survive so long under this
onslaught from our sun? Well, throughout its history, our planet
has always had its magnetic field to cushion the impact of coronal ejections – think of it as planet-sized bubble-wrap. But . . . if
that magnetic field is severely weakened then . . . well . . . well,
no one really knows what the implications are.'

An immaculately dressed, grey-haired man with a trim beard
sitting across the table from her cut in. 'Ah, come now, Dr
Maitlin, please do not lecture us.' He had addressed her in English, she realized; her United Nations-issue AR informed her
that he was Ashraf al-Magribi, the Egyptian Minister of the
Interior. He spoke in a clear, confident voice, as though accustomed to being listened to. 'We already know all we need to
about these coronal ejections and how and why they are formed.
That is not why you have been asked onto this committee.'

Sarah felt momentarily winded, not quite knowing how to
respond to this sudden hostility. A woman sitting next to the
Egyptian turned to admonish him. She looked about the same

age as Sarah, but even from across the table Sarah could tell that she'd had extensive tissue-engineering work and skin nano-implants. However, it was her voice that betrayed the decades her face was hiding. 'There's no need for such an insulting tone, Mr Magribi. We have invited Dr Maitlin to join our committee, so at least do her the courtesy of listening without interrupting.' Her voice was soft, yet commanded immediate respect and al-Magribi sniffed and stroked his beard, trying not to look as though he'd just been put in his place.

Sarah's AR informed her that the woman was Filomena Crespo, the immensely powerful Brazilian vice-president of Samsung, and she wondered whether her representing a multi-national company rather than a nation state meant she was less encumbered by politics and thus more likely to be sympathetic. Maybe she just felt it necessary to defend a fellow woman – after all, Ms Crespo would have started her career back at a time when women needed to work twice as hard to prove their worth in reaching the very top of the career ladder. Whatever the reason, Sarah was grateful.

She guessed that an Egyptian representing a population of a hundred and twenty million would be particularly keen to have some reassurances. After all, his country's agricultural infrastructure was in tatters since the disappearance of much of the Nile Delta a decade ago, one of the first regions to fall victim to the rising sea levels, which had put an almost unbear-able strain on an already fragile economy.

She resumed her presentation: 'Of course, not all Earth-bound CMEs are dangerous. We think about one in five would cause us major concern. The issue is that everyone is probably looking in the wrong place.'

Now she had their full attention. *This is it. This is where I get to shake them from their smug complacency.* 'You see, you've been worried about the coronal ejection's impact on the magnetic field itself, causing a geomagnetic storm.'

'You're still not telling us anything new, Dr Maitlin,' the Chinese ambassador said coldly.

Sarah felt her face get hot as anger suddenly rose inside her again. *For fuck's sake, it's not like I asked to come onto this bloody committee. What would they do if I just stood up and walked out?* She took a deep breath and composed herself. 'My *point*, Ambassador, is that geomagnetic storms are not necessarily what should be concerning us right now. The communication satellites taken out last week that caused the crash of Flight AI-231 were fried by the direct impact of high-energy particles in the ejection itself and *not*, as everyone seems to think, by a geomagnetic storm.

'Catastrophic though they can be, our focus now should not be on the more predictable problems of disruption to power grids or disturbance to radio signals that we've had to worry about during geomagnetic storms in the past, but rather the threat of *direct* exposure to the burst of CME radiation hitting the Earth.'

She flicked on to the next holo image. It showed an animation of the Earth with its surrounding magnetic field, which was represented by flux lines emanating from the Earth's poles and curving round in ever larger loops. The shape of the field was shown compressed on the Earth's Sunward side to a distance of about ten Earth radii. 'The reason the side of the Earth's magnetosphere – its magnetic field – facing the Sun is squashed is the pressure of the solar wind. But on the night side of the Earth you can see how the field lines are stretched out so that the magnetosphere extends like a tail behind us.

'But . . . this is what the magnetosphere *should* look like at full strength. Now watch what happens in the event of a direct hit from a CME.' As she spoke, the animation showed an approaching coronal mass ejection, a colourful cloud of plasma far larger than the Earth. When it slammed into the magnetosphere it caused the field lines to distort and stretch, compressing even more on the side that took the full impact. 'The high-energy particles in the CME are deflected around the Earth by the field, like water parting around a rock in the middle of a fast-moving stream.

'Even though the majority of these particles don't get through to us, the highly charged plasma of the CME sets off a geomagnetic storm – a disturbance in the magnetosphere that causes powerful electromagnetic currents to flow around the planet.

'Now then, you might expect that a *weaker* magnetic field would mean less violent geomagnetic storms. And you'd be right. But . . .' She ran the animation again, but this time there were fewer field lines surrounding the Earth. '. . . a weaker field is also less effective at stopping the high-energy bombardment of the subatomic particles. So, instead of them being deflected around the Earth by the magnetosphere, more of them can punch through it.'

She paused briefly to see the reaction on the committee's faces. Yes, she certainly had their complete attention now.

She added, 'Maybe *this* is something new, or does everyone know this already? In which case, I really don't know what my role is here today.'

She realized that she had probably raised her voice a little too much, but so what? They wanted the truth, and they'd got it, with no sugar coating.

The room suddenly erupted in a hubbub of questions, mostly directly to her, and Senator Hogan needed to call the meeting to order. 'I think, ladies and gentlemen, that the point Dr Maitlin makes is very important, and can potentially be seen as encouraging news.'

'Encouraging? In what possible way can it be encouraging? Or have I just completely misheard Dr Maitlin?' said the Finnish delegate, a slim woman with cropped white hair sitting off to Sarah's left.

Hogan smiled. 'The reason we asked Dr Maitlin onto this committee was so that she could tell us just how precisely she and her team could forecast the arrival time of a CME, so that the world can take the necessary precautions. If the main threat is therefore from the initial CME impact, then I would guess that is a far more reliable thing to predict than any subsequent geomagnetic storm it might cause. Am I right, Dr Maitlin?'

Sarah had a sinking feeling. OK, here it comes. Clearly, she had already not endeared herself to most of the committee, and they sure as hell weren't going to like what she had to tell them next.

She decided to just give them the facts as calmly as she could. She took a deep breath. 'Ejections aimed at the Earth are called "halo events" because of the way they look to us. As the approaching cloud of an ejection looms larger and larger it appears to envelop the Sun, forming a halo around it. This means that, unlike with one heading off, say, at right angles to the line between the Sun and the Earth, predicting its speed is difficult, because we can't see it moving from a side-on view. With something coming straight at us, we just *can't* predict precisely when it will hit us.'

It was Aguda's turn to interrupt her. 'But don't we have solar orbiting satellites that can give us enough of a side-on view? They'd be beyond the path of the ejection – outside of the line of fire – and therefore safe from being fried. They can track the ejection and give us an accurate approach velocity.' To illustrate his point, he extended his arms, pointing his two index fingers towards a point in front of him, and brought them together.

On cue, Sarah clicked to the next image, which showed the Earth in its orbit around the Sun and the location of two satellites in the same orbit, one ahead of Earth and the other lagging behind. 'That's true,' she said. 'We have the STEREO2 spacecraft that give us just this view, but by the time the CME is close enough for this to be useful, it's too late and the ejection is almost upon us.'

Even though she was having to relay unpalatable news, she nevertheless felt on much firmer ground now, science she'd spent her entire career working on.

'So, instead, we have to make predictions based on simulations. These can take into account everything our AIs can learn about an ejection, from the Sun's own magnetic field to the solar wind, to the size and strength of the ejection itself. All this just so we can get one number out at the end: the SAT, or Shock Arrival Time.'

The Chinese ambassador interrupted her again. 'But of course, the number we all want from you, Dr Maitlin, is a different one, and is based on the accuracy of this prediction. How wide is the arrival-time window? How much advance warning do we get?'

Sarah took another deep breath. 'Since CMEs can travel at a wide range of speeds – anything from a few hundred to several thousand kilometres per second – our best estimate, based on a combination of computer predictions and satellite data . . . is a window of eight hours.'

Everyone stared at Sarah. Al-Magribi broke the silence. 'Do you mean to tell us we will know we're *going* to be hit, but not *when*? This means it could hit anywhere?'

'That's correct, I'm afraid. We must face up to the fact that the population of entire continents will need to stay indoors if they are to avoid a potentially fatal dose of radiation. And that's not to mention the damage done to animal and plant life. No single country will know if it'll be hit until it is too late to act. And this is something that is likely to happen again and again in the coming months.' Once again, everyone started talking at once. Her uncompromising assessment had clearly been both unexpected and unwelcome.

'But I still don't understand,' cut in the Finnish delegate loudly. 'How does this eight-hour uncertainty come in?'

Sarah manipulated her fingers on the touch-sensitive section of the table in front of her to retrieve the very first holo image she had shown of the Earth slowly rotating about its axis. 'Our planet takes twenty-four hours to complete a full revolution, right? So, over the space of eight hours one whole third of the planet's surface could be exposed to the impact.'

An uneasy ripple of conversation spread around the table. This was as good a time as any to hit them with the *coup de grâce*.

'And I'm afraid there's one more thing.' She had to raise her voice to be heard. 'Before the CME even reaches Earth, we'll be bombarded by a stream of high-energy protons, the vanguard of the pulse. Because these particles will be travelling at near light speed, they'll reach us about ten minutes after the CME is ejected by the Sun. Normally, they'd be deflected by the magnetosphere, but in its weakened state some will get through and pose a serious radiation risk.'

This new revelation left everyone stunned. After a few seconds, Hogan was the first to speak. 'None of this really changes anything. We already knew we would have to put in place various emergency strategies and procedures in the event of a direct hit. All this means is that more individual governments are going to have to do this than we thought.'

'And even if there is a strong chance a CME will miss us,' continued Aguda. There were a few reluctant nods around the table.

'But,' continued the senator, 'we still need to write our report and agree on a united plan of action.'

Sarah felt a wave of relief that she'd finally got this off her chest. The world was in peril, but at least it was no longer just her worry.

# PART II

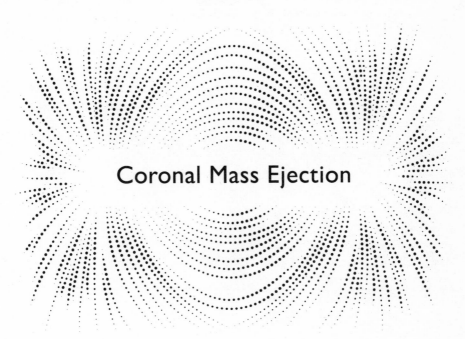

# Coronal Mass Ejection

# 13

QIANG LEE HAD ARRIVED EARLY AT MCCOSH HALL ON Princeton University Campus, where the dark-matter conference was being held. He felt relieved to have made it at all as so many flights into New York had been cancelled due to fears of what Hurricane Jerome might do next. The superstorm was all anyone seemed to be talking about at the moment and was certainly the only topic on all the AR news feeds.

His name badge read 'Prof. Lee, Qiang (IHEP)', which made him smile. The Institute for High Energy Physics in Beijing now had a strong enough international reputation that its rather generic acronym was sufficient to place the wearer. After turning away from the registration desk with his conference bag, he took a look inside it. There was a time when it would have been filled with useless pieces of paper: maps, leaflets listing the best pizza restaurants in town and glossy brochures of 'Things to do while in Princeton' – mostly open markets, art exhibitions and community amateur dramatics events. By contrast this one was almost empty, but he was pleased to see that along with a folded plastic e-pad containing the programme and the rest of the conference information there was a pad of notepaper and pen. Hardly any delegates used such pads any more, but Qiang liked to doodle or work on dense algebraic derivations while only half listening to the talks.

Strolling back outside the building, he wondered how his old friend and collaborator would be. He'd heard about Marc Bruckner's marriage breakdown, and how he'd fallen out with several people in the Physics Department at Columbia and had finally escaped to his late parents' summer home in New Zealand for some much-needed convalescence. Having spoken to him last night, Qiang decided he did look and sound a lot better than he had dared to expect. Was that just an act for his benefit? Could sufferers from depression recover so quickly? He doubted it. Maybe it was more to do with the anticipation of seeing his daughter Evie after the conference.

Their brief online exchange had brought back memories of those heady days in the late twenties when the two men had made the biggest breakthrough in particle physics research since the discovery of the Higgs boson, that dark matter self-interacts, creating normal matter in a burst of high energy.

He spotted Marc striding purposefully across the grass towards him and waved. Marc waved back and grinned broadly. As soon as he was close enough Qiang extended his hand, but Marc pulled him into a bear hug.

Qiang smiled, feeling a little awkward. 'It's good to see you. And I'm glad you could make this meeting. We've got a lot of catching up to do.'

Both men had long since given up on the idea that a scientific conference was about listening to the talks. They could find out about other people's research any time and from anywhere. No, conferences were about renewing acquaintances, discussing the politics of academia and, of course, knocking around new ideas in the bar. Qiang wondered whether Marc could still outdrink everyone else.

The two men walked into the building where thirty or more delegates were milling around greeting each other. There was an audible drop in the level of background chatter as Marc was spotted. He didn't seem to care and Qiang was relieved, although he felt certain that had it been him on the receiving end, he'd have been devastated. Maybe Marc was just good at hiding his feelings.

They picked up coffees and wandered into the lecture theatre to claim their seats – not too close to the front or the rear,
but always to one side in case they needed an early escape if a
talk was particularly boring.

As soon as they were seated, Marc turned to Qiang. 'So,
how's Chyou doing? And the kids . . . they must be school age
now?'

'Yup, the boys are both at school and doing well. And Chyou
is fine. Although I think she still misses New York.'

'What? Are you crazy? What's to miss?'

'When were you last in Beijing, Marc?' chided Qiang. 'Chyou
says she misses Manhattan's clean air and provincial feel.' They
both laughed.

'How about you? When you said that you'd moved back to
New Zealand I expected you to turn into a hermit and shut
yourself away from the world.'

Marc sighed. 'Yes, I did think about leading a life of solitude and focusing full-time on feeling sorry for myself . . .' His
eyes took on a distant, glazed look. Then he shrugged and smiled.
'But, you know what? Fuck it. Life is only as bleak as the lens
you look at it through, right? Anyway, did you know Evie turns
sixteen next week?'

'Wow, sweet little Evie? I remember babysitting her when
she was the same age as my boys are now.' Qiang thought back
to those times when Marc and Charlotte seemed to have the
perfect marriage and family life with their young daughter. He
looked closely at his old friend.

Marc smiled self-consciously under Qiang's scrutiny. 'Time
marches on, my friend,' he said. 'I see you've got the odd grey
hair yourself now.'

Qiang shrugged. 'That's just Chinese bureaucracy for you, and
the never-ending writing of grant proposals. Not something I
guess you're too worried about these days.' As soon as he'd said
it, he regretted it and started to apologize. Marc cut him off.

'Hey, don't be silly; it's true, I don't. Anyway, I haven't
decided what to do next. I haven't entirely ruled out getting
back into academia.'

Other delegates were starting to filter into the hall. 'So, what's new with you, Qiang? I saw your last paper before Christmas. What are you working on now?'

Qiang couldn't hide his change in demeanour and it was clear Marc had picked up on it. There was no point keeping what he knew to himself any longer, so he dropped his voice to a whisper. 'That's why I was so relieved when you told me you'd be here. If you hadn't come I would have flown down to New Zealand to speak to you.'

He wondered what Marc would think of his crazy idea.

# 14

MARC WAS INTRIGUED. IT TOOK A LOT FOR QIANG TO OPENLY show emotion in this way. Looking down at the programme of talks for the morning he groaned inwardly. 'Look,' he said, 'this session is basically welcoming speeches and a couple of plenary overview talks – nothing we don't already know. Come on.' He stood up and ushered his friend out into the aisle and up the steps at the side of the lecture theatre.

The two men strolled out of the building, now walking against the stream of delegates entering through the glass doors. Once outside in the crisp morning sunshine again, Marc said, 'Well, it seems my rehabilitation into the dark-matter community didn't last long. But then I'm really not ready to sit through all that drivel just yet, especially not forty-five minutes of crusty old Goldstein telling us how everything we know about the subject is down to him; and certainly not when you've got something important to tell me. So, come on, spill the beans.'

Qiang shook his head and watched in silence as a few late-running delegates hurried past them, nodding their greetings as they went. Marc thrust his hands into the pockets of his coat, hunching his shoulders against the chill air, and waited for Qiang to talk. When they were finally alone, Marc turned to his friend, puzzled at the apparent need for secrecy. 'Well?'

Qiang had pulled his collar up against the cold, which made

him look even more conspiratorial, like an old-fashioned spy. Marc suppressed a smile.

'OK, but I must first ask you to promise to keep what I say confidential.'

Marc shrugged his shoulders and frowned. What could be so important? 'Of course, but why do you even need to ask me that? How can you worry that I would ever talk about your work before you'd published?'

'It's not something that will *ever* get published.' Qiang looked around nervously as though he feared they were being watched. 'Several weeks ago, I was invited to Shanghai with a group of other scientists – mostly geologists, but still a surprising spread of expertise. Anyway, we had a couple of meetings with some high-level government officials. It was clear they wanted us to put our heads together to address the implications of the weakening magnetic field.'

Marc raised his eyebrows. 'What? Oh . . . I see. Well, you know you've really made it in the world of science when your government asks you to solve a problem you're no more qualified to tackle than my plumber,' he chuckled. Qiang frowned. Whatever he was involved in, it was obviously something that concerned him. Marc gripped his arm and looked his friend in the eyes.

'Sorry, Qiang, I didn't mean to suggest that you— OK, look, this doesn't sound too sinister to me. I mean, everyone's talking about the Flip and when it's going to happen. They're saying later this year. And after this horrific hurricane, which may or may not be linked to the weakening field, not to mention the CME that brought down the Air India plane . . . well, it can't happen soon enough, I guess.'

He now saw something in Qiang's eyes that unsettled him. There was a wild excitement that looked somewhat out of place. Qiang grew suddenly animated and started walking more briskly. 'And *that's* the issue,' he almost shouted. Then, as though remembering what a risk he was taking, suddenly dropped his voice back to a whisper. 'What I learned from these meetings is that they believe the Flip may not happen as soon as we hope.'

'What do you mean? Are there new data?'

'No one is saying as much, but . . . Well, let me just say that the secrecy we've all been sworn to would suggest that we're not being told everything.'

Marc tried to suppress his impatience. 'OK, look, I know what the Chinese authorities are like with secrecy and I can understand that you feel you're taking a huge risk by talking about it, even to someone I hope you feel you can trust. But I'm also guessing you have good reason for wanting to confide in me. So come on, what the fuck *is* it you're trying to tell me?'

Qiang drew in a deep breath of the cold morning air and slumped his shoulders in resignation. 'Well, I don't know what they are basing their information on, but they've been looking at putting plans in place to cope with a drastically weakened magnetosphere over a three- to five-year period.'

Marc stopped abruptly in his tracks. 'Sorry, did you just say three to five *years*?' He stared incredulously at his friend.

Qiang gave him a grim nod. 'I know. This dramatically conflicts with the official line, which is that we just need to ride this out for a few months before the Flip and the field rights itself, not several *years*.'

Marc rubbed his hand slowly against his stubbly cheek. Why would the world be told things would start returning to normal in a few months if it was really going to take years? And what further damage could be caused if the field continued to weaken? Would life be fried by cosmic radiation? Would the ozone layer be stripped away? He stood gazing out across the campus, contemplating the ramifications of what he was hearing.

Qiang had carried on walking without slowing and Marc hurried after him, falling into step with him just as he began talking again. 'They encouraged us to come up with various proposals, from protective shields in orbit, to excavating vast underground bunkers. I didn't really have much to offer. But on my return to Beijing, I started thinking. What if, for the sake of argument, we *had* to do something about the magnetic field itself? What if we simply couldn't wait around for the planet to right itself?'

Up ahead, jogging towards them, was a young couple, probably lost in music only they could hear. But Qiang nevertheless waited until they had passed and were a safe distance away before he continued.

'I've been doing some digging around in the scientific literature. Did you know it's only in the last ten years or so, thanks to advances in neutrino imaging, that we've properly understood how the Earth's magnetic field is generated?'

He didn't wait for an answer. 'Well, the liquid metal core of the Earth is basically a giant dynamo. As it swirls around it generates electric currents and magnetic fields, which push more conducting liquid metal around to create even stronger currents, and so stronger fields, and so on. It's a gigantic feedback loop.'

Despite the seriousness of the subject, Marc couldn't help but feel a little amused. Qiang's deep expertise in particle physics was so specialized, so niche, that, brilliant scientist though he was, he was only now discovering basic high-school geomagnetism. He was animatedly waving his arms around and wiggling his fingers to simulate various circular motions. His enthusiasm reminded Marc of those early years when he would pop into his office at Columbia first thing in the morning with a new idea and start scrawling Feynman diagrams on the board, while Marc tried desperately to keep up. But the subject matter now was far more important than a theoretical curiosity about the structure of dark matter.

'But,' continued Qiang, 'if this liquid core gets disturbed, the magnetic field gets weaker. And right now, turbulent vortices thousands of kilometres below our feet are disrupting its smooth circular flow.

'So, my question is this: if we really had to, is there a way of kick-starting the core again? How could we deliver a massive boost of energy to the right spots at the right time to push the liquid metal in the right direction?'

Marc was intrigued. 'I guess it's a bit like sticking your finger into emptying bathwater above the plughole and stirring it to recover the steady circular vortex after it has been messed up.'

'Exactly,' said Qiang with a small smile. 'Only it's not so

easy to stick a giant finger into our planet. So, the problem is how to deliver that energy. In the old Hollywood movies, there'd be an expedition to the centre of the Earth, in which some kind of manned subterranean craft would blast its way to the core with a laser beam. Of course it's a fun idea, but you and I both know it's quite unrealistic. I mean, even today, the deepest boreholes in the Earth's crust don't penetrate beyond about twenty kilometres. Compared with the six and a half thousand kilometres to the centre, that's barely a pinprick.'

They had left the large academic buildings behind and were now walking through rows of student apartments. They passed a Starbucks, busy with university staff and students picking up breakfast on their way to offices, labs and classes.

Qiang stopped again and looked around, as though only now noticing how far they had walked. He turned to face Marc and put a conspiratorial hand on his arm. 'Maybe we should start heading back.' Marc shrugged, and they turned to retrace their route. Qiang continued. 'So, if you wanted to deliver energy to the centre of the Earth without it being lost en route, what would you use?'

'You mean like proton beam therapy to treat tumours?'

'Exactly. Deliver energy into living tissue without obstruction, then dump it exactly where it's needed inside the body at a precise location. What if, instead of a human patient, you were dealing with the entire planet?'

Marc was puzzled. He was clearly missing something obvious. 'OK, we already use neutrino beams for imaging the interior of the Earth, but that wouldn't work here. Hardly any energy loss. Most of the particles in those beams pass straight through.'

He sensed that Qiang was waiting patiently for the penny to drop. And it suddenly hit him like a bombshell. 'Of course!' he shouted. 'Fucking hell, Qiang . . .'

A woman walking her dog on the other side of the road stopped to look over at the two men. Qiang gave her a friendly wave.

Marc was oblivious, finally realizing what Qiang was getting at. Of course there was a way to reach the Earth's core. But it would involve a beam of particles trillions of times heavier and yet far more elusive than neutrinos. More to the point, they were the particles to which the two men had devoted their research careers.

'Neutralinos!'

Qiang stared up at him, bright-eyed. Expectant. Knowing he no longer needed to say any more.

For the past twenty years, the two physicists had dedicated their lives to studying dark matter – more specifically, seeing what would happen when beams of neutralinos, the particles of dark matter, smashed together at high energy. Like their tiny cousins the neutrinos, these particles hardly interact with normal matter at all and so would pass through the Earth unobstructed. But, cross two beams of neutralinos together . . . Marc liked to quote Spengler, the character from the old movie *Ghostbusters*: '*Don't cross the streams.*'

His mind was racing. What if you aimed multiple beams of neutralinos down into the ground from different locations around the planet, all meeting at one point deep in the core? They would each travel through the Earth as though it were completely transparent, but if they met . . . He tried to do the calculations in his head to determine how big a bang that would make. Big enough to kick-start the Earth's core again? He couldn't tell whether the idea was even feasible; he knew too little about geophysics. It was certainly a daring idea. Actually, scratch that, it was a crazy idea. Even if it worked, it would take years to put it into practice.

He realized Qiang was still staring at him, waiting for him to say something. He exhaled noisily. 'I'm assuming you've not shared this ridiculous suggestion with anyone else.'

'Of course not. But what if we had no choice but to try it?'

Marc felt a strange mix of terror and excitement. All thoughts of going back to New Zealand were gone for now.

# 15

SHIREEN HAD BEEN ON THE RUN FOR THREE DAYS. SAVAK, the recently resurrected and feared Iranian secret service, had been on her tail and getting closer all the time. It hadn't taken her much effort to hack into surveillance cameras to monitor locations around the city that she had passed through and watch as they clumsily followed clues she had deliberately left as bait to throw them off course. So far, it had worked, and she had managed to stay one crucial step ahead of them. But unless everything went according to plan, which she admitted was a long shot, especially since the plan itself was still so hazy, it would only be a matter of time before they caught up with her.

Her world had started caving in when Majid hadn't shown up for class on Friday, the morning after her successful hacking session in his apartment. But it wasn't until lunchtime that a mutual friend on the dark web informed her that Majid had been arrested after receiving a visit from Savak late on Thursday evening. How close had she been to getting caught too? They must have very quickly traced the security breach to his computer. Poor, innocent Majid. She felt wretched about getting him mixed up in all this, and at the same time terrified by the speed with which the authorities had reacted. Clearly, she hadn't been quite as careful as she'd thought.

Majid must have tried to cover for her, otherwise she'd have been picked up too, but he had bought her a few precious hours – enough for her to put a rough plan of action in place with the help of several cybs on the dark web whom she felt she could trust. By Friday evening she had yet to look at the files she'd obtained, now buried deep in her little corner of the dark web where even the most sophisticated AIs wouldn't find them. Or so she hoped. After all, *she'd* managed to acquire them, hadn't she? But she hadn't allowed her paranoia to get the better of her. One of the advantages of the dark web was its sheer size – layer upon layer, world upon world, like a multi-verse of realities coexisting in the same cyberspace yet never interacting, allowing millions to hide their secrets away from prying eyes.

She hadn't gone back home on Friday. Savak agents would be there waiting for her, she was sure of it. Of course, her parents would have been sick with worry, but for now, the less they knew the better. Instead, she'd headed for the most secure place she could think of: an internet café called Nine Nights – a typically geeky play on the '1001 Nights' stories, but with the number interpreted in binary. It was a popular haunt of the Tehran cyb community, run by a retired coder by the name of Hashimi who in an earlier life had been an associate of her father's.

Hashimi was a tall, thin man, with a grizzled grey beard that used to scare her as a young girl when he would come round to their house. The beard had always made him look much older than his years. Even now, she figured, he had to be only around sixty. But he had kind eyes that shone with a deep wisdom she found reassuring. A few years ago, he and her father had fallen out over Hashimi's shady dark-web activities and she hated to think how disappointed her father would be if he knew she had come to Hashimi for help instead of confiding in him.

She had no choice now but to trust the man. He had been very pleased to see her when she had turned up just as he was closing the café. But his mood changed to one of concern when he'd seen the look in her eyes. He'd ushered her inside, locked up the café and sat her down. She had told him about the files without giving him too much detail about exactly how she had acquired them. Although he'd been initially reluctant to get involved, the look in his eyes gave away his palpable admiration for what she had achieved, and he was clearly as intrigued as she was by what the files might contain. Nevertheless, it had taken all her powers of persuasion to stop him from contacting her father. He'd led her through a dimly lit corridor to a door at the back of the building that required biometric access. The room they entered looked like a cross between a junkyard and NASA's Mission Control Center. It was filled with an array of old computers with old-fashioned physical display screens and cables covering the floor. She could swear that much of the hardware looked older than she was. And yet the familiar electronic hum and glowing LEDs left her in no doubt that this was a working environment. Every square centimetre of surface area was filled with a mix of electronic gadgetry, empty food cartons, beer bottles and coffee cups. Along one wall was stacked a bewildering mountain of defunct hardware that presumably Hashimi couldn't bring himself to get rid of. On the other side of the room was an unmade bed and a small sink. Shireen had wondered under what circumstances he might have needed to spend the night in this electronic bunker when his own apartment was just upstairs.

She'd felt overwhelmingly grateful when Hashimi left her alone to read the contents of the files in privacy. But he'd insisted she come and get him if and when she needed his help.

It had taken her about an hour to access and scan through all the files. Among them was high-resolution satellite footage, magnetic-field data, graphs and tables, scientific papers in preprint form, emails, internal memos and confidential reports. By the end, she had been left in no doubt what she had. Nor did it take her long to work out why people at the very top of the food chain wouldn't want this information to get out.

The facts were simple enough. Here was solid evidence that powerful individuals, and possibly entire governments, had been hiding the truth about the Earth's weakening magnetic field: it was not about to flip, but was instead slowly dying, probably permanently. The official line to the public seemed to be that quite the opposite was taking place: that pockets of the magnetic field in the southern hemisphere were recovering fast and that the crisis would be over by the end of the year. These files told a very different story, however, and it terrified Shireen. She had sat staring into space for a long time, trying to clear her head and calm her nerves. She didn't understand all of the science, but it didn't take much effort to piece together what this implied: without a magnetosphere, all life on Earth would eventually be wiped out.

Shireen had lived her entire life in a world struggling to cope with the severe consequences of climate change, and humankind was finally winning the battle to turn things around. Was it now about to face an even greater challenge to its survival? What she had not been able to find was the source of the cover-up. Who had ordered it, and why?

She had to form a rational plan of action. But she didn't have much time. For a few minutes she had even seriously contemplated turning herself in and handing over the files. She was clearly out of her depth. But she doubted she'd have got away with a simple reprimand. After all, she couldn't now unknow the contents of the files, nor could the authorities be sure she hadn't already released them on the dark web. No, that wasn't ever really an option.

The only alternative was to make the files public and hope that there were still people in power uncorrupted by this secret and who could protect her.

What would happen next, she had no idea, but the world needed to know. Later that evening she had confided in Hashimi and showed him the contents of the files. He had agreed it would be naive to think she could simply make them public by releasing them online. Their contents would be instantly discredited and branded as fraudulent – just another attempt by cyberterrorists to embarrass the global order alongside the millions of other conspiracy theories, fake 'leaks' and elaborate hoaxes that were part and parcel of the online world these days. And disseminating them across the dark web, which would have been very easy, was an even worse idea. No one would take it seriously. It would just be lost in the noise. No, the only way was for the files to be leaked by a source of utmost reliability – someone in a position of power who was beyond reproach.

But finding the right person wasn't even the difficult part. The files would have to be delivered *in person*. She couldn't risk simply emailing them and hope they would be taken seriously. Besides, that would involve retrieving the files from the safe depths of the dark web and sending them across the surface web where they would certainly be tracked and intercepted by monitor AIs before they reached their destination.

She couldn't risk getting in touch with her parents herself, so she had asked Hashimi if he could do so as surreptitiously as possible, letting them know she was OK and warning them to go dark. She knew full well that they would have been watched very closely by Savak, but the one thing she was confident of was that her parents were more than capable of disappearing off-grid for a few days. She guessed they would know how to shake off Savak surveillance and head up to the mountains north of the city where they had friends they could rely on to hide them. She had begged Hashimi to share with them only the sketchiest of information – enough for them to take the matter seriously. The less they knew, the safer they would be.

After a little digging, Hashimi had informed her that Majid had been released, causing fresh waves of relief and guilt to wash through her. Poor Majid. It wouldn't have taken Savak long to get the truth out of him, or what little he knew of it. And they wouldn't have needed to use force: a simple chemical relaxant that affected his higher cognitive functions, followed by an fMRI scan, would allow them to read his thoughts like an open book. It was hardly telepathy – all they had to do was to see which parts of his brain lit up in answer to yes/no questions. They'd have learned quickly enough that he was an innocent accomplice who knew nothing about the content of the secret files. She just hoped he would escape serious punishment.

Now, she hoped, she had only herself to worry about. Almost anyone else would have been picked up within the hour: hooking up to the Cloud for anything as simple as purchasing a bus ticket or a sandwich would instantly reveal their location. It wouldn't help much staying offline either; the thousands of miniature cameras hidden throughout the infrastructure of the city could locate anyone within seconds.

But Shireen wasn't just anyone.

She would need to keep on the move, and to stay hidden from prying cameras. A simple disguise wouldn't be enough to hide her – pattern-recognition software running Grover algorithms would sift through a CCTV database of twenty million people going about their daily business throughout the city to find her just by the way she walked.

No, she needed a squelch jammer, an illegal electronic device that could disrupt the video-feed signal from any cameras close enough to biometrically identify the person possessing it. As a favour to her father and knowing how damaging her information could be for the hated Savak, Hashimi had provided her with his own jammer. But he had warned her that even being constantly on the move was risky – it wouldn't take long for the trail of signal interference to be traced and extrapolated. The jammer needed to be used sparingly.

He had persuaded her to get a night's sleep first and had made up the bed in the back room, then cooked her a late supper.

The following morning was the closest that Savak had yet come to catching up with her. She was awoken by raised voices at 5 a.m. The café couldn't be open yet, which could only mean that they had found her already. She didn't stop to think about how. Scrambling out of bed, she stood in the middle of the room among the stacks of cardboard boxes and tried to make out the conversation outside. Her eyes darted about the room for an escape route. Grabbing her shoes and the rucksack containing the jammer along with the few personal belongings she had with her, she ran for the small back window. It didn't look locked, but still resisted her attempts to open it. She considered breaking the glass, but finally managed to prise it free of the rust and layers of paint that had kept it closed for what must have been years, and swung it part-way open. She couldn't make out much in the darkness beyond other than that it gave onto a narrow alleyway.

The voices outside were growing louder and suddenly the door to the room flew open. Leaping up onto the window sill, she squeezed her waiflike body through the narrow gap and out into the cold early-morning air in one clumsy motion and jumped down into the alleyway.

She hit the ground running, stumbling over several garbage bags and just managing to stay on her feet, her arms cartwheeling about wildly as she ran, trying to regain her balance. Her surroundings took on a dreamlike quality, but this was no immersive VR game – it was really happening. Pure animal instinct took over and she kept running. The panic she felt made her chest constrict and she found it harder to breathe than the physical exertion of the running would account for. As soon as she had covered several blocks, she stopped to slip on her shoes, then pulled the rucksack off her back, reached in and flicked on the jammer.

She then continued at a brisk walking pace. She needed to put as much distance as she could between herself and her pursuers.

The last thing Hashimi had done the previous evening was give her a contact he said might be willing to help get her out of the city, so when she reached a local park, she had found a bench hidden within high shrubbery and sat down to gather her thoughts. She could no longer risk using her wristpad and AR – that would instantly give her location away. Instead, she had to do this the old-fashioned way. She pulled out the small tablet that Hashimi had given her and fired it up. She knew she wouldn't be able to hide her position for long, so she simply displaced it. It was an old trick – a simple case of electronic ventriloquism: suggesting that she was accessing the Cloud from several kilometres away. For now, the best she could do was keep them at arm's length and guessing what her next move would be.

That had been Saturday morning.

Now, forty-eight hours later, it seemed like a lifetime ago.

She had hardly slept since then and was feeling cold, hungry
and in desperate need of a shower, but she had so far stayed
out of Savak's reach. And she was at last about to meet the cyb
whom Hashimi had recommended and who had thankfully
agreed to help her. Her contact was a legend on the dark web
and, despite her exhaustion and anxiety, Shireen felt excited to
be meeting her. Known only as Mother, she never stayed in
one place long and had evaded the authorities for over a decade, so Shireen had no idea whether the meeting would be
face-to-face. Contact had been established on Saturday morning but they had exchanged very little information. Although
Shireen hadn't told her about the files, she'd got the impression
that Mother knew more than she was letting on. What she had
told her was that she needed to get out of the country and
across to America. What she hadn't told her was why.

Shireen had chosen her target carefully, using Hashimi's tablet
to carry out a search of potential candidates around the world.
It had to be someone she could entrust with the files, but also
someone who fulfilled certain other criteria. A scientific training
was vital, or they wouldn't understand the implications of the
satellite data. But it also had to be someone who couldn't have
been part of the cover-up in the first place, someone she might
have a half-decent chance of convincing that the files were genuine, who could be then trusted to do the right thing and, most
importantly, who would be listened to by the world's media.

If this was a worldwide cover-up then she couldn't go to any
one government since she didn't know who was involved. No,
it had to be the United Nations. She had discovered a new UN
committee set up to tackle the weakening-field crisis, but it had
only two scientists – the rest of its members being politicians.
And it hadn't taken her long to settle on the younger of the two:
a British solar physicist by the name of Sarah Maitlin who, until
a fortnight ago, had been an anonymous academic working at a
research institute in Brazil modelling coronal mass ejections, who
had been suddenly plunged into the media spotlight after the
Air India plane crash and now seemed to have been recruited
onto the UN committee that was examining future threats. The

other scientist, a geologist by the name of Aguda, seemed to have the more relevant credentials, but he appeared to have been involved in UN work for several years, which meant he could conceivably also be part of the cover-up. Anyway, Shireen would trust a woman over a man any day. Had she had more time, she was sure she could have come up with a more foolproof plan than simply betting everything on someone she had never met, but this was the best she could do with her limited time and resources.

Now, two days after establishing contact with Mother, it seemed half the global cyb community already knew Shireen very well. News spreads fast. The dark web was awash with stories about the young Iranian cyb who'd achieved what no one had believed possible: cracking a high-security quantum-encrypted website and gaining access to secret files, with speculation and rumours about their contents growing ever more outlandish.

For her part, Shireen knew very little about Mother other than that the woman was Turkish in origin and was currently in Tehran – something that Hashimi must have known. The rest was a mix of mythology, rumours and conspiracy theories.

Mother had agreed to meet her at a secret location – which was on the other side of the vast metropolis, but Shireen had managed to make it there on foot, resting overnight on park benches, mingling with the city's homeless, always keeping her hood pulled up to hide her face and avoid any prying surveillance cameras.

She arrived at the address just before dawn. It was an old apartment block on the corner of two quiet roads. Pausing for a moment at the bottom of the steps, she scanned her surroundings. There was no one in sight. The narrow door's paint was peeling and the large brass knocker had seen better days. Just as she was wondering whether to knock, the door buzzed and she heard a lock click, so she pushed it open and ventured nervously inside.

The hallway was in semi-darkness and she peered around her. Suddenly a man stepped forward out of the shadows, startling her.

He was tall and spindly with a thick beard and shaven head. In the dim hall light he looked to be in his late twenties. He spoke softly. 'You are Shireen?'

She nodded. 'Then please follow me. We must not keep Mother waiting.'

Without waiting for her, the man started up the chipped marble staircase, taking the stairs three at a time, his footsteps echoing around the quiet hallway. Two floors up, at the end of a gloomy corridor, he stopped and unlocked a shabby-looking door.

She followed him into a sparsely furnished apartment. There were no curtains at the window and the room was lit only by a street lamp outside. In the centre was a flimsy-looking table laden with electronics. The man directed Shireen to a chair next to it. 'Please, sit down and put on the visor.' She spotted the VR helmet and suddenly understood what this implied. Of course she would not be meeting Mother physically – how naive of her ever to have thought that. The cyb could be anywhere in the world. She felt an odd mix of disappointment and relief.

Her guide then turned and left the room without saying any more, closing the door softly behind him.

Picking up the visor, Shireen sat down on the edge of the chair and placed the helmet carefully over her head. It instantly moulded itself to the shape of her face, blocking out the light from outside and plunging her into darkness. She activated the switch beneath her left ear and her field of vision suddenly lit up. At first, she could only make out a kaleidoscope of colours, but they quickly resolved themselves and a virtual world came into sharp focus. She recognized the rudimentary details in the surrounding landscape. It looked like thousands of other generic virtual reality worlds both on the dark and surface webs and there was something reassuring and comforting about its familiarity.

In fact, this one looked more basic than most. It was a bright, sunny day and she was standing in the middle of an empty courtyard surrounded by imposing grey buildings that could have represented just about anything, anywhere. A door in the building to her right opened, through which a woman appeared and walked briskly towards her. She was wearing a splendidly colourful long robe, a traditional Turkish *entari*, with gold buttons done up from the waist to the throat. Below the waist was an equally bright and patterned long skirt covering leather boots. Shireen knew better than to project a person's avatar onto their real-life persona, but this woman was tall, elegant and handsome-looking – everything Shireen had imagined 'Mother' to be.

The woman smiled and greeted Shireen in perfect Farsi, the software translating whatever language Mother was physically speaking in. 'Hello, Shireen, I'm Evren Olgun. Well done for making it this far, but you are far from out of the woods yet.' Shireen didn't need to be told this. But at least she now stood a fighting chance of completing her task.

'Thank you for agreeing to help me. It's a real honour to meet you, Mother . . . er . . . I mean Evren.'

Evren's avatar tipped her head back and laughed. 'Well, Shireen, I am sure you're smart enough to know that my motives are not purely altruistic. You have achieved something many of our smartest cybs across the world have failed to do – you've found a way to break through the tightest quantum encryption security. And, while I am certainly intrigued by whatever is in those files, I know that if everything goes according to plan then I, along with the rest of the world, will know about it soon enough. So, for now, what is of far more interest to me is *how* you did it.'

Shireen had guessed all along that the price to pay for getting Mother's help would be to share with her the details of the Trojan horse software. It made sense that Mother would want to make as much use of the quantum hacking trick as she could before the authorities discovered the weakness in the system Shireen had exposed and closed the door for good. But to do that they would have to catch her first. That was why she hoped she could trust Mother not to double-cross her. It was in her interests to keep Shireen from being captured for as long as possible.

Evren continued. 'You must know that we have very little time. After all, it's not just Savak, or even Interpol, that you should be worrying about. At this moment there are many other special-interest groups and cyber cells trying to track you down too. Word will have quickly spread that you have a way of cracking encrypted secrets and everyone wants to get their hands on it. So, here's the deal. I will get you out of the country and safely to America if you hand over the code. But it has to happen now.'

The sudden insistence in Evren's voice sent another wave of panic through Shireen. What if she told her everything she knew and then was kept prisoner in this room, a sure-fire way to guarantee her not getting caught. But she had no choice now other than to trust the older cyb. What other option did she have?

A large transparent display screen appeared, hovering in the space between the two avatars. 'So, show me,' said Evren.

It took just a few minutes for Shireen to access her Trojan horse software on the virtual screen within the virtual world. Line upon line of code scrolled down the screen as she explained, proudly, what she had done. When she finished, the older woman was silent for a few moments. When she finally spoke, Shireen detected more than an undertone of admiration in her voice, which had taken on an excited fervour.

'This is astonishing! And you can be sure we will put it to good use, and it will help our cause immeasurably. There are too many secrets these days that are being kept from the people.'

Shireen wondered what Mother would say if she knew the contents of the files she had uncovered – the biggest secret of them all.

Evren's voice suddenly softened. 'You know, you really are a quite remarkable young woman and I'm sorry that you are in this situation. Maybe, if you succeed in getting the files' contents out, we may one day be able to work together. For now, I must go, as there is much work to be done.'

'Wait! What am I supposed to do now?'

The point of the deal with Evren had been to receive help in getting to New York to meet Sarah Maitlin. Evren couldn't just leave her now.

As if reading her mind, the older cyb said: 'Don't worry.

Lambros, the young man waiting outside, will give you a small gift from me that will help you get out of the country. You can trust him.'

Without further explanation, Evren spun round, her robe twirling rather more impressively than it would in the physical world. Shireen watched the woman walk away, and she was suddenly consumed with doubt, and feeling more alone than at any time in her life. She lifted the VR visor off her head and allowed herself a few seconds for her eyes to readjust to the gloomy room.

She walked to the door, half expecting it to be locked. It wasn't.

Lambros was standing just outside and nodded to her. Before she had a chance to say anything, he said, 'She is quite something, isn't she?' The awe in his voice was obvious. 'Now hold out your wristpad.'

What did he need it for? Had she just made a huge mistake trusting these people? A new wave of panic swept through her. Lambros must have caught the look on her face because he smiled broadly. 'You do want your ticket to America, don't you?'

Shireen was astonished. He must have been there during her VR meeting with Evren. But, surely, he couldn't have set this up so quickly?

'How could you have known . . .'

'. . . that you need to get to New York? To meet Dr Sarah Maitlin? But we've known all along. We've been monitoring all activity on Hashimi's pad since you first started researching Dr Maitlin's background and we guessed, correctly as it turns out, that she would be the one you would reach out to with your, um, new revelations.

'Oh, don't worry,' he added when Shireen recoiled in horror, 'Savak have no idea. And as far as we can tell, neither do Interpol. They don't have the sort of access to the activities of our community on the dark web that we do. Nor do they have loyal friends like Hashimi. If they did, we wouldn't survive for long.'

Reluctantly, Shireen held out her arm and he held his wristpad above hers for a couple of seconds.

'There you are. Your new ID and flight ticket to New York. Now then, there's something else you're going to need if you're to stand a chance.'

He was holding a tiny capsule between his thumb and fore-finger, which he now held out to her. She felt a surge of excitement as she carefully took the small metal cylinder from him. Follow-ing his mimed instruction, she twisted open the top to reveal a grey sphere smaller than a garden pea, which she tipped into her palm.

She'd heard rumours of such e-pills. Their micro-SD cards had a storage capacity of half a zettabyte, equivalent to the capacity of the entire internet thirty years ago. But this was the first time she had seen one. So, this was her reward, the piece of nanotechnology that was to help her deliver the files. Evren must have been very confident she would tell her everything she wanted.

'You must swallow it now,' said Lambros. 'It has micro-grappling hooks that will activate when it hits the lining of your stomach to anchor it. It then sits there, drawing power from your body heat, for forty-eight hours before detaching itself.

'As you know, wherever you are, biometrical scanners are in constant operation – facial recognition, iris identification, gait, everything. The pill detects the scanners and sends them fake information. This technology will be much more effective than that squelch jammer you've been using.'

Shireen let the remark slide. She still had Hashimi's jammer in the rucksack and was hoping to be able to keep hold of it. She stared at the tiny device in her hand. 'What you're saying is that it essentially makes me invisible?'

'Not quite. What it cannot do, of course, is help you if you undergo a DNA g-scan, so let's hope that isn't necessary.' Shireen knew full well that a physical DNA sample could not be faked; if she had to go through one at the airport then the game was up.

'But surely, getting through security means I'll need to pass through a scanner. Won't the pill itself show up?' Shireen guessed that the pill's developers would have thought of this but wasn't expecting the answer she got.

'Don't worry, the pill itself is completely undetectable.'

Shireen shook her head in disbelief. 'But . . . ultrasound scanners are *designed* to look for just this sort of thing. They'd see it even if it was the size of a grain of sand. It's—'

Lambros held up his hand, interrupting her. 'The pill is coated with a metamaterial layer.'

Shireen had heard of the new smart materials that could be used as cloaking devices. Their optical properties meant they could bend light around them and make themselves invisible. 'But . . . the scanners I'll have to go through at the airport are not electromagnetic. The pill may be invisible to light, but not to high-frequency ultrasound.'

Lambros grinned, his white teeth gleaming in the dimly lit corridor. 'You ask too many questions. The pill is coated with a tuneable metapaint that reacts to soundwaves rather than light. Its properties are altered as soon as it detects the high-frequency signal hitting it and it takes less than a microsecond for it to adjust and react to that wavelength. Then . . . well, for all intents and purposes, it simply disappears.

'Your flight is in four hours, but the e-pill won't activate for another hour or two, so you'll still need your quaint jammer to get you to the airport, I'm afraid.'

Shireen stared at him while her brain processed this information. Neither of them had moved from outside the door of the room she had exited. Lambros was still looking down at her expectantly. When she couldn't think of a reason to stall any longer, she placed the pill on her tongue and swallowed.

# 16

*Monday, 11 February – Tehran*

THERE THEY WERE AGAIN – THE TWO SAVAK AGENTS, A MAN and a woman, that she had spotted earlier. They were getting uncomfortably close. Luckily, they hadn't actually seen her yet, having, she hoped, only tracked her to the busy shopping mall from the trail of blocked CCTV cameras where she'd used her jammer. Pulling her hood up to hide her face, Shireen kept walking as briskly as she dared, out of the mall and across the street, following the signs to the maglev station. She hardly noticed the driving rain.

At the station, she was relieved to see there were no biometric scanners and she was able to purchase a ticket with her new ID while keeping her face hidden under the hood. Boarding the maglev train, she found a seat – near the door just in case a hasty exit was required. Wiping the rain from her eyes, she took off her rucksack. For all her tiredness, it felt as if every nerve in her body was on high alert. Only when the doors closed and the train started to move did she begin to relax. As they picked up speed, gliding smoothly above the busy Tehran streets, Shireen closed her eyes and thought back over the events of the past few days.

Her hope was that Savak would fail to anticipate that she'd try to leave the country, that they'd assume she was smart enough not to attempt something so preposterous. She looked around the maglev carriage again. She'd have to change seats soon since jamming any camera for more than a minute or two would raise alarms. Luckily the fifty-kilometre journey out to the airport wouldn't take long. She turned to look out the window. Rivulets of water ran horizontally on the outside of the glass as the maglev skimmed silently along its monorail track at three hundred kilometres per hour.

She was snapped back to reality when a shrill shout behind her pierced the hubbub of conversation in the carriage. 'SHIREEN DARVISH, STAND UP AND TURN AROUND SLOWLY.'

Turning, she saw the female Savak agent standing a few metres away, stun gun aimed directly at her. Fuck. What a fool she'd been. Raising her arms slowly, she stood and faced the agent.

She heard a woman behind her scream and was aware of several other passengers in her peripheral vision slowly and silently edging away from their seats and moving to the far end of the carriage. A sudden, unexpected calm washed over her and the analytical part of her brain immediately began to rationalize why this might be. Was it relief that this was finally Game Over? Or was it just her way of coping with extreme stress? After all, the situation was so ridiculous that it didn't seem real. Yes, that was it. It just didn't feel like any of this was really happening. In fact, she had encountered scenarios like this on numerous occasions while immersed in VR gaming simulations.

She contemplated the stun gun pointing at her chest and ran through her options. What would she do if this really were a computer game? An urgent voice in her head told her that the only sensible option was to surrender, then this whole futile adventure would be over.

She surprised herself by deciding to ignore the voice. Had she really come this far just to give up now? But what were the alternatives? Maybe feigning docile compliance before suddenly striking? No. Ridiculous. This was the real world and she was just a computer nerd, not a highly trained assassin with special skills or hidden weapons. The woman was small and stocky, not much taller than Shireen, and Shireen didn't fancy her chances in a fight, even without a gun pointing at her.

However, the choice was made for her. The train suddenly decelerated as it approached its stop. Shireen grabbed the side of the seat to steady herself, but the agent, holding the stun gun up with both arms, lost her balance and fell forward. It was all Shireen needed and instinct took over. Bending forward, she charged, her leading left shoulder connecting with the agent's chin with a crunch. The agent gasped and stumbled backward, hitting her head hard on a handrail in the middle of the carriage and landing on the floor with Shireen on top of her.

Shireen sat up, astride the dazed agent's midriff, and looked around. The train had now stopped, and the carriage doors slid open. Most of the passengers were scrambling to leave, and the few standing on the platform ready to board took one look at the scene in the carriage and hesitated. However, a handful had decided to gather round and enjoy the action, gawping at the two women on the floor, by their glazed stares each making a retinal recording, no doubt for immediate uploading on social media. But thankfully, no one tried to intervene.

Shireen spied the agent's gun lying on the floor a metre away and smiled to herself. She'd wasted countless hours playing 'shoot 'em up' video games and regarded herself as something of an expert on all types of firearms, whether standard issue or illegal. This was a Leyden Taser. It fired two tiny needles, delivering a painful electric shock, instantly incapacitating the victim for a few minutes.

The doors closed, and the train began to move again. The agent let out a groan and lifted her hand to her head. Shireen rolled off her and reached for the gun just as the agent opened her eyes and sat up. Without thinking, she pointed it and pulled the trigger. The stun gun fizzed, and the darts embedded themselves in the agent's neck.

The agent jolted and arched her back as the electromagnetic pulse shot through her body, then quickly slumped back into unconsciousness. Shireen stood and turned to face the other passengers. She felt trapped. Even though the gun would need reloading, she held it up, arms outstretched, and swivelled round, taking it through 360 degrees. Most of the passengers took a step back, but a couple simply held their ground. She knew she wouldn't be able to stop them uploading their footage immediately, each one trying to be the first to report the incident in the hope of it going viral. So, she had very little time to do what she needed. Her mind was racing. One more stop before the airport: Rahahan Square and the Central Station where intercity trains left for Qom, Isfahan and Shiraz in the south, Mashhad in the east and Tabriz in the west. Could she still pull this off? She had to try. 'You all saw what happened. I'm not a criminal, but I need to get away to clear my name. Please don't stop me getting off at Rahahan. I have to catch my train out of the city.'

To her astonishment, several people began to applaud. Others nodded approval. Of course. People hated Savak. Those of her grandparents' generation had many stories to tell, but even they admitted that the agency had gained further notoriety in recent years, as though trying to make up the lost forty-five years of Islamic state rule during which it had been disbanded. She walked slowly towards the doors as people backed away, opening up a route for her. She never once lowered the gun. After all, she had not spotted the second agent yet. He must by now know what had happened.

The two minutes to the next stop were the longest of her life. Police at Rahahan station would surely have been alerted by now – would there be a welcoming committee on the platform already? At least no one on the train seemed interested in trying to overpower her; they were a passive audience eager to see how the incident played out.

Just as the train began to slow, a crazy idea popped into her head. It could make all the difference and it might just work. She returned quickly to the unconscious agent. The woman was far heavier than she'd expected, but she summoned up all her energy reserves and slowly pulled her up into a sitting position against a seat where she would have a clear view of the maglev doors. However, she needed the agent conscious for what she had in mind. She slapped her across the face. No response. She slapped her again, harder this time, and the agent's eyes slowly flickered open. Good. She was pinning her hopes on the woman not being able to move very quickly just yet, while her muscles recovered from the electric shock, but she would hopefully be conscious enough to activate her AR and record the next few seconds.

Shireen grabbed her rucksack from the seat and rushed towards the doors just as they swished open. Moments ago, she had felt utterly exhausted – now, she was buzzing. Without looking back, she squeezed through the throng of passengers trying to board. No welcome committee, thank God. Once on the platform, she pushed her way past the crowds towards the exit, ignoring their curses and angry shouts. Looking back, she caught a momentary glimpse of the Savak agent stumbling from the carriage before she was hidden from view. Shireen had no time left. If the agent managed to keep the train at the station it would be all over. She felt a wave of relief on hearing the warning bleeps signalling departure. At the last moment, she dived back onto the train through the doors of the last carriage just as they were sliding shut. The train began to move again, and she turned to hide her face from the platform side.

Had she done enough? The agent had seen her get off and the passengers would corroborate her stated intention to catch a train out of Tehran. If all went to plan, the authorities would be hunting for her in and around the vast Central Station for long enough to buy her the time she needed to board her flight. She chose a seat towards the back of the carriage and, for the second time in the space of a few minutes, slumped down exhausted, grateful that the other passengers were ignoring her.

The squelch jammer could still do the trick of disrupting the airport security cameras, but she should now assume the new identity that Evren had provided for her. There would surely be heightened security at the airport, but if the e-pill she'd taken did what it was meant to then any cameras and scanners running surveillance software would register her fake ID. She sighed inwardly: it was a big *if*. She just hoped that there were no Savak agents at the airport, as they wouldn't need to rely on biometric software to identify her.

On arrival, she made her way through the airport terminal without further incident. Reluctantly, she dropped the jammer into a bin as she passed. It had taken her this far, but she couldn't afford to be caught with it at security. Next hurdle: the departures gate. Ahead of her, just as she'd anticipated, were the ultrasound scanners. Crunch time. The e-pill should have activated by now, but would it get picked up in the scanner? She had no choice but to keep going. She stepped into the pod, and the reinforced glass screen swished closed behind her as she followed the pictorial instructions and raised both arms above her head. Time stood still. The scan took only a few seconds, but it seemed to last for ever. Lowering her arms, she turned to wait for the exit door to slide open. Instead, a disembodied voice above her head announced: 'Scan inconclusive. Please turn around, placing your feet on the marked spots again, and raise your arms over your head.'

She resumed the position. Her heart was pounding. *Stay calm. Stay calm.*

Finally, the door swished open and she was through, her panic replaced with euphoria. That clever little pill had come through after all.

Her flight had already begun boarding by the time she reached the gate. Joining the back of the queue, she shuffled along with the other passengers, most of whom looked like businessmen and -women, and all seemed preoccupied with their retinal feeds. She wondered why boarding was so slow.

It was only when she got to within a few metres of the gate that she saw the reason for the delay: a security guard holding a DNA g-scanner, taking micro skin samples from each passenger.

*Fuck. Fuck. Fuck.*

So near, and yet so far. She was overcome with a sense of despair and felt close to tears. Was the genetic scanner a recent addition? Was it there for her? Turning around as casually as she dared, she started heading back the way she'd come. She just needed a few moments to think and regain her composure. She hadn't come this far only to fail now.

She had reached the end of the queue and was almost back in the open departure area again when she felt a firm hand on her shoulder.

'Excuse me, miss, could you come with me?' The burly security guard towered over her. He was in his thirties and looked to be wearing a uniform several sizes too small for him. His cap, pulled down over his eyes, covered a mop of long, unruly hair.

Panicking, she jerked away from him, trying to twist her body free, but the hand on her shoulder tightened with a steely grip, his fingers digging into her painfully. 'I wouldn't try that if I were you,' he hissed, 'you really wouldn't get very far.' Several passengers turned to stare. She looked up at the guard and nodded weakly. With his hand still firmly gripping her shoulder he led her away from the gate.

As they walked, he said quietly: 'You are Shireen Darvish, aren't you?'

She looked at him silently. So the game was up.

'That g-scan would have revealed your identity, so you panicked, right?'

*You were clearly picked for this job because of your astonishingly sharp intellect.* Shireen no longer had the stomach for her usual defiance. 'Did I look that guilty?'

The guard grinned. 'No, I knew what you looked like because Mother Cyb described you to me. I've been expecting you.' He took his hand away from her shoulder.

Shireen recoiled in shock. How could Evren betray her? *Why* would she betray her now? Why let her get this far? It didn't make sense.

The guard saw the shock on her face and his grin grew even wider, showing several crooked teeth. 'Hey, stop panicking. My job was to ensure you boarded this flight safely, which means bypassing the g-scan. To be honest, we weren't expecting this level of security just yet, but you must have triggered something.' Then he added, somewhat sheepishly, 'You know, I'm a big admirer of what you've done, as are all of us in the cyb community.'

Shireen opened and closed her mouth in utter bemusement

but couldn't think of anything to say. The guard was clearly
not expecting a response because he had already turned away
and was looking around to check if the coast was clear. 'Come
on. Let's get you on board before anyone gets even more suspicious.'

When she finally managed to get words out, all she could
say was, 'Thank you.'

He led her through an adjacent gate, which he accessed with
a security pass, and down a deserted corridor that led on to
the walkway to the plane. A minute later, she was in her seat
on the flight to New York.

She sat still, hardly daring to breathe. She knew that all the
time the e-pill was working, she could remain anonymous. What
happened after its forty-eight-hour lifetime she had no idea.
She hoped that by then she would have achieved what she'd set
out to do. For the first time in a couple of days, she wondered
how her parents were doing. Had they remained out of sight?
She wondered who else would now be looking for her. Maybe
she'd even made it onto Interpol's most-wanted list. *I guess I'm
now officially an international cyberterrorist. Mum and Dad
will be so proud.*

Sighing, she turned to look out of the window as the plane
taxied towards the runway. She half-expected to see Savak agents
sprinting towards her across the tarmac to stop the plane. Suddenly she was pressed back in her seat as the plane accelerated.
The relief of take-off was so overwhelming that she at last began
to cry. No one was watching so she let the tears flow freely,
silently. Then, without warning, exhaustion overcame her and
she fell into a deep, dreamless sleep.

# 17

*Sunday, 10 February – New York*

THE SUNDAY AFTERNOON THAT MARC HAD BEEN SO LOOKING forward to, spending time with his daughter, started badly. How could he have been so deluded as to think that Evie would rush into his arms, all forgiveness and smiles, as soon as she saw him? He'd picked her up at midday from the smart terraced address that had been, until a few months ago, his home for seven years. Instead, all he received was a brief, perfunctory hug.

And yet he was determined to try and lift her mood from this brooding, standoffish resentment to at least get a glimpse of the bubbly, ebullient Evie he knew was somewhere underneath.

'I thought we'd spend the afternoon in Bryant Park. You know how much you used to enjoy our Sunday afternoons there.'

'That was when I was five years old, Dad. Maybe you hadn't noticed, but I'm not a kid any more.'

He tried desperately to work out the last time they had actually spent time together as a family and realized he couldn't recall it. Instead he said, 'Well, you'll always be my little—'

'—Don't, Dad. Please,' she said in a pleading voice, and he sighed. They walked in silence for the next couple of minutes.

When they reached the junction, he had to stop himself from instinctively grabbing hold of her hand to cross the road.

*Shit, she's right. I still think of her as a young child.* He decided to tackle full on the issue that was such a barrier between them.

'Look, I know what a disappointment I must be to you, and I know it'll take time for you to fully forgive me. But you will, when you see I'm not such an arsehole any more.'

'Dad, you're not a disappointment, honest. And I know more than you probably think I do about depression and how it can control people. But . . . well, can't you see that your leaving us – well, leaving me – and going off like that was taking the coward's way out? Running away from your problems won't make them disappear, or suddenly make you well again.'

She was right. Of course she was. His little girl was now a mature young woman with her own blossoming wisdom. He felt a mixture of shame, as her words hit home, and pride in this wonderful person walking alongside him. He resisted the temptation to put his arm around her and instead he tried to make light of the situation. 'Well, if you really wanted to help make me feel better, you'd let me buy you pizza for lunch and then allow me to spend an afternoon with my favourite human being on the planet.'

Evie finally smiled. 'Oh, planning on spending the afternoon alone then, are you?'

'Yeah, yeah. OK.'

After pizza they went for a walk around Bryant Park. Despite a promising start to the weather that morning – the first blue skies seen since the remnants of Hurricane Jerome had drifted back out into the Atlantic – things were now taking a turn for the worse. The wind was picking up and the sky had turned grey. Marc hoped the rain would hold off for a few hours. At least Evie's mood had thawed considerably.

'You know it's glorious summer weather down in Waiheke at the moment. I've been doing a lot of work on Grandma and Grandpa's house, and the boat. I'd love it if you could come over to visit.'

'Dad, you do know I go to school, right? And by the time we break for summer it'll be turning colder down there. Geography isn't my strongest subject, but I know that much.'

Marc shrugged. 'Still, you'll love it. I bet you can't remember too much from your only trip to NZ. You'd have been . . . um . . .'

'I was seven. Don't you remember, Dad, we celebrated my seventh birthday at Grandma and Grandpa's house? They held a party and there was no one my age and you got drunk and got into an argument with Grandpa and—'

'—OK, yes, I remember. Sorry.'

'I miss them, you know: Grandma and Grandpa. Even though I didn't see that much of them.'

'Yeah, me too,' he said quietly.

Time to change the subject. 'So, anyway, how're you getting on with Jeremy Golden Balls these days?'

Evie giggled. 'He's fine, Dad, honest. He can be a bit overbearing at times, but mostly he's OK. And Mum seems happy. She's very tired, but . . .'

Marc looked at his daughter, wondering what it was she was reluctant to spit out. 'But, what?'

Evie looked down at her feet. 'Well, the house is a lot quieter these days, that's all.'

Ah, yes, of course. He and Charlie had done a lot of shouting in the last few months before he'd moved out. But he'd been locked too deeply in his own dark world to think much about how it might have affected Evie. The truth was he did feel better knowing that Evie, and Charlie for that matter, were happier now.

Bryant Park was still Marc's favourite place in Manhattan. There were so many memories of happier family times spent there, picnicking on the grass during the summer. After feeding the pigeons, he'd queue for ice cream while Charlie took Evie for a ride on the carousel. That still seemed like yesterday and he felt a sudden wave of melancholia at the thought of how much his, and Evie's, life had changed in recent months. He managed to push it away.

Today the park looked very different. Although still full of joggers and dog-walkers, it now looked bleak under the leaden sky. The cold wind whistled through the bare branches of the tall trees on the outer edges of the park. During the summer months, they blocked out the surrounding skyscrapers, but their leafless skeletons exposed the glass and concrete buildings beyond. They walked slowly around the park, twice, with Evie starting to do more of the talking.

By the time they made it back to the apartment, the skies had begun to clear again, and the threat of rain had receded.

'Do you want to come in for a bit? Say hi to Mum? Jeremy isn't around.'

'Probably not a good idea, Evie.'

'No, probably not.' She gave him a hug, this time for a little longer. He didn't kid himself that all was well again between them, but today had been a good start. She turned and ran up the steps to the front door.

'I'll stop by on Tuesday if that's OK,' he shouted after her. 'And I expect you to have some idea what you'd like for your birthday.' He made a mental note to ask Charlie what she had got her.

She waved without looking back. A moment later she was inside with the door closed behind her.

It must have been the familiarity of the street and the house, and the near-normality of the time he'd just spent with his daughter, but Marc just stood there outside his old apartment for several minutes feeling flat. It seemed the girl who'd laughed at his jokes, and who'd announced gleefully on every occasion: 'You're *so* weird, Dad', which had been a default reaction to almost anything he said or did, was growing into an independent young woman who no longer needed him. He thought about going up the steps and knocking on the door. What would he say? Would he apologize again, ask for things to go back to the way they were? Too late for that.

He sighed, wondering what to do with himself for twenty-four hours. He'd decided against the offer to stay with an old friend while in town and had checked into a hotel instead. But he was starting to have serious misgivings about what Qiang had roped him in for the following evening. His younger colleague had been invited to a reception held by the Chinese ambassador, and Marc was his plus-one. Whoopie-fucking-doo. All that banal small talk with politicians and diplomats. He wondered what the protocol was at events like that regarding sloping off early.

Still, it was great that Qiang was moving up in the world. His involvement with the Chinese investigation into the Earth's magnetic field had obviously got him fast-tracked along the corridors of power. And if Marc could help him in any way – then it was the very least he owed him. He was also desperate to discuss further with Qiang his idea about neutralino beams. It was all too crazy to be taken seriously, of course, but it was an interesting hypothetical problem to consider.

# 18

*Monday, 11 February – New York*

IT HAD BEEN JUST 48 HOURS SINCE SARAH'S UN MEETING, and she already had several high-level meetings lined up in her diary, mostly about what sort of contingency plans to put in place to cope with a whole range of scary scenarios. She found it infuriating that the politicians she spoke to were still more worried about what the geo-storm after a direct hit from a CME might do to global electronics networks and telecommunication satellites than they were about a potentially catastrophic exposure of entire populations to the radiation itself. At least they acknowledged the very real danger of secondary threats like hurricanes and tsunamis, and it was a relief to see so many other scientists being drafted in.

What she hadn't been prepared for was the secrecy. While her warnings about the heightened danger of coronal mass ejections hitting the Earth were being taken very seriously within the corridors of power, both at the UN and elsewhere, in public and across the networks politicians were actively downplaying the threat. Not that this seemed to have much influence either way – most people were immune to what they read or heard on their AR feeds and were cynical about anything politicians said, preferring to just get on with their own lives.

That was something Sarah could identify with. Right now,

all she wanted was to curl up in her hotel room with a book and glass of wine and pretend this was all a bad dream. But that wasn't going to happen this evening. Spending an afternoon shopping for something to wear to a fancy cocktail party, as she had just done, was the last thing she'd felt in the mood for and it all seemed rather surreal. But a last-minute invitation to Ambassador Xu's reception this evening meant a necessary trip into town.

She'd been a little surprised to receive the invitation, but assumed it was Aguda's doing. After all, she hadn't exactly endeared herself to the Chinese ambassador so far. Hopefully, Aguda and one or two of the other scientists she'd met at the UN would also be there.

Her frustratingly extended stay in New York was at least more comfortable now that she had been upgraded to the Plaza Hotel on Fifth Avenue. She estimated she would need another two weeks to finish writing her section of the report the committee had been asked to produce. She had been checking every day with her young research colleague Miguel in Rio and was itching to get back to her own research again. The sooner she could escape from the political machinations of the UN, the better.

She tapped her wristpad and checked the invitation on her AR. The Chinese Embassy was sending a car at seven, so she had just under an hour to kill.

Suddenly her wristpad pinged as a text message came through. Odd. It was on her private account, and only her parents had access to that. It must be her father. She hoped everything was OK. She quickly focused her eyes on the AR display in the top right of her field of vision, but the message wasn't from her parents.

It was short, as though composed in a hurry:

*My name is Shireen Darvish. I wish you no harm.*
*I know you are leaving the hotel at seven. Meet me*
*downstairs in the female bathroom near the lobby*
*at 6.50. I have information you have to see.*
  *Please. I have no one else to turn to.*

She squeezed her eyes shut and took a few deep breaths. Alarm and anxiety quickly morphed into curiosity and she read the message again. *OK, think. Someone has got hold of your private contact details. Fine – there are plenty of smart hackers out there. But this all sounds very cloak and dagger.*

Of course she wouldn't be able to resist this. Anyway, what's the worst that could happen in a hotel bathroom with people coming in and out all the time? She spent a few minutes online trying to learn a little more about this Shireen Darvish, but drew a blank. Very strange. It was unheard of for an individual to leave not a single footprint on the net.

At a quarter to seven, she grabbed her coat and bag and left the room.

The hotel lobby was busy and noisy, with a number of new guests arriving, leaving their islands of suitcases clustered around the reception desk as they checked in. Other guests were heading out into the early New York evening. Sarah stopped to look around. She couldn't see anyone who looked remotely suspicious or who might be watching her. She glanced at the time. 6:50. She turned and strolled as casually as she could to the door marked 'Ladies'.

A well-dressed middle-aged woman was coming out just as Sarah entered.

Once inside and the door closed, she looked around. She couldn't see anyone, but two of the cubicle doors were shut. She whispered, 'Hello? Ms . . . Ms Darvish? Are you in here?'

Silence.

Puzzled, she waited a few seconds before turning back towards the door.

Suddenly she heard the click of a lock and the far cubicle door opened slowly. A diminutive girl, in her late teens or early twenties, stepped out very cautiously. She had an unruly crop of bright pink hair and several nose rings. Sarah's first impression was that she looked exhausted and very, very scared. She watched her carefully while at the same time making sure she could make a run for the exit if she needed to.

'Please. We don't have much time.' The girl spoke in a soft, halting voice in perfect English with what sounded like a Turkish

or Persian accent. She sounded, and looked, on edge, her eyes
darting around nervously. She quickly ducked down to look
under the only closed cubicle door and, presumably satisfied
that it was empty and that they were alone, gestured to Sarah
to approach her. 'My name is Shireen Darvish and I'm a computer science student from Tehran. You must believe what I am
about to tell you.'

Sarah remained rooted to the spot.

The girl took a step towards her and began to speak faster,
as though reciting a prepared speech. 'I have in my possession
highly secret documents that I have gained access to. I don't
have time to explain how, but you need to see them. The world
needs to see them before the information is erased for good.'

Sarah must have looked incredulous, but what the young
woman said next sounded even more preposterous.

'I know how this must look to you but believe me when I say
I am not crazy. It's possible that the fate of humanity depends
on you getting this information out and using your reputation
to back up its authenticity.'

*Yup, that sounds exactly that. Crazy.* As though humanity
wasn't in enough trouble already. And yet there was something
about this woman: a desperate, haunted look in her eyes. She
might be deluded or unstable, but Sarah was willing to bet she
genuinely believed what she was saying. Her AR was giving
her no information at all as she stared at the young lady. She
was clearly being very careful at keeping her identity a secret.

Sarah took a deep breath, her curiosity stronger than ever
now. 'OK, tell me a few things first. Who do you work for?'

'No one. I told you, I'm a student at Tehran University.'

Sarah realized she had not made herself clear. 'No, I mean
who else is involved in this?'

'I am working alone.'

Sarah stiffened in surprise. 'You mean you were able to gain
access to such highly sensitive information without help?'

Shireen looked at her quietly, her big brown eyes now shining in defiance.

'Oh, come on, I wasn't born yesterday. If this information is

as sensitive as you say it is, then the firewalls would be so impregnable that even Google and SonyIntel would struggle to get past
them, so who's backing you?' Sarah wondered what sort of organization could be behind such a high-risk operation. Did this
young woman belong to one of the many global cyberterrorist
cells or could she really be an exceptionally talented cyb acting
alone? In any case, in today's world with its ubiquitous electronic
surveillance, it would have been almost impossible for a fugitive
from the law, as she must be with all this cloak and dagger secrecy,
to travel halfway across the world without being caught. So,
either she had help from powerful people or she was in possession of superpowers. Either way . . .

Just then the bathroom door opened, and two elderly women
walked in. One went into a cubicle while the other looked at
Sarah and smiled, then headed to a large mirror to check her
makeup. Sarah walked over to the far corner of the bathroom
and began washing her hands. The young Iranian followed her
and turned on an adjacent tap.

When Sarah felt confident they couldn't be overheard she
whispered, 'Do you really expect me to believe you travelled
thousands of kilometres, risking so much, to meet me *physically* when you could have just contacted me from Iran?'

Shireen answered quickly, as though she had been expecting
the question. 'And would you have believed me if my avatar had
popped up in your AR space? Hi, I'm Shireen and I'm a cyber-
hacker who has a secret to share?' When Sarah didn't reply she
continued. 'Can't you see? Anyone could have done that. You'd
have thought it was fake and ignored me. And I couldn't risk just
sending you the files in case they got intercepted. I had to come
in person, to deliver the files to you physically. And, yes, since
you mention it, I've risked everything to get here.'

'But why me? If you were so desperate for this information
to get out, why not simply release it?'

'And what do you think would have happened then? It would
have made no difference if it had gone viral and been seen by a
billion people. Whoever is behind this is powerful enough to
have immediately discredited the story as fake and replaced it

with a watertight counter-narrative. So, I needed someone who
would be believed – someone who couldn't be silenced. Someone who cared as much about the truth as I do.'

'But you don't even *know* me,' whispered Sarah loudly, and
jerked her head around quickly, realizing she could have been
overheard. But the woman by the mirror had now left and the
other was still in a cubicle. 'How dare you presume what my
motives might be and try to involve me in whatever this is about.'

The second woman emerged from the cubicle and walked
over to wash her hands. Sarah waited silently until she had left
and they were alone again, then turned to Shireen and sighed.
'OK, give me something to go on. What's in these files?'

Shireen began to speak quickly, picking up her well-rehearsed
speech where she'd left off. 'I follow the news. I know about the
threat of the weakening field. I know you sit on a powerful UN
committee that's looking into it. But as far as I can tell you're
not a politician and you don't serve any political interests. So,
you're the only person I can hope to trust to get this information
out. The data I've sent you show that the recent measurements
of the Earth's magnetic field have been tampered with. I don't
know who's behind it, but there's been some cover-up.'

Sarah stared at her. What the hell was that supposed to mean?
'If this is some sort of ridiculous conspiracy theory bullshit—'

Shireen tapped her wristpad. 'You need to see the files. Please,
Dr Maitlin. I have them here—'

'Wait a minute.' Sarah felt a rising panic. 'Before you impli-
cate me in this, this . . . whatever it is, I'll ask you again. You
mentioned the UN committee I'm on, but there are plenty of
people who are more powerful and better placed than me to go
public with your information. Dr Gabriel Aguda for one – he's
a geologist after all and he understands a lot more about the
magnetic field measurements. So, why me?'

Shireen was nodding vigorously, as if she had anticipated
Sarah's response. 'A mixture of gut instinct and logic. I needed
someone who couldn't possibly have been involved in the cover-
up. I'm not saying that Aguda is part of this – it's just that, well,
you've just joined that committee, so I knew you would be, um,

clean.' After the briefest of hesitations, she added, 'Also, I feel I can trust . . . another woman.'

Sarah wasn't sure how to respond. But Shireen hadn't finished. 'The files can only be accessed by me biometrically. But I'm now copying them over to your Cloud space. I had to do it this way – only by meeting you physically could I get them over to you directly. Any other route would risk interception. Now please, I beg you, look at them. You will understand why they need to be released to every organization, media outlet and scientist you can think of, as quickly as possible. I don't know how much more time we have before it's too late and I'm silenced.'

Sarah tapped her wristpad and saw that several folders had been downloaded. Each looked like it contained many files.

She was aware that Shireen was still staring at her intensely, but knew she didn't have time to look at the files now. She quickly checked the time. 'OK, I have to go. But how will I be able to get in touch with you?'

'You can't. But, maybe you can help secure my release from custody. As soon as this goes public it will be clear that I am in New York.' Then she added, almost too quietly for Sarah to hear, 'And I am too tired to keep running.' All the intensity in the girl's manner just a minute ago now drained away, as though a fire had just gone out in her eyes. That scared Sarah more than anything Shireen had told her – that she must have risked so much coming this far to entrust her with information, while knowing for certain that she would be arrested for doing so. What the hell was in those files?

Sarah didn't know what else to say. She nodded at Shireen, turned quickly and walked out.

Her car was waiting outside the hotel entrance. As she walked out to it she ran through the strange encounter again. The young cyb had clearly been through a lot just to get these files to her. She might well be a completely deluded conspiracy theorist convinced about yet another ridiculous global cover-up, but there was something about her that Sarah recognized: an intelligence and defiance in the girl's eyes that reminded her of her own young self.

As soon as she was alone in the car and it had pulled away from the kerb, Sarah opened the files and began to scan them. There were three separate folders, each containing hundreds of documents. Some of these were data files, some were graphs, some were images showing colour-coded maps of magnetic field strengths around the Earth, and some were reports, in both Chinese and English. But only half a dozen or so were marked as priority. They had been flagged by Shireen and gathered together in a bundle under the heading 'READ THESE FIRST'. She worked her way through them with growing shock, trying to digest the information as quickly as she could.

As she did so, she started running through her options. Of course, this might all be completely fabricated. It would be a simple matter to concoct such a story, with bogus data and fictional reports, something a cyber group intent on causing disruption would be more than capable of doing.

But what if this was the real deal?

No, she decided, what she was looking at was genuine: these were raw satellite data stretching back over the past two years and they flew in the face of what Aguda had told her a week ago in the diner. Equally shockingly, there were reports making it clear how the data should be changed so that the officially released statistics gave quite the opposite result: that field measurements in the southern hemisphere showed regions where the magnetic field was *gaining* in strength, rather than weakening, in readiness for a pole reversal, probably sometime later this year – something these files suggested wasn't going to happen.

Well, whoever was behind this – and she guessed it had to go far up the chain of command – had lied to Aguda and the rest of the world.

*Damn it, Aguda, are you in on this too? Oh, what the fuck have I got myself mixed up in?*

She looked out of the car window to get her bearings. She was passing Central Park on her left. It was beginning to snow but she was too deep in thought to notice.

She went over the 'facts' again. The satellite data had been tampered with, that much seemed clear. In fact, it seemed that the original measurements contained in these files showed un-equivocally that the field was getting weaker . . . *everywhere.* But that was just crazy. If the Earth's magnetic field was really dying . . . No, that was too horrifying to contemplate.

As a scientist and now a member of a highly influential UN committee, she knew it would be utterly irresponsible, not to mention dangerous, to make this information public without checking its validity carefully first. On its own, of course, the data would not have meant much to a non-scientist. But there were other documents and emails, from anonymous senders to equally anonymous recipients, demanding emphatically that the original data be buried.

She knew she had to do something, to trust someone. The obvious choice was Aguda. He would, she hoped, know what to do, and who else she could trust.

She attached a few of the files to a brief voice message, explaining her meeting with Shireen, and pinged it to Gabriel. She was taking a huge risk with this and couldn't be certain about Aguda's trustworthiness. Nor could she be sure the files wouldn't be intercepted on the way to him. After everything Shireen must have gone through to get the files to her . . . But what else could she do? Who else could she turn to? She slumped back in her seat and waited for a response. While she did so, her mind drifted. There had been just two occasions in her life when she had experienced this deep feeling of foreboding. One was nine years ago, when her mother had been diagnosed with advanced Hodgkin's lymphoma. The other was when she was fourteen and had been called into the headmistress's office at school to be told that her brother Matt had been in a road accident. On both occasions, her anxiety had eventually turned to relief. Somehow, this time she didn't believe there would be a happy ending.

A thousand questions tumbled over each other in her head. How widely did this conspiracy stretch? Who knew about it? How many countries had been colluding to keep this information from getting out? And, most importantly, why? What possible good would come of hiding the truth? Was it simply to avert mass panic while the authorities dealt with the crisis? *I have to think sensibly about this. I'm part of the establishment now, not some disillusioned cyber anarchist trying to bring down corrupt global powers. Shit.*

The car glided along silently. She rested her head against the window pane, briefly enjoying the refreshing coolness of the glass against her temple. Her heart was racing and her stomach was churning. She thought about scanning the web for more information, but quickly dismissed that idea as a waste of time.

Just then, her wristpad pinged and Aguda appeared on her AR feed. He was dressed in a tuxedo and at first she hardly recognized him. So, he was going to the reception too, or most likely he was already there. He looked more solemn than she had ever seen him. She tapped her pad to connect and instantly the cameras in the car picked her up and linked with her feed.

'Hello, Sarah. I see from your surroundings that you are on your way here. Please don't do anything until you arrive. I will meet you and we can discuss this in private properly.'

'No, just tell me please, did you know about this?'

There were a few seconds of silence, as though he were weighing up different options. Then he said, 'Yes, Sarah, I did know. I'm afraid I lied when I told you the field was regaining its strength. But please, can this wait until you get here when I can explain more carefully?'

Sarah felt sick. 'Damn it, Gabriel, if you're in on this, what's to stop me from just sending this information out, right now, before I get to you and you talk me out of it, or, or God knows what? I mean, does everyone else on our committee apart from me know the truth – that the Earth's magnetic field is fucking dying and not getting ready for the Flip at all?'

'No, Sarah, not everyone. And please try to stay calm and not do anything you'll regret.'

But she couldn't help herself, her indignation and fury growing by the second. 'How could you deliberately keep this from me? Everything we're putting in our report is to do with temporary measures to deal with the consequences of a weakened field for a few months. Not this – not the end of the fucking world!'

Aguda nodded sympathetically. 'Look, I know what you must be thinking right now. But I'm asking you not to do anything rash. Please.'

Sarah took a deep breath. She would be at the reception in ten minutes. Maybe this was the sensible, measured thing to do. After all, what could 'they' do to her?

She didn't register the two jet-black vans that sped past her in the opposite direction.

Still furious, she didn't know what else to say to Aguda, so she disconnected. It occurred to her that the Chinese government, as the dominant player on the global stage, would be in on it for sure. It was unthinkable that the world's last remaining superpower wasn't at the heart of this cover-up. In which case, she was now heading straight into the lion's den.

# 19

*Monday, 11 February – New York*

SHIREEN FELT DRAINED, AS THOUGH EVERY LAST DROP OF strength and will-power that had sustained her over the past few days had finally been used up. The e-pill inside her still had a day to go, but she almost didn't care any more. She was no longer concerned whether she was caught now – her fate was in someone else's hands. She just prayed Sarah would do the right thing.

Wondering what to do next, she decided she would find a quiet corner in the hotel lobby and check the news outlets. If Sarah had released the files, it would only be a matter of minutes before someone picked it up and reported it.

She found a wide sofa hidden away behind a couple of large potted plants to the side of the hotel's grand staircase. Sitting down, she tapped on her AR feed and started scanning various networks. To make herself more comfortable, she rested her head on the soft cushions and quickly felt herself drifting off. She didn't resist.

Almost immediately, she was pulled sharply out of her doze by loud shouts. She jerked upright to be confronted by four armed FBI agents. It couldn't have been more than ten minutes since Sarah had left. So, she must have released the files almost immediately. Or had she just betrayed her? But her head was too foggy to try and think anything through. She looked at the men in front of her passively, feeling numb.

'Stay exactly where you are and don't move a muscle,' said one of the agents, holding a stun gun directly at her chest. She had no intention of moving, so she stared back at the man. Two others approached her and pulled her roughly to her feet. She didn't put up any resistance as her arms were yanked painfully behind her back and her wrists cuffed.

The fact that she had been found so quickly meant one of two things: either Sarah Maitlin had indeed released the files and her movements had been traced back to the hotel where its cameras had identified Shireen . . . or Sarah had sold her out and just informed the authorities. She hoped her instincts had been right and that she had chosen Sarah wisely.

Of course, there was a third possibility: that Sarah had been naive enough to hold back from releasing the files just yet, or, worse still, to put her trust in people who would try to stop her. Whatever had happened, it was too late to worry about it now, and she wouldn't have long to find out. She wondered whether her backup plan had been needed and, if so, whether it had worked. She allowed herself to be led off through the hotel lobby and out to a waiting black van.

# 20

*Monday, 11 February – New York*

IN THE GATHERING DARKNESS OUTSIDE, THE SNOW WAS COMING down a little heavier now and the traffic was moving slowly. Sarah was looking out, deep in thought, at the early-evening Manhattan lights, a glistening kaleidoscope of colours diffracted and reflected by a thousand drifting snowflakes, when she suddenly caught sight of a tiny drone through the falling curtain of snowflakes. It had appeared from nowhere and was now hovering about a metre from the window, level with her eyes and keeping pace with the car's slow progress. No sooner had she identified it as a media drone than she spotted several others joining it and hovering alongside the car, all with their miniature cameras focused on her. Confused, she touched the window to opaque, hiding herself away from their prying eyes.

What on earth would they be following her for? She checked her AR. What she saw was astonishing. Her mouth went dry and she felt a tightness in her chest as the horrid truth of what was unfolding hit home. Her entire conversation with Aguda just a few minutes earlier was being relayed live across the net and was spreading like wildfire. The information that Shireen Darvish had been so desperate to release to the world was now well and truly out there, for better or worse, and the world was reacting. But it was Sarah's face and name, not Shireen's, that was spreading exponentially across both the official and social media networks. No doubt it wouldn't take very long for AIs to analyse the footage and determine that it was a genuine exchange between two scientists working for the United Nations.

She'd been played. Presumably by Shireen. Had that been the young cyb's intention all along? And anyway, how could she have known that Sarah would confide in someone rather than release the files? It certainly wouldn't have been difficult for someone of Shireen's obvious ability to copy a spyware code over with the files – one that would activate as soon as she made contact with anyone, sending the footage to a site that linked to major hubs around the world. The decision on what to do with the files had been taken out of Sarah's hands. *But no one has the files themselves yet, unless of course Shireen has released them, now that their authenticity has been endorsed by my outburst to Aguda and his admission. No. Wait. Shireen wouldn't need to do anything. If my conversation has been leaked out then the files could also have been released, from my account. Oh, this is all just fucking great.*

Sitting back, she closed her eyes. Shit. Too late to do anything about it now. Maybe the world did need to know the truth. After all, if a patient is diagnosed with a terminal illness, doctors have no right to hide it from them.

It certainly hadn't taken the media long to locate her. She checked her feed and saw that she was already being pinged to respond to a growing cacophony of requests for statements. Any attention she'd received over the past two weeks was going to look pretty lame compared to what she was going to have to face now.

Clear of the heavy traffic, her chauffeurless limo suddenly picked up speed as it headed northwards along First Avenue to the reception in Manhattan's Upper East Side.

# 21

*Monday, 11 February – New York*

SENATOR PETER HOGAN STOOD IN FRONT OF THE FULL-LENGTH mirror and adjusted his bow tie. He smiled, liking what he saw. These days he felt an inner strength and tranquillity in knowing he was in complete control of his own destiny. He flicked a speck of dust off the shiny silk lapel of his dinner jacket.

Looking back, he had to admit that his career had gone exceptionally well. He was intelligent and ambitious and had used both traits well to build up his power base. But, despite appearances, he was still very much a loner. His only true friends were his three dogs. Animals understood him. They asked nothing of him other than to provide them with food and shelter and, in return, granted him obedience and loyalty. Humans were different. Too many of them failed in life because they allowed emotions to cloud their judgement. To him, traits such as compassion and empathy served no purpose when it came to survival of the species. Sure, altruism could be found among many creatures, like bees and termites, but that was simple kin selection: ensuring the propagation of an individual's genes by helping those closest to it genetically to survive. But human culture had tried to push this idea too far. And that was always going to be its downfall. Selflessness was overrated.

By any measure, his career in politics had been meteoric. After graduating from the University of Notre Dame back in '26 he'd started out by serving on the Indiana State Election Board before working as an attorney in practice, mainly dealing with environmental cases pushing for the closure of the State's remaining coal-fired power plants, the last of which shut its gates in '34. He ran for the US Senate as a Democrat in '37 on an anti-corruption ticket, sweeping to victory to become the youngest member of Congress at that time at the age of thirty-two.

While it seemed that just about everyone in politics now considered themselves to be an environmentalist, they had different ways of showing it. In a state like Indiana, which along with West Virginia had been at the bottom of the Green League Table of America for many years, standing for election as a champion of the environment was now a good political move. But Peter Hogan was smart enough to know that he could not reveal his true feelings. A passion to protect the biosphere from further destruction by humankind was one thing, but to let slip his contempt for humanity itself would not have been a particularly wise move. Instead, he made sure that his green credentials were just what the administration, desperate for allies in Congress, were looking for: someone who could help lift the country out of the doldrums after the failure of The Walls project, which of course he had opposed from the outset. That two-trillion-dollar, overly ambitious scheme to build five-metre-high sea walls to protect the country's coastal cities was doomed before it got started. He had spoken out vociferously against it, when other politicians saw it as the only solution. Now, of course, southern states such as Louisiana and Mississippi were bankrupt and unable to fund their huge repopulation programmes to deal with the displaced inhabitants of lost coastal cities like New Orleans and Gulfport.

People who had never met him thought Hogan came across as charming; smart and ambitious, but likeable and warm. Those who did know him would have agreed with the first three attributes but would have struggled to apply the last two to him. Senator Peter Hogan was anything but likeable and warm.

In recent months, he'd felt particularly good about life. In fact, the charm button was so much easier to switch on now that the fate of humankind was sealed. It would certainly serve no purpose for the public to know the truth about the dying magnetic field. What would be the point of panicking billions of people? After all, nothing could be done about it now. Far better for everyone if the world remained in its innocent ignorant slumber, hoping as always that things would eventually turn out for the best.

Well, amen to that.

He left the bedroom and walked downstairs, checking the time as he went: seven-fifteen. Time to leave. He didn't like to be too late, but always enjoyed a grand entrance. He uttered a command as he entered the kitchen and the French windows slid silently open. His dogs, who had been sitting patiently out on the patio, ran in. They were hungry.

As he walked out of the front door of his luxury apartment, just ten minutes' walk away from Ambassador Xu's mansion, his wristpad buzzed. It was Gabriel Aguda. The man looked highly agitated.

# 22

DESPITE THE CHILL, MARC WAS FEELING UNCOMFORTABLY warm under the tightly buttoned collar of his dress shirt as he walked up the mansion steps with Qiang. He'd struggled to find a dinner jacket at short notice and had ended up borrowing the whole outfit from a former Columbia University colleague. Now he wished he'd just worn the old grey suit he'd packed back in Auckland. After all, he wasn't planning on impressing anyone this evening.

Qiang also appeared out of place and awkward, despite looking the part, complete with a resplendent bright red bow tie. The Chinese physicist must have seen the amused look on his face.

'I really do prefer the familiarity of a traditional scientific conference dinner, you know, where all I have to do to smarten up is to put on a jacket and tie—'

'—Yup, preferably one with a science-themed image on it, like a Feynman diagram or the periodic table,' laughed Marc.

Qiang nodded in fake seriousness. 'That's the beauty of ties like that, they're so terrible, they go with whatever shirt you've been wearing during the day.'

They joined the throng of well-heeled guests arriving at the reception, all of whom seemed to exude that same casual air of

confidence and entitlement that always marked out the wealthy
and powerful.

The Chinese ambassador's mansion was an impressive building. Technically a townhouse, it had been built in 1911 in
neo-French Renaissance style by an American billionaire whose
family had finally sold it to the Chinese government ten years
ago, just one example of so much of America's prime real estate
these days that was now owned by the East. Its imposing steps
led up to the main entrance, where an equally imposing doorway was set back from a stone arch. Spotlights high on the
roof of the building bathed everything in an insipid bluish hue.

Marc and Qiang presented themselves for retinal scans by
the two muscle mountains at the door and then had to pass
through a security scanner. Once inside the ornately decorated
grand hallway they were accosted by half a dozen bots carrying trays of drinks. Picking up a glass of champagne, Marc
surveyed his surroundings. His eyes were first drawn to the
fabulously colourful floor, which was covered in beautiful and
intricate mosaic tiles. All around him were symbols of wealth
and power. There was also no shortage of antique Chinese art
on show: colourful Qing Dynasty paintings, Ming vases on ped-
estals and glazed ceramics of Chinese warriors on horseback.
All this ostentation made Marc feel angry, although he couldn't
figure out why.

He looked over to see Qiang already chatting to several other
guests. Marc knew the protocol at occasions such as these. He
would be expected to use face-recognition software in his retinal AR to find people he should be introducing himself to and,
glancing around, he was amused to see that most people were
doing just that. With a tinge of nostalgia, he thought back to
the time, not so many years ago, when you could walk up to a
stranger at a party and ask them how they knew the host or
what they did for a living. Better still, if conference delegates
were wearing name tags, you could try to sneak a glance down
at it without appearing to break eye contact with the person,
especially if you felt it was someone you should know. He had
a secret and reluctant admiration for the younger generation,

for whom the skill of simultaneously scanning their AR while seemingly engaging directly with the person in front of them came so naturally.

Qiang must have noticed him watching and walked over. Marc put his hand on the younger man's shoulder. 'It's OK, you know. You go and do the necessary schmoozing. Just don't leave me alone all evening – I haven't got to perform any social niceties at this party, but don't forget I am supposed to be your date for the night.' Qiang grinned and wandered off into the main reception room where most of the guests were gathering.

Marc wandered over to one of the pictures on the wall to take a closer look. It depicted a Chinese man sitting at the base of a crooked tree. He guessed it was an original and probably worth a fortune. His thoughts drifted back to his afternoon with Evie and how long it would take to fix their relationship. Still feeling flat, he strolled among the guests. Everywhere he heard the usual sycophantic and nauseatingly forced greetings and exchanges of pleasantries – always necessary to establish the social order at such occasions. But apart from the odd polite nod or smile from a few guests who either didn't know who he was or didn't feel inclined to chat to him, he was invisible. He maintained a faint smile frozen on his face that, he hoped, gave him the air of someone at ease with his surroundings and who attended such functions all the time. And he hated himself for doing it.

One or two of the guests were now starting to raise their voices in more animated conversation and a number of them were standing still to focus on their AR feeds. Was some piece of news breaking?

He decided he wasn't interested enough to check right now and drifted back outside to get some fresh air. As he stood at the top of the steps, a limo pulled up with another VIP guest. An elegantly dressed woman in a knee-length black cocktail dress got out. She was carrying her coat over her arm, clearly not feeling the cold. Her blonde shoulder-length hair looked silvery under the building spotlights. She was surrounded by a flurry of tiny skeeter drones hovering over her head, mechanical dragonflies recording her every move and presumably beaming their feed to news networks. Marc watched as several security guards ushered her quickly up the steps towards him. She looked vaguely familiar, but he couldn't quite place her. Was she an internet star? A politician? There was something about her body language and defiant expression, however, that didn't quite fit. She gave off a sense of aloofness that was less self-importance, and more nervous resolve.

As she reached the top of the stairs she passed within a metre of where he was standing, and he saw a steeliness to her posture – her head held high. She had been looking straight ahead, not speaking, not smiling, but for the briefest of moments, their eyes met. It seemed to Marc to last an embarrassingly long time but couldn't have been more than a second. She had a glazed look suggesting her thoughts were very far from her immediate surroundings.

After she was swept inside, he followed her back in, just catching her being led up the grand staircase, which had only a few minutes earlier been roped off. Many of the guests around him were now talking in excited voices and Marc tapped a passing man's shoulder. The man turned, his eyes clearly more than half focused on his AR feed.

'Sorry, but could you tell me what's going on? Who is this woman?'

'Check your feed, pal. That's Sarah Maitlin, one of the scientists involved in some scandal.'

At first, it didn't register, but then it hit him. Of course! She was the British scientist who'd been in the news a couple of weeks ago talking about the geomagnetic storm. But what was she doing at a reception held by the Chinese ambassador to the United States? And why was she the belle of the ball? Surely her media appearances hadn't earned her such A-lister status? And anyway, what fucking scandal?

He walked into the main reception room, where he spotted Qiang in conversation with an elderly couple on the far side. His friend broke off when Marc approached, and introduced the pair as the Portuguese ambassador and her husband. They nodded to Marc but were clearly not in the mood for small talk.

Qiang sounded agitated and excited. He'd already removed his bow tie, as though whatever was now unfolding trumped any pretence of the formal occasion this was meant to be. 'Have you been following the news, Marc? If true, this is huge.'

'What? You mean in the few minutes since I last spoke to you? No, of course I've bloody not. I've been too preoccupied wondering why I am the only bloody person here who seems to be clueless.'

He watched as Qiang pulled out and unfolded a plastic e-pad and activated it with his wristpad. He moved his fingers over it and brought up a live news feed, then passed it to Marc. At the bottom of the screen, alongside the words 'Breaking News', was the scrolling headline:

*SECRET FILES REVEAL STARTLING COVER-UP.*
*IS THE EARTH'S MAGNETIC FIELD DYING?*
*HAS THERE BEEN A CONSPIRACY TO HIDE THE TRUTH?*
*NEURAL NETS REVEAL AUTHENTICITY OF SCIENTISTS*
*AT CENTRE OF SCANDAL.*

The footage was of Sarah Maitlin in an online video chat with a man, and they were arguing about what to do with new revelations about the Earth's magnetic field. Marc noticed that Sarah was wearing the dress he'd just seen her in, so this footage must have been from earlier this evening.

It was followed by live footage of a reporter standing outside the Plaza Hotel in downtown Manhattan talking excitedly about a cyberterrorist group that had obtained top-secret files containing highly sensitive information. He claimed this group's plot had been foiled and arrests had been made.

On the one hand, this sort of thing wasn't unusual; the networks supplied a steady stream of conspiracy stories and devastating cyber threats, but this time it seemed different, as though people could sense this was the real deal. As far as Marc could tell, as he quickly tapped and scanned his way through various news outlets on Qiang's e-pad, it appeared that Sarah Maitlin had been at the Plaza Hotel too, but it wasn't clear what her connection was. The reporter he'd seen first had claimed that she was some sort of whistle-blower, a hero, but there were other reports that she was in fact part of the cyberterrorist cell itself. Marc tried to dismiss all this speculation as the sort of rubbish that news networks would come out with at the start of a breaking story, in the frenetic skirmish to secure the lead coverage spot, with the billions of advertising revenue that would bring. At this very moment, network producers were probably frantically talking to their bosses, who were talking to their lawyers about what their position should be. After all, everyone in the news had to be either hero or villain. It didn't really matter which, as long as a choice was made quickly.

Marc was aware that all around him the sound of conversation was dropping away as more people stood around like zombies reading their feeds.

He exchanged a look with Qiang. If this was true and the earth's magnetic field really was dying, then the cover-up was far worse than the prospect of a mere *delay* to the Flip that Qiang had been so concerned about during their conversation in Princeton two days earlier. Marc turned to the Portuguese ambassador, who had just finished speaking on her phone in a low, urgent voice. 'Is there any more you can tell us, Madam Ambassador? The news seems pretty confused right now.'

'I'm afraid we are all confused, Professor Bruckner. In fact, I'm needed back in my Washington office immediately.' She turned to speak to her husband and they both excused themselves and left. The room did indeed look like it was thinning out as politicians and dignitaries were recalled to their posts to deal with the inevitable shit-storm. Perhaps he and Qiang ought to be taking their idea a little more seriously. Perhaps, despite the utter outlandishness of the very notion of firing beams of dark matter into the Earth's core, it might turn out to be the only way to save the planet.

# 23

*Monday, 11 February – New York*

THE YOUNG WOMAN IN THE SMART BLUE SUIT WHO HAD MET
Sarah at the entrance of the ambassador's residence had insisted
she follow her upstairs to a private conference room immediately. She had said it was for Sarah's own safety, given the
'sensitivity of the current situation'. Sarah's first instinct was
to turn and run, but where would she go? Who could she turn
to for help or moral support? She thought about asking for a
lawyer to be present, but decided she would just have to cope
with whatever was coming. After all, what could they possibly
do to her? She had done nothing wrong.

She was led into an empty conference room on the second
floor of the residence. The woman walked half a pace ahead of
her and didn't speak a word. Instead she exuded cold efficiency.
Was she embassy staff, FBI, Homeland Security or something
more sinister? The room Sarah entered was cavernous and felt
somewhat out of place in a large stately home like this. It
exuded power and efficiency, less of a traditional boardroom
and more of a high-tech command centre, similar to the room
at the UN where she had first met Hogan and his committee,
but larger and with portraits of important-looking figures in a
range of power-stance poses adorning the walls. An interactive
conference table took up more than half the room. She guessed
it would normally have been lit up with an array of vid displays,

e-docs and overlaying colourful graphics, but its graphene coating was now jet black. The woman pulled out a chair and gestured to her to sit down. 'Can I get you a drink, Dr Maitlin?'

'A glass of water, please.' She hoped her voice didn't betray the nervousness she was feeling. It felt like she was back at school and being hauled into the head's office for a reprimand. The woman went over to the sideboard. Sarah heard the chink of ice in a glass and moments later was handed her drink in silence. 'Thank you,' she said.

'Please wait here. Someone will be along shortly.'

The woman then turned and walked briskly out of the room, closing the door softly behind her.

*Well, so much for the new cocktail dress. This is turning into one fun party.* Sarah couldn't have felt more inappropriately dressed had she turned up at a funeral in a clown's outfit. She checked the time. It was seven-thirty – probably long enough for the world's media to have gone into meltdown over the satellite data revelations. Or maybe not. Maybe whoever had been behind burying this in the first place was also more than capable of putting a new spin on it, or even discrediting it. She took a deep breath to calm her nerves and wondered who she would be meeting. Was this to be a discussion among equals or were they going to blame her for the leak?

After a few minutes alone with her thoughts, she summoned up the courage to check her feed. Sure enough, all across the net no one was talking about anything else. Some commentators were claiming that this was the biggest international cover-up since the Vatican scandal of 2029. And Dr Sarah Maitlin was the main protagonist in this drama. Just fucking great.

It seemed like an age before the door to the conference room finally opened and two men walked in: Senator Hogan and the party host, Ambassador Xu. There was no sign of Aguda. Whatever was going on, this meeting was clearly meant to be far from the ears and eyes of journalists and other politicians.

So, what was this going to be? A debriefing or an interrogation?

Hogan paused and looked across the table, before sitting

down. 'Good evening, Sarah.' The intensity of his reptilian stare made her skin crawl and it took every bit of her will-power to meet his gaze, but she was determined not to be cowed by him. When he spoke, his voice was flat and toneless, his tight grin more a rictus than a smile. 'It would appear that we have something of a crisis on our hands.'

She decided to say nothing for now. *Let's see how this plays out.* Hogan certainly didn't look like a man who'd just discovered that the world was about to end. Nor indeed did Xu Furong, whose face betrayed no emotion whatsoever. Like Hogan, his eyes never left Sarah. If they were deliberately trying to intimidate her, they were wasting their time.

After a pause, it was the ambassador who broke the silence. He spoke in perfect English. 'We are giving you the benefit of the doubt in assuming that it wasn't you who deliberately recorded and transmitted your conversation with Gabriel a few minutes ago.'

Sarah frowned, suddenly realizing how that might be one interpretation. 'Of course you bloody assume correctly. If I had wanted it leaked I'd have done it myself. I chose to speak with Aguda first because . . . well, because I needed to know the truth for certain before the rest of the world did.'

Hogan raised a hand towards the ambassador and smiled. 'Come on, Furong, we know full well that Dr Maitlin didn't do this. Besides, it will be easy enough to see if there was any spyware downloaded with the files placed there by the cyb.' He turned to smile at Sarah again. 'Something this big, this, ah, *scandalous* – the cyb couldn't possibly take the chance that you might betray her, and so it appears she's dropped you in it. And I have to say that Gabriel doesn't come out smelling of roses.'

The ambassador stared at Sarah, stone-faced.

Hogan continued. 'Still, Dr Maitlin the scientist, the seeker of truth and objectivity, not corrupted by the lies and deceits of the world of politics like the rest of us – you must surely be quietly relieved by this outcome. After all, the secret is out, and you presumably see yourself as playing the role of an innocent and blameless participant – the hero, even.'

The sarcasm in his voice was nauseating and she glared at him. So this was how it was going to be, was it? His tone suggested that Hogan most certainly did not see her as an innocent and blameless participant. He sat back in his chair. Was he deliberately trying to goad her?

She tried hard to keep her voice steady as she spoke through gritted teeth. 'Are you accusing me of wrongdoing, Senator? Seriously? You invite me onto your committee to provide my scientific expertise, and for what? This whole business has been a sham from the start. I'm the one to demand answers here, not you two. And where the hell is Aguda?'

'Gabriel will be joining us shortly. He's currently engaged elsewhere. In fact,' added Hogan, 'we are all going to be rather busy tonight, as you can imagine. Of course, we hope to count on you too.'

'What? You expect me to cooperate with you? To smooth this over? Damn it, we've been discussing recommendations to world governments about how to cope with potential CMEs *until the Earth recovers*, and yet it seems you knew the whole situation was futile? Tell me which bit I've got wrong.' Anger and indignation welled up inside her, threatening to overflow.

Then she added, before either man could respond, 'And in any case, just so we're clear, this is absolutely *not* about me. You're damn right I've done nothing wrong. But you . . . I mean, how dare you fabricate scientific data and lie to the world? And just how far does this lie stretch? What else are you hiding?'

'Oh, come on, Sarah,' said Hogan. He sounded almost amused by her outburst. 'I gave you more credit than that. Firstly, yes, of course we knew. But, you're playing in the grown-up world now, so save that touching moral outrage of yours for your pathetic world of liberal academia.'

Sarah felt an overwhelming urge to reach across and punch his conceited, supercilious face, but instead she sat back in her chair and closed her eyes. Her opportunity would come, she was sure of it.

Hogan lowered his voice and spoke softly. 'Listen to me carefully, Sarah. You are going to help us put this mess right. You're smart, and so I have no doubt that you will understand what I have to say. There are people around the world, people in positions of stupendous power, working within, and even above, world governments, who have been trying to ensure that nine billion people don't descend into collective mass hysteria. Tell me, what did you expect to happen – what is no doubt already happening – when those nine billion people found out what was being kept from them? That before this century is halfway through, the Earth will witness the fastest and most dramatic mass extinction since life first began four billion years ago? Please, do tell me what you expected them to do? At this very moment, I predict there will be potentially hundreds of extremist groups and cults springing up and promoting their own version of how to avoid the apocalypse or how to punish the authorities for bringing it on.'

Xu added, 'Not to mention how this news will be received by the Purifiers. If they are persuaded that the Sun is taking care of things for them, they may lose their *raison d'être*. On the other hand, this might embolden them and things could get far worse.'

Like most people, Sarah was familiar with the terrorist organization generally known as the Purifiers, although many people still referred to them by their original Arabic name of Almuta-hirun. In their basic ideology they were not so different from many other radical groups and end-of-days cults that had come and gone since the dawn of civilization, inasmuch as their central message was beautifully simple: humankind was destroying the planet, and the world was approaching *Yawm ad-Dīn* (the Day of Judgement) and *Yawm al-Qiyāmah* (the Day of Resurrection). Many world religions shared this belief that there would be a final assessment of humanity by God, which would begin with the annihilation of all life, followed by resurrection and judgement. But the Purifiers were impatient. They believed their role was to hasten the arrival of the Day of Judgement by whatever means necessary. The revelations about the Earth's magnetic field would only lend strength to their cause. Sarah wondered whether it would give them fresh impetus. Would they want to find some way to hurry things along? After all, their fatalistic philosophy was based on all hope in this life being abandoned and instead looking to a plentiful afterlife that awaited the faithful.

Hogan's cold voice cut through her thoughts. 'So, I guess we now need to know. Can we still count on you?'

'*Count* on me?' she burst out. 'To do what, exactly?'

As she was debating whether she could trust any answer Hogan gave, he leaned forward across the table, his arms folded, and rested his chin on them. 'To clear up this mess you've been duped into creating, of course. Jesus, Sarah, are you really so naive?' He turned to Xu and gave him a quick look, which was meant to be one of innocent exasperation. He sighed, then said, 'OK, Sarah, you ask us what the truth of the situation is. Well, here's the truth. Yes, of course a plan to save the planet is in place.'

She noted that his demeanour had now changed to one of intense sincerity, like a parent dishing out important advice to an errant child, something he must have practised on the campaign trail to get elected to the Senate. 'We still want you to be part of that plan, Sarah.'

Again, he held her gaze for a few seconds before releasing her from his hypnotic stare. He sat back in his chair and, again, his personality switched. This time the chill was back in his voice. 'In return, you are going to help us clean up this mess. You see, between us, we will be going on a charm offensive to try to calm the world down. There will no doubt be unrest. Some governments that are, shall we say, less than well prepared will topple. And yes, people are going to die. Our job now is to sell a prettier, more optimistic future to the media, to calm nerves and to play down the consequences. People across the globe are going to need time to digest this. And they will be looking to those of us in charge to tell them everything will be OK. A statement is being carefully prepared as we speak.'

He paused to let his words sink in. Then, 'Of course, it will naturally be more convincing coming from you. You will see that what is being developed is a quite ambitious rescue plan – one that would benefit from your expertise as a solar physicist. It goes without saying that you don't have to agree to this. So, we'll give you a minute or two to think the matter over.'

But Sarah knew she wasn't going to get the chance to mull it over, sleep on it or 'phone a friend', as her mother was fond of saying. In the end, her cold rationalism and survival instincts took over. Maybe she could be of more use working on the inside. Hogan was almost certainly right about the mass hysteria these revelations would now cause. He might be a cold-hearted bastard, driven by blind political ambition, but he certainly wasn't stupid. In the end none of these ethical questions were what decided it for her – it was her elemental scientific curiosity about the plan Hogan had hinted at. But she couldn't admit to that. It would be as though she had just rolled over and surrendered to these two bullies, and she was still angry at their arrogance. Suddenly, she saw a faint glimmer of salvation and clutched at it with the desperation of a drowning person grasping a lifebelt. 'OK, but on one condition.'

Hogan snorted in amusement. 'Bless you. Did you really think you were in a position to barter?'

Xu raised a hand. 'Wait a minute, Senator. I'm intrigued. Please continue, Dr Maitlin.'

Sarah sat upright and stared Hogan in the eye, hoping that she sounded and looked braver than she felt. 'The young cyb, Shireen – she was only doing what she believed was the right thing to do – and, for what it's worth, what I still believe was the right thing to do. I assume you have her in custody. I want her released, and all charges against her dropped.'

Hogan's laugh was that of someone who'd never in his life found anything funny. It was cold and unnervingly high-pitched, like the bark of a fox.

'I can see why that would play on your conscience. Again, you're not thinking this through. This cyb is going to be hailed as a hero. We wouldn't be able to keep her locked away for long anyway. So, yes, that sounds like a reasonable request, especially if you feel it will buy your redemption . . .' He laughed again, then sat back and kicked his chair away from the table.

'Well, we have work to do, don't we?' He pinched his thumb and forefinger together to activate a nano-mike on his nail, which he spoke into. 'Gabriel, you should join us.'

A few seconds later, Aguda came into the room, followed by the young woman Sarah had seen earlier and several other aides who had been waiting outside.

Sarah and the Nigerian geologist exchanged a glance. She didn't know what to say. She just knew she could never trust him again.

# 24

*Saturday, 16 February – New York*

SARAH STARED OUT OF THE WINDOW OF THE FBI LILIUM E-Jet as it came in to land at JFK. Across the aisle from her, Shireen had been sleeping soundly for the duration of the one-hour flight from DC. A few minutes earlier Sarah had needed to pull down her blind to block out the bright mid-morning sun as the aircraft banked at the start of its descent. But, now that it had dropped down through the thick grey cloud cover, the scene outside, and her mood, suddenly turned gloomier. She was looking across to where the Manhattan skyline should have been visible in the distance. Instead, she was greeted by a thick blanket of falling snow that dramatically reduced visibility.

She wondered what the weather was like in Rio, realizing how desperate she was to get back to the Institute and her research.

It had been a week during which her life had been turned upside down: not content with finding out that the fate of humanity hung in the balance, she'd had to make a public statement, with Aguda by her side, aimed at calming the nerves of billions of people around the world. Governments in many countries had put their military on high alert, but that hadn't prevented the inevitable unrest and widespread rioting that had broken out. There'd been a large number of deaths reported in both Nairobi and Istanbul and huge demonstrations in most large cities. People were demanding to know what was being

done to avert catastrophe. And Sarah felt personally responsible. Maybe Hogan had been right – wouldn't it have been
better for the world to have remained in blissful ignorance of
its fate? She looked over at the sleeping Iranian cyb. *You thought
you were doing the right thing, didn't you? Well, for better or
worse, it's out now.*

Sarah didn't blame Shireen for transmitting her conversation
with Aguda to the world. She understood the girl's motives. But
then Shireen wasn't the one who'd been getting death threats.
Sarah had been shocked to the core by the first one she'd received,
less than two hours after her broadcast statement late Monday
evening. Someone had managed to hack through her security
firewall to send her a colourful personal message about what
they would do to her. And while she had immediately demanded
heightened security, it hadn't prevented several other nasty
threats getting through in the following couple of days. Thankfully, they seemed to have stopped now.

There had been frantic debates among world leaders as to
whether they should continue to deny the truth – in fact, the
official news networks in some countries were still maintaining the whole thing was fake. But from what Sarah had managed
to learn from Aguda and Hogan, and to pick up on the more
in-depth newscasts, most governments now knew that the genie
was out of the bottle. Researchers in South America and Aus-
tralia were analysing data from independent satellites over
the South Pacific, confirming the continuing weakening of the
magnetic field.

But over the past few days she'd had bigger issues on her mind
than the leaked documents or her own safety. Her thoughts
drifted back to the 'rescue' plan she was now a part of. Now
that the world knew about the dying field, the authorities saw
no reason to keep their mission to save the world a secret
either. Indeed, it was now vital that the public had some hope
to cling to. The plan was audacious in scope.

The ambitious idea, as first explained to her by Aguda, was
to perfect the design of a giant magnetic pulse device that
could generate a powerful magnetic punch, strong enough to

block a coronal ejection. Aguda had given her the MPD report and had even asked her to comment on it.

The following day she'd met up with him in his UN office. She had expected the atmosphere to be frosty when she walked in and had been taken aback by Aguda's friendly demeanour.

'Ah, Sarah, good morning. Please come in.'

She'd tried to clear her head of the multitude of emotions still swirling around: exhaustion from lack of sleep, worry about the ramifications of the Pandora's box she had played a part in opening, anger at Aguda for keeping the truth from her, and above all a deep-seated feeling of foreboding about the fate of the world. She had nevertheless tried hard to be professional and objective. He had been sitting behind a desk so impressive it made even his frame seem diminutive.

'I know I'm coming to this late, Gabriel, but I've read the report and, well, I just don't see how the sums stack up.'

Aguda had nodded sagely. Was this still an act, or could she finally trust him? 'I know it seems preposterous. But I'm proud of the progress that we've made so far, and I think you will be too when you see more. As you will have seen in that report, work on the device is already advancing on several fronts.'

'By "several fronts" I suppose you mean where it would be built.'

'Yes, that's still the main sticking point. There's still no agreement on whether it should be based on Earth or in space, or whether it would be one device, or many scattered around the globe.'

'And is that a technical or an economic issue?' she'd asked, certain that no one could possibly be thinking about putting a price on the only hope to save humankind.

'Oh, it's definitely the engineering challenges that are proving the issue. You see, while I'm personally against it, the front runner for a working MPD is to build it in space.'

'But the report says nothing about *how* we get the components for such a large structure out to . . .'

'. . . four times the distance to the Moon and then assembling and testing it there, all in the space of a year. Exactly.'

Aguda sat back, as though pleased that he had an ally. 'It's technologically possible, of course,' he continued. 'The best suggestion seems to be to get the components to the Moon in multiple trips and then assemble most of them at the Chinese moonbase, which has the necessary construction equipment and heavy industry already in place from their mining operation.'

Sarah had been astonished by the sheer scale of the proposal. 'So, why not just build an Earth-based device?'

'Oh, a number of countries are pushing for this, believe me. The problem here is that the magnetic pulses they would be aiming out into space would damage any satellites flying overhead at the time.'

Sarah felt she didn't know enough about the technical specifications yet to comment on this. But, 'Surely knocking out a few satellites is the least of our problems?'

Aguda said nothing.

This had been the point when Sarah had voiced her central misgivings about the entire plan. No one appreciated the sheer strength of the punch that a massive coronal mass ejection could deliver better than she did. Were they really naive enough to think they could stop one?

'I know you aren't expecting me to comment on the engineering challenges. But I simply don't believe the basic physics.'

'Well, Sarah, this is something we do need your input on. The computer simulations that have been run so far suggest that if a magnetic pulse powerful enough and timed just right could be aimed at an incoming CME then it could slow it down, and even disperse it.'

Sarah shook her head in frustration. 'But that's not the issue. Your scenario will only work if the CME is moving in a straight line from the Sun, but if it spirals in from a slight angle, as it can do, then an e.m. pulse would be much less effective.'

Deep down she felt the whole enterprise was futile. Defending Earth against a really powerful CME with electromagnetic pulses would be like standing in torrential rain and trying to stay dry under a cocktail-stick umbrella.

The CME that caused the great solar storm of 1859 or the

near miss of 2012, which – had it been ejected nine days earlier – would have met the Earth full on, frying the world's electronics and bringing much of human civilization to a halt, would both, if they struck today, be catastrophic. With the magnetosphere in its current sorry state, civilization on Earth wouldn't stand a chance.

Yet no one seemed to want to listen to her. Over the following days she had tried to get this point across, but there seemed to be no political will to take her warnings seriously, while the scientists and engineers working on the project were too busy trying to solve the thousand and one other technical problems they were facing. No one wanted to accept that the plan was doomed to failure from the outset.

What no one wanted to admit either was that dealing with CMEs was just the start. Even if this particular threat could be averted, it didn't stop the slow but constant bombardment of the atmosphere by cosmic-ray particles from deep space, coming from all directions, which would inexorably erode the atmosphere until the Earth eventually resembled its sister planet Mars: dead and lifeless. With no atmosphere, even the oceans would quickly evaporate. Apparently, that was a longer-term problem to worry about at a later date.

Her thoughts were now interrupted as Shireen stirred and opened her eyes. She looked a little embarrassed and self-conscious at having slept through the flight. Even though they had only met on three occasions, the two women had begun to develop a mutual bond, born out of a sense of 'us against the world'. Sarah was still impressed with the cyb's strength of character and unbending, principled determination, which had made her feel even more wretched about the way she had folded so compliantly to Hogan and Xu's demands.

Shireen had spent the past few days at a facility outside Washington, DC, run by the National Security Branch of the FBI. She had initially been questioned about her Trojan horse code, so they could shore up security loopholes before cyber-hackers unearthed any more awkward revelations. Sarah had persuaded her to tell them everything as a condition for her release, and Shireen hadn't needed too much convincing. She seemed genuinely proud of what she had accomplished, and her main concern now seemed to be ensuring her parents' safety back in Iran. On some level, she even appeared to enjoy the admiration of her interrogators – one of them, a nerdy computer scientist, had been unable to hide his approbation.

Sarah had been relieved to hear that Shireen was to be released without charge and that while she wouldn't be able to fly back to Tehran just yet, she could at least come and go as she pleased. Shireen had requested that she be released into Sarah's care for the time being.

Shireen grinned at Sarah and she smiled back weakly, not that she had much to smile about at the moment.

# 25

DESPITE FRANK EGELHOF'S EXHAUSTION, HIS MIND WAS buzzing. It was late. Had his simulation not just finished running he'd have called it a night anyway. The drive home from the Max Planck Computing and Data Facility would probably take a further hour, even around the A99 Munich ring road. At least the traffic would be relatively light on a Saturday evening.

The computer simulations of the magnetic pulse device he'd been working on for the past seven weeks were finally running reliably, and his results looked conclusive. He was one of a number of scientists at the Max Planck involved with the MPD project, but his simulations were bound by a level of secrecy above those of his colleagues, a situation he found exhausting. He hated that he couldn't even talk about it to his wife, Rachel. But he could see why this was necessary – his job was to determine whether the space-based device was even feasible in principle, and there were, as far as he could tell, a lot of political careers, scientific reputations and investors' fortunes riding on his results. Removing his glasses, he stood and rubbed his eyes. He only used the glasses for desk work and didn't feel the need to have the routine surgery. Besides, he was very squeamish about that sort of thing.

He tapped the plasma screen to black and walked out of his office, remembering to touch the thumb pad on the handle; hearing the reassuring click of the lock, he wandered off down the corridor to the bathroom. Even though it was the weekend and very few people were around, particularly this late in the evening, he couldn't be too careful with security.

For days, he'd been hoping against hope that his results wouldn't confirm what he had suspected deep down all along. But finally he knew the project was doomed to failure. He'd had his doubts from the beginning but hadn't been allowed to voice them. Now he just felt flat. Of course, his paymasters still wouldn't want to hear what he had to tell them, but what could he do? His simulations were unequivocal. More than ever, he was aware of the need for discretion – bad enough that the world knew that the magnetic field was dying, but how much worse would things be if people were told that one of the two hyped plans to avert disaster wouldn't work? He just prayed that the Earth-based MPD project was still a viable alternative to the one he'd been working on.

The basic physics behind the project was simple enough, and on paper it had initially looked to Frank like it might actually work: gigantic toroidal superconducting magnets out in space that would send out intense electromagnetic pulses timed to meet any incoming coronal mass ejections and deflect them, just as the Earth's natural magnetic field had done for billions of years. The advantages of having the device in space were clear, and putting it at the first Lagrange point made obvious sense.

Situated a million miles from Earth on a straight line between the Earth and the Sun, the L1 point has a very special geometric property. Normally, any body closer to the Sun than the Earth would orbit it faster – basic Newtonian dynamics – but this ignores the effect of the Earth's own gravity. If the body is sitting directly between the Earth and the Sun, then the Earth's gravitational pull in the opposite direction weakens the Sun's attraction on the body and so slows down its orbital speed. At the L1 point, the orbital period of the body exactly matches that of the Earth and so it remains always sitting on the direct line between the Earth and the Sun throughout the orbit.

Placing the MPD at the L1 point would mean it provided a

permanent protective shield for any incoming CMEs from the Sun. It also had the added advantage over an Earth-based MPD that its magnetic pulses would always be directed away from the Earth so would not damage any Earth-orbiting satellites.

His computer models were meant to show the effects of bombardment of cosmic radiation on the ceramic material of the superconducting magnets, and it didn't look good. It was a catch-22 situation. Without substantial shielding, the magnets wouldn't survive very long in the harsh environment of the solar wind. But the necessary protective shielding would itself then prevent the magnetic pulses from getting out with sufficient strength to stop an incoming CME. Basically, the device wouldn't work out in space, and that was that.

Hurrying down the flight of stairs, he looked forward to getting home. When he returned to his office he would have to send a secure email to his bosses with these latest results, then encrypt all his codes and output data files before he could leave for the night. He was one of a team of twenty computer scientists working on the MPD simulations, but right now it seemed he was the only one still in the building after 9 p.m. on a Saturday. He wondered whether Rachel would be asleep when he got home. She had been very patient with him these past few weeks as he spent increasingly long hours at work. He pushed open the door to the bathroom and walked in as the lights flicked on. The place smelled of disinfectant and was sparklingly clean. The evening janitor bots must have just finished their cleaning round.

Despite the quietness of the building, he didn't hear the man who had followed him in until it was too late. He'd unbuttoned his flies by the urinal and begun relieving himself when he was suddenly aware of a shuffle of footsteps behind him. Surprised, he turned his head to look and in so doing ensured that the first bullet entered his right cheek, exiting the front of his face and leaving behind the remains of what used to be his nose and jaw. Egelhof fell back against the urinal, gurgling with pain as blood filled his throat. This was cut short by another bullet, which passed through his left eye and into his brain. The third bullet to his head as he fell was unnecessary. He crumpled to the ground in a pool of blood and piss. The sounds of his brief cry and the three silenced gunshots were heard by no one else.

The simple message scrawled on the note that was then pinned to his body, and which was found by the security guard doing his rounds later that evening, was a mix of English and German:

*Delaying the inevitable is pointless.*
*Die Welt wird der Menschheit gereinigt werden.*
*The Purifiers.*
*[Delaying the inevitable is pointless. The world will be cleansed of the human disease.]*

It is one of those sad ironies that had the assassin waited just another twenty-four hours, his own sources would have been able to inform him that there was no need for this mission to sabotage humanity's last chance of survival – that neither Frank Egelhof nor the MPD project posed any threat to their dream of letting nature take its course.

The murder of a respected German computer scientist hardly made the news the following day. Besides, far more interesting to those at the top were the demoralizing revelations discovered on Frank Egelhof's computer – and these were kept quiet.

# 26

*Monday, 18 February – New York*

MARC PUSHED THE CHAIR BACK FROM THE DESK IN HIS HOTEL
room, stood, stretched and yawned. He was in desperate need
of a decent night's sleep. Evie's birthday celebrations on Friday
had been a welcome distraction from the anxiety and stress
that so many were feeling these days, although it was clear
that everyone was putting on an act, pretending that life was
continuing as normal. The afternoon had indeed seemed a
little surreal at first, especially so for Marc. For a start it felt a
little weird to be just another guest – along with twenty of
Evie's friends, a few family friends and his ex-wife Charlotte's
elderly parents – in the house he'd called home for so many
years. Thankfully, Charlie had been gracious and friendly
towards him and he'd even managed to have a civil conversation with her partner, Jeremy, the smarmy politician.

Most importantly, Evie had seemed genuinely pleased to see
him, although he couldn't help but notice the slightly surprised
look on her face when he'd walked in, as though she hadn't
expected him to keep his promise and show up. At least the
birthday present he'd bought her, an elegant gold locket on a
chain, had been a success.

'Oh, Dad, it's beautiful.'

'I thought I wouldn't risk getting you anything techie or

anything within VR as I know I'd probably get it wrong. And that's despite your mum's detailed suggestions.'

'Yes, you would definitely have screwed up. But this is lovely – real Old School.'

'I'm pleased you like it, not to say bloody relieved.'

He'd hardly had the chance to chat to Evie after that for the rest of the afternoon, but the highlight of the day had been when he was leaving, one of the last to do so: Evie had given him a tight hug and had told him she loved him. He'd walked the twenty blocks back to his hotel with a spring in his step he'd not felt for many months. All too briefly, the world seemed a little brighter. But by the time he'd reached his room the usual concerns had returned, and his thoughts drifted inevitably to the plan he and Qiang were putting together.

Qiang had arrived early the following morning and they had started their mini-research project to save the world.

Now, over forty-eight hours later, he surveyed his surroundings. The hotel room looked chaotic. The large entertainment screen occupying one wall had been turned into an interactive display with diagrams, graphs and colourful graphics packed together and overlying each other; his king-sized bed was buried under a patchwork of sheets of paper full of algebraic symbols written in his illegible scrawl. He preferred to see his calculations laid out the old-fashioned way: writing his equations down in longhand, which of course had meant finding a store that sold paper.

In the middle of the floor sat Qiang, immersed in his own calculations, wearing his VR visor and haptic gloves, manipulating virtual screens in mid-air, which he controlled with deft fingers. The two physicists had settled back into their old research routine, bouncing ideas around, each setting up hypotheses or mathematical arguments to be knocked down by the other – only this time they weren't just being driven by intellectual curiosity; this time the fate of the planet was at stake. They had spent all weekend running through their equations and computer codes, only leaving the room for food or fresh air.

Marc was relieved that Qiang hadn't needed much persuading

to keep their idea a secret until they were completely satisfied it was at least scientifically feasible. But he also knew they were in a race against time, and after the most intense and sustained effort that either man had experienced in his life, their wild plan was finally coming together – maybe even getting close enough to something fully workable. But exhausting though it was, Marc was feeling invigorated by the intellectual effort he was putting into the work. And while he couldn't admit as much to Qiang, he was guiltily aware of a lightness of spirit and renewed sense of purpose he hadn't had for years, despite the magnitude of the project and the grim consequences if it failed.

He'd kept the 'Do Not Disturb' sign hanging outside his door because he didn't want any of the sheets of hand-written calculations touched until he was confident that his final numbers were correct. The previous night, after Qiang had left around midnight, he'd slept on the sofa to avoid having to disturb the bed.

Someone must have reported the three-day-long sign, however, because he'd received a visit from the hotel manager earlier in the day. He'd had to let him into the room to show him that he wasn't engaged in anything illegal and promised that it would be ready for cleaning by the following morning.

Marc knelt down beside Qiang and groaned at the stiffness in his knees. 'How's it going in there? I don't know about you, but I am ready for a coffee.'

Qiang, blind to the outside world, waved him away. 'Almost finished. I promise. I'm just recompiling this fluid-dynamics code. One of the subroutines kept returning floating point errors, but I think I've fixed it.'

Marc stood up again. He needed to get out, get some fresh air, maybe even go for a run. Above all, he needed some coffee. Things had finally calmed down on the streets of New York and the city was slowly returning to a semblance of normality after the demonstrations and riots of the previous week.

Marc wandered over to the interactive screen on the wall, pretty sure it had never been used for anything like this before. He stared at the dense combination of graphs and equations. Were they ready to unveil their scheme to the world? He hoped they wouldn't have to reopen the heated argument they'd had last night about who they would tell first.

'Marc, we have to be realistic. Why do you still have issues with approaching the Chinese?' Qiang had wanted to know.

'Come on, Qiang. It has nothing to do with that and you know it.'

'But my contacts in Shanghai recruited me to look into exactly this sort of idea. So, they are very unlikely to dismiss it out of hand.'

'I understand that, Qiang. But please, let's take things slowly. Let's see if there's even an appetite for something as outrageous as this. We need to talk to other scientists before we approach the politicians.'

'And you are convinced it has to be this Sarah Maitlin. Why? Neither of us has even met her. How do you know we can trust her?'

'I don't. But who can we really trust these days anyway?' Certainly, as a physicist, she would understand the merits of their plan and the urgency of getting it off the ground, but more crucially, of course, she was a UN insider who would know who to take it to.

'Listen, you agree that timing is crucial, right? So, I just don't think we can afford for this to go through all the levels of bureaucracy that would mean it possibly taking months before anything even gets started. No, we need a shortcut. Someone who has the ear of those who can make a fast decision.

'Why don't we at least set up a meeting with her? If she doesn't think she can fast-track this through her UN committee then it's your Shanghai boys.'

Qiang had finally been worn down rather than won over. He sighed. 'OK then, Marc, but only provided she's still in New York. We would need to meet her face to face. Any other way would be too risky at this stage.'

And so, it had been settled.

Marc wondered what Sarah thought of the MPD proposal that everyone was talking about. As far as he could see, it would, even if successful, be at best just a temporary fix – deflecting coronal mass ejections was not a permanent solution to the loss of the magnetosphere. The planet's atmosphere would continue to be gradually eroded by the solar wind. Over time, the entire biosphere would suffocate and die. No, the only hope for humanity was to kick-start the Earth's core again and bring the magnetosphere back to life.

It was then that Qiang let out a quiet whoop of triumph, snapping Marc out of his reverie. He turned back from the screen. 'OK, I'm happy with the numbers,' Qiang said, deftly touching and swiping to one side the virtual displays floating around his head, then removed his visor and gloves. He stood up, stretched his arms over his head and turned to Marc. 'It checks out, just like you predicted. Correcting for relativistic kinematics for the energy pulse in the core isn't necessary.'

Marc grinned at his friend, whose hair, following the removal of his visor, was in a state of dishevelment impressive even by his high standards. 'I fucking knew it,' he said, clenching his fist and punching the air. 'Then we're all set, right? We can't take this any further without carrying out full simulations. And we're going to need help with that.' Qiang grinned back and nodded enthusiastically. He looked tired, with dark bags under his eyes from the lack of sleep, but his eyes were shining with an inner fire.

Marc rubbed his chin, feeling the three days' growth of beard. 'I don't suppose you could do a coffee run, could you?' he asked. 'I feel I need a shave and a shower before I do anything else.'

Qiang smiled. 'Yeah, OK.' He headed for the door.

'And close the door carefully behind you. Last time it slammed, and the breeze blew a couple of pages off the bed.'

Qiang grinned and nodded slowly. When he'd gone, Marc stared down at the mass of paperwork spread out on his bed and tried to summon the energy to move to the bathroom. This was a rewarding kind of exhaustion, though, the type that followed a long and sustained period of creativity, just like the old days, when nothing got in the way of his research once he was on to something big. He'd tried hard not to allow himself the luxury of believing their plan might actually work, but now he couldn't help but think of Evie again. Maybe this would give her back a future she probably wouldn't otherwise have.

But if he were truly honest with himself, Marc would have to admit that these past three days hadn't really been about saving the world, or even saving his daughter – but rather more selfish motives. This had always been where he felt happiest: waist-deep in mathematics. And once he was 'in the zone' the outside world faded away, leaving just him and his equations. He was in an abstract, enchanted world, rich with symbols and beautiful in its logic. The creativity he experienced at such times was not so different from that of a sculptor, poet or musician, and his sense of achievement no less than that of an explorer or mountaineer.

He began to gather the sheets of paper carefully together. *I really need to number these pages, or I'll regret it.* He thought about what he and Qiang had achieved. Strangely, the particle physics aspects, which he knew best, were the easy part. What was tricky was figuring out how to set the whole thing up: there would need to be a suite of dark-matter accelerators, all producing beams of neutralinos and firing them straight down into the ground from different locations around the globe. The mathematical problem was twofold: what was the minimum number needed and where should they be located?

Of course, whatever the answer, it would make the project stupendously expensive. Several new particle accelerators would have to be built from scratch, and ridiculously quickly. The sheer audacity of the plan made it sound crazy.

He knew the physics would work, and he knew it wouldn't take long to convince other scientists of its feasibility. The more pressing issue was whether there was the political will to do it, and to have it up and running in a matter of months.

For some reason, an image from his childhood obsession with *Star Trek* floated into his consciousness as he pictured the Starship *Enterprise* with her shields up. If they weakened, it would leave her exposed to a Klingon attack. Now, the Earth was the *Enterprise* with her shields down and the Sun was the Klingon ship waiting to strike.

Once he'd finished stacking the papers neatly on the desk, he headed for the bathroom. Staring into the mirror, it occurred to him that they needed an appropriate acronym – something the politicians and media could latch on to. After all, every great scientific project, space mission, telescope or particle accelerator had to have a name. But he felt too tired for any more creativity just now. He finished shaving and jumped in the shower, welcoming the sensation of the hot water as it washed away his aches and tiredness, only half thinking about a name for their project.

Qiang had calculated that eight different neutralino accelerators would be needed, spread across the globe, all firing their beams into the centre of the planet to deliver enough energy to set off a seismic shock wave that would kick-start the flow of the molten core. However, Marc could think of only three laboratories that could currently do that job: CERN in Switzerland, Fermilab in the US and J-PARC in Japan. Their locations were ideal, but it was almost inconceivable to think that five new accelerators could be built, in under a year. And yet it was even more inconceivable to think that humanity wouldn't come together to try.

As he stepped out of the shower it finally hit him. He ran naked and dripping to the desk and found a pen and scrap of paper. That was it. They would call it the Odin Project.

Marc had read a lot of Germanic and Norse mythology and his favourite deity had always been the god Odin who, with his staff and broad hat, reminded Marc of Gandalf in *The Lord of the Rings*. And Odin, the god of death, knowledge and healing, was the perfect choice for an experiment that, through physics knowledge, could heal the planet and pull it back from the brink of death.

He scribbled down a list of relevant words beginning with each of the four letters and quickly came up with a winning combination: The O.D.I.N. Project would stand for Octangular Directional Ignition with Neutralinos. It was perfect.

He then scampered back to the bathroom to finish drying himself off. He didn't want to give his young friend a scare.

The one thing that Marc had only privately contemplated, and suspected Qiang had too, was the possibility that the project would go ahead, but still fail. Because there would be no second chance. For example, what happened if any one of the eight neutralino beams misfired or missed the central collision point thousands of kilometres deep within the Earth's core, even by a single millimetre? The eight beams had to come together, each from a different direction, and meet simultaneously at precisely the same point to create a burst of pure energy that would be directed around the molten core. But without this careful balancing act from their combined momentum, a shock wave would instead be sent outward towards the planet's surface. It would be like firing a bullet up at a glass roof: the Earth's crust would be shattered, bringing about the end of most life on the planet far more efficiently than the dying field could do.

*The question is whether the rest of the world can be persuaded that this is a risk we have to take.*

Dressed and feeling half human again, he decided to look up Sarah Maitlin while he waited for Qiang to get back. He sat down on the bed and activated his AR. It took him just a few seconds to locate her, and he sent a brief message.

*Dr Maitlin, my name is Marc Bruckner, a particle physicist. I apologize for getting in touch with you out of the blue and hope you don't dismiss me as a nutter. Please check my academic credentials. I have strong reservations about the MPD project, and suspect you might do too, although of course I have nothing to base this on. But, there may be another solution. I think you may currently be in New York, as am I, and I wondered if you might agree to a brief meeting. Please contact me as a matter of some urgency so I can tell you a little more.*

*Best wishes, Professor Marc Bruckner.*

As soon as he'd sent the message he lay back on his bed and closed his eyes.

He was awoken from sleep by his wristpad pinging. He tapped it and Sarah Maitlin's face appeared. He sat bolt upright and self-consciously rubbed his eyes. How long had he been asleep? And where was Qiang?

'Professor Bruckner, hello. You wanted to talk to me,' Sarah said in her British accent. He noticed she had activated surround block to ensure that all he saw was her face and not where she was. She looked distracted and sombre.

'Ah, Dr Maitlin. Thank you for getting back to me. I appreciate that this is all a little unconventional, but then we live in, um, interesting times.'

Sarah didn't answer, so he decided this wasn't the time for pleasantries or small talk and ploughed ahead. He hadn't rehearsed what to say and realized he needed to tread carefully, both because he didn't want to scare her off and because he didn't know who else might be listening in.

'My colleague Professor Qiang Lee and I have a scientific proposal to put to you. We feel that your research field, your public profile and your position in the UN all mean you're the ideal person to make things happen.'

'I see. Of course, firstly, let me say I know of your work, Professor Bruckner, so I'm satisfied you're genuine, despite your recent personal problems.'

So, she had checked up on him and clearly wasn't going to be pulling any punches. But then her voice softened a little. 'In fact, I attended a talk you gave on dark matter when I was a grad student in Cambridge about fifteen years ago.'

*Way to go to make me feel old.* 'Wow, OK, so—' He tried to recall what the occasion might have been but gave up.

'Sarah, if I may, listen, I don't want to say any more at the moment. Is it possible to meet with you in person to discuss this matter? And, yes, I know how this must sound.'

There was a pause. Then, 'OK, but give me something to go on first.'

'Well, we – that is, Qiang Lee and I – think that—' Even as he searched for the words to say, he realized how ludicrous it all sounded. 'Look, I really would prefer it if you heard the details from both of us.' Then he added, 'Let's just say you can't afford *not* to hear us out.'

In his mind, Marc heard her say, *Oh, but I most certainly can, Professor Bruckner*, but she didn't. Maybe it was something in his voice she had picked up, or maybe she just sensed his desperation, because her face grew larger on the screen as she lifted her wristpad closer to it and at the same time dropped her voice a little – an interesting conspiratorial gesture, although quite pointless if anyone was indeed listening in. Then she said, 'There's a diner on the corner of Madison and East Twenty-Seventh. They do great pancakes. It'll be busy, so I can guarantee anonymity and privacy. How about tomorrow morning at eight?'

'Sounds perfect. See you tomorrow . . . And thank you.' Marc resisted the temptation to say anything else.

Her face disappeared from the screen.

Two minutes later, there was a knock on the door and he opened it to Qiang, who was holding two large paper cups of coffee.

'Ah, the wanderer returns,' he said. 'You took your time.'

'Sorry, I couldn't find anything open. It seems that with all the unrest of the past few days, a lot of the shops haven't re-opened yet.'

Marc seized one of the cups from his friend and took a deep sip. It tasted wonderful, despite being only lukewarm. He wondered whether the place Sarah had suggested they meet tomorrow would also be closed. Then he realized he'd have to break the news to Qiang that he'd gone ahead and set up the meeting without consulting his friend. He decided to stall.

'So, the "Odin" Project. Whaddaya think?'

Qiang shot him a puzzled look.

'That's what we're going to call it,' said Marc, taking a second sip of coffee and wandering back to his bed. 'Oh, and we get to discuss it with Sarah Maitlin over breakfast tomorrow morning.'

# 27

QIANG LEE APPEARED LESS ENTHUSIASTIC THAN HIS OLDER colleague about talking openly to Sarah. Maybe he was just naturally shy. At first, she thought it might be because he had reservations about their audacious plan, but soon realized he was just uneasy about trusting her. And why should he? She'd had to learn herself not to trust anyone these days.

Marc Bruckner, on the other hand, was far more candid. 'I know how this sounds,' he said after they had ordered breakfast. 'A stupid plot from an old Hollywood disaster movie. But we really believe it can work.'

'Firstly, why me?' she asked, recalling the number of times she had asked that question over the past few weeks: of the world's media obsessed with hearing her views, of the British government, of Aguda when she had been recruited onto the UN committee, of Shireen who had singled her out with the revelations about the dying field . . . How lovely that people seemed so naturally drawn to her. 'Why not go further up the chain of command to people who can actually make things happen?'

Qiang grunted, but Marc was clear about his motives. 'Look, you're a physicist too, so we felt—' He gave Qiang a quick sideways glance. '—*I* felt that you would at least see it as feasible in principle. Plus, of course, we think the magnetic pulse plan is useless – even if successful, it's nothing more than a temporary measure, and we can't just sit around waiting for the planet to die. If we do nothing, the Earth will end up a dead planet like Mars. But, hey, I'm not telling you anything you don't know.'

Sarah didn't reply. She pondered how she had so quickly morphed from innocent ingénue to influential figure in world politics. What was it that people saw in her that made her the target of such attention, and trust?

They were sitting at a table not far from the one she'd shared with Aguda ten days earlier, but the diner was much quieter this morning. In fact, she'd noticed far fewer people out on the streets these past few days; the civil unrest – which had been particularly bad in New York – triggered by the satellite data revelations, and further exacerbated by the ensuing political uncertainty and turmoil, meant that many people were either anxious about leaving the safety of their homes or simply too dispirited to go to work. Trouble had erupted hard on the heels of her leaked conversation with Aguda and their subsequent network appearance, and had got so bad in various parts of the city that the National Guard had had to be called in.

Marc began to give her the full sales pitch and seemed unashamed to do so, waxing lyrical about high-energy beams of dark-matter particles produced by accelerators around the globe, $E=mc^2$, seismic waves and liquid metal cores.

Sarah listened as they described the Odin Project. No one in the world knew more about dark matter than Bruckner and Lee – hell, they were still in the running for the Nobel Prize – but the idea of firing beams of high-energy particles into the Earth's core made the MPD proposal sound almost reasonable. This plan was nothing short of crazy. And when had the ability to do world-class research ruled out the possibility of pushing a crackpot theory later in life? There were plenty of examples of geniuses going off the rails . . .

Having read the stories of Marc's broken marriage and his long struggle with depression, she was quite surprised by his disarming charm and openness. But it was clear that behind the breezy façade lay a complex character that he kept carefully locked away. And yet, there was something in his eyes that made her want to believe him – a fiery zeal that he couldn't quite hide. He was good-looking, in a rough-round-the-edges way, as though he couldn't be bothered to put in the effort any more. She tried to work out how old he must be – probably mid-forties. She also knew he had a teenage daughter and wondered what part she played in stoking his desire to make this plan work.

In the end, what persuaded her to take their idea seriously wasn't so much the science – that was for others to assess – but the fact that she knew better than Marc how ineffectual the MPD project really was. She had seen the negative results from the simulations of the space-based MPD produced by the murdered German computer scientist.

So she promised to take their proposal, with her own endorsement for what that was worth, to Peter Hogan and the committee, in the hope that they would agree for Marc and Qiang to give a more formal presentation at the UN.

'But please don't get your hopes up. They could well dismiss it out of hand as being too outlandish, too risky and too expensive to take seriously.'

Qiang leaned forward, slamming his fist on the table. 'But how could they *not* listen to us? What's the point of worrying about cost, if the world is coming to an end?' Marc rested his hand on the younger man's shoulder to calm him. But Sarah understood his frustration.

'Look, I didn't say they won't listen, just that you have to prepare yourselves for disappointment.'

'We have other options, you know,' said Qiang. 'It may be that the Chinese government is more receptive than your UN committee.'

Sarah shrugged. 'Possibly. But just remember that the current international stance is that the MPD project is still the only official solution, whether space-based or terrestrial.'

But for how much longer, she wondered. Would there come a time when the MPD option was shelved for good and Marc and Qiang's Odin Project would be seriously considered?

# 28

*Wednesday, 13 March – Rio de Janeiro*

SARAH HAD BEEN WOKEN UP BY HER TWO CATS – ONE scratching at the open bedroom door, knowing this would eventually prompt a response from her, and the other purring loudly in her ear as it curled up on the pillow between her head and the back wall.

*No, it's too early, you little rascals. Leave me alone.*

She pushed the cat off the bed and lay staring up at the ceiling, letting her vision swim into focus. It had been over three weeks since she had first met with Marc and Qiang in New York and there still hadn't been any progress in getting their plan heard by the right people. It had been extremely frustrating. Although other scientists had acknowledged that it was theoretically feasible, most governments simply didn't have the appetite to switch from the MPD plan to what Peter Hogan had referred to as science fiction.

She promised Marc that she would keep pushing for it but she had been needed back in Rio to monitor and gather data on the latest, unusually high, solar activity. She had left Shireen to stay on in her New York apartment. The FBI were still watching the young Iranian closely, but it seemed unnecessary for Sarah to act as a full-time chaperone. Now, back in her own apartment, she at least felt a semblance of familiar routine returning to her life after the past anything-but-routine weeks.

But the deep-seated sense of dread and impending catastrophe never left her. If anything, it was worse now, invading her dreams most nights. On several occasions she had woken up in a sweat from a nightmare of a dystopian post-apocalyptic world, helpless to do anything about saving humanity. She had found herself talking to her parents more regularly too, with each of them hiding their anxiety and keeping up the pretence of normality.

Even though there was no reason why she should be held personally responsible for saving the world, she still felt frustrated by her helplessness. But all she could do was what was asked of her, to provide information about potential CMEs, which she fed back to the UN task group working on the magnetic pulse devices.

She crawled out of bed and plodded to the bathroom. The photovoltaic glass of her large bedroom windows had already reacted to her movements and changed from opaque to clear, allowing the early-morning sun to stream in, and she guessed it was already about six-thirty. 'Coffee on. Latest solar update,' she croaked. Reassuringly, her home AI had no problem recognizing her voice and responded with a breezy Good morning, Sarah, and she heard the reassuring sound of the coffee machine clicking on in the kitchen. The cats wouldn't even let her sit on the toilet in peace and were now both weaving in and out of her legs. *Serves me right, being away for so long. They've got used to being fed at this ungodly hour by Mrs Azevedo.* That reminded her: she made a note to check that her upgraded house bot was ready for collection, although she had to admit she'd been enjoying getting back to her old household chores, away from the media spotlight and polluted UN politics.

She tapped the big bathroom mirror and its interactive screen burst to life, showing her several images of the latest solar activity. The European Space Agency's Solar Orbiter satellite, the closest man-made object to the Sun, was revealing an even higher flare activity than yesterday, which meant an increased risk of CMEs. Even more worrying was the fact that several CMEs over the past couple of days had been ejected from a region close to the Sun's central disc and were being sprayed out in the plane of the inner planets' orbits, although so far none towards Earth. She had stressed in her report to Hogan that few CMEs ever scored a direct hit on Earth. And the seriously disruptive and dangerous ones occurred on average once a century.

She tapped off the interactive screen on the mirror and the technical display was replaced by her half-awake and dishevelled reflection staring back at her. She turned away and headed for the shower. It was going to be another warm and sticky day and she enjoyed the invigorating coldness of the water. Then, dressing in an old pair of jeans and T-shirt – it was a relief to be back in her normal scruffy clothes again – she headed into the kitchen to grab a coffee. She'd pick up breakfast when she got to the Institute.

Five minutes later she was ready to leave. The traffic shouldn't be too bad this time of the morning, especially since she was able to weave around the cars on her bike. Besides, the roads were significantly quieter these days. The Rio riots had been particularly violent, with vehicles set on fire and shops ransacked. So, many people were still afraid to go out. She picked up her crash helmet and two lithium-air batteries from the induction pad they had been charging on. 'Leaving apartment. Back this evening,' she said hastily, and her AI system responded with a warm, Thank you, Sarah. Enjoy your day. She hurried down the two flights of stairs, and then thumb-activated the door down to the small basement carpark. It was seven-fifteen.

In the basement, she walked over to the dimly lit far corner where she kept her motorbike. The 100bhp Yamaha was her pride and joy and probably the thing she had missed the most while in the States.

Just then she heard a familiar voice behind her. 'Hi, Sarah, when did you get back?'

She turned to see Luca Aumann, the Austrian journalist from the ground-floor apartment, who was with his young daughter. 'Oh, morning . . . Luca. Yes, I got back a couple of days ago.' She smiled at the girl, whose name came to her just in time. 'Hello, Laura. Ooh, I like your hair.'

Laura smiled back shyly and held her blonde pigtails one in each hand. 'Papa helped me do them,' she said in a soft voice. Sarah recalled that the girl spent half her time with her father and the other half presumably with her mother, somewhere.

She turned back to meet Luca's eyes and was instantly lost for words. Luca Aumann always made her feel like an awkward teenager and she was suddenly conscious of how scruffy she must appear to him in his expensive-looking jacket and open-neck shirt. How did he stay so cool in this humidity?

She suddenly realized she had been staring at him without saying anything and felt her cheeks begin to flush. But Luca put an end to her discomfort. 'Well, it's good to see you again. Laura and I are off to the park to feed the ducks before school, aren't we, Laura?' The girl nodded and showed Sarah the paper bag she was holding. 'Anyway, now that you're back, Sarah, you should come down and have dinner with us one evening.'

'That'd be lovely, thank you. Say hello to the ducks for me, Laura.' Sarah gave the little girl a brief wave before turning to her motorbike. She heard their car door close as she clicked the batteries into position. She put on her helmet, swung her leg over and fired up the engine, relieved that it started on first go. She sat for a moment enjoying the artificially generated rumble of a fossil-fuel internal combustion engine. Reversing quickly, she headed up the ramp, out onto the road and into the morning traffic.

# Interlude

## Wednesday, 13 March – STEREO2 spacecraft

AT 10:28 COORDINATE UNIVERSAL TIME – 07:28 IN RIO DE Janeiro – the two Solar Terrestrial Relations Observatory spacecraft moving in separated heliocentric orbits, one far ahead of the Earth and the other lagging behind, recorded the approach of a large coronal ejection which, a few minutes earlier, had been expelled by the Sun and then immediately picked up speed as it travelled through space. Their combined data placed the CME on a trajectory that would almost perfectly rendezvous with Earth.

At about the same time that the two spacecraft first detected the ejection, which was just over eight minutes after it had actually left the Sun's surface, high-energy photons, both ultraviolet and X-ray, hit the Earth's upper atmosphere, ionizing its gases. In itself, this caused no harm to the biosphere, but the levels of ionization were so severe that over half the world's radio communications were temporarily wiped out, disrupting the information flow from many satellites. And with much of the global internet connectivity now using dual laser–radio technology, with data being sent and received between thousands of drones that filled the sky at an altitude of 20 km, the disruption to radio signals was enough to shut down large parts of the internet too.

This meant that when the warning signals sent by both STEREO2 spacecraft that a CME was on its way arrived at the near-Earth satellites thirty seconds later, they went no further.

*So, no one knew that just eleven minutes after that, the CME's vanguard of high-energy particles – protons moving at close to the speed of light – would hit the Earth. Many of these protons would collide with molecules of air in the upper atmosphere, causing a shower of new particles, such as muons, to rain down to the surface. But with Earth's depleted magnetic field unable to deflect them, many of the original protons from the Sun would themselves also make their way to the ground. They would be deadly.*

*For many years, several strategies had been in place to cope with a CME-induced geomagnetic storm. These had been reviewed and revised in the light of the Earth's weakening magnetic field. The Hogan committee had then recommended further strategies following the Air India disaster, including a shut-down of all non-essential communications and switching from large electricity grids to local generators. Cloud communications and data transfer would also switch from a combination of laser and radio transmission to laser only, since drone–drone and drone–Earth radio signals would be dramatically compromised by any large geomagnetic disturbance. None of this was implemented, since no one knew this particular coronal mass ejection was coming. Until it was too late.*

# 29

*Wednesday, 13 March – Rio de Janeiro*

JOINING THE ORDERLY AI-CONTROLLED MORNING TRAFFIC, Sarah enjoyed the freedom of being, almost, in complete control of the bike. She turned off her AR feed as she focused on the road – the chances of the Sun misbehaving during her half-hour journey seemed slim. As in most big cities, Rio de Janeiro's entire transportation system was run by an AI Mind that linked together and coordinated all the autonomous traffic on its roads, as well as all the traffic lights, which were needed for those vehicles still under the control of their human drivers. And the Mind would not allow her to exceed the speed limit or jump any lights even if she had wanted to: it would take over her bike's computer, commanding it to activate the brakes and slow down.

The traffic was light as she sped north up Rua de Santana, passing the abandoned and burnt-out vehicles on the side of the road – a reminder of the civil unrest the city had endured over the past few weeks. But she would soon hit the commuter rush hour when she reached Avenida Presidente Vargas, which ran into the city from the west. As she reached the intersection she dropped the revs on the bike's throttle in anticipation of the Mind taking over control of her brakes. She still found this mix of manual and remote control of her bike disconcerting and preferred open country roads away from AI control, where she could manually apply her own brakes if and when necessary.

The first sign that something was wrong was when her brakes failed to activate automatically as she approached the busy intersection that got her onto the freeway. Strange. She was always stopped here by the Mind, even if for just a few seconds. Dropping down to a lower gear, she edged forward carefully. There was heavy traffic on the four lanes of the eastbound side of the road, which she had to cross, and it was completely stationary. It had been a long time since she had witnessed such an old-fashioned traffic jam – it just wasn't the sort of thing that happened in large cities any more. It occurred to her that, not so many years ago, this sort of scene would have been accompanied by a cacophony of revving internal combustion engines and car horns honking impatiently while drivers leaned out of their windows to shout at each other. This morning, everything was eerily quiet. People had quickly got used to relying on their cars' computers to do all the driving while they sat in comfort within their air-conditioned environment.

Weaving her way carefully around the stationary cars blocking her path, she noted the bemused looks on the faces of the passengers, suggesting that whatever had stopped the traffic had only happened recently. None of the cars on the westbound side were moving either, so it had to be a problem with the city's AI. But the Minds that ran the very largest megacities around the world simply didn't go down. Ever. She felt a creeping unease. Pulling over, she dismounted and blinked on her AR. The feed was dead.

*No reason to freak out just yet, girl – just because the entire net is down!*

She steadied her breathing. *Logic before panic.* After all, she'd spent the last few days worrying about the Sun's abnormal activity, but that did *not* mean that this internet blackout was in any way related.

*OK, think. If a solar blast really has knocked out radio-wave connectivity, then maybe I can still use my wristpad.* Like her computer back in the apartment, it had a direct lasercom link to the STEREO2 spacecraft, which meant it didn't have to route through any Earth-orbit commsat. She quickly established a link and scanned recent solar activity.

*Fuck.*

She examined the data streaming across her vision and gasped. The incoming CME was a monster. Its size, speed and energy density were off the charts. Could it be a mistake? No, the stats would have been cross-correlated between the STEREO2 spacecraft. Her heart was now pounding as she did a quick mental calculation, trying to suppress her growing panic. The spacecraft had first detected the CME and begun sending their alert to Earth a few minutes ago, which would also have been when the electromagnetic pulse that must have brought down the net had hit.

*Oh, shit . . . this is really, really bad. It means we've got at best ten to fifteen minutes before the proton blast.* She knew that others at her institute and elsewhere who had direct links to STEREO2 would also be aware of the incoming CME, but they'd have little time to do much.

Under normal conditions, with a healthy magnetosphere, the proton shower that preceded the arrival of a CME would not be cause for concern. But in its weakened state, the field would not provide an adequate shield. She estimated that it could potentially be worse than the radiation fallout from a thermo-nuclear blast. And that was before the main ejection hit the Earth in a day or two. Worst of all, with the net down there was no way to warn people. It was the stuff of nightmares.

She surveyed her surroundings on the highway. Everywhere, people were getting out of their cars. *They have no idea what's about to happen. And they can't stay here, exposed. Even in their cars they'll be like sitting ducks.* It would be like hiding inside a cardboard box on a firing range.

She ran to the nearest group of half a dozen well-dressed businessmen and -women and, instead of speaking in English and relying on their universal translators, she started to explain as best she could in her broken Portuguese that she was a sci-entist and she knew what had caused the blackout. Things were about to get very bad and they needed to find shelter – anywhere that could give them protection from the radiation from the sky.

They just stared at her as though she were mad. She switched to English in the hope that some of them would understand, either directly or through their UTs, and could pass on what she was saying.

'Please. I work at the Solar Science Institute. We're about to be hit by dangerous radiation from the Sun and we only have a few minutes. Everyone needs to get off the road.'

One young man turned to the woman next to him and muttered something that caused her to raise one hand to her mouth and conceal her laughter. An overweight middle-aged man who was already starting to sweat in the warm morning sun spat an impatient insult at Sarah in Portuguese, which she understood perfectly well and chose to ignore. She knew how she must sound; these days the world was full of doom-mongers preaching that the end of the world was nigh, some more wildly than others. But these people *had* to listen. She grabbed a well-dressed middle-aged woman firmly by the shoulders and spoke as clearly as she could. 'Listen to me. The internet blackout is because of the Sun. And it's going to get worse . . . and if you're exposed to it you could die. Please . . . *please*. Everyone needs to find some shelter. *Now.*'

She realized she was ranting, and the look on the woman's face confirmed how crazy she must sound.

She felt a hand on her own shoulder pulling her away and she let go of the woman. She stumbled backwards, losing her balance, and fell heavily, grazing her hands as she reached down to break her fall.

More people had gathered to check what the commotion was. A few, who had heard part of what she'd said, were now in animated conversation. A mother pulled her two young children from a car and, holding their hands firmly, began pushing her way through the crowd to the side of the road. Sarah sat, dazed, on the ground as a circle gathered around her and stared, while others lost interest and returned to their air-conditioned cars. A few people were looking up at the sky, shielding their eyes from the sun's glare.

She was helped to her feet by an embarrassed-looking young couple. Feeling both humiliated and enraged in equal measure, she began to explain to them, 'Please, you have to listen—', but they smiled awkwardly and retreated back down the road.

Time was running out. What more was she supposed to do?

Instead, a primal survival instinct kicked in, snuffing out any feelings of moral obligation. *Well, fuck you then. Stay out and enjoy your suntan.* She picked up her helmet and ran back to her bike. She knew where she needed to get to.

She swung her leg over the bike, hit ignition and revved the engine, ignoring the soreness in her right hand from her stumble. She turned the bike around and looked frantically for a route to get across the multiple lanes of traffic. She needed to head back the way she'd come, back to the Santa Barbara tunnel, but by now traffic was backed up in both directions along Rua de Santana, which had been so comparatively empty a few minutes ago.

People were standing around in the road ahead of her but, realizing that she had no intention of slowing down as she sped between the stationary cars, they scattered as she bore down on them. She left a tirade of obscenities in her wake. Tough. No time for pleasantries.

Suddenly, a car door swung open in front of her without warning and she had to slam on her brakes and swerve, still clipping the door sharply with her back wheel. The young occupant of the car jumped out and looked for a second like he was going to pull her from her bike. She ignored him and weaved her way onwards.

Up ahead of her several cars had tried, unsuccessfully, to turn around, causing utter chaos. Already voices were being raised and the first punches thrown. How quickly the rule of law broke down – how volatile the public mood was at the moment. The road looked completely blocked. She let out a scream of frustration.

With less than ten minutes before she needed to get to safety she knew she had to get off the highway. The narrow winding lanes of the Santa Teresa district were above her and she gunned the bike onto the pavement, up a steep grass slope and across flower beds. Suddenly, she was on a quiet residential road.

As the crow flies, the tunnel was less than a kilometre away, but would she have enough time to make it along the twisting steep roads on the Santa Teresa hill? She had to try. Revving the engine with renewed purpose, she sped off.

Twice her bike skidded as she wrestled to keep it on the winding road. Adrenalin was now surging through her, the single-minded determination to reach the tunnel blocking out all other emotions. She braked hard approaching another sharp U-bend, then gunned the throttle again with a twist of her right wrist even before she had straightened up. Too late to react, she saw a group of young boys playing football in the middle of the road. She slammed on her brakes again. Too hard. The tyres screeched as the bike swerved one way then the other. There was nothing she could as she lost her balance, still travelling at speed, and fell onto the road with the bike on top of her.

The bike slid along the road with her leg trapped underneath, ripping her jeans and cutting into her leg. Miraculously, the boys somehow managed to jump out of the way fractions of a second before woman and machine ploughed through them. She felt a sharp pain in her elbow as her arm displaced a brick that had been acting as a makeshift goalpost. Finally, Sarah and motorbike came to a stop in a shallow ditch by the side of the road. Dazed, she was vaguely aware that the boys were gathering around her. One or two were shouting, asking if she was OK, but a few were laughing. With her head pounding, she dragged her bloodied leg out from beneath the bike and forced herself to stand up. Lifting the machine up caused a spasm of pain to shoot up her left arm. She was pretty sure her elbow was fractured.

She turned to look at the boys. She wanted to scream at them, to tell them to get home, to find shelter, but they were already going back to their game. Ignoring the intense pain in her arm and leg, she heaved the bike back up and somehow managed to get back on. The engine was still running. Twisting the throttle, she flicked into gear and took off down the road again.

How long did she have? No time to check now. Just keep going.

Suddenly, there was a flash of light in her left eye, followed by two more in quick succession in her right eye. Please no, not yet.

For three quarters of a century astronauts had reported these flashes: high-energy particles from space travelling through the eyeball and hitting the back of the retina. So, this was it – the first and fastest particles from the Sun were arriving now, like the first few drops of rain before a downpour.

She turned a corner and felt a wave of relief as she saw the tunnel entrance on the road below her. The flashes were arriving more regularly. She gunned the throttle of the bike yet again, joining the road just a hundred metres from the tunnel entrance. The tailback of traffic now extended all the way into the tunnel. Without coming to a complete stop, she leapt from the bike, falling again and rolling over on the verge. She struggled to her feet and ripped off her helmet. Ignoring the searing pain in her leg, she half ran, half hobbled as fast as she could manage along the side of the road, pushing her way past commuters who had abandoned their cars. Many were rubbing their eyes, while some turned to stare at this wild woman in the torn and bloody jeans with dishevelled hair and panic in her eyes.

Consumed with pain and frustration, her breathing loud and laboured, she ran. She shouted to people to follow her towards the shelter of the tunnel. No one did. In a week, two weeks, maybe more if they were particularly unlucky, many of these people would be dead from radiation exposure.

She could see the tunnel entrance looming larger. Almost there. The spots in her eyes were coming thick and fast now.

At last, she had made it. Plunging into the cool darkness, she kept on moving deeper inside, until she was sure that the mass of rock above her head was sufficient to provide enough shielding. She finally slumped back against the tunnel wall, gasping for air. She wondered what the occupants of the cars stuck in the jam here would think when they discovered how lucky they were.

Later that night, lying in hospital along with hundreds of people who, unlike her, appeared sick from radiation exposure, she drifted in and out of a fitful sleep. Her dreams were haunted by the memory of those young Brazilian boys playing football in the street and how they would probably have all died painfully and horribly of radiation exposure soon after. They had laughed at her and she had left them to die.

And she dreamed too about how much worse things were going to get.

# Interlude

THE CORONAL MASS EJECTION HAD BEEN HEADING TOWARDS EARTH *for twenty-one hours. As it passed the first Lagrange point, a million miles from Earth, it washed over the Chinese Kuafu satellite. The satellite dutifully carried out the task it had been put there for and sent back data on the CME – to a mostly deaf humankind. Less than a minute before the CME reached Earth it began to feel the effects of the magnetosphere. Yet it hardly slowed down at all. Instead, it compressed the field ahead of it as though it were a car air-bag with not enough air in.*

*The CME blasted through the weakened outer Van Allen belt tens of thousands of kilometres above the Earth's surface, destroying it. Charged cosmic-ray particles – protons and electrons – trapped by the magnetosphere in this radiation shell for millennia, were now set free and quickly scattered into space like autumn leaves whipped up in a storm.*

*With the magnetosphere squashed so thin ahead of the CME, many of the thousands of satellites in orbit were left exposed to its full force, and their electronic circuitry was instantly fried.*

*Although the particles making up the CME were lower in energy than the initial wave of protons that had arrived the day before, their sheer intensity meant they were just as deadly. There would have been an even greater number of fatalities had populations not been warned in time following the initial proton blast, but nothing could stop crops from being destroyed and livestock wiped out in many parts of the world.*

*Happening so close to the March equinox, the effects of the blast were felt most strongly around the equator. In South America, the final tally would reach two hundred thousand dead, mostly in eastern Brazil, where it coincided with the morning rush hour, with many people simply ignoring the warning messages. Luckily for those further west, it was too early in the day for many people to be outside their houses, which mostly offered them adequate protection. The same could not be said for sub-Saharan and southern Africa, where the radiation blast hit in the middle of the day. It was estimated that up to seven million people across forty countries suffered fatal exposure – dying either from lethal radiation poisoning in the immediate aftermath of the event or from cancers brought about by the ionizing radiation, over the following months, making it the world's worst natural disaster in recorded history.*

*A taste of things to come.*

# PART III

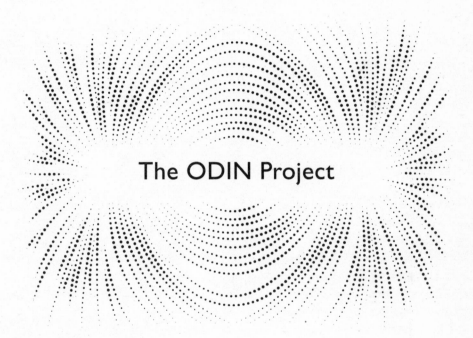

# The ODIN Project

# 30

MARC MADE HIS WAY PAST FAMILIAR BUILDINGS THROUGH the site of the vast laboratory complex of the Conseil européen pour la recherche nucléaire, where he had spent much of his early career, and considered how much had changed in his life over the past three months. In fact, it struck him that he felt pretty good about himself right now, in part due to his work on the Odin Project, but also because of his growing feelings towards Sarah and his continuing rehabilitation in the eyes of Evie – who seemed to be revelling in her father's new-found fame.

Things had moved rapidly in the days that followed the events of 13 and 14 March. With the world reeling from the shock of such a cataclysmic loss of life, rumours spread fast that this was not a freak event – that unless the magnetosphere recovered, more devastation was inevitable. Across the world, the sense of unease grew stronger. Fresh riots broke out; looting became so widespread that many governments were powerless to stop it; and few people were prepared to believe the official line, that the March CME really was a once-in-a-century event.

It quickly became clear that the magnetic pulse devices still being worked on would not offer the protection needed from any future threat from the Sun of similar magnitude. At best, an Earth-based device would provide a temporary preventative measure – a local shield protecting the lucky few beneath it – but never a permanent global solution.

One group revelling in all this chaos was the Purifiers. The end-of-the-world prophecy they held by was coming true, and they rejoiced. But that didn't dampen their enthusiasm for giving nature a helping hand. They upped the ambition and frequency of their attacks on government facilities and research labs working on potential solutions to the dying field, always driven and cajoled by their spiritual leader, Maksoob. Little was known of this shadowy figure, a man who had kindled a warped passion among his growing band of followers. He had recruited them carefully from around the world, mainly from among the disaffected and disillusioned in poverty-stricken areas: those in the once oil-rich nations of the Middle East and the millions displaced from coastal homes in southern Asia lost to the rising seas.

For several weeks after the Event, as it was now being referred to, Sarah had remained in Rio, in part to recover from her injuries – a fractured elbow, a sprained ankle and deep gashes in her leg – but also, as Marc had discovered when he'd visited her, because of her crushing feelings of guilt that she hadn't done enough to warn people about the deadly radiation from the sky on that fateful morning.

Despite her pleas to be discharged, she had been kept under observation in hospital for a week to ensure that she wasn't suffering from any radiation effects. Amid the chaos and disruption to travel in the days following the Event, Marc had somehow managed to get on a flight down to Rio, in part out of a genuine desire to see Sarah and check up on her, but also in the hope that he might discuss the possibility of resurrecting the Odin Project.

Within minutes of seeing her sitting up in bed, he could tell that her physical injuries would heal quickly enough, but her mental state was a different matter. In contrast to the zest and determination he'd admired in the woman he'd got to know on the few occasions they'd spent time together in New York over the previous weeks, Sarah was now quiet and withdrawn. It was as though she'd put up an impregnable wall around her to block the outside world out while she battled her inner demons.

No one knew better than Marc Bruckner about the futility of trying to talk someone out of depression. But he had tried.

'Anyone would have done what you did. How could you possibly convince people in the few minutes you had out on the streets? And why risk fatally exposing yourself too?'

Sarah hadn't answered. Instead, she'd cried a lot that day.

The day after he'd arrived in Rio, Marc had received a call from Qiang.

'We've been asked to attend a briefing meeting at the UN tomorrow. It sounds like our idea is back on the table.'

'Says who?'

'Says . . . Well, I don't know who's made the decision. All I know is that they are now ready to listen to us, properly.'

Marc wasn't sure how he felt. 'Well, yes, I suppose desperate measures require desperate solutions, right?'

Qiang was quiet for a second, then he said, 'You know, that's exactly what they said to me!'

Marc had promised Sarah he'd come back to see her as soon as he could.

One week after the Event, news of the new plan to save the world had gone viral. Within days, everyone was talking about how dark matter was going to rescue humanity. The Odin Project had been born. It hadn't taken long for the feasibility of the science to be checked and confirmed. The official view was that it *could* work, in theory at least. And that was enough. It had brought governments together in a way never seen before. Marc had been astonished by the speed at which consensus had been reached. Not since the Second World War had so many nations rapidly invested so much time and resource into a single objective – but this time they were all working on the same side. The scale of the task made mid-twentieth-century technical achievements like the Manhattan Project and the space race seem like amateur diversions.

*

It was a warm June morning in Geneva and, despite what was at stake, Marc felt excited. He found it hard to believe just how rapidly the Odin Project had evolved from crazy speculations about firing beams of neutralinos into the core of the Earth to serious discussions about how this might be achieved and where facilities would need to be built, to designing and carrying out the first feasibility tests. Today, the results of the first real tests of his and Qiang's idea were being presented.

People were already taking their seats in the main auditorium as Marc made his way down towards the front. He quickly spotted Qiang in animated discussion with Gabriel Aguda and noticed the dramatic contrast in size between the two men. Aguda had consistently voiced his reservations about the Odin Project. Unlike the MPDs, which he claimed at least gave the world a stay of execution, he'd argued strongly that this was too expensive, too uncertain, could not be achieved in time and, most importantly, diverted attention from the more 'reliable' MPDs option. Marc found it hard to read what the man was thinking.

Scanning the hall to see if Sarah had arrived, he soon spotted her sitting by the middle aisle on the far side. She mouthed, 'Good luck.'

As he navigated his way down to the stage area through the throngs of delegates standing around in the aisle, the irony of how his fortunes, and mood, had improved as a consequence of the situation that was sinking the rest of humanity into pessimism and anxiety was not lost on him.

Qiang had admitted that he too felt the same sense of purpose about the Odin Project – and argued that it was OK for Marc to feel positive. 'After all,' he'd said, 'if we don't have faith in the science, then we've lost.' Marc didn't buy this cheap psychology, but knew what Qiang had meant. They were, after all, leading the most ambitious and important scientific undertaking the world had ever known, one that would determine the future of the planet, which was, by any measure, pretty fucking awesome. If nothing else, it put his own demons into perspective.

He had been somewhat surprised at the speed of his re-acceptance among the international community of high-energy physicists as soon as the Odin Project had taken off. The reputation of a research scientist was a fragile thing which, like one's virginity, could only be lost once. He'd certainly lost his. But here he was again, back at CERN where he'd spent the first fifteen years of his research career and the centre of attention for the world's leading scientists once more, and realizing that he still enjoyed it. He adjusted his tie as he walked. This was probably the first time ever he had given a physics talk in a jacket and tie, but he felt the occasion merited some sort of formality.

Of course, there was a dark backdrop to all this sanguine enthusiasm. Marc knew better than anyone just how outrageously ambitious the Odin Project truly was. There were simply too many unknowns, too many challenges, and too little margin for error.

And it was now clear that security was an even bigger problem than the science. As soon as the Odin Project was announced the Purifiers had issued a statement outlining their intent to sabotage it. So, they had begun to target the new facilities being built and the scientists and engineers working on the Project. In the past week alone, two accelerator physicists in Paris had been murdered and a research lab outside Tokyo had been extensively damaged by a bomb. Worst of all was the devastating destruction of the half-built Dark Matter Facility in Texas, which had been expected to play a central role in the Project. The vast underground lab had been obliterated by a huge blast, which the Purifiers claimed responsibility for, and which had buried alive three hundred workers and technicians. The depth of the facility underground meant that even in the unlikely event of there being any survivors, all hopes of rescue were futile.

Now, global security had been ramped up to near preposterous levels, almost doubling the cost of the Project. Armies had been mobilized and all travel restricted. The distribution of the financial burden had yet to be settled, but governments understood that they couldn't afford to delay.

Marc sat down in the front row of the auditorium next to Qiang, sweeping aside the sheet of paper with the words 'Reserved. Professor Bruckner' on it. The atmosphere of anticipation in the big hall was palpable, and Marc knew that the world outside was also holding its collective breath. The talks were being streamed live to billions.

He turned to his friend. 'Morning, Qiang. All set?'

Qiang merely nodded nervously, but Aguda, one seat along, said, 'It's OK for you two, Marc, you get to promise to save the world. I'm just the guy who has to make sure as few people as possible find out about the catastrophic consequences if you boys get anything wrong.'

'Well, so far, so good, right?' Marc had been more relieved than excited by the results from the recent Antarctica test.

Qiang turned to him. 'But there wasn't so much at stake, was there? We can afford to get it wrong for the test, but when we do the real thing . . .'

Mark said nothing. Qiang was right; they'd only have one shot at this. He turned to survey the audience behind them. The four hundred seats were all occupied now, and there were people still streaming in, packing the aisles and filling up the rear of the auditorium. Most were CERN scientists and engineers working on the Odin Project, but there were also groups representing various governments and media bodies. Marc had already met many of the movers and shakers the previous evening at dinner – including, for the first time, the leader of the American delegation, Senator Hogan, who he saw was now seated just two rows behind them and deep in conversation with CERN's director-general. Sarah had been right – there was something unsettling about Hogan's manner, a cold detachment that Marc had found disturbing. He'd taken an instant dislike to the man.

The noise began to subside in anticipation of the start of proceedings.

Qiang was fidgeting, cracking his knuckles as he always did when nervous. His task today was straightforward: he was to report on the first successful test in which the only three operating dark-matter accelerator labs – here at CERN, Fermilab near Chicago and J-PARC north of Tokyo – had all successfully fired their invisible beams down through the Earth. Everything had gone exactly to plan with three synchronized neutralino bursts, each passing unhindered through ten thousand kilometres of solid planet, converging just before they emerged at a point one hundred metres below the surface of the Antarctic ice.

Marc and Qiang had flown out to Antarctica to witness the experiment at first hand. It was the most nervous Marc had felt in his life. If this test had failed that would most likely have spelled the end of the Project.

The chosen spot for the dark-matter beams to converge, just south of the Kraul Mountains in the Norwegian dependency of Queen Maud Land, was a remote enough site, yet close enough to the British Halley Research Station eighty kilometres away to be carefully monitored from a safe distance.

After a twenty-four-hour delay due to a security breach at J-PARC, the three labs had fired their dark-matter bursts into the ground. When the pulses met, a split second later and thousands of kilometres away, they created a burst of energy so great it vaporized a volume of the remaining Antarctic ice, leaving behind a lake of hot, but rapidly cooling water three kilometres wide and two hundred metres deep. Under normal circumstances, such devastation would have horrified environmentalists, but these were not normal circumstances. Marc found himself wondering whether Oppenheimer, Fermi and the rest of the gang on the Manhattan Project had experienced the same feelings of awe and dread at such pure, unleashed power, as they gazed out at the first mushroom cloud in the New Mexico desert a century ago. The difference now was that, unlike the Manhattan Project, this test was meant to save humankind rather than incinerate it.

And yet he had to remind himself that this test had been with just three dark-matter beams rather than the eight he and Qiang were proposing, not to mention the fact that they had been operating at a fraction of the intensity that could be achieved, and which would ultimately be needed when the time came.

Marc's thoughts were interrupted when the lights dimmed, and he heard a familiar voice over the PA system. Despite the importance of the event, proceedings began just as all CERN

conferences had done for some years past: with a welcoming
address from the lab's Mind. The holographic human avatar
representing the AI that controlled every aspect of the vast
laboratory complex was, in contrast, simple and understated.
The original programmers had created it in the stately image
of a woman with white hair tied efficiently in a bun at the back
of her head. Those listening to her without the use of the universal translators would hear her speak softly in English with
a hint of an Italian accent. It was said that this was a deliberate
nod by the programmers to the laboratory's first female director, Fabiola Gianotti. They had even given it her name. The
real Dr Gianotti had retired several years ago but still came to
the lab regularly. Marc had once asked her what she thought
of the avatar created in her image.

'I'm very flattered,' she'd replied. 'If only it had been around
when I was director. I could have taken longer holidays and
left it in charge. It knows far more about how to run CERN
than I ever did.'

Like everyone else in the room, Marc now saw the Mind's
avatar in augmented reality and listened as Fabiola gave a brief
introduction to the lab.

'Many of you will know that CERN was conceived in the late
1940s as a laboratory to be shared by many nations when particle physics research became too expensive for any one country
to pursue alone. So, it is fitting that today it is the centre of
operations for a new type of experiment – one that involves a
truly worldwide collaboration between eight laboratories spread
around the globe. Many of you will know that we have this type
of connectivity in science already, with our largest radio tele-
scopes linked together to effectively act as a single Earth-sized
telescope to look deeper into space, but humankind has never
attempted something as audacious as Project Odin.'

As the Mind went on to introduce Qiang and invite him to
present the latest test results, Marc's attention drifted once
again. The great human technological achievements of the past,
such as the space exploration programmes to the Moon in the
1960s and Mars in the 2030s, had been driven by nothing more

than national pride and economic supremacy; this current race against time was different. Unlike with the Moon and Mars programmes, failure now quite literally wasn't an option.

Sitting there, only half listening to Qiang describing the results of the Antarctic test, he felt a sudden unexpected surge of panic. This entire project really was quite insane. He tried to recall the confidence and excitement he'd experienced during that weekend of feverish activity in his New York hotel room, when the two men had conceived the plan. But despite their calculations being checked and verified by hundreds of other scientists, he now felt more nervous than ever.

Still, what choice did the world have? Secretly, a small part of him was hoping that someone else would come up with a better plan – one for which the chances of success were higher and where failure would not mean the end of the world. At least if something went wrong and one of the beams did in fact miss the intended rendezvous spot deep in the Earth's molten core, he wouldn't have too long to blame himself for destroying the planet.

Loud applause dragged him back to the here and now. Qiang had finished his short presentation and was returning to his seat. It was time. Standing, Marc waited for a second or two, trying to calm himself and collect his thoughts. He was conscious of hundreds of pairs of eyes burning into the back of his skull as he made his way to the stage. Pausing at the lectern to pick up the holo-control pad, Professor Marc Bruckner turned to face his audience and smiled.

'Ladies and gentlemen,' he began, 'I'm aware that many of you are not scientists and will therefore not appreciate the subtler details of dark-matter physics, particle decay pathways and the role of superconducting bending magnets. In any case, the documentation you have all been given lays this out in clearer detail than I am able to do.'

A murmur of light-hearted approval rippled through the audience, which would have come mainly from the non-scientists.

'As you know, ODIN stands for Octangular Directional Ignition with Neutralinos. This means eight beams of neutralinos, the particles of dark matter, all directed into the core of the planet from different points on the surface. But as you have just heard from Professor Lee, we currently have only three accelerator laboratories capable of producing these particles at sufficiently high energy and intensity.'

He wondered how what he was about to say would be received. After the tragedy in Texas, they had needed to come up with a revised plan. Many in the audience would now be hearing the new details for the first time.

He clicked the pad in his hand and a giant three-dimensional globe appeared suspended in the air in front of him, slowly rotating. Created by several holo-projectors around the stage, the bottom of the sphere hovered a metre above the ground, but its top almost reached the roof of the auditorium seven metres above the stage.

Marc walked across from the podium to stand in the centre of the projection, so that the globe's South Pole cut through his midriff. And because his eyeline coincided with the southern oceans, as the Earth spun he looked out at the audience through a blue translucent wall. He was aware that his actions might seem overly theatrical, but he had a practical reason for positioning himself inside the hologram. With a click of the pad in his hand, three bright lights lit up at the appropriate locations on the surface of the globe, depicting the sites of the only three labs capable of producing beams of dark matter.

He continued, 'The challenge is how to turn three beams into eight, each one aimed into the Earth's core from a different location.

'Those further five locations have now been identified. They were chosen for two reasons. The first is of course their strategic location on the surface of the planet. The second is that they all have much of the infrastructure that is needed already. You see, we won't be building five new dark-matter accelerators. Instead, we're using the beams from the three we already have, only we're splitting them up.'

As he spoke, he clicked his pad and five new lights appeared on the globe.

'All we need . . .' He paused to give the audience the chance to realize he'd meant those three words sardonically. This time the ripple of laughter came from the other physicists, who knew only too well the immense scale of the task. '. . . All we need . . . are giant superconducting magnets to bend the particle beams fired from the three main labs downward into the ground.'

A subdued buzz spread around the auditorium as people leaned in to each other, whispering, pointing at the globe. Marc began warming to his task.

'For example, the beam produced here at CERN will be split into three: one heading to the north coast of Norway in the Arctic Circle . . .' A red line lit up, joining the light that marked Geneva to another in the far north. It traced a perfect straight path that passed below the surface of the Earth instead of following its curvature above ground. '. . . a second to the deserts of Jordan just outside Amman, and a third to Cape Town in South Africa.' Two more bright lines appeared, radiating out from CERN.

A few people clapped enthusiastically, and then, feeling self-conscious, stopped again.

'Across in America, the Fermilab beam will be split in two: one heading straight down to the core directly beneath the lab and the other sent south to the Andean Plateau in Peru.

'Finally, the Japanese beam will also split into three, one directly down and the other two to facilities located on Big Island, Hawaii, and Dunedin in the south of New Zealand.

'Once the beams from the labs reach the six remote locations, powerful magnets will bend them downwards, aiming them into the ground.'

As he spoke new red lines appeared around him pointing radially inwards from each location, to meet at the centre of the hologram at a point high above his head.

He now stepped back out of the holo image. 'As you can see, the eight beams,' he indicated back to the red spokes of light inside the sphere, 'two from the existing facilities and the other six from the new locations, all meet in a single spot in the Earth's core.'

Marc paused to join the audience in admiring the image. 'I could stop here and just ask you to wish us luck. But since I have you as a captive audience I feel I should share with you the *really* cool stuff.'

He looked out across the auditorium. There was a mixture of admiration and concentration on the sea of faces in front of him. His own earlier anxiety and pessimism about the Project had evaporated and his missionary zeal was filling him with a reassuring belief that this could really work. Marc Bruckner had spent his entire adult life testing and prodding the laws of nature. Now was the chance to put his years of study and research to the ultimate test.

He caught sight of Aguda sitting in the front row. The geologist's stony expression contrasted with the animated features of those around him.

*Oh well, can't please everyone.* For some reason his eyes drifted across to where Peter Hogan was sitting, but he found it impossible to read the man's blank expression, which he found somewhat unnerving. To counter his unease, he quickly glanced up at Sarah, who gave him a reassuring nod of encouragement. He took a deep breath.

'You see, ladies and gentlemen, for the magnets to bend the trajectories of our beams from their original direction so that they enter the ground, the particles need to know the magnets are there and react to them, right?

'Yes, I know that sounds obvious. But, as I hope you all know by now, dark matter doesn't feel the presence of normal matter, by which I mean it's not affected by the electromagnetic force. So, just as dark matter passes through normal matter as if it weren't there, it will also be oblivious to the presence of the magnets, regardless of how powerful those magnets are.'

The background murmuring began afresh as many in the audience suddenly understood what seemed to be a fundamental flaw in the scheme.

Marc took a couple of steps closer to the front of the stage. 'So, here's the plan. We don't make beams of neutralinos, the usual dark-matter particles, to begin with, but heavier versions of them. These are called, somewhat unimaginatively I'm afraid, *heavy* neutralinos. Think of them as the normal neutralinos' overweight and short-lived cousins. Beams of these heavy particles will be created in all three accelerators, surviving just long enough, if produced at the right energy, to travel out to the six magnets.

'Then, just as they arrive at the magnets, and rather like Cinderella's coach at midnight, each of them transforms into yet another type of particle called a chargino.'

There was a smattering of laughter at this and Marc acknowledged it with good grace. 'Yes, I know, it sounds like I'm just making this stuff up as I go along, but I promise you I didn't invent these names.

'What's important,' he continued after the audience had settled, 'is that these charginos, as their name suggests, have an electric charge, which means they will be bent downwards by the magnets, but they too live for such a short time that they will almost immediately transform – we say decay – into the light neutralinos that we want. This step is crucial.'

Marc knew that the better the job he made of explaining things now, the easier his life would be in the press conference later. So, he ploughed on. 'The point is that the solid ground will appear to the charginos as just that: *solid*. If they don't transform in time to neutralinos they will be stopped dead in their tracks. This is because their electric charge interacts with the atoms that make up the stuff of the planet. Luckily for us, these charginos transform very quickly back into neutralinos. Once they do, it will be as though the earth suddenly becomes transparent again and they continue on their path unobstructed, but this time in their new direction towards the core.

'The eight neutralino beams travel downwards until they meet, slamming together in the mother of all bangs. The energy this produces in the planet's liquid core will be a hundred million times greater than the burst that melted that chunk of Antarctica. We've calculated – that is, Professor Lee and I have calculated . . .' Marc nodded towards Qiang. '. . . that this would be enough to create a seismic pulse that kick-starts the

Earth's inner dynamo, and switches the magnetosphere back on.'

As an afterthought he added, with a theatrical wave of his hands, 'And that's how we're going to save the world.'

There was wild and enthusiastic applause, even from colleagues who knew the science inside out. A few were standing, and he noticed that Sarah was among them.

He waited patiently for the applause to die down. When it was quiet again he asked, 'Right, does anyone have any questions?'

'Excuse me, Professor Bruckner.' A man in the second row was leaning towards the microphone by his seat. Marc recognized him as a Swiss journalist from *Le Temps* who had interviewed him a couple of years ago. 'Could you please explain something to us lesser mortals? How can you know precisely when these different particles transform from one type to the other? From my basic understanding of quantum physics, this is not something you can control.'

Marc nodded. Unbidden, a famous quote came to him. He had a feeling it was from a Kurt Vonnegut novel, but couldn't remember the character or what the story was about. It was along the lines of: any scientist who couldn't explain to an eight-year-old what he was doing was a charlatan.

'You are right, of course, that particles decay according to the rules of quantum mechanics, which state that this takes place at an indeterminate moment. This is not to say that quantum mechanics is an imprecise theory, but rather that Nature herself hasn't decided when such individual quantum events will happen.'

The sage-like slow nodding from the journalist suggested to Marc that he was still following, or at least pretending to, so he ploughed on. 'Quantum mechanics tells us that the world of subatomic particles is a fuzzy one ruled by probability and uncertainty. So, while we cannot control or predict when any *given* particle will decay, we do know the *average* lifetime when we have lots of them. So, we produce very many heavy neutralinos in a tight bunch, all travelling at just the right speed, such that *most* of them will decay just before arrival at the magnet. Of course, some won't decay until it's too late and they'll overshoot the magnet. Those are lost. Others will decay too soon and won't even reach the magnet because they will interact with other atoms in the ground or the air and be knocked off their course. But most will make it, transforming just in time for the magnets to do their bending job on them.

'They enter the facilities as a pulse of dark-matter particles travelling through the air, which passes into a sealed beam pipe kept under high vacuum. Only once isolated inside this do they transform into charginos that get bent by the magnets, following an arc within the enclosed, curved pipe that carries them down to the ground.

'And because we know the speed and lifetime of these charginos we can calculate how far they will travel, on average, before they transform back into neutralinos, and so we just have to make sure the beam pipe and the surrounding magnets are high enough above the ground. We've calculated that raising them by about a hundred metres would be enough to give most charginos the chance to decay. Only then do they decay back to dark matter again and the pulse passes through the other end of the beam pipe like a phantom and continues down into the earth.'

He paused to let the information sink in.

The journalist interjected: 'But isn't that quite a tough engineering challenge?'

Marc laughed. 'The whole project is something of an engineering challenge.' A number of people laughed too. 'But you're right. And so, there's an alternative plan that might be easier. The magnets are kept at ground level, but instead we bore a vertical tunnel into the ground, down which the beam pipe of charginos is directed, to give them that extra breathing space. Again, some longer-lived charginos won't have decayed in time. They hit the sealed end of the beam pipe and are lost.'

Marc wished he'd been able to give a more traditional seminar to an audience of physicists alone. That way he wouldn't have had to choose his language carefully and skip so much of the interesting technical detail. For example, he'd conveniently left out the fact that the heavy neutralino beams would decay into a host of other particles besides charginos, like W and Z bosons, which in turn would quickly decay into other more familiar particles like quarks and electrons, all of which would be slamming into the magnets at incredible energy. Hopefully they wouldn't destroy the electronics before the magnets had served their purpose.

All the other questions he fielded over the next fifteen minutes were easier to deal with, mainly because he was unable to give definitive answers. He could not say what the Odin Project's chances of success were, when it would be completed, and the beams fired for real, or whether he knew of other ways of getting energy to the Earth's core. He batted away the other obvious questions: yes, he was confident the Project could be kept secure; no, there had been no political pressure on the choice of the magnets' locations – the decision had been entirely scientific. And he also stressed that the original idea of using neutralino beams had been Qiang Lee's, not his.

The question he dreaded being asked didn't come up and he was relieved when the session ended. The one major detail he had deliberately left out of his talk was what happened if anything went wrong. If just one of the eight beams misfired, or missed the central collision point, then the energy pulse produced by the other seven would be out of kilter and . . . well, he tried not to think about that.

# 31

*Monday, 17 June – CERN, Geneva*

As the audience filtered out of the lecture theatre, Marc excused himself from the throng who had come down to talk to him. Qiang was engrossed in a spirited technical discussion with several CERN physicists, so he wandered out into the concourse where people were gathering and headed for the long coffee table on the far side. A serving bot glided towards him on the other side of the table.

What would you like to drink, Professor Bruckner? it asked in a singsong voice.

The bot was little more than a white plastic cube, the size of a human torso, with arms. It reminded Marc of a headless Bender, the robot from the animated TV series *Futurama* that he'd enjoyed as a teenager. These days, he'd got so used to the wide range of humanoid bots that worked behind bars and shop counters around the world that he'd forgotten how little CERN cared about anthropomorphizing their service robots, opting instead for minimalism and practicality.

'Black coffee, please,' he said to the cube.

Taking a sip of the strong brew, he wandered around in search of Sarah, quickly finding her in conversation with a group of younger men and women whom he recognized as local CERN scientists. Sarah was holding her coffee mug in both hands, laughing at something one of them was saying. He sensed an inner self-assurance and resolve about her that was in stark contrast to her feelings of helplessness and worthlessness in the weeks following the Event. He also noted as he approached that, despite the plainness of her clothes – a pale blue blouse over comfortable-looking black trousers and flat shoes – and her hair pulled back in a ponytail, she looked stunningly beautiful.

Just before he reached the group he was intercepted by an eager-looking young man who grabbed his hand and shook it enthusiastically. 'That was a great presentation you gave, Professor Bruckner. Do you really think it can work? I mean, will we get the necessary luminosity if we need a double in-flight decay?'

'You mean, are we sure we will still have enough neutralinos after the losses in the beam before and after the bending magnets?'

The young scientist nodded earnestly.

'At each stage there will inevitably be some loss, so we need to build in some redundancy when we generate our initial beams. But in answer to your first question, yes, I do believe it will work. All the simulations say it is possible . . . just. In any case, it *has* to work. What other choice do we have?'

With a parting nod, Marc retreated before the man could ask him anything else. When he joined the cluster around Sarah he noted that three of the group had adopted the familiar expression of people focusing on their retinal AR feeds. Then, almost in unison, several pulled out pocket pads and tapped a few commands on them. Marc looked over at Sarah, but she was watching the physicists expectantly.

'Excuse us . . .' said a man Marc recognized as a senior CERN technician called Carlo '. . . but it looks like the beam is about to be turned on shortly for today's run and we need to get back to the VENICE control room.'

Sarah looked perplexed. 'Venice?'

'Sorry,' said Carlo with a wry smile, 'VENICE is the name of our dark-matter detector. It stands for Very Energetic Neutralino-Ion Collider Experiment – basically a giant underground camera the size of a fifteen-storey building.' He saw the amused look on

Sarah's face and added, 'Yes, I know. Sometimes it seems like we spend as much time inventing acronyms for our experiments and equipment as we do carrying out the science itself.'

'Huh, that's nothing,' said Sarah, 'you should hear some of the names of our space missions.'

Marc turned to her. 'They're colliding a beam of dark matter onto an iron target and analysing those highly rare collisions when they take place.'

'And how is this related to the Odin Project?' she asked.

'Well, we still need to understand how the unstable, heavier dark-matter particles decay, so this sort of routine experiment is a vital part of the Project.'

Carlo nodded at them. 'Why don't you come along? You can see for yourself.'

'OK,' replied Marc. 'Let me first go and let Qiang know I'm disappearing for a bit.'

The dazzling sunshine contrasted with the dim lighting inside the lecture theatre complex and the polarizers on Marc's contact lenses kicked in within seconds.

'The VENICE building is about a klick away, so we'll take the buggies,' said Carlo, leading Marc and Sarah across the quad to where several of the CERN vehicles were parked. The three of them climbed into the first one. Carlo tapped the destination on a small display screen on the dashboard and the car moved off silently.

As they joined the CERN perimeter road Carlo pointed to a large grey structure in the distance that looked more like an aircraft hangar than a science laboratory. 'The VENICE complex is housed inside that building over there.'

'Presumably we won't see much of the detector itself,' said Sarah, 'since all the action is deep underground.'

Carlo nodded. 'Afraid so. You'll have to make do with the inside of the control room. Definitely not advisable to go down to the guts of the accelerator since this is the dangerous form of dark matter, the stuff that decays into nasty products that will do a lot of damage to living tissue.'

The rest of the short drive was covered in silence. Marc looked over at Sarah, who was staring out of the window lost in thought. He followed her line of sight – patterns of colourful lilies lined the roadside – and he wondered what was going through her mind. He had hoped to be able to spend more time with her, to get to know her, but they had both been incredibly busy recently.

They arrived at the VENICE building and followed Carlo inside. Marc enjoyed telling visitors that the aircraft hangar-sized structure was just the tip of the iceberg – the top bit of the VENICE complex that was above ground and which housed the all-important control room. And it was to this centre of operations that Carlo led them, their footsteps echoing around the building. Once inside the air-conditioned room, Carlo excused himself and went over to talk to several scientists who were staring up at two large screens displaying a myriad of scrolling numbers, graphs and colourful diagrams, showing the status of the experiment. Marc and Sarah stood and watched as about twenty other scientists busied themselves with their computer screens. Several turned and nodded to Marc then quickly returned to concentrate on their tasks.

'This is all just official protocol, you know,' Marc whispered to Sarah. 'Because Fabiola, the CERN Mind, will have everything under control. She always does.'

Sarah nodded. 'Not surprising really. An AI, plugged in and networked to millions of electronic components, is much better placed to fix any technical problems herself rather than rely on us flawed humans.'

On a whim, Marc grabbed Sarah's hand. 'Come with me. I want to show you something.' She looked puzzled and amused but didn't resist. He escorted her back out of the control room, down a ramp and across the cavernous building past an area filled with cranes and other heavy lifting equipment. He knew the perfect spot to get a closer look at the VENICE detector. Anyway, they would just be in the way in the control room. Their route eventually led them across a twisting metal gangway where they had to duck under pipework and tread carefully over hundreds of thick cables on the ground.

As they walked, Marc talked about the CERN Mind. 'As you can probably guess, Fabiola isn't networked to the Cloud, so there's little chance of cyberterrorists or hackers getting into her systems.'

'I think Fabiola is brilliant,' said Sarah. 'There's an air of confidence and control about her that's reassuring.'

Marc grinned. 'Well, that's the idea, of course,' he said. 'The human-looking avatar's appearance and voice were designed to exude complete competence. In fact, I sometimes think of her as supernaturally omnipresent.'

They climbed up a metal staircase and onto a walkway that stretched across a vast concrete chasm in the centre of the building. After a few metres, the walkway widened out to a viewing platform. They had arrived at one of the twenty holo stations scattered around the lab. 'Watch this,' he said, touching a wall display, and two overhead projectors began to hum. Like a phantom materializing in between them, the CERN Mind suddenly appeared as a human-sized holographic projection, startling Sarah, who stumbled back a step.

'Hello, Marc. Hello, Sarah. What can I do for you?' said Fabiola in her gentle voice with its unmistakable Italian accent.

Sarah looked delighted with this party trick. 'I know I shouldn't be surprised. She's running the entire CERN complex and so can identify everyone who's on site, but it's still nice. Hello, Fabiola.' Fabiola smiled. She'd always looked to Marc so much like the real person on whom she was based, and whom he knew so well, that he sometimes had to remind himself that he was talking to a computer and not a human being. But for people who had never met the real Fabiola Gianotti, the avatar looked like a kind, elderly aunt from some fairy tale.

He addressed the hologram. 'Fabiola, can you tell us what's happening here today?'

'Certainly, Marc. We're carrying out a routine experiment. In ten minutes, I'll be generating a neutralino beam at a luminosity of ten to the power of eleven particles per pulse and directing it onto atoms of iron in a target at the centre of the VENICE detector located beneath us.'

'Thank you, Fabiola. Well, in that case we won't take up any more of your time as we know how busy you are.'

'On the contrary, Marc, I am happy to discuss this with you, if you like. Unlike humans, I am able to multitask.'

Marc winked at Sarah. 'I know, Fabiola. That was a joke.'

Just then they heard a loud metallic ring, as though something heavy had been dropped. Its echo resonated around the giant building. Marc quickly tapped the hologram off and they both leaned over the railings of the walkway and peered into the large concrete cavern, twenty metres below.

'Was that the dark-matter beam hitting the iron target?' joked Sarah.

'Oh, very good. You solar physicists are so droll,' chuckled Marc, but he continued to concentrate on the floor far below them. Although he hadn't ever been down there, he knew it formed the roof of the shielding above the giant particle detector itself. He could see several manhole covers that would provide ways down into the bowels of the colossal instrument, deep underground. *Hmm . . . probably nothing. Just strange that there would be anyone down there right now—* Just then, he caught a glimpse of movement over on the far side. Someone – it looked like a man – disappeared into an open hole in the floor.

*What the fuck? . . . Who would be crazy enough . . . no, stupid enough . . . to go down there just as a run is about to start? If the beam was switched on now that would be a suicide mission.*

He felt Sarah touch him lightly on the shoulder. 'Hey, you OK? You look like you've seen a ghost.'

He shook his head. 'Not a ghost, no. A real live idiot climbing down into the detector.' He kept staring over at the open manhole through which the man had disappeared, hoping he would emerge again.

As he watched, another thought bubbled up to the surface of his consciousness, and now it hit him like a freight train.

Fabiola had said that the beam of neutralinos had a luminosity of ten to the power of eleven. What to mere mortals would be just numbers with lots of zeroes, was for Marc Bruckner a world of mathematical symbols, colliding particles, heat and light. Such a high luminosity was one hell of a lot of dark matter concentrated onto one spot – in fact, a million times more 'punch' than there should be. It had to be a mistake. Yet that's what Fabiola had said, and Fabiola was a powerful AI that wouldn't just make a mistake like this. What the hell was going on?

He turned to look at Sarah. 'I know for sure he shouldn't be down there. But I think something else is very wrong. I have a horrible feeling *we* shouldn't be here either.'

Sarah stared back at him. 'What is it?'

He took a deep breath. 'The intensity of the neutralino beam is too high. It's even higher than the beams we used in the Antarctic test, and they caused one hell of a bang. The information Fabiola gave us can't be right.'

He spun back to the wall and tapped the pad to reactivate the holo. When the avatar of the CERN Mind materialized again, he said, 'Fabiola, why is the beam intensity so high?'

The silver-haired avatar smiled again. 'This luminosity is required to achieve optimum results for the current run.'

'What fucking optimum results?' Marc shouted. He was starting to panic. 'You do know what sort of energy would be produced with a ten to the eleven luminosity, right?'

'Yes, Marc. When the first pulse hits the target, it will release an energy equivalent of twenty-three kilotons of TNT – the power of a small thermonuclear warhead. I have estimated with 99.97 per cent certainty that this will happen. No other pulses will be necessary.'

His mouth suddenly went dry and tasted acidic. Was he going mad? Did the CERN Mind just say she was about to generate a dark-matter beam that would destroy CERN? For a moment, he was lost for words. Then, 'You bet your digital ass there won't be any more pulses. Because there won't be any more CERN! Fabiola, switch off the beam, now. I command you.'

'I'm sorry, Marc, you don't have the authority.' The hologram smiled sweetly, like a mother telling her small child he
couldn't have another cookie.

He looked over at Sarah, who was just staring at the holo.
She now turned to him. 'We should get back to the control
room and warn people.'

'This is quicker,' he said and, keeping his voice as steady as
he could, he addressed the Mind: 'Fabiola, patch me through
to the control room.'

Instantly, an image of the control room appeared on a screen
on the wall behind the hologram. He knew at once that he
wouldn't be telling them something they didn't already know.
All around the room, people were shouting. Some were relaying
data, others barking orders. One or two were just sitting back
helplessly staring at computer screens no longer under their control. Carlo suddenly appeared in close-up, sounding frantic and
scared. 'Marc, sorry, can't talk now. We have a crisis.'

'I know, Carlo. Some fucker has just hacked Fabiola! Look,
I'm closest to the detector, so I'll see what I can do.'

'Hang on,' replied Carlo. 'We're trying to get back into the
system, but it seems Fabiola has locked us out. None of the
standard override protocols seem to be working. We're sending
a team over. You should stay where you are.'

'Sod that, Carlo. Anyway, someone's already down there now.
You do know that, right? Just tell me this: how long do we have
until the beam comes on?'

'Just under eight minutes. Marc, if we can't get in and stop
the run in the next two or three minutes we will have to evacuate.'

'Evacuate to where?' screamed Marc. 'If this is the work of
the Purifiers and they destroy CERN then that's curtains for
the Project, and humanity.'

He turned back to Sarah. 'I'm going to try to switch off the
beam manually. You need to get the hell out of here, quick.' He
wondered whether the man he'd seen had realized what was
about to happen and was already a step ahead of him. Or was
he part of whatever was going on?

'The hell I am. You might need my help,' said Sarah. 'Besides, if this thing goes off where did you think I was supposed to go?'

Marc didn't stop to argue. Nodding, he said, 'Shit, Sarah, I'm sorry I've got you mixed up in this. OK, come down after me.'

He opened a gate in the railings, turned around and started to climb down a metal ladder bolted to the wall. He could hear Sarah's feet just above him. His hands were sweating, and he almost lost his grip. It didn't help that he was shaking too. He didn't like heights at the best of times, but he managed to push aside the thought of how far he would fall if he slipped.

He jumped the last five rungs and landed awkwardly. But he was up and running straight away across the featureless expanse of concrete towards the manhole cover. Without looking back, he heard Sarah running a few paces behind him. Their footsteps echoed off the walls of the chamber. Marc reached the opening where the man had disappeared and knelt down to peer into the blackness.

'Hello? Who's down there?'

No response. Shit, they'd have to go down into the detector – there was no way back now and the seconds were ticking by. He spun round and dropped his right leg in, feeling with his foot for the ladder rung. As soon as he found it, he lowered the rest of his body into the blackness and started the climb down. No time to act the gallant gentleman and wait for Sarah.

Three metres later he hit the ground and gave himself a few seconds to get accustomed to the dark. The room was crowded with instruments blinking their coloured telltales, and the minimal lighting lent everything an eerie alien glow. He was accosted by a dozen different sounds, from the hissing of vacuum pumps and the hum of magnets to the beeps of detectors, sensors and alarms. It seemed every bit of space was being used. He was fighting off his feelings of claustrophobia as Sarah joined him.

They quickly followed signs pointing to an elevator. When they reached its wide metal doors, Marc pushed the button and heard the whirring of a distant motor. It seemed to take for ever for it to arrive, but at last the doors slid open and they stepped into its spacious interior. It was clearly designed to transport many people at once, or large pieces of kit, in contrast to the narrow entrance in the roof they had just used.

'Where does this take us?' Sarah asked as they began to descend.

'Down six storeys to the core of the detector. The dark-matter beams haven't been generated yet, but the energy of the protons circling in the main ring is already being ramped up. A siren goes off when the dark-matter beam is on, and if we're still down here then— I don't know how long we've got or even what we can do, but we have to try.'

'Well, given what Fabiola just told us, I don't suppose it matters whether we're down here or back in the control room. We'll be vaporized either way,' said Sarah in a cold, flat voice.

The elevator doors rumbled open, and they were greeted with the sight of a vast underground cavern. On any other occasion it should have taken their breath away, but Marc wasn't in the mood to admire feats of technology. The hum of the electronics here was even louder than it was at the top. Sweeping his gaze around the chamber, he suddenly caught sight of movement over on one side. It looked like there were two people, a man and a woman, with their backs to him. They were crouched down in front of a piece of equipment and hadn't heard the arrival of the elevator over the background noise. Marc's initial reaction was one of relief, that someone was already here dealing with the situation.

'Hey,' he shouted, hurrying over to them, 'how's it going? Can you override things from here?' But they still seemingly couldn't hear him.

'Hey!' he shouted, louder this time.

The pair twisted their heads around. They appeared startled by the interruption. Marc could see clearly now that they had been working on what looked like an old-fashioned laptop perched on a wooden stool.

The man – who had a wiry frame and pale face beneath lank dark hair and who looked like he could be any other regular accelerator scientist – suddenly jumped up to face him and, with a cry of rage, picked up a metal bar lying on the ground next to him, then rushed at him like a wild animal protecting its domain.

'What the—?' Marc watched, hypnotized, too stunned to move.

As he ran towards Marc, the man twisted his body, lifting the bar above his head with both hands like a medieval knight wielding a longsword. By the time Marc came to his senses it was too late and his attacker was upon him.

The man's mistake was not to slow down as he approached. As he began to swing the heavy bar towards Marc's head, it didn't respond quickly enough. The split second it took for it to arc round was all Sarah needed. She crashed into him from the side, sending them both sprawling, and the bar clattered across the floor.

Marc didn't hesitate. He ran towards them, picking up the bar on his way. 'Right, you're going to tell me what the fuck you're—'

But the man had already scrambled to his feet and was sprinting towards the still open elevator doors. Marc thought about giving chase, but decided he had a more pressing issue to deal with. He turned to Sarah, who was getting to her feet and rubbing the side of her head.

'Thanks for that. Are you OK?'

'I'm fine. Look, the woman's gone too.' She pointed to the abandoned laptop a few metres away.

They ran over to it and stared at the still open command windows on the screen.

Marc's heart was pounding, and he tried to clear his head. He couldn't afford to panic now, in what little time they had left. 'Right, we have to assume that whatever they were doing is connected with hacking into Fabiola. But I don't get this. It's all just so low-tech. Why would sophisticated cyberterrorists use decades-old technology . . . and why would they need to be down here in person, knowing that they would be caught up in the blast if they succeeded?'

'I think I can guess,' said Sarah, still breathless. 'Fabiola can't be accessed from the outside world, so the only way to hack her would be to get into her base-level machine code, from the inside.'

Marc nodded. 'And they would have assumed there'd be no interruptions down here.' He knelt down by the laptop and stared at the screen filled with lines of code.

'Ah, shit. What the hell are we supposed to do? We don't have network access down here inside all this shielding, so we can't get help.' Marc's mind was racing. But maybe he could still shut Fabiola down. Their only hope was if the laptop was indeed plugged deep into her command level.

He began to type and executed various Unix commands, but nothing he did seemed to have any effect.

Behind him, Sarah suddenly stood up and shouted, 'Look, I'm no use to you here, so I'm heading back to let the guys in the control room know where you are. We need their help.' Without waiting for a response, she turned and ran towards the elevator. For a split second Marc thought about stopping her. What if she bumped into the terrorists? What good would it do if she made it back to the control room in time? How many more minutes, possibly just seconds, did they have, anyway? He pushed the thoughts away and turned his attention back to the screen.

Suddenly, he heard Fabiola's voice, loud and echoing above the background noise. It had the same gentle, almost reassuring quality as ever, which made it all the more chilling.

'You are accessing forbidden code, Marc. Please desist now.'

*Good*, he thought to himself, *I'm getting under her skin.*

Fabiola's repeated warnings reverberated with increasing urgency around the chamber. He tried to ignore them. He knew he just needed to find the correct reboot commands. His fingers danced around the keyboard as he tried to recall his almost forgotten programming knowhow.

Then, just as suddenly as it had started, the AI's voice went silent, and the computer screen went completely blank. Marc's fingers hovered above the keyboard, waiting. Had he done it? Had he really reset an AI Mind? Suddenly, two words popped up in the top left corner of the screen. He recognized them as the two best-known words in computer science, representing the output of the most basic program anyone could write – two words that became famous decades before he was born, but which still carried significance for anyone with coding knowledge. They said simply:

```
hello, world.
```

Marc stared at the screen for a few seconds. Of course, even a sophisticated AI like Fabiola would operate fundamentally on deep neural net architectures using reinforcement learning. Rebooting her really did mean wiping her memory clean.

His hands were now shaking uncontrollably, and he felt beads of sweat running down his temples. The deafening noise had stopped, as though a number of the machines had shut down. It had to be the scientists back in the control room. They had taken over manual control and stopped the run. Euphoric relief washed through him and he started to stand up, aware that his knees felt stiff. But he didn't get very far. He felt a sudden bolt of excruciating pain in the back of his head and everything went black.

For a few seconds after he came to, Marc couldn't figure out where he was. All he knew was that he had a splitting headache and the bright lights above him were not helping. As his surroundings swam into focus he made out a sea of concerned faces hovering over him. He recognized Carlo and tried to sit up, to speak, but a wave of dizziness overwhelmed him, and he flopped back down again. 'Don't try to move, Marc,' said Carlo. 'Enough heroics for one day, eh? You've been out cold for an hour.'

He tried to recall what had happened. He'd been down in the bowels of the VENICE detector. And he'd shut down the CERN Mind.

'Is the beam shut off?' he croaked. 'Is everything OK?'

'Yes. Thanks to you. We had less than fifty seconds to spare before we'd all have been vaporized.'

It came back to him now. 'What about those two who tried to sabotage the experiment? Were they Purifiers? I guess one of them hit me.'

'We don't know. There's no sign of them yet. But lab security and Geneva police are searching the lab. In fact, they would
like to speak to you as soon as possible to get an ident.'

Marc tried to sit up again, more slowly this time. 'Where's
Sarah? Is she OK?'

He saw her pushing her way in to him. 'I'm here, Marc. I'm
fine. These guys showed up just in time, but not before one of
the two we interrupted had hit you over the head.'

Marc grunted. 'Out of sheer bloody spite because we'd ruined
their party.' He was relieved Sarah was safe. Hell, he was
relieved CERN was safe. Those Judgement Day nutters seemed
keen to sabotage any plans that would rescue humanity. If this
was the work of the Purifiers, then maybe they had yet to realize that there was an option B – that the best way to ensure a
quick and decisive end to humanity would be to wait for the
endgame when the Odin Project was ready, then strike. Maybe
they weren't as smart as people thought. Hacking a Mind with
a museum-piece laptop and hitting people over the head – presumably with that fucking iron bar – didn't sound like the work
of sophisticated cyberterrorists. But they'd still come close to
succeeding. Too close.

By attempting to destroy one of the three labs capable of
producing beams of dark matter they were clearly still aiming
to prevent the Odin Project from getting off the ground in the
first place. But it wouldn't take long for them, and the rest of
the world, to realize just what a risk this entire venture was.

# 32

*Wednesday, 3 July – Juliaca, Peru*

DESPITE THE EVEN TIGHTER SECURITY AFTER THE CERN attack, the Project continued to move forward rapidly. But with only two months to go now to the planned Ignition, there was still so much to do. Sarah was relieved not to be directly involved with operational matters, or the messy world of politics, any longer. She had, however, found herself inescapably grouped with Marc and Qiang as one of the talismanic global representatives of the Project. She still loathed all the media attention this entailed, but she knew she really had no choice. Anyway, Marc and Qiang were good company. She continued to work hard at not falling for Marc's charms, but she sensed deeper feelings for him growing inside her that had nothing to do with any superficial physical attraction. Still, she had kept them locked away. These were no times for starting up a relationship, particularly with someone she had to work with professionally.

Having dealt with the world's press at CERN following the failed attack, their attention was now focused on Mag-4, under construction high on the Andean Plateau in southern Peru, one of six facilities around the world housing the giant magnets that would bend the beams down into the ground. The three physicists had come to the site to witness the next test: to see if a pulse of heavy neutralinos would indeed behave in the way Marc and Qiang had proposed – that the particles would decay at just the right moment to be bent by the magnets. Their official brief was to offer encouragement, discuss the science with the locals and generally provide the media with the charm offensive so vital in the face of continuing public opposition and widespread, but understandable, fear. Along with the other countries on the Pacific coast of South America, Peru had got off relatively lightly during the CME back in March. The initial devastating radiation burst had hit before 6 a.m. local time and most of the population had still been in bed, not out in the open.

As soon as she got off the plane at Juliaca Airport, Sarah could sense that the atmosphere was thinner. And despite the coolness of the air inside the bustling terminal, once out in the harsh sunlight she felt its warmth. They'd been warned of the discomfort they were likely to feel at such altitude – four thousand metres above sea level – and not to exert themselves for the first few days until they had acclimatized. So, she was grateful that a couple of bots took their luggage on ahead, weaving smoothly on their treads through the crowds entering and leaving the terminal building.

She didn't feel tired. The one-hour, ten-thousand-kilometre hyperskip from Geneva to Lima had been uneventful, as indeed had the much shorter heli flight across to Juliaca.

The city of Juliaca, in the Puno region of southern Peru, lay to the northwest of Lake Titicaca. It was a sprawling metropolis of over a million inhabitants and a thriving trade centre, forming the hub that linked Peru's three largest urban areas of Lima, Arequipa and Cusco to La Paz across the border in Bolivia.

A man in dark sunglasses was waving to them from across the road outside the terminal. Sarah noted that, in contrast to the three scientists' casual attire, he was wearing a three-piece grey suit, its buttoned-up jacket straining against his waistline and the fabric so shiny it glinted in the bright sunshine. She assumed this was their host, Dr Arnau Diaz-Torres, the Mag-4 chief engineer. He stood beaming at them as they approached, his thick, well-groomed moustache speckled with grey.

'Welcome. Welcome to Peru,' he said in his heavy Spanish accent, extending a hand to Sarah. 'Dr Maitlin, it is a pleasure to meet you. I have watched you on the news so much in recent months that I feel I know you.' He turned to Marc and Qiang. 'And, of course, you two gentlemen are my physics heroes. You are true giants of science.'

'It's a pleasure to be here,' replied Sarah. 'I hadn't quite expected it to be so warm, given this is your winter and we are so high up.'

'Oh, just wait until the sun goes down. The contrast in temperature between day and night up here is greater than in any desert.'

The doors of the car waiting alongside slid open and Sarah was a little surprised to see a driver inside. Diaz-Torres saw the look on her face. 'Because of the heightened security, we have decided that a human driver is the safer option. Humans are less likely to be hacked.' He laughed. 'Especially when we have such important visitors. We will of course have an army escort too.'

Sarah noticed for the first time the two jeeps on either side of their car, each one containing several heavily armed soldiers. They only slightly reassured her. She hadn't truly felt safe in a while, despite her round-the-clock protection. If the Purifiers wanted to strike, she was sure they'd find a way. Since the failed attempt to destroy CERN, they had been quiet, but no one believed they had given up. And yet the authorities were no closer to defeating them.

As they pulled away, Diaz-Torres said, 'You will be staying in accommodation within the high-security Mag-4 compound. But if you don't mind, we will go straight to the facility and I can show you how the Peruvian sector of the Odin Project is progressing.'

She detected more than a hint of pride in the man's voice. He then reached into the satchel on the seat beside him and took out various items and passed them around. 'I have taken the liberty of providing you all with sun hats and sun-block pills. These days the dangers of UV radiation are even greater than usual so far above sea level.' Sarah accepted her provisions and thanked the Peruvian, but when he turned his attention to Qiang, she exchanged a quick glance with Marc. They didn't have the heart to tell Diaz-Torres that they had everything they needed already in their rucksacks. Still, it was a sweet gesture.

They drove out of the airport and along the busy roads that skirted around the city centre. She stared out of the bullet-proof glass window, only half listening to Diaz-Torres as he explained how life had changed in Juliaca over the past few weeks. 'The city's population has been swelled by many thousands. And it isn't just all the scientists, engineers, technicians and the three thousand Mag-4 construction workers. We have bus-loads of tourists arriving each day, as well as many traders from around the region.'

It also looked to Sarah that a large fraction of the Peruvian army was making its presence felt. Groups of armed soldiers stood on every street corner and army vehicles rumbled up and down the main streets.

After about twenty minutes, they were on the winding highway north of the city. Sarah had visited the astronomical observatories in Chile, high in the Atacama Desert, but this landscape was even more spectacular. The Altiplano, or 'high plain', was more commonly known throughout the world as the Andean Plateau, where the seven-thousand-kilometre-long Andes mountain range was at its widest. On both sides, beyond the barren hills bulging up indiscriminately over the otherwise flat ground, were impressive peaks: to her left, like an array of giant shark's teeth, was a chain of majestic-looking volcanoes, and to her right, in their dramatic, serrated, snow-capped splendour, rose the Andes mountains themselves. The only vegetation she could see, stretching into the distance, was highland grass. Diaz-Torres explained that this was the *ichu*, the staple grazing food for the herds of llamas and alpacas.

They passed a picturesque lake and surrounding marshland almost entirely covered by a vast flock of pink flamingos, a sight Sarah found enchanting. Then, without warning, they were there. The view that greeted her around the next bend was impressive: a wide, flat plain surrounded on three sides by fierce-looking mountain ranges. At first, it was difficult to appreciate its scale, but she estimated it was about five to six kilometres deep and three kilometres wide. Along the entire length of the road, an imposing high fence had been erected, isolating the area from the outside world.

The car slowed down as the driver negotiated the dense traffic of other vehicles and people surrounding the compound. It looked as though an entire town had suddenly sprung up outside. Sarah's senses were bombarded with a sea of colour, sound and activity. There seemed to be everyone from tourists, well-wishers and curious onlookers to demonstrators and religious fanatics – including a group of end-of-the-world doomsayers in their long grey gowns and shaven heads, who were being watched carefully by the soldiers lining the fence. All these people mixed with the locals, and all seemed curious to witness the wonder of engineering in the distance that was part of the plan to save the world.

She watched as street traders tried to catch the eye of anyone venturing close enough to their colourful displays of traditional Peruvian hats, ponchos and pan pipes alongside hastily manufactured miniature models of the giant magnet and other Project-related souvenirs, all laid out on makeshift tables. The tourist industry seemed to be thriving, and it gave her an odd sense of faith in humanity. She even spotted tourists paying locals to take their picture posing with docile and cute-looking llamas. Even during such uncertain times, some things don't change.

Qiang laughed. 'The circus has come to town.'

'The biggest circus South America has ever seen,' agreed Diaz-Torres. 'And over there is the main attraction.'

Sarah followed his gaze beyond the crowds and the high-security fence towards a giant grey dome in the distance, inside which Mag-4 was being built.

'If this is a circus, then that is the Big Top, yes?' said Diaz-Torres. 'Did you know the locals already have a name for Mag-4?

In our native Aymaran and Quechuan languages, they call this place *Ukhupacha waka*, which means "Temple of the Inner Earth".'

Sarah watched Qiang practise the words under his breath; then, turning to Diaz-Torres, he said, 'I'm afraid the only words I know in Quechuan are *Machu Picchu*.'

The Peruvian smiled. 'We are still proud of our Incan heritage, you know. Locals have great affection for Pachamama, the Earth Mother, our ancient deity, and many in my country believe the dying of the Earth's magnetic field is due to mankind's misuse of Nature, which has been an affront to Pachamama.'

'They're not the only ones,' agreed Sarah. 'Everywhere you look, new and old religions are gaining followers. We've raped and pillaged our planet; we've changed our climate; we've destroyed so much. You'd think people would be *losing* faith.' Then, after a moment's hesitation, she added, 'I suppose it's only natural, given the threat we're facing right now. People want to trust the science, but if there's a chance that a higher power can lend a hand . . .' She turned back to look out of the window.

Driving through several gates with increasing levels of security, including biometric checks and sniffer bots, they finally entered the vast compound and a wide, newly tarmacked road that led in a straight line to the Mag-4 facility. From this distance, its scale was deceptive since it was dwarfed by the mountains behind it, but Sarah realized that it must be further away, and therefore much larger, than she had first estimated. As if reading her mind, Diaz-Torres said, 'The reason it has to be so big is because of all the shielding.'

Sarah nodded. 'And at the risk of sounding naive, that's presumably to block all the synchrotron radiation produced when the charged particles are bent by the magnets, right?'

'Precisely,' enthused Diaz-Torres. 'This is basically the world's biggest X-ray machine, but it has nothing to image. The X-rays are an unavoidable by-product when the charginos are forced to change direction. But we still need to stop this radiation from zapping everything in its path.'

They pulled up outside the front of the dome. Sarah stepped

out of the car into the bright sunshine and quickly reached for the sunglasses in her pocket. She looked back along the road they had come, to the perimeter fence and the crowds outside it. They were too far away for their sounds to carry and all she could hear was the faint whistle of wind around the dome and a deep hum of machinery coming from within. She arched her neck back to look up at the structure and, despite her sunglasses, still needed to squint. It was huge.

She turned to see Marc and Qiang already following Diaz-Torres towards the entrance and hurried to catch up with them. Just outside the door they were met by a young man who handed them hard hats.

Sarah donned hers and removed her sunglasses. 'Hard hats suit you,' smiled Marc as he adjusted the strap on his. 'You look like you mean business.'

'I always mean business, Bruckner. And don't you forget it.'

They followed Diaz-Torres in. Sarah had expected to walk into semi-darkness after the bright daylight outside, but it was quite the opposite – the centrepiece of the vast chamber was illuminated by powerful LED floodlights from all angles, giving it an almost supernaturally bright aura.

'Oh, my God . . .' she whispered. Her two companions also stopped suddenly in their tracks, speechless.

A hundred different sounds assaulted their ears. A huge drilling rig at the centre of the dome was the loudest, but backing support was provided by the hum of other machinery, the throb of electric currents, the shouts of the workers, and the incessant sirens and alarms of equipment – ranging from low-frequency horns to high-pitched, ear-piercing bleeps.

Sarah realized Diaz-Torres was smiling broadly as he watched them, clearly happy with their reaction. He had to raise his voice to be heard above the cacophony of sound. 'The roof of the dome is as high as a thirty-storey building,' he shouted, 'just over a hundred metres. As you can see, the concrete shielding is not yet in place, but you get to see the magnets for now. There are twelve dipole magnets, each one forty-two metres in length and five metres in diameter.'

It felt to Sarah almost like a spiritual experience, here inside this vast cathedral to science. The magnets, suspended high above their heads, resembled black missiles arranged along three separate arcs, one above the other, each arc consisting of four magnets, and all held in place by high-tensile carbon nanotube scaffolding.

Sarah put her mouth close to Marc's ear and shouted, 'It looks like some crazy art installation.' He grinned at her.

'As you can see,' continued Diaz-Torres proudly, leading them further in towards the magnets, 'the beam, which will have travelled here from Fermilab in Chicago, comes in from over there.' He waved his hand vaguely.

Sarah and Marc had followed him, but Qiang remained rooted to his spot near the entrance, staring up as though hypnotized by the structure.

Diaz-Torres, now in full flow, continued his lecture. 'And the beam, as it comes in, has three opportunities to be bent. The neutralinos that decay quickly into charginos will get bent by the first set of four magnets in sequence, with each one in turn deflecting the particles by thirty degrees, until they are travelling downwards towards the centre of the Earth. For those neutralinos that decay a little later and which pass straight through the first array of magnets, the second and third set provide further opportunities to catch and bend them. And so—'

Sarah interrupted him. 'Sorry, I thought you said each magnet bends the beam by thirty degrees,' she shouted. 'There are *four* magnets, and four times thirty makes a hundred and twenty degrees. But don't you need to bend the beam by a right angle: just ninety degrees? So why use four magnets when only three should be enough?'

'You are correct, Dr Maitlin, but don't forget the curvature of the Earth. The beam coming from Fermilab is actually travelling along the shortest path to get here – a perfect straight line – and since it does not have to follow the curvature of the Earth's surface it can tunnel straight through the ground. This means it arrives here from underneath us at an angle of just under thirty degrees to the horizontal. So, it has to be bent back by the magnets by more than a right angle – in fact, by a hundred and twenty degrees, which makes our job even harder.'

With the impromptu geometry seminar ended, Sarah excused herself and wandered over to the giant drilling rig positioned directly below the magnets at the very centre of the dome. A circular barrier stopped her from getting too close, but she could see the hole it was boring into the ground. It looked to be about a metre in diameter. So, this was where the beams from all three sets of magnets would be focused and combined as they began the vertical leg of their journey. She recalled the latest Project plans: the early estimates of a one-hundred-metre borehole had been deemed too conservative. Unless the charginos decayed back to neutralinos quickly, they wouldn't get very far once they hit solid matter. So, to be safe, it was decided that five-hundred-metre-deep vertical shafts would be created at each of the eight facilities to accommodate the beam pipes, which would be maintained under vacuum as empty as interstellar space, so as not to disturb the beams. Then once the charginos decayed back to neutralinos the world would suddenly become invisible to them again. Sarah felt she was getting the hang of all this dark-matter physics.

She heard Marc, Qiang and Diaz-Torres come up behind her. Diaz-Torres was still proudly explaining the workings of the facility to Marc and Qiang. He had to shout even louder over the noise of the drilling. 'All the shielding, along the quadrupole focusing magnets, goes in next week, and once that is calibrated we can start our first test run.

'Eventually, when we have to synchronize with the other seven beams we will need to control the pulse energy very carefully. Did you know we are twenty kilometres further from the centre of the Earth here than Mag-5 in Norway?'

Sarah watched Marc's carefully modulated reaction. Of course they knew. He and Qiang must have been through the geometry a thousand time, so it was sweet of him not to wish to hurt Diaz-Torres's feelings. 'Ah yes, of course, we are on the bulge of the equator here,' he shouted back, nodding his head gravely.

'As well as being at high altitude,' said Diaz-Torres, 'which means our beam heading into the Earth must travel further, so we must give it an extra boost of energy to make sure it arrives at Point Zero at the same time as the other pulses.'

Then he added with a flourish, 'In fact, even the tidal forces due to the Moon's gravity are included.'

He stood back, hands on hips, seemingly taking a personal pride in having surmounted so many difficulties.

Sarah was keen to find out what the next stage in testing was. As a solar physicist used to studying whatever the Sun deemed fit to produce and send Earthwards, she wasn't accustomed to designing this sort of experiment and found it fascinating to be reminded of the many problems that had to be overcome. She walked closer to Diaz-Torres, so he could hear her. 'What is this first test designed to check?'

'Ah,' replied the Peruvian enthusiastically, 'if all goes to plan, a pulse of heavy neutralinos fired from Fermilab will be sent here to see if the magnets can do their job. Of course, with just the one beam, it should travel straight through the Earth to the other side, coming out in the South China Sea.'

Qiang nodded vigorously. 'Of course. And that's where Darklab will be waiting!' he shouted. Sarah now remembered why he was so excited. His institute in China had been developing a mini dark-matter accelerator for the past five years and he'd been heavily involved in getting it funded. Now it seemed that it would play its part in the latest test of the Odin Project. It was to be placed on-board a ship that would float above the point where this beam would emerge on the other side of the planet. Darklab would itself produce a small amount of dark matter and fire it down into the sea to meet the Mag-4 pulse head-on. The tiny energy created would then be picked up by the vessel's detectors.

She turned to Qiang. 'But if it's just to see if two colliding dark-matter beams can create energy inside the Earth, wasn't that what the Antarctic tests confirmed last month?'

As soon as she said it, she realized she knew the answer. She held up her hand to Qiang, indicating she didn't need him to respond. Of course, this test was to do two things: firstly, to make sure the magnets were doing their job of bending the beam and that neutralinos were indeed being created; and secondly, to check that they were being sent in precisely the right direction through the Earth.

Unbidden, the sheer scale, complexity and downright conceit of the entire Odin Project hit her, sending her mind reeling. *Is humankind truly capable of pulling this off? Maybe we're kidding ourselves if we think we can play God with our planet.* It was an unexpected notion. She came from a long line of agnostics and atheists and had always dismissed the term 'playing God' as nonsense. And yet, and yet . . . All the time the Project had been just an idea in Marc Bruckner and Qiang Lee's heads – a set of equations and computer simulations – she'd been fine, but seeing it take shape like this now suddenly unsettled her. A billion things could go wrong, a malfunction in a small component somewhere, one simple miscalculation, a bug in a line of code – and it would be curtains. She looked up at the giant magnets suspended high above her head. *What the hell were we thinking?*

# 33

*Tuesday, 10 September – Bletchley Park, Buckingham-shire, England*

A FAINT BREEZE RUFFLED THE TOPS OF THE TREES LINING the cycle path, but the sky was clear and blue. It was going to be another hot day. The temperature in western Europe had broken all records this summer and had nudged above 40°C in Britain for the third year running. Now, the country was in the middle of an early-autumn heatwave. As she cycled to her new job, Shireen wondered what Majid would say if he saw her now, working at one of the world's top cybersecurity organizations. Her old friend had gone back to his university studies after his release. They constantly chatted, but everything they said was now closely monitored and she couldn't tell him any details about where she was or what she was working on.

While she wouldn't go so far as saying she was happy – no one ever talked about being 'happy' these days – her life had become increasingly interesting. She still missed home terribly, of course, and had even managed to visit her parents over the summer. It had been wonderful, despite being accompanied throughout by Savak agents. Even her mother and father didn't know what she was really working on, and although relieved that all charges against their daughter had been dropped, it still puzzled them. All she could do was reassure them that everything was fine. The official line was that she was simply helping the UN on a cyber-security project.

She didn't mind that her university studies had been put on the back burner for now; it was the same for most people these days – all plans, hopes and dreams were currently on hold. It was as though nine billion humans were holding their collect-ive breath, waiting to see whether there even was a future.

And the world didn't have long to wait. The Odin Project was nearing completion, and the moment when the dark-matter beams would be switched on for real, Ignition, was drawing nearer. Now it was just one week away and no one could see beyond that moment.

For her part, Shireen had made little progress of note so far. And time was running out. Whoever the Purifiers were, they appeared to be both well organized and well funded, and her attempts at hacking into their communications network on the dark web had so far proved unsuccessful.

After the CERN incident she had been one of an army of cyber experts assigned the job of uncovering who had been behind it. The Purifiers had not claimed responsibility, but then what group *would* claim credit for a botched attempt? But now, as Ignition approached, security was being ramped up to feverish levels. And work at Bletchley Park was no differ-ent. It suited Shireen just fine being able to come and go relatively freely, even though she knew that every move she made was being monitored and scrutinized. At least she'd been allowed to block out the intrusion into her augmented reality feed and get some privacy back.

She overtook a couple of joggers. It was only a fifteen-minute cycle ride from her apartment, but she was already feeling uncomfortably warm. She wondered what the rest of the cyb community would think if they knew what she had been doing these past few months: working for 'the enemy' to root out cyberterrorism – poacher turned gamekeeper. But then the rules of the game had changed.

Here at the CICT, Shireen almost felt at home. The work at the

Centre for Intelligence on Cyberterrorism was in a high-security compound just outside the city of Milton Keynes, north of London, where she was part of a team of frighteningly brilliant young coders, mathematicians and cyber espionage specialists. Of course, no one ever used the organization's unflattering acronym and the place was known locally by its more popular name of Bletchley.

Everyone here, as far as she could tell, was doing pretty much what Bletchley Park had been famous for one hundred years ago when it was home to an equally brilliant group of young British cryptanalysts and codebreakers led by Alan Turing. Today, Bletchley was a United Nations of geeks, all working together to monitor worldwide cyberterrorist activities.

Most of the people seemed friendly enough. A few, like Koji, a Japanese mathematical prodigy who sat at the desk next to her, were her own age and quite fun to be around. But she seemed to have very little time for socializing.

Arriving at the front gate, she jumped off her bike and wheeled it through the biometric scanner. She locked it alongside dozens of others in the yard, then entered the cool, air-conditioned building. She nodded a greeting to an older man who'd come in just ahead of her. All she knew about him was what Koji had told her in the staff canteen the day she'd arrived, that he had been one of the original MIT team behind the first AI Sentinel.

For the first couple of weeks in June, after the UN had recruited her to work on protecting the Project, Shireen had been something of a celebrity herself. It seemed everyone had heard about her Trojan horse code, and everyone had ideas about how to improve it.

But here at Bletchley she was just another cyb prodigy. The remit of the scientists at Bletchley was clear. In fact, the need for their existence had been starkly highlighted by Shireen herself: that while the AI Minds around the world that ran and protected the infrastructure of society, from transport and financial systems to defence and security, were themselves mostly adequately protected by the Sentinels, there was still a place for human ingenuity to work alongside them.

Most of the time, of course, the Sentinels did a far better job at cybersecurity than any human ever could, since they were able to carry out tasks billions, and often trillions, of times faster, as well as being in constant communication with each other, exchanging the information content of an entire library of books in less than a nanosecond.

She still vividly remembered with nostalgic fondness a hiking trip with her father in the Alborz Mountains when she was thirteen. She recalled being cold and tired, but the scenery had been stunning. They had spent hours discussing AI and the way the world was changing. Her father explained to her that the notion of artificial general intelligence, when machines could do everything humans could, required AIs to be sentient, to develop self-awareness. Otherwise, they would stay just very clever zombies, with no true understanding of what they were doing. All the time this remained the case, humans could keep one step ahead of them. True machine consciousness, he'd said – she recalled this was the first time she'd heard the term 'the singularity' – would not be achieved for many decades.

Since that hiking trip just seven years ago the line between artificial and human intelligence had become increasingly blurred. Passing the Turing test had not meant that computers were now sentient, but it had highlighted instead that what most people thought of as consciousness was no longer so clear-cut. Sure, AIs now had very crude emotional states, but these had mostly been programmed in rather than learned. At best, the most powerful Minds were more like benign yet extreme psychopaths (those scoring close to the maximum of 40 on the Hare psychopathy checklist), in that they lacked the ability to feel basic emotions such as compassion, or to empathize with the emotional states of humans.

But Shireen's job was not to protect or monitor the AIs. She had been given a quite specific task: to infiltrate the Purifiers' network. She knew she wasn't the only one at Bletchley working on this and it was a little frustrating that she couldn't discuss anything with others. Surely pooling their mental resources would be more effective? But she also understood that it was probably safer for her to be doing this alone, following her instincts as she navigated her way through the vast dark web.

Later that morning, just as she was thinking of taking a short break, she received notification of a message sent to her dark web account. It was one that she only used very rarely and which few people had access to.

It was from Sarah. Shireen had suggested she contact her that way if she ever wanted to say something in private. This was the first time Sarah had used it.

She stared at her screen and her heart started beating faster. The message was brief and obscure:

> *Shireen, we have to meet today. Covent Garden 3 p.m.*
> *Tell no one.*

She hadn't even known Sarah was in London, but thanks to her own past experience in avoiding the prying eyes and ears of drones and sensors Shireen immediately understood Sarah's choice of venue. Covent Garden was one of the busiest places in London – ideal if you didn't want to be spotted easily. But what might warrant such secrecy? She quickly sent back a reply.

> *OK. I can be there. What's going on?*

She waited a couple of minutes for a response, but nothing came back. What the hell? Sarah would have sensitive information about all sorts of details relating to the Project, but the only reason she might want to contact Shireen at this point was if she knew something about the Purifiers and their plans.

For her own part, if she was going to get to Covent Garden without raising suspicion, Shireen decided the best course of action was to keep her story as simple and as close to the truth as possible. All staff at Bletchley were on call twenty-four hours a day and had been working around the clock for several weeks now as Ignition drew closer. And while officially everyone was still being positive about the outcome of the

Project, it was also understood that many would want to have short visits to see family and loved ones to say their goodbyes, just in case. Everyone therefore was allowed a few hours off each week on compassionate grounds. Shireen had an aunt who lived in Soho, just a few minutes' walk from Covent Garden, whom she had been meaning to visit for several weeks past. It was the perfect cover.

Within half an hour she was on the high-speed shuttle from Milton Keynes to central London. Staring out of the window and lost deep in her thoughts, she didn't register the city's suburbs flying past. If required, she could go dark – disappear for a few hours so that she was untraceable – but there was nothing to suggest that was necessary yet. Not having any idea what Sarah wanted was frustrating. Anyway, for now let them keep track of her movements. Someone would no doubt have already checked out her cover story, but that was in hand. Her aunt had been delighted when she'd called her to say she would be dropping in.

The train slowed as it approached Euston Station and she checked the time. Midday. She could spend a couple of hours at her aunt's swapping family stories before she had to leave to meet Sarah. Every minute was going to feel like an hour.

# 34

*Tuesday, 10 September – London*

WITH ONE WEEK TO GO TILL IGNITION, MARC HAD BEEN IN
Geneva with Sarah to discuss final arrangements with the rest
of the international task force. Although their relationship had
remained platonic so far, Marc had been finding it increasingly difficult to hide his feelings for Sarah. He still wasn't
entirely sure whether she felt the same but hadn't wanted to
jeopardize their friendship by suddenly coming on strong. On
the one hand, now really was not the time for romance, but
then, if the Project failed and the world was destroyed, he
wouldn't want anything to be left unsaid.

He'd been looking forward to the coming weekend when he
planned to catch up with Evie in London. His daughter was
over in Europe for a week with her high-school art class visiting museums and galleries in several capitals. Last night, he'd
spent an enjoyable hour sharing in her delight as he watched
the retinal video feed she had posted of her day at the Tate and
National Portrait Galleries. He was amazed not only at the
resilience and relaxed attitude of the young towards the Project, but that most schools around the world continued to
function normally during these times.

It was then that his world had come crashing down.

First came the news from the London police that Evie had
gone missing from her hotel. The alarm had been raised by her

school party earlier that evening when her roommate had returned to the hotel from a shopping trip to find her not there. But, as the officers were very keen to stress, she could well have just gone out for a walk without telling anyone, although they acknowledged it was strange that she had also gone off-grid.

Within an hour of talking to the police he was back in his Geneva hotel making arrangements to fly to London – Sarah had insisted on accompanying him and the two of them had packed as quickly as they could. He'd clung to the hope that Evie would return, that she had just gone for a walk and got lost. But his wristpad had pinged as they were about to leave the hotel room. He'd stopped halfway out of the door to look at it.

*Professor Bruckner, congratulations on cheating death in CERN. But now you will help us ensure that Mother Earth cleanses herself of the plague of humankind. If you want your daughter to live long enough to witness Mother Earth's glorious rebirth you will do exactly what we ask. If you inform the authorities about this message she will not live to see another sunrise.*
*Further instructions to follow. Acknowledge.*

Marc had felt his world begin to swim and he'd stumbled against the door, then slumped to the floor. Sarah's voice, asking him what was wrong, had sounded as though it was coming from a great distance. He'd read through the message again. What did they want? What did the message even mean? The mention of Mother Earth indicated that this was from the Purifiers, or someone trying to pass as the Purifiers.

In a shaky voice, he'd spoken into his wristpad. 'Acknowledged.'

He didn't remember much more of that evening, or the flight to London. He had received a call from Charlotte in New York and had tried his best to hold himself together as he spoke to her. She had been hysterical with worry, wanting to catch the next flight over herself. She told him the police in London had spoken to her too and were keen to know if Evie was having any friendship problems, whether there were any girls on the school trip with whom she might have fallen out and which might have prompted her disappearance. Of course not, she had told them. Evie was popular and as well-balanced and sensible as any teenage girl could be. He'd managed to persuade his ex-wife that, for now, there would be absolutely no point in her coming over to London. Evie was bound to show up soon. Maybe her wristpad had been stolen and she couldn't find her way back to the hotel or contact anyone. He knew he hadn't sounded very convincing, but until he had more information he just couldn't risk telling her any more.

'Listen, Charlie, I'll be in London in a few hours and will call you as soon as I hear something.' He hoped he'd sounded calm enough.

So, here they were, sitting outside a café in one of the busiest locations in the crowded metropolis. Waiting. But not just for contact from the terrorists. Sarah had persuaded him that he . . . they . . . should enlist the help of her young cyb friend, Shireen; that if anyone could infiltrate the group and find his daughter, she could.

Marc had taken a lot of convincing. 'Sarah, we don't know what their demands are yet. All we do know is that the Purifiers will stop at nothing to get what they want.'

But Sarah had won the argument. 'Shireen is one of the world's smartest cyberhackers.' She lowered her voice to a conspiratorial whisper. 'I'm sure you know she's working for UN intelligence to infiltrate the Purifiers' network, so no one on the planet is better placed than she is to find Evie. And you know as well as I do that the vital thing now is time. The longer we wait the harder it will be to trace them.'

And so they waited for Shireen. And they waited for instructions from the kidnappers. Marc stared down at his wristpad willing a message to arrive – anything, just as long as he knew Evie was still alive. After a few minutes, he stood up. 'I'm going to get another coffee. You want one?'

'No, thanks,' said Sarah. 'I'll try to eat some of this salad. It's already looking a bit sorry for itself.'

Marc disappeared into the café. He'd been standing in the queue for no more than a minute when his wristpad buzzed. He looked down at it and what he saw made his blood run cold.

*You really should eat some lunch, Professor. We need you at your sharpest.*
*Stand by . . .*

They were watching him.

That meant they would see him meeting Shireen too. He rushed back out again, his heart pounding. Several people turned to stare as he pushed his way through the crowded café entrance. Were the kidnappers among them? And how long had they been tracking him?

The look on his face must have betrayed the panic he felt, because Sarah froze. 'What is it?'

He showed her the message then slumped down in his chair and put his head in his hands. None of this seemed real.

Sarah put her hand gently on his arm and whispered, 'They can see us, but I don't think they can hear us. Remember, we chose this table ourselves, so it couldn't have been bugged in advance, and all the noise around us means no drone mike could pick up what we say if we speak softly.'

Marc looked up at her. She was right, but it didn't reassure him in the least. 'You know we won't be meeting your friend now. It's too risky. You can see that, right?'

Sarah held his gaze for a couple of seconds, then nodded.

Suddenly, his wristpad pinged again. He forced himself to look down at the new message.

*Professor Bruckner, your Odin Project is an abomination and it will not succeed. As its architect, you will now become its destroyer. You will do exactly what we, the Purifiers, tell you, because you love your daughter. If you do then she will come to no harm, but you will only see her again once we are satisfied your task is complete.*

The stomach-churning dread and anxiety he was feeling about Evie was now supplemented by an even deeper sense of foreboding. He tasted bile rising up in his throat. What was it they needed from him? It was clearly something they were confident he would agree to. Until recently, he would have said that a group as ruthless and resourceful as the Purifiers would have had a thousand ways of stopping the Project, but not any more. Since their failed attempt to reduce CERN to a giant crater, the eight Project sites had become physically impenetrable fortresses and surveillance within and around them was bordering on the omniscient, while the security clearances necessary to access any aspect of the Project were becoming so tight that many of the scientists and engineers involved now found it difficult to do their jobs properly. Every conceivable weakness, from cracking quantum encrypted data files to hacking the Minds themselves, had now been addressed.

And yet . . . Had the Purifiers just found the Odin Project's Achilles heel: one of its two creators?

When the third message came through a minute later, he didn't know what to make of it at first.

> *In exchange for your daughter's life, we ask for a simple thing from you. You must give us access to your REAPER-9 code.*
>
> *It would be a shame if you allow some misplaced sense of moral duty to humanity to cloud your judgement. Your daughter's death will not be pleasant.*
>
> *You have 24 hours.*

He stared at it for a few seconds, his mind in turmoil. Then he understood.

When he raised his eyes to meet Sarah's, all he could feel was a numbing sense of hopelessness – it was an experience he knew well, only this time the demons were all too real.

She had read the message too because now she spoke softly and calmly. 'Take a deep breath, Marc, and tell me about the REAPER-9 program.'

He gathered his thoughts as best he could.

'It's a computer code that Qiang and I developed about fifteen years ago. It calculates dark-matter particle properties – their lifetimes, decay schemes and so on. It's a big code – over twenty thousand lines. It's what we used in the work that led to our breakthrough prediction.'

'Your discovery that dark matter self-interacts?' Sarah asked. 'But what's that got to do with the Project? I mean, that's all established science now, right? It's out there in the public domain.'

'It's not as simple as that.' He sighed, still trying to work out how the Purifiers had found this weakness. There were now hundreds of research teams around the globe working day and night on the Project; thousands of engineers were building the giant superconducting magnets, several in some of the remotest parts of the world; accelerator physicists, geologists and engineers were teaming up to finalize the finer details of the dark-matter beams to ensure that each pulse was aimed in precisely the right direction for all eight to meet within a single nanosecond at 'point zero', a volume the size of a peppercorn deep within the molten core of the planet. And yet, the Purifiers had still known exactly what, or rather whom, to target . . .

'You know, their plan is quite beautiful in its simplicity,' he said finally. 'The REAPER-9 program is still a vital part of the calibrations. And they want me to give them access to it. And I can guess why. All they'd need to do is change one line of code – a single line out of over twenty thousand.'

He saw the shocked look on Sarah's face. 'Many years ago,' he continued, 'I was involved in the calculations that first predicted the lifetime of the chargino, the particle that has to be bent by the magnets. The relevant subroutine in the code deals with something called R-parity conservation and it's my numbers that feed into the main program. Changing that line of code would make our estimate of the chargino lifetime wrong.'

'And? What are the implications? I mean, you seem to be talking about lines of code – a simulation – but we will have real beams of particles doing what they do and the entire mission has been set up to make sure nothing goes wrong. What am I missing?'

Marc chewed his lip and shook his head. 'No, the REAPER-9 code is much more than a simulation. If it is altered so as to predict that the charginos will decay back into neutralinos more quickly than is really the case then the energy of the beams, the speed of the particles, will be adjusted to suit the prediction, and the beam will still consist of charged particles when it hits the ground.'

Sarah shook her head. 'I still don't get it. Why calculate lifetimes during the run itself? Why not hardwire these numbers into the accelerator design in advance?'

'Because then we would have no control. The energy and luminosity of the beams will always have tiny error bars and so all parameters have to be constantly adjusted. Remember, for the run to work, all eight beams need to coincide, and these particles are travelling at close to the speed of light. There is no margin for error.'

'OK, so it doesn't work. We'd just try again, right? Once we know, it can be corrected again.'

'Ah, but I know now what they will do. Or at least I can guess. They only want to tamper with the code controlling the CERN beams. They know I still have the access passwords to the codes being run at CERN. The beams from the other two labs would be unaffected.'

Sarah jerked back in her seat. 'What?' She had said it too loudly and a few people seated nearby turned to look at her. She leaned forward and lowered her voice again. 'But if not all eight beams meet at point zero then the perfect balance is destroyed, and the energy pulse gets sent back out again – to the Earth's crust.'

Marc nodded. 'If the CERN beams don't get through then that's three of the eight that are knocked out. The remaining five wouldn't cause a catastrophic event, but there would still be serious seismic activity: earthquakes and tsunamis wherever it emerges. But it's survivable.'

He saw the blood drain from Sarah's face. 'You mean "just" millions might die, rather than billions?'

Marc felt a sense of despair. 'That's what they seem pre-pared to risk – and, more to the point, that's what they seem confident *I* would be prepared to risk in order to save Evie.'

But now that he had explained what he thought their plan would be, he realized there was something bugging him. At first, he couldn't quite articulate it. Then it came to him. 'What I don't understand is why do it this way? Why not knock out just one of the eight beams and bring about the quick annihila-tion of the entire planet? Why three?'

'Maybe because this is easier,' replied Sarah. 'And it still ensures the failure of the Odin Project. Maybe they don't want humankind to bring about its own, sudden demise. Maybe the Purifiers themselves want to survive long enough to see their mission through, to be a part of the slow suffocation of all life as the planet loses its atmosphere. I don't know, Marc. It's all so fucking sick.'

Marc felt he was grasping at straws. 'But this way, we *would* try again. We would have to.'

'No, Marc, we wouldn't. Global opinion would swing away from the Odin Project, maybe back to the MPDs, and that would be that. You know how hard it was to make the case for the Project in the first place. Do you really believe they would sanction a second attempt? Besides, how can you even contem-plate signing the death warrant of millions of innocent people? I know I can never forgive myself for not doing more in Rio back in March. I watched so many people die and just saved myself. This is different. You would be knowingly committing genocide.'

Marc felt anger rise up to the surface. What was she saying? That he would instead sacrifice his own daughter?

'Please spare me the moral philosophy, Sarah. I can't think beyond Evie for the moment. Can't you see that?'

They sat in silence. Finally, Sarah whispered, 'You know we can still find Evie, if you allow Shireen to help. Don't be fooled by her age – that young woman is astonishingly resourceful.'

Marc felt broken and emotionally drained. 'I have to, now, don't I? Otherwise, if I do as they say I will be buying my daughter's life with the blood of millions of others . . . other Evies and their families – people I will never meet. And you know what gets me most? It's that the kidnappers are so sure I would make that choice.'

Suddenly his wristpad buzzed again. But this time instead of a message it showed a grainy-looking video feed. It was very dark and hard to make out, so Marc cupped his hand around it to block out the harsh sunlight. His mouth went dry and he let out a quiet whimper. 'Oh, Jesus, no!' It was her. It was Evie. His daughter was lying unconscious on a rug on a filthy brick floor. Or was she just sleeping? He hoped she was sleeping. The lighting was just good enough for him to make out the gentle rise and fall of her chest. At least she was alive! Behind her, a stained brick wall and curved archway led into darkness. It looked to Marc like a cellar. Or a dungeon. Then, without warning, the screen went blank.

'Oh, my God, Marc, where *is* that?' said Sarah softly.

He was too shocked to answer. Seeing his daughter like that had brought the full, horrible reality of the situation clearly into focus. Finally, he looked up at Sarah, a fire burning in his eyes. 'What time is it? We need to meet your friend.'

As if on cue, Sarah received a message. It was Shireen. She showed it to Marc.

*Go dark. Turn off your devices and disconnect your AR feeds. Then leave your table and walk around to the other side of the piazza. It's busier there and we can lose whoever it is that seems to be watching you.*

Sarah looked at Marc. 'I told you she was good. She's been watching us too. Come on, it's time we fought back.'

# 35

GAINING ACCESS TO SEVERAL COVENT GARDEN SURVEILLANCE cameras had been straightforward enough. Now, standing in the shadows on one side of the bustling piazza, Shireen studied her retinal feed carefully. On one side of the split screen she had a bird's-eye view of Sarah and Marc sitting at their café table, while on the other half she could see the two men who were watching them. One was an older man with a shaven head who seemed to be in charge; the other, younger with a wispy beard, looked like the tech guy. She smiled to herself. The watchers were now the watched. She had no idea what they wanted, but whatever the issue, it was serious. Marc and Sarah seemed tense and animated. She'd hopefully find out soon enough.

She'd realized as soon as she arrived that she wasn't the only one using the camera aimed at the two scientists' table and had tracked down the source of the other hack to a bar on the south side of the piazza – far enough away for what she had in mind. But the timing had to be right. Having sent Sarah the message to go dark she waited until the very last moment before she and Marc stood up to kill the feed from the café camera. She watched as the two men, after a moment's blank shock, broke into an animated discussion, presumably about why they no longer had eyes on their quarry. Shireen smiled to herself. *Not so clever now, are you, boys?* Suddenly, they both jumped up from their table and made their way out of the bar in a hurry, but it would take them a couple of minutes to reach the café – ample time, she hoped, for Sarah and Marc to lose them.

Making sure her baseball cap was pulled down to hide her face, she came out of the shadows into the harsh sunshine. She briefly caught sight of Sarah and Marc and made a beeline for them through the crowd. As she brushed past them she spoke under her breath without slowing or looking up. 'Follow me.'

A minute later, she was standing near the back of a throng of people gathered around a street performer. She couldn't see him clearly through the crowd but whatever he was doing – some conjuring trick, most likely – his patter was so infectiously enthusiastic that he had drawn a large audience. She had flicked on the squelch jammer in her rucksack as soon as she'd arrived. It was more sophisticated than the one Hashimi had given her in Tehran and she was now invisible to any drones or satellites overhead. She hoped it would also shield Sarah and Marc from being spotted once they were within range. Hopefully, it would give her enough time to find out what was going on.

It was just after 5 p.m. by the time Shireen arrived back at Bletchley and she was eager to get started. There were at least ten people still working at their desks, but no one had noticed her come in, their VR visors locking each of them away in a world only they could see.

Back at her desk, she pulled on her visor and accessed the vast repository of information she had built up on the Purifiers' network. For the first time, she now had a real lead to follow, only she had hours rather than days to infiltrate their cyberspace.

Her first task was relatively easy. Before she could find where Evie was being held, she needed to locate the kidnappers, and it didn't take long for her to trace the IP source of the original message sent to Marc the day before. She wasn't surprised to find that the kidnappers had put in place clever diversions, trapdoors and firewalls, but there was nothing she hadn't nego-tiated a gazillion times before. It appeared that whoever these people were, they had covered their tracks in a hurry, and that meant they would have been sloppy somewhere along the line. If she kept prodding and probing, she knew she would find what she was looking for. The Trojan horse spyware she was currently using had been modified significantly by the team at Bletchley. It was now more powerful than the original code she'd created.

Humming along to music as she worked, she let it guide her movements until she was swaying and manipulating her virtual displays in sync with the beat. She had recently become a fan of fusion punk, a synthesis of West African rock and angry Asian K-pop, and she found the urgency of the beats just what she needed to stimulate her thought processes when immersed in the dark web. Despite the magnitude of her task, Shireen felt happy, at one with cyberspace. Almost omniscient.

And while she worked, her spyware code flowed silently through the dark web, a digital ninja searching and probing for weaknesses, following leads, building up correlations, looking for patterns.

By 5:45, she had pinned down the origin of the messages to Marc. They had come from somewhere inside the British Library on Euston Road in the centre of London. And, whereas cyber-hackers would normally build in a delay to make it hard for anyone to determine the exact timing of the hack, in this case, the messages had been created and sent in real time. There. That was very sloppy. It took her less than two minutes to access the library's computer system and locate the record of everyone who had used it during the one-hour window between 2 p.m. and 3 p.m., which was when the final messages had been sent to Marc.

Of the one hundred or so people who'd used the library's computers, only seven had blocked their idents. Of those, five had left several minutes before the final message was sent, which meant there were just two suspects. Both had left the library just after 3 p.m.

All she had to do now was hack into the data from street cameras in the neighbourhood of the library to catch them leaving. Simple. Sure enough, they had left the library separately: a man and a woman, both in their early to mid-thirties. She now had sufficient biometric data to search for them.

The search for a match among the more than ten million Londoners captured on the city's many thousands of cameras took just a few seconds; she found the woman first, in a coffee shop across the road from the British Library. She was sitting in a corner with a milkshake, reading a book and looking like every other customer in there. Nothing suspicious. Shireen was almost certain she could rule her out as a kidnapper.

In contrast, the man was on the move. Each time-coded feed showed him at a different location, enabling her to plot his route across London. The most recent footage was just ten minutes ago when he'd entered the site of what looked like an old warehouse. The satellite data she accessed allowed her to survey the area and a quick search told her that it was near Tower Bridge, south of the Thames, a neighbourhood that had been among the worst flooded in London ten years earlier. Much of it was apparently still abandoned. Very private. Very convenient. She quickly accessed and commandeered a high-flying surveillance drone and zoomed in as tightly as she could onto the derelict building. Was this where they were holding Evie?

Piecing together a sketchy profile of the man from the information she could find on the dark web wasn't so easy. But while she couldn't yet link him to anyone or anything to do with the Purifiers, there was enough to suggest he had much to hide.

Removing her visor, she sat back in her chair and rubbed her eyes. It was almost 7 p.m. and there were five or six other people still working in the office. It occurred to her that she hadn't had anything to eat since the slice of cake at her aunt's apartment at lunchtime. But food could wait; like a lioness, she was closing in on her prey and couldn't afford to stop now. She slipped the visor back over her eyes, leaving the physical world behind again.

# 36

*Tuesday, 10 September – London*

ENTRUSTING HIS DAUGHTER'S LIFE TO A STRANGER – A GIRL barely five years older than Evie herself – terrified Marc. But what choice did he have? This past twenty-four hours had been a living nightmare.

Shireen had told them to avoid going back to the hotel, which was most likely being watched by the kidnappers. They needed to find somewhere with no surveillance cameras and wait for her call. Sarah suggested they take refuge at the Helios Institute, the solar research laboratory in the grounds of University College London where she was a regular guest and could gain access with her visitor's pass.

They had walked the two kilometres from Covent Garden to the Institute in silence. Marc couldn't get the image of Evie lying on that filthy mat out of his mind and was grateful to Sarah for leaving him alone with his thoughts. They didn't meet anyone on their way in. Sarah led him up to the fourth floor then heaved a sigh of relief when her thumbprint was recognized and the door of the office she had used on her last visit clicked open. The office was empty, and Sarah quickly closed and locked the door behind them.

Marc slumped onto a chair by the window and stared down at his wristpad. Shireen had done something to their devices to make sure they were secure. But he kept expecting at any moment to get a message from the kidnappers telling him they knew what he was up to. Within minutes, he was on his feet again, pacing around the small office, stopping every few minutes at the window to stare out at the city bathed in late afternoon sunlight. *Evie is out there somewhere, frightened and alone, and I'm stuck in here. Or maybe she isn't even in London any more?*

Sarah was sitting at the desk, nursing a mug of coffee and staring into the distance, clearly not knowing quite what to say to make him feel any better. He shouldn't have dragged her into all this, but not for the first time he felt grateful that she was with him.

It was just after seven and fully dark outside when he got the message from Shireen via the secure route she'd set up. His heart missed a beat as he read it. 'My God, Sarah. She's found her! Shireen's found Evie already.'

'I told you she was good,' said Sarah, rushing over to him.

He showed her the message.

*Marc, I think they're keeping Evie in an abandoned warehouse south of the river. I've sent you the coordinates.*

Sarah looked up at Marc. 'So, what do we do now?'

There really wasn't much to discuss and he hoped Sarah would understand. '*We* aren't going to do anything. I am.'

'Come on, I know she's your kid, but we're a team now. And I'm not your dutiful fucking sidekick—'

'Don't do this, please, Sarah. You must know I would readily sacrifice my life if it meant saving Evie, but I can't ask you to do the same. I need to see this through. Alone.'

'Let me guess, I stay here where it's safe, while you do your Indiana Jones routine and go beat up the bad guys?'

'It's not like that,' said Marc, with no hint of a smile. 'I know you can take care of yourself . . . It's just—'

'Fuck you, Marc Bruckner.'

'Look,' he said, holding her shoulders gently. He pulled her closer to him and looked into her eyes pleadingly. 'She's my baby girl. And I know you want to help, but if they even get a whiff of what we're up to I don't know what they'll do. And I can't risk that. Not even to spare your pride. I'm sorry.'

Sarah seemed to relax a little and sighed. 'So, what's your plan, Indi? You haven't got a gun or a whip. Dammit, you don't even have a hat.'

Marc smiled weakly. 'Look, if Shireen is right, then I can make it there by myself. At least I have the element of surprise on my side. If I find the odds are stacked against me then we can think of calling in the cavalry.'

Sarah suddenly reached up and kissed him gently on the lips. Somewhere deep inside him was a thrill that Sarah felt the same way about him as he did about her, but right now he was consumed by his fear for Evie. Sarah grinned at him as she pulled away.

'For luck,' she said. 'Please don't try anything stupid.'

*I'm about to go after a bunch of maniacs who are holding my daughter captive, unarmed and with no plan. Define stupid.*

He did his best to give her a wry smile and hurried out the door.

It was a warm and sticky evening and beyond the Institute's courtyard the roads and skies were busy with traffic. It suddenly occurred to him that he couldn't risk getting a road or air cab in case the kidnappers traced him when he paid the fare. He had to stay as inconspicuous as possible. He looked around the courtyard until he found an unlocked bicycle, which he commandeered and wheeled out as quickly as he could, hoping the jammer Shireen had given him did its job. This would take him longer, but he couldn't take any risks. And it meant he could arrive unannounced. He hoped he wouldn't live to regret the delay.

He quickly worked up a sweat as he cycled in the early-evening humidity. He tried to stay as focused as he could, but the image of Evie locked away in the dark warehouse somewhere kept resurfacing. What did he expect to find when he got there? What would he do if the place was guarded, or if there were several people?

The traffic had thinned out dramatically by the time he reached Tower Bridge. He'd not been south of the Thames before and was shocked by the wasteland of abandoned office buildings, warehouses, and tower blocks. The rising sea levels had overwhelmed the Thames estuary, now five times larger than just a few decades ago, with much of the surrounding countryside in south-east England now underwater. London's flood defences had done a reasonable job of minimizing the impact on the capital, but large swathes of land south of the river had been sacrificed. He checked his surroundings against the map on his lenses, trusting Shireen that, like his wristpad, it was now safe to use his AR without being detected.

Many of the roads in this part of the city had become shallow waterways – a poor man's Venice – and he needed to negotiate a route through the few streets remaining accessible to road traffic. The area was deserted and appeared devoid of surveillance cameras, the ideal location to hide someone.

Just then, he heard Shireen's voice in his earphone.

'Marc, I'm tracking you and I can see you're nearly there. I'm still monitoring the warehouse and there's no sign of activity yet. I think you're safe to approach.'

His AR told him that the warehouse was just up ahead. Abandoning the bike against a wall, he ran the rest of the way. Keeping as close as he could to the buildings as he approached, he almost tripped over someone sleeping in a doorway. The man sat up, grunted and waved a large kitchen knife in Marc's direction. Already on edge, the incident gave Marc a scare. He didn't slow down.

The warehouse was in the middle of a fenced-off derelict site. He stood by the open gate for a few seconds to catch his breath. There were no windows on this side of the building, so he sprinted across the open yard to the nearest wall and waited to make sure he hadn't been spotted. Shireen's voice came through again.

'Marc, I can see you at the building. I have no idea what's waiting inside. Please be careful.'

He didn't reply. Instead, he peered around the corner, spotting a small window at about shoulder height just a few paces away. With his back tight up against the wall, he edged towards it and peered inside.

At first, the place looked empty, but then a flicker of artificial light caught his eye. There, in the gloom in the far corner, sat a fair-haired man in a T-shirt. He had his back to Marc and seemed to be staring intently at a computer monitor. On the floor around him was a haphazard array of electronic equipment. Marc couldn't be certain, but it looked to him like surveillance kit. It all seemed very makeshift. If this was their centre of operations, then they were clearly either moving in or moving out.

A surge of anger rippled through him. The man appeared to be alone. But where was Evie? Was there a basement? All thoughts of the folly of what he was about to do now evaporated. He threw caution to the wind and sprinted round the building to find a way in.

*Right, then, dickhead, it's showtime.*

The entrance was a large metal door and he eased it open until the gap was wide enough to squeeze through, relieved that it made no sound. Once inside, he stood still and tried to control his breathing. It took him a few seconds to adjust to the gloom. He was in a narrow entrance hall with what looked like a small kitchen off to his left. To his right was a corridor leading through to the main warehouse. He searched around for a weapon, realizing too late just how unprepared he was for this rescue mission. A filthy plank of wood leaning against the kitchen door looked sturdy enough to do some damage. He picked it up quietly, satisfied with its reassuring solidity, and crept slowly across the hallway. Detritus and broken glass, hard to avoid in the dim light, crunched as he walked and he cursed under his breath as he tried to cross it on tiptoe.

When he emerged into the main open space of the warehouse, he stood still in the shadows while his eyes darted around, searching for any sign of Evie, but he could see no obvious route down to a cellar. At least the man at the computer screen, who was still unaware of Marc's presence, appeared to be alone.

But the element of surprise didn't last.

Without warning, the man suddenly swivelled around in his chair and looked directly towards where Marc stood. Marc had no time to think. Luckily, shock had temporarily immobilized his antagonist and it was all Marc needed. With a howl of rage, he charged.

The world took on a dreamlike quality as everything seemed to slow down. He had halved the distance between them when the man snapped to his senses and reached across the table for a gun. There wasn't enough time to cover the remaining ground and instinct took over. With an underarm swing, he propelled the plank of wood at the man with all his strength. It arced upwards through the air, catching him with a loud crack under the chin, throwing him backwards against the chair behind him and leaving him crumpled in a motionless heap.

Marc was by now on top of him. Snatching the gun off the table, he held it ready to fire, but his caution wasn't necessary. The man was out cold. His mouth was bleeding and hanging open at an unnatural angle – a broken jaw. Marc stood over him for a few seconds then swung round to examine the warehouse space once again, consumed by the need to find his daughter.

'EVIE. EVIE. CAN YOU HEAR ME? IT'S DAD.'

Silence.

After several minutes of desperate searching he gave up. Had he just come on a wild-goose chase? He tapped his wristpad and contacted Shireen. 'Shireen, I'm OK. But there's no sign of Evie here.'

'Shit. Tell me how I can help.'

'OK, stay with me.'

He considered reviving the still unconscious man and beating the information out of him, but instead turned his attention to the computer on the table. There had to be some clues there. The screen showed several windows of live video feed. The one that caught his attention first was a view of the interior of the warehouse itself. He was looking down on himself from above. He craned his neck back and, sure enough, hovering silently a few feet above his head was a tiny skeeter drone recording his every move. *That's how the man knew I was here.*

He looked back at the screen. Another window showed a view of Evie's prison: the rug she had been lying on and the stained brickwork behind it. But there was no sign of Evie. In the top left of the window were the words 'St Pancras'.

His heart sank. 'Shireen, I'm in the wrong place. I'm looking at what appears to be live footage of where Evie is, or was, being held, but I can't see any sign of her. It's definitely the same place as that video footage of her they sent me and it just says, "St Pancras".'

'OK, I am accessing that computer through your wristpad so that I can trace the origin of the feed. Give me a minute.'

Marc felt helpless. The man he'd overpowered was clearly one of the kidnappers, but if Evie wasn't here, what was this place? Some kind of safe house? Was Evie being kept captive in a temporary location and set to be moved here later? A sudden tiredness overwhelmed him as the adrenalin that had been surging through his body just a few minutes earlier, and which had sharpened his senses, now drained away. Had he missed his only chance of finding Evie?

Suddenly a woman's face appeared in a corner of the screen and she was staring straight at Marc. *And they know I'm here. Great.*

He jumped from the chair, not quite knowing what to do with himself. He couldn't stay here, that's for sure. Had he just signed his daughter's death warrant?

*But where am I supposed to go? St Pancras Station? Is that where Evie is, or at least where she was? Stay calm and think, dammit. Think!*

Then Shireen's voice again. 'Marc, I've found it. It's not St Pancras Station, it's St Pancras Church. She's being held captive in the crypt beneath it.'

'And where the hell is that?'

'There was a reason why Evie's captors contacted you from the British Library. The church is just across the road from it.'

'Oh, no,' moaned Marc. 'And that's just a couple of blocks away from the Institute, where Sarah is, where I just spent the past few hours. I've just been on a wild goose chase.' He stumbled out to the road. But Shireen hadn't finished.

'Marc, listen. Firstly, we wouldn't have found the place had you not gone to the warehouse. But there's something else. There wasn't just one of the kidnappers in the library this afternoon. There was a woman too. But I had stupidly discounted her.'

'How do you know this?' He was suddenly finding it hard to breathe and his head began pounding.

'Because I just hacked into her wristpad and put in an auto-track. She's just left the coffee shop where she's been all afternoon. It's up the road from the church. She must have been hanging around to keep an eye on things, and now it looks like she's heading there.'

It was the same woman he'd seen just now and who'd seen him too, he was sure of it. He'd run out of time. He couldn't get there before the kidnappers.

But Sarah could.

'Shireen, tell Sarah. Tell her—' He didn't know what he expected Sarah to do. He would be putting her directly in danger, and in some corner of his brain a warning voice told him this was a grave mistake, that it was not fair to ask her to do this. But what other choice did he have?

'Tell her to get to the church, but to stay out of sight. And if she sees anyone, not to do anything. I'll be there as quickly as I can. And Shireen, call the police. Our cover's blown now so there's no point in being careful any more.'

'OK,' said Shireen, 'I'll get eyes on the church too.' She disconnected.

Never in his life had Marc Bruckner felt so powerless.

# 37

*Tuesday, 10 September – London*

SARAH WAS OUT OF THE HELIOS INSTITUTE BUILDING AND running before Shireen had finished briefing her, the information continuing to feed through to her retinal AR as she ran. In one corner of her field of vision was a map of the block between University College and the church; in another, she watched a live feed from a drone hovering above the church. She could be there in less than a minute.

The church was on a quiet, tree-lined avenue at its junction with the busy Euston Road. She slowed to a walk as she emerged from a side-street opposite, and approached the church more cautiously. She'd seen no one on the drone feed, so with luck she'd beaten the kidnappers back here. The churchyard was blocked off from the road by an imposing metal fence and a padlocked gate looked like the only entrance point. She rushed along the fence and around the side in search of another way in while Shireen told her what she could about the place.

'There's a crypt beneath the church. And images of it online show that its walls match those in that footage. It seems it was originally used as a catacomb and there are still over five hundred bodies entombed down there! But it's been abandoned for the past ten years, the perfect prison. Evie was down there, I'm sure, but I don't know if she still is.'

'Thanks,' panted Sarah. She stood still for a moment to take stock. Staring through the railings it struck her that there was something forsaken, sempiternal, about the place that she found deeply unsettling. All she could hear was her own heavy breathing.

Just then, Shireen spoke in her ear. 'Sarah, it looks like you've got company. You'd better hide.'

She ducked behind a tree just in time, because a second later she heard the sound of an engine. Peering from the shadows she saw a large anonymous black van pull up alongside the fence. A man jumped out and unlocked the gate, pushing it inwards. The entrance was wide enough for the van to drive into the churchyard and out of her line of sight. Were they about to move Evie to another location now that they knew Marc was on to them?

'Sarah, I've taken the drone up to two hundred metres in case they hear it, and its camera resolution isn't good enough to make out details, so it's just your eyes now.'

Sarah looked up and down the street. It was deserted. She edged her way back round to the front gate. There was no one visible in the yard and the van looked empty, so its occupants must have gone inside, down to the crypt presumably. She took a deep breath. Her heart was still racing from her run and was showing no sign of slowing down. Had it been just one person, maybe the woman from the coffee shop that Shireen had mentioned, she might have stood a chance. After all, she still had the element of surprise on her side. But she had no idea how many kidnappers there were.

'Sarah, I can just about make you out at the gate. Please be careful. There's nothing you can do right now so get back out of sight. The police are on their way.'

Shireen was right. But the decision was made for her. One of the kidnappers suddenly appeared from behind the van and pulled open the sliding door on its side. She realized all too late that she was caught in no man's land and in plain sight. He had spotted her. For what seemed like an eternity, neither of them moved, and the spell was only broken when two more of Evie's captors appeared – the man who had unlocked the gate and a woman. They were half carrying, half dragging Evie between them. Her clothing was dishevelled, and her face and hair smeared with dirt. At first, Sarah almost didn't recognize her. The girl looked dazed, as though drugged.

The sight snapped Sarah back to her senses. She was within arm's length of the gate and the open padlock was still dangling from the bolt.

Sprinting forward, she reached out and pulled the gate shut, slipping the padlock off the bolt as she did so. The driver, seeing what she was doing, started running too. She had no more than a couple of seconds. The gate clanged shut and she pushed the bolt across. Despite her fingers fumbling, she managed to slip the padlock back onto the bolt and click it shut just as the man reached the other side of the gate. He snarled and thrust both arms through the bars to grab at her, but she had already stepped out of his reach. She now watched transfixed as he pulled out a key from his pocket and tried to manipulate his hands through the bars to reach the padlock, but thankfully the angle was too awkward to allow him to get the key into it from inside.

The second man now released Evie from his grip and the girl dropped heavily to her knees. Sarah stood rooted to the spot in horror as he walked calmly around behind Evie and pointed a gun at the back of her head.

'That was a very stupid thing to do, Dr Maitlin,' he called over to her. 'My associate is going to pass you the key to that padlock and you will unlock it again, or your boyfriend may find it hard to forgive you with his daughter's blood on your hands.'

What choice did she have? What on earth had she been thinking anyway? That they would just sit around, imprisoned in the churchyard until the cavalry arrived? She slowly walked up to the gate again, her whole body shaking with anger. The man on the other side smiled cruelly at her as he stuck out his hand through the bars, offering her the key.

Just as he did so, she heard a sudden buzzing sound overhead. At first, she thought it must be the surveillance drone Shireen had commandeered. Looking up, she saw instead a weaponized police drone skim over the fence. Without slowing, it fired twice at the armed man standing behind Evie. He was thrown backwards in a spray of red, gun flying from his hand. The driver lunged at Sarah through the bars, but she stumbled backwards out of his reach once again and his hand snatched at thin air. Within seconds, more police drones dropped out of the sky and a cold mechanized voice ordered the two remaining kidnappers to lie down on the ground with their hands over their heads.

Sarah stood frozen to the spot. A robotic voice from one of the police helis above her head boomed out, 'Dr Maitlin, step back from the gate now.'

It snapped her out of her stupor, but instead of obeying, she without thinking rushed over to the gate and unlocked it, then dashed past the dead man to Evie. The girl just stared up at her, eyes wide in shock.

'Come on, Evie, let's get you out of here. You're safe now. I'm Sarah. Your dad has told me so much about you.' Helping the girl gently to her feet, she supported her limp frame and guided her back out to the street.

They hurried across to the other side and sat down on the kerb. The police had now physically arrived on the scene and were pouring into the churchyard. A small crowd of onlookers was beginning to gather outside.

Sarah watched numbly and hugged Evie tight. She could feel the girl shivering as she sobbed silently against her chest.

It was almost midnight by the time Sarah and Marc got to the hospital to be with Evie. Marc had understandably not wanted to leave his daughter's side but had to endure a thorough debriefing at Scotland Yard. Sarah had told them everything she knew and was confident that her story would tally with both Marc's and Shireen's, who were each being interviewed in separate rooms.

Now, perched next to Marc on the edge of Evie's hospital bed, Sarah watched the heavily sedated girl as she slept.

Marc spoke softly. 'One way or another this will all be over in a week.' His attempt at a smile was no doubt meant to be reassuring. Was he trying to convince her, or himself?

'A week suddenly seems an awfully long time, though, doesn't it?'

Marc rubbed his eyes and nodded. 'You know they'll keep trying, don't you?'

Sarah wondered whether the arrest of several of the Purifiers in London would provide enough intel to bring down their entire network. She doubted that very much.

# 38

*Monday, 16 September – Amman, Jordan*

MARC AWOKE JUST BEFORE DAWN AND LAY STILL FOR A FEW
minutes. He thought about the trauma the terrifying ordeal of the
previous week would have inflicted on his daughter. Charlotte
had told him that Evie hadn't been sleeping well, even under mild
sedation, and was waking up regularly from disturbing nightmares. Not surprising really, considering what she had been
through. But given the current situation so close to Ignition, they
had not been able to arrange any counselling for her. Still, she
was a tough kid and if they got through all this, then there'd be
time to worry about any lasting psychological scars. He had to
keep telling himself that this was not his fault and that at least
she was safe now. It had been quickly decided that families and
loved ones of all key personnel connected with the Odin Project
would be taken off-grid and moved into secret protective custody
until after Ignition. But he missed Evie, now more than ever.

He listened to Sarah's soft breathing in bed next to him and
turned to face her. She looked even more beautiful when she
was sleeping. Had they just spent the night together because
they might never get another chance? Or was it the only way
they had of dealing with the stress they were under? Maybe it
would have happened anyway at some point, under more normal circumstances. For him it was probably a combination of
all three reasons.

He thought about going for a run to ease the tension he was feeling but knew that was no longer possible – the hotel was under heavy guard to protect the assembled scientists, journalists and politicians staying there and no one could leave or enter without good reason and without ridiculously tight security. Instead, he climbed quietly out of bed and padded across the cool marble floor to the window. Pulling up the blind, he opened the casement wide and took a deep breath, instantly feeling the contrast in temperature between the air-conditioned room and the warmth outside. He gazed out across the ancient city bathed in sepia early-morning light. After the heavy thunderstorm overnight, the sun was now rising above the distant desert skyline with its usual intensity and belligerence, signalling another swelteringly hot Middle Eastern day. Ignition had almost arrived: thirty-three hours to go. He wondered whether tomorrow's sunrise would be his last, and quickly pushed the thought away. *No, the Project will work.* He'd spent his career trying to tease out the secrets of dark matter and hadn't come this far for his life's work to count for nothing. He closed the window and wandered off to the shower. As he did so, he heard Sarah stirring and turned towards her.

'Hey.'

'Hey to you too.' Sarah stretched and smiled sleepily, the sheet that had been covering her now slipping down.

*I'd better make that a cold shower.*

Seeing him looking at her, Sarah grinned as she pulled the sheet back up. 'What time is it?'

'Early enough. Don't forget, we're meeting Qiang for breakfast before we head off.'

For both political and practical reasons, Mag-8 in Jordan had been chosen as the main centre of operations for the entire Project as the final countdown got under way. There was nothing more that could be done at this point. All the tests and checks were complete, and security was now so tight that nothing barring a major incident was going to stop Ignition going ahead. But the world could not afford for anything to go wrong, so it had been agreed that *if* any of the eight facilities was compromised or developed an unforeseen last-minute glitch, the entire run would be called off.

The threat of a strike of some kind by the Purifiers was uppermost in everyone's minds. But Marc also worried about another aspect of the Project. Tomorrow, control would pass over to the eight AI Minds, one at each facility around the globe. At T-minus three hours, the entire operation would go into Lockdown, meaning that while the Minds could communicate with each other, to raise any last-minute problems that might trigger a postponement, there would be no means whatsoever to intervene from outside. It was a radical decision. But the very real threat of cyberattack by the Purifiers meant that this was deemed to be the safest option.

And so, the fate of *Homo sapiens* would for the first time be in the hands, metaphorically speaking, of artificial intelligences. Marc would never have believed that such a day would come during his lifetime.

For a few days last week there had been a real possibility of delay to Ignition. First Mag-6 on New Zealand's South Island and then Mag-7 on Hawaii's Big Island had had to deal with mild earth tremors. Neither site was geologically ideal, but they were the only two locations in the vast Pacific Ocean that could host the bending magnets. The tremors hadn't persisted, and they didn't seem to be precursors of more serious seismic activity that could have disrupted the alignment of the bending magnets, so the decision was taken not to postpone.

Then, just three days ago, Marc heard that J-PARC Laboratory, the site of one of the primary dark-matter accelerators, had problems with one of the superconducting magnets in its proton beam booster ring. Sections of a fifty-kilometre-long niobium cable wound around its central solenoid seemed to have degraded and had had to be replaced. The problem was quickly fixed, with the only damage being to the pride of the Japanese accelerator engineers.

And now everything appeared to be on track. After months of intense worldwide activity, the most ambitious, and certainly the most consequential enterprise ever attempted by human-kind was ready. He hoped.

It all came down to this now. The waiting.

Over breakfast, Qiang looked agitated and irritable. 'I can't understand why so many VIPs have come to Jordan,' he said. 'I know Mag-8 is the designated epicentre of the whole operation and I can understand the need for the world's media to be here to report on it, but everyone else . . .?'

Marc didn't respond. Qiang was right, of course.

'. . . I mean, either the ground opens up under our feet, and that will be that, or nothing happens, and we won't know if it's been successful for months.'

Marc nodded. 'True. But a lot of people want to be part of history. They will be able to say they were there when the world was saved. Anyway, don't forget that most people have chosen the sensible option of spending what might be their last days at home with their loved ones.' Again, he thought about Evie.

It was Sarah who asked: 'For that matter, why are *we* even here? It's not like we can do anything now.' She had been intending to return to England to be with her family, until she realized she'd left it too late to travel.

Marc sighed. 'I guess it's our moral obligation to see this through. Well, mine and Qiang's anyway. But, hey, we'll all be global heroes when we save the world! And besides, if I'm going to be witness to the *end* of the world then what two better people to share the experience with.'

He'd meant it as a light-hearted joke, but it fell flat.

The decision to choose Mag-8 as the focal point of the operation had been made carefully. It was agreed that giving just one of the eight Minds, the one here in Jordan, override control was the only way to ensure the run couldn't be compromised. Every decision made by any one of the other seven Minds had to be passed through the Mag-8 Mind. The isolated location of the SESAME facility in the Jordanian desert also made security easier.

And meanwhile, the rest of the world became ever more

nervous. All transport had now come to a virtual standstill; banks, offices and schools had closed; in many countries, the military had assumed control. All but essential emergency services had ground to a halt as entire communities gathered together for comfort. Old scores were settled, and differences resolved, sometimes peacefully, sometimes violently. Some people partied, some prayed, while others couldn't shake off an overwhelming sense of nihilism and futility. The number of suicides, by those not willing to wait around to witness the destruction of the planet, soared. A few hid themselves away in underground bunkers in the misguided hope that they would be protected if the Project failed.

Most people, however, remained resolutely optimistic about the success of the Project, unable to contemplate failure. Marc regularly heard the 'hope for the best, prepare for the worst' philosophy, where in this case the superlative 'worst' really meant that. No one could see beyond 12:45 Coordinate Universal Time on Tuesday, 17 September: the moment when all the waiting, all the preparation, all the testing and checking of formulae and calibration of instruments, was over. The moment of reckoning. Salvation or Armageddon.

It would be 15:45 here at Mag-8.

Two Jordanian military approached their table. The younger one, a soldier in army fatigues holding an impressive-looking semi-automatic M26 gun against his chest, stood just behind the senior officer, a man in his forties, immaculately dressed in khakis and sporting a magnificent thick black moustache. He spoke to them in perfect English. 'Excuse me for interrupting your breakfast, but we're about to depart for SESAME in a few minutes and we need all guests accounted for in the lobby.'

Marc and the others nodded their thanks, finished their coffee and readied themselves.

Situated an hour's drive outside Amman, the SESAME facility had begun its scientific life as a synchrotron source, with its first beams produced in early 2020 after many delays and huge political stumbling blocks. Now a major high-energy facility and the largest in the Middle East, it was still one of the few places in the world where Israeli, Saudi and Iranian scientists worked in close collaboration. So, if there ever was a place that symbolized humankind's ability to come together in the face of global adversity, this was it. What also made it an ideal location was that it already had the necessary infrastructure in place to build one of the giant bending magnets.

Marc, Sarah and Qiang arrived together with an army of other dignitaries, politicians and journalists in a large convoy of military vehicles and were ushered inside the building by nervous-looking soldiers. The main reception hall resembled the entrance to a grand palace. Marc marvelled at the high sheen of the luxurious patterned tiles on the floor and could smell the walls had been freshly painted in readiness for the eyes of the world.

As they shuffled along with the other guests he noticed Sarah stiffen. He followed her line of sight: on the far side of the room stood Senator Hogan, talking to a group of men and women. Marc touched her arm gently, making her jump. 'Ignore him, Sarah. I know he can be an unpleasant bully, but as soon as this is over you won't need to have any more to do with him.'

Sarah didn't respond.

They were led through to the main conference centre and asked to take their seats while 3D visors were handed out. They were to be given a virtual tour through each of the eight facilities. Marc had seen this several times before but placed his visor over his head anyway. He found it hard to believe that it was only seven months ago that Qiang had outlined his crazy idea of firing beams of dark matter into the Earth. And yet here they were. It had become a reality. He sat in his seat while he was transported around the world. At each of the eight sites, the local Mind in human avatar form acted as their guide, explaining the physics involved. Right now, any distraction that helped eat up the remaining hours was welcome. He reached out to Sarah, who was sitting next to him and, finding her hand, gave it a squeeze.

# 39

WHILE THE WORLD HELD ITS COLLECTIVE BREATH IN THE final hours before Ignition, Shireen had been busier than ever. The cybercrime centre in Washington, DC, was larger and far busier than Bletchley. No more sedate cycling into work for her. She hadn't left the building in days and hadn't slept for forty-eight hours. Nor could she afford to – not now that she had finally found a way into the Purifiers' network.

Following the events in London the previous week, she had been informed that her unique skills were needed now more than ever. The authorities were certain the Purifiers would try something again, but when, where and how? Frustratingly, there had been no major breakthroughs following the arrests in London. The kidnappers had obeyed instructions without any knowledge of their chain of command. Now, a whole army of cybs had been recruited to try to break into their network using what meagre leads they had.

Since Shireen's role at Bletchley had been leaked following Evie's kidnapping, she'd been informed she could no longer continue to work there and had instead been flown to Washington. She had desperately wanted to get back home to Tehran to be with her parents before Ignition, but all commercial flights had been suspended. She'd had a long and, she admitted, tearful chat to them two nights ago. Yes, she'd assured them, she was being looked after and treated well.

She estimated there had to be hundreds of international cybersecurity organizations now working alongside the Sentinels to ensure that both the hardware and the software of the Project were secure from attack. Many wanted to believe that the threat from the Purifiers had lessened – that the Project was safe.

But Shireen knew better. She had learned early on that this cult was not one to boast about its ideology or one that felt the need to spread its propaganda. After all, its whole *raison d'être* was to bring about the end of humankind, not to recruit new followers. Not any more. And whatever they planned to do, it would already be in place.

Paradoxically, as Ignition Day drew nearer the task of hacking into the Purifiers' network had become easier. As security surrounding all aspects of the Project tightened, the options available to the Purifiers narrowed. Shireen thought of it as a game of chess in which her opponent was losing pieces from the board, limiting the moves available to them.

It was quite clear to her, along with almost everyone else here in DC, what the Purifiers hoped to achieve. Their mission was simple. They saw the dying field as a fulfilment, a vindication, of their ideology. To start with they had tried everything they could to stop the Odin Project from getting off the ground. The slow, certain death of the *entire* human race had been their safest option. But now, with time running out to stop the Project, the quick, albeit incomplete annihilation of life brought about by a catastrophic malfunction if one of the eight beams failed was far more appealing. And with just a few hours left before Lockdown, when all eight facilities would be completely isolated from the outside world, Shireen knew that time was running out for the Purifiers – by deliberate design, no human intervention or interference would be possible after Lockdown.

But that also meant time was running out for her.

Then, just before midnight, she had her first real break. It was so unexpected that, at first, she thought it was a hoax. She'd found an obscure dark-web forum whose members displayed all the right ideological views. By hacking into the account of one of its members, a Texan white supremacist who believed that God was about to destroy everyone apart from the chosen few, of whom he of course was one, she was able to read all the postings. That was when the message came through. It appeared to have been distributed throughout the Purifiers' network, and it was all she'd needed to track it back to its source. Within minutes she'd found it. She stood and raised her visor. She needed a drink of water, needed to clear her head and try and make sense of it.

Shireen returned to her desk. She couldn't speak to anyone here. Not yet. She tried to calm down, hoping no one had noticed her excitement. But all the other cybs in the vast open-plan space had their visors on. The air-conditioned office suddenly struck her as very cold and she shivered. Feeling both elated and horrified in equal measure, she had to decide, quickly, what to do with the information. She needed to speak to Sarah and Marc. Her eyes flicked to the display on her visor. It would be early morning now in Jordan. The morning of the day of Ignition.

She pinged Sarah, and moments later the solar physicist's face appeared in the top right quarter of her visor display. The picture quality was poor, but all but essential communication drones had been switched off to limit net traffic, so the secure line she was using didn't have the necessary bandwidth. But she could still make out dark shadows under Sarah's bloodshot eyes. Shireen wasn't the only one unable to sleep, then.

Not having given any prior thought to how she was going to break the news, she decided to take it slowly.

She spoke softly so as not to be overheard. 'Hello, Sarah. Is Marc with you too?'

'Hi, Shireen. We haven't got you in vision. Are you contacting us through a visor?'

'Yes. Sorry it's a bit rude, but I'm, you know, still working.'

'Ah, OK. Of course, it must be gone midnight for you. But yes, Marc's here too.' The picture shifted as Sarah lifted up her wristpad so that Shireen could see Marc behind her. He smiled weakly and gave a little wave.

Suddenly aware of those around her, she took a deep breath.

'OK, listen. I've found something. The Purifiers are definitely planning some sort of attack.'

Sarah gasped, and Marc's face loomed large on Shireen's display as he leaned closer to Sarah's wristpad. '*What?*'

'I don't know any details yet, but I'm working on it. I picked up a brief message that suggests they have something in place.' She paused, gathering her thoughts. 'You're the first people I'm telling about this. I mean, it's not so much what the message says as who it's from. Let me read it out to you.' She slid the window containing the message up her display alongside the video link so she could see it clearly. 'It says: "To all those who seek to purify Mother Earth of the scourge of *Homo sapiens*: Rejoice. The Day of Judgement is almost upon us. Tomorrow, we witness humanity's destruction by our own hands." And it's signed "Maksoob".'

Marc spoke first, his voice echoing. 'OK, it's from their top dog. But it doesn't really say anything. For all we know, this is just propaganda. There's nothing there to suggest they actually have a plan in place.'

'I agree. But that's not why I've contacted you,' Shireen said, a little too loudly. She pulled her visor up and quickly scanned the room to make sure she hadn't been heard. She'd got away with it. She lowered the visor, and her voice. 'It's who the message comes from! Everyone knows that Maksoob is this near-mythical leader, right? The man behind the Purifiers who is most likely much more than just a talismanic figurehead.'

She paused, her heart pounding. 'This is why you both needed to know. You see, I've found the source of the message. I know who he is now. Maksoob . . . it's Gabriel Aguda!'

Sarah and Marc seemed to freeze. They were aghast. Then Sarah spluttered, 'Aguda? It can't be. Surely that's ridiculous?'

Marc was frowning. He looked as if he was puzzling over a particularly difficult equation. 'Come on, Shireen, seriously? This sounds like some weird conspiracy-theory bullshit. What's

the link between a respected academic geologist and a geno-
cidal maniac terrorist? I mean, I've had my doubts about Aguda
ever since the satellite data episode, and everyone knows he
prefers the MPD option over Odin, but this . . . It's ludicrous.'

Shireen tried to control her frustration. She hadn't expected
this reaction. 'Well, you're wrong, Marc. I know it.'

'OK, Shireen,' Sarah interjected. 'The question is what do
we do about it? No one knows about this apart from the three
of us, right? So, tell us, what evidence do you have?'

'I know this sounds crazy, but I traced the message back to
Aguda's personal account—'

'Hang on, Shireen,' interrupted Sarah again. 'If he is Maksoob,
why would Aguda be so stupid as to send an incriminating
message from his personal account? Is this message enough to
arrest and interrogate him?' Then after a pause, she added, 'It
would of course mean postponing Ignition, until we could find
out what they planned to do.'

Once again Marc's face loomed large on her screen. 'Another
thing. Don't we need to consider the possibility that the Purifiers *want* you to think Aguda is Maksoob by constructing a
bogus link? That they want to, you know, sow the seeds of
doubt, just to postpone Ignition? That may be the best they
can hope for now.'

Shireen couldn't understand what seemed to her like a defence
of Aguda. Of course, they knew him better than she did and
so might have been prepared to give him the benefit of the
doubt, but . . . She tried again.

'Even if there's the slightest possibility Aguda is behind this
and there is a sabotage plan in place, we have to let the authorities know. You know that, right? If Ignition is postponed,
then so be it – at least we would be sure.'

Sarah shook her head slowly. 'Two problems with that. Firstly,
if we go to the authorities now and demand that Aguda is
arrested and interrogated, who are they going to believe? It's
his word against ours. And we need to remember that Gabriel
Aguda is vice chair of the Odin Project Committee. All we
have is an inflammatory statement traced to the account of

one of the world's most influential scientists by a young cyb who came to prominence when she hacked into government secret files. I'm sorry, Shireen, but that's what people will think. And we simply *don't have time before Lockdown* to persuade the right people, whoever the hell they might be.

'Secondly, and more crucially, if the Purifiers are indeed planning something then we still have hope, and a few precious hours, to find out what it might be *without* raising their suspicions. As soon as Aguda is arrested, and assuming he *is* Maksoob, then the game may be up. They will almost certainly have planned for that eventuality.'

Shireen couldn't believe what she was hearing, but Sarah hadn't finished her train of thought. 'Besides, we just need to keep the Project safe until Lockdown. The whole point of the Lockdown is that they would have to do something *before* then. After Lockdown, *no one* can interfere.'

Shireen had already considered this. It was what scared her more than anything else. She tried to keep the desperation out of her voice. 'But . . . what if they have something in place, some virus maybe, that only activates *after* Lockdown? And what if the Mag-8 Mind is infected or compromised, like the CERN Mind in the summer? Then there'd be nothing to stop it and we'd be helpless.'

This time Marc shook his head. 'Even if we could stop Ignition after Lockdown,' he said, 'and I have no idea what would be needed to do that, short of ordering a missile strike against Mag-8, then even that wouldn't be enough.'

Sarah turned around to face him, so the angle of her wrist-pad meant they were both out of vision now, seemingly having forgotten about Shireen. But she could still hear them. 'What do you mean?' asked Sarah.

'I mean we would have to knock out the other sites too. Think about it – if the Purifiers are capable of sabotaging Mag-8 in some way then we must assume they're capable of overriding any instruction to the other seven Minds to abort in the event of only Mag-8 being destroyed. Stopping just one of the eight beams is the nightmare scenario, remember. And even if we could avoid Ignition with such drastic measures then the Purifiers will still have won. The Project would be over.' He sounded exhausted.

'Jesus. So we lose either way.'

'There may be another way,' Shireen interjected. The idea had been swirling around in the back of her mind ever since she'd decided to contact Sarah and Marc. 'What if you could get something out of Aguda? I don't mean a full confession, just something incriminating enough to convince the world to listen to us and stop Ignition. He's there with you in Mag-8, after all.' They didn't reply, so she added, 'But you have less than six hours.'

# 40

SARAH KNEW THAT SHIREEN WAS RIGHT. THEY HAD TO FIND a way of confronting Aguda. And even if she was wrong about him, they couldn't afford to do nothing. It had taken her and Marc almost two hours of arguing before they settled on a plan, and Sarah could tell that he was unhappier than her by far. But they were running out of time discussing it, and she knew he could see the sense in her line of reasoning. It was the only card they had left to play.

The only way to entrap Aguda, she had argued, was if he felt safe and unthreatened. For that, she had to be the one to meet him, alone. Playing to his self-confidence, his *amour-propre*, might just force him to let slip something they could use. But to get him to meet in the first place was trickier. How could she do that without raising suspicion?

'He has to think I know more than I do – that I am a threat—'

'A threat he will want to deal with,' Marc reminded her.

'Marc, we've been through this.'

He didn't respond. Instead, he drew her close and held her. She knew how uncomfortable he was feeling about the plan: allowing someone else he cared for to put themselves directly in danger like this. He'd just been through a major trauma in which he'd almost lost the person he loved most in the world.

But Sarah wasn't Evie. And a father's love for his daughter was hardly the same as this ill-timed and misplaced chivalry.

Sarah knew Aguda had arrived at the Mag-8 facility an hour after them, along with Peter Hogan and an entourage of high-ranking officials. Most people were gathering in the vast viewing hall that overlooked the central chamber itself. The giant magnets loomed high above them like an alien space fleet hovering silently and menacingly; and below were the aluminium beam tubes, glistening under the bright lights that were suspended on the walls and roof of the chamber. All three tubes, each with its surrounding bending magnets, split off in sequence from the main cylinder whose sealed front end faced the north-west, ready to allow in the beam of heavy neutralinos arriving from CERN. The other ends of the three tubes pointed vertically down into the focusing chamber, where they merged again into a single cylinder, down which the beam of charginos would pass into the ground. The entire construct was an exact replica of the Mag-4 facility she'd seen before completion in Peru.

There were six hours to go before Ignition and three hours before Lockdown. The atmosphere was tense. People huddled in groups talking in hushed tones, as though even a raised voice might jeopardize the mission. The occasional laughter she heard sounded forced. Technicians and engineers went about their business carrying out final checks while they still could before Lockdown. Marc had found Qiang and taken him outside to talk to him away from prying eyes and ears. He'd insisted that since his colleague was the only other person they could really trust he needed to be brought up to speed.

Sarah hadn't wanted to confront Aguda in public in case he detected something in her manner that scared him off. So, they agreed she should stay out of his sight and send him a brief message instead. She found an empty meeting room to hide away in and composed the message:

*Gabriel, I don't know who else to turn to, but I need to speak to someone urgently. There's a plot to sabotage*

*Mag-8 that we've uncovered, and we have to warn*
*people. Can we talk privately?*

Waiting for Aguda's response was almost unbearable. The
minutes ticked by and she wondered whether he was deliberately ignoring the message. Did he suspect anything? Possibly.
Would he be considering the possibility that they were trying
to entrap him? Marc and Qiang joined her in the room.

'Damn it, Marc, it's been almost twenty minutes. He's not
responded. Have we just made a terrible mistake?'

Marc began pacing up and down. 'Right, if we haven't heard
from Aguda in another ten minutes, we'll have to go to security and insist he's arrested. They'd be crazy to ignore us.'

And then Sarah received a message:

*Meet me in the old electron booster ring building.*
*Fifteen minutes.*

Relief mixed with fear washed through her. This was it. The
game was on.

The booster hall was situated within the old SESAME
building – an artefact of a bygone era despite its microtron
accelerator still being used to produce the electrons that were
injected into the much larger storage rings of the new accelerator. But from the start of the Project several months earlier,
these experimental buildings had been sitting dormant and
deserted, with all the large superconducting magnets being
appropriated for Mag-8's construction.

The building was quiet when Sarah walked in, and the air
smelled stale and suffocating. She could see the central area of
the hall, the site of the accelerator ring, a circular tube forty
metres in circumference and threaded through multiple magnets like a necklace. Hidden within high concentric shielding
walls, it was accessed by following a winding corridor, like
walking around the outer layers of a circular garden maze, but
with two-metre-thick concrete walls instead of green hedges.

Aguda obviously knew his way around the SESAME complex –
the hall was certainly far from prying eyes and ears.

Despite feeling terrified, Sarah made her way to the
experimental area. She rehearsed her lines. She couldn't afford
to let her guard slip and nervously checked her AR feed to make
sure it was recording everything she saw and heard. She wasn't
surprised to see the network signal drop out as she walked
deeper into the building. Marc and Shireen would by now
have lost contact with her. Had Aguda chosen the location
so that no one outside could eavesdrop? Did he suspect
something? Did he even have any intention of letting her
go? She knew the risk she was taking, but it had seemed the
only way.

She wondered if Gabriel was already there. The shielding
corridor opened up into a large hall. Looking about her, the
only accessible floor space was a narrow walkway squeezed
between the outer wall and the accelerator ring itself, which
was situated about waist high all the way around. The chamber
was crowded with instrumentation: stacks of shelving over-
flowing with electronic equipment connected by a multi-coloured
spaghetti of wires and cables. Nothing seemed to be switched
on. There was none of the usual comforting hum or the colourful glow of LEDs. There were tables on which lay abandoned
tools and dormant computer displays.

The only sounds Sarah could hear were her own footsteps
and the blood rushing in her ears. The lighting was poor
on this side of the ring and, at first, she thought she was alone.
Gabriel hadn't arrived yet. Maybe he wouldn't come. Maybe
he planned to imprison her here until after Lockdown. No,
he wouldn't be foolish enough to believe she was the only one
who knew about the plan.

Then she saw a figure moving out from the shadows.

'Ah, Sarah. You came.'

She stopped dead in her tracks. At first, she was confused.
Confusion that was quickly followed by a dreadful dawning
realization. She felt a strange, prickly tingling as though elec-
trodes had been attached to every part of her body.

It was Hogan. Senator Peter Hogan. And he was smiling his broadest smile.

He was wearing a stylish cream suit and was studying what looked to be a small display pad.

'I hope you're not too disappointed to see me instead of Gabriel. He felt this was just too important for him to deal with, and so he asked me.' He winked at her conspiratorially. Every nerve in her body yelled at her to run, but she knew she had to hear him out.

Resting the display gently on the table, Hogan walked slowly towards her. 'OK, Sarah, here we are, just the two of us.' He held his hands out to either side of him. 'So, I think we can be frank with each other, yes?' He didn't wait for an answer. 'Now then, you believe there's been some sort of security breach here at Mag-8 and that the Project is in jeopardy? This, just a few hours before the most portentous moment in human history. Don't you think you're leaving it rather late in the day to be worrying about monsters under the bed?'

To her relief, he stopped a couple of metres from her.

She managed to find her voice and to her surprise it sounded steadier than she could have hoped. 'Please don't be facetious, Senator. I needed to speak to Gabriel urgently because—'

'—because he's the person you go to when you dig up secrets, right? Just like you did with those files about the satellite data?'

He smiled again, flashing his shark's teeth. 'Well, I don't think Gabriel is in any position to help you right now. Poor Gabriel, a man always aiming higher than his limited intellect would allow. A man without the imagination to be anything other than a foot soldier.'

At first, Sarah wasn't quite sure what he'd meant. Then it hit her like a juggernaut. She didn't know how she knew, she just knew – as sure as she had been of anything in her life. *Oh, shit. Aguda isn't our man. He never was. I'm looking at Maksoob right now.*

She didn't need to rationalize how or why a successful American politician was also the leader of a terrorist organization intent on wiping humankind off the face of the earth. A fresh rush of adrenalin coursed through her body. And it gave her courage. *I have to hold it together. Otherwise we'll have nothing.* Somehow, she managed to compose herself. She refocused her eyes to check her retinal feed was still recording. *OK, let's see what you've got, you bastard.*

'Then maybe you can help instead, Senator. After all, you're clearly the one with the real influence. A man people will listen to.'

When he didn't answer, she carried on. 'Of course, we don't want to trigger an unnecessary postponement of Ignition, because that would mean weeks of delay before we could try again, and I saw what happened in Rio. We can't risk waiting around for a catastrophic event like that to happen again.'

'Ah, of course, you were in Rio during the March Event. How awful for you. All that *tragic* loss of life you weren't able to stop . . .'

*You bastard.* White-hot anger rose up in her and she had to use all her resolve to keep it from bubbling over.

He smiled again. 'And tell me, Sarah. How, may I ask, has this information come to your attention? Given that the entire world's cybersecurity effort is at this very moment focused on ensuring today goes smoothly.'

She breathed deeply. 'I have reason to believe the Purifiers are here at Mag-8 and are planning some sort of act of sabotage.'

'Oh? And this is something *you* have discovered? That neither the Sentinels nor the rest of humanity seem to have picked up?'

Did she detect a slight rise in the level of his voice, as though he were becoming excited by this game? Good. And he hadn't yet asked her what the nature of her suspicions were. Was this an acknowledgement that there really was a plan in place?

'It would appear so, yes,' she prodded. 'Although Marc Bruckner believes the Purifiers know they've failed and that it's too late to stop Ignition now.'

'And what do you think, Sarah?' His eyes glittered.

*Right, this is it. It doesn't matter that it's Hogan, not Aguda.*

This was what she had rehearsed. She needed to get under his skin. 'I'm not so sure,' she replied as calmly as she could. 'Personally, I just don't think we can take that chance. They've shown themselves to be very . . . resourceful. But then their failure so far also suggests they don't have the knowhow, intellect or imagination to strike the killer blow. Their acts seem too clumsy and random, too uncoordinated.'

Hogan's pale blue eyes drilled into hers. He seemed to be enjoying this. She had to keep going. She had just switched tack from claiming to have uncovered a plot, to arguing that the Purifiers weren't capable of carrying it out. And she didn't think Hogan had noticed.

'Personally, I wonder whether their supposed leader, Maksoob, really exists. He sounds more like a concept, invented by a group of desperate individuals. Of course, if he does exist and is planning something, then I would expect him to want to reveal himself at the end, to bathe in the glory of achieving his ultimate aim.'

For the first time in their conversation, Hogan didn't respond immediately. He appeared to be mulling over what she'd said. Aware of his own hesitation, he suddenly straightened himself and took a casual step closer. She called upon every ounce of determination not to back away from him and somehow managed to keep her feet rooted to the spot.

'This is getting boring, Sarah, and frankly I don't have the time for it. So, please stop playing the tiresome amateur psychologist.'

This was her chance.

'Oh, I'm not playing. I'm deadly serious. Strange that you haven't yet asked me what it is I know – what I may have uncovered – Senator Hogan. Or perhaps you would prefer to be addressed as "Maksoob"?'

It was as if a switch had been flipped. His smile evaporated to be replaced by a look of pure malevolence.

'Oh, Sarah,' he snarled, 'how very clever of you. And yet you were expecting to meet Gabriel. Did you find his message to the Purifiers? It's a little insulting that you fell for it so quickly – to think that Gabriel Aguda could control the destiny of the entire planet. Although of course I'm rather pleased you realize your mistake now.' His expression suddenly softened, and he turned his gaze upwards as though recalling a fond memory. 'Poor Gabriel, he's been useful in so many ways – always eager to play with the big boys, and oh so desperate to make his mark on the world.'

She had to think fast. *If Hogan sent the message out from Aguda's account to deflect attention, why do it at all? Why risk exposure at the last minute? Wait. Maybe it's obvious. Maybe he had to reach out to his followers – a last rallying cry from their prophet. His ego was too big not to.*

Then the cold psychopathic stare was back. She felt his eyes bore into her. 'So, tell me, Sarah, what's your plan? Is your knight in shining armour going to dash in and rescue you from my evil clutches?' He shook his head again as though reprimanding an errant child. 'I should inform you that I took the liberty of locking the door remotely as soon as I heard you enter. After all, we wouldn't want anyone disturbing our friendly chat. So, I'm afraid no one will be able to come in or out. It's just you and me until after Ignition.'

Despite her terror, she found the strength from somewhere to blurt out, 'Why? What is it you plan to do?'

He laughed. It was a blood-curdling laugh, devoid of human emotion. 'Oh, Sarah, is this where the good guy convinces the bad guy to reveal his master plan now that he thinks he's got away with it? How sweet. But that wouldn't be so much fun.'

Somehow, he was now just an arm's length away and she took an involuntary step back, feeling the cold metal of the accelerator ring against her back. She was trapped. And like a wolf moving in for the kill, Hogan sensed her panic. 'Sweet, innocent Dr Sarah Maitlin. You are so out of your depth right now. Did you really think that you could stop the inevitable?'

She needed to stall for time. She needed to find out what the inevitable was. She could worry about escape later. She couldn't give up now.

# 41

WHEN SHIREEN LOST CONTACT WITH SARAH, SHE FIRST assumed it was just the net being taken down for added security, but Sarah's retinal feed had dropped out as soon as she had entered the booster hall, so it had to be because of some sort of shielding inside the building. Had Aguda chosen to meet her there because he knew any transmissions to and from the outside world would be blocked? Marc didn't sound surprised when he contacted her a few seconds later. 'Shireen, I have no signal from Sarah – I assume you don't either.'

'No, I've lost signal too. What happened?'

'I could kick myself for not seeing this sooner. The radio frequency generated by the particle accelerator in there, when it's running, means that the whole building must have been acting as a giant Faraday cage to stop any radio waves escaping and interfering with the electronic instruments outside.'

'So Sarah's in there, alone with Aguda, and we can't see or hear what's happening.'

'You don't need to tell me that. I've got to go in after her.'

'No, wait!' She felt her voice rise. 'I mean you can't. If he sees you before Sarah can learn anything, it's all over.'

'It may be all over already, Shireen. If Aguda chose the location so as not to be heard, then maybe he knows we're on to him. And that means Sarah's life is in danger. I can't risk it.'

She knew she couldn't stop him. She switched her display to Marc's retinal feed, even though she knew it would be pointless as soon as he too went inside the building.

So, she saw the closed doors of the booster ring building at the same time that he did.

'Fuck. I'm locked out.' Marc's voice crackled through her earpiece. 'And Sarah's trapped in there with that monster. Shireen, is there anything you can do from your end?'

She didn't answer right away. A thought had suddenly occurred to her. If the doors were locked, then Aguda was definitely on to them. In which case, wouldn't he have simply locked Sarah inside, alone? She quickly traced his whereabouts from his wristpad.

Yup, she was right.

'Marc, Aguda's not in there with her. He's still somewhere in the main building, but I can't pinpoint his location any better than that.'

'You mean he's locked her in there alone? To keep her out of the way until Ignition? That doesn't make sense. Wouldn't he want to know what she knew?'

Marc was right. Aguda couldn't be sure who else knew.

She watched through Marc's eyes as he turned away from the doors and made his way back to the Mag-8 building. He said, 'OK, see if you can get those doors unlocked. I'm going to track down Aguda.'

'OK,' said Shireen, 'I'm sending through a map of the site with his location to your AR feed. But you're on your own after that. I have another idea. Contact me if you need to.'

Shireen knew trying to get Sarah out would be a waste of time. Hacking into the central control system at SESAME in order to release those doors wouldn't work. Even before they went into Lockdown, the Mag-8 Mind or its Sentinels would be on to her instantly. Sarah was locked in there – alone but, as far as Shireen could tell, safe. And with just a few hours to go, they were getting nowhere. Still, maybe there was something she could try. It would be the most outrageous and foolish thing she'd ever attempted in her life. She shivered. Indeed, it might well mean the end of her life, but she had no other option. And she couldn't do it without help. First, she had to get across town to the FBI's National Security Facility.

She slipped out of the building in which she'd spent the past five days and into the cool night air. The streets were eerily quiet. The entire population of the city seemed to have decided to wait it out and watch events unfold on the few official media networks still operating. There were hardly any cars around either, but she found one that seemed to have been abandoned in a hurry near a charging pod. She climbed in, hacked its computer and headed for the Facility. On the way, she called the one person who might be willing to help her.

Zak Boardman picked up almost immediately. Like everyone, he sounded on edge, and was certainly surprised to hear from her. But he was also prepared to listen. Shireen smiled when she heard the young FBI man's voice. They had quite a bit in common. A few years older, Boardman had shown an almost embarrassing degree of admiration for her during the two days of interrogation after her arrest back in February. Of all the FBI team who had questioned her, he had been the most impressed with the Trojan horse code. She saw him as a kindred spirit and was now thankful that she'd kept in touch with him.

She pinged him the message from Maksoob and gave him a brief outline of what she knew.

'We can safely assume that *if* the Purifiers have done something as crude as planting a bomb inside Mag-8, then the Mind or its Sentinels would have found it by now, right?'

'Of course. So then what exactly *are* you suggesting they could do?'

Shireen hesitated. How much should she divulge? Too much, and he would try to talk her out of what she had in mind. More likely still, he would just think she was mad.

She took a deep breath. She had to take the chance. 'Zak, how much do you know about swarm technology?'

'Huh? Um . . . well, not my area but I know we have a lot of people working on it. So do the Chinese and Indians. It's no big secret. But why are you asking me this now? We're just hours away from Lockdown after all, and—'

'I know, Zak,' she interrupted. 'And I know anyone can look up the details online: flying nanomachines, manufactured in huge numbers, probably up to a billion in a single "swarm" – independent entities, acting in unison, but each obeying remarkably simple rules—'

'You mean like staying at a constant distance from their surrounding neighbours, which gives the illusion of choreographed motion?'

'Exactly. Like a murmuration of starlings weaving those stunning patterns in the sky.'

As she spoke, she only half registered the outside world. The car sped along its programmed route, manoeuvring around hastily parked, probably abandoned vehicles. The scene on the deserted Washington streets was like something from a post-apocalyptic horror movie.

'But that's wrong,' said Zak. 'A nanoswarm is much more like a single artificial organism, a cloud of programmable matter. Each nanobot processor has the storage capacity and power of an insect's brain. And yet, because it doesn't need any of this brain power for keeping itself "alive", or hunting for food or finding mates, its entire focus can be on its mission.'

It was what Shireen had feared. 'So, a swarm would be more like an army of a billion *telepathic* killer bees acting as a single unit?'

'Yes, but wait a minute, Shireen. Are you suggesting the Purifiers could have got their hands on a nanoswarm to send into Mag-8?'

When Zak said out loud what she had only toyed with in her mind, it made it sound both terrifying and so much more real.

'I don't know, Zak. I just think that, logically, it's the only option available to them if they want to evade detection by the Mind.'

'I still don't understand. How would that be possible?'

'I'll explain later. But I need to get into your TID Lab, and you're going to help me.' She knew she sounded more bright-eyed than she felt.

He was silent for a few seconds, then, 'OK, I'm listening.'

She checked the on-board map. She'd be with Zak in just over thirty minutes, enough time for her to outline what she had in mind and convince him that she wasn't completely crazy.

She got the car to drop her about fifty metres from the front gate of the NSF compound. Shireen had decided to walk the rest of the way. No need to spook the guards. As she approached, she spotted the skinny figure of the young agent standing in the glare from the harsh arc lights above the security gates.

Zak Boardman walked towards her, flanked by the two heavily armed sentries, both of whom looked like they'd rather be anywhere but here, tonight.

'That's far enough, Ms Darvish,' said one of them, who stood back, levelling his gun at her while the other approached. He held a biometric scanner in front of her face. He nodded as though satisfied and turned to Zak. 'OK, Agent Boardman, she's cleared to come in, but she stays with you at all times, understood?'

Zak thanked him and signalled to Shireen to follow him through the barriers into the compound.

Shireen fell in behind him, checking the time as she went. It had taken her longer than she'd expected to get here. Less than ninety minutes till Lockdown. Looking across at the imposing building, she could see a lot of activity inside. But Zak led her along a diagonal path that took them away from the main entrance towards the far side of the grounds. As they approached, she could make out the sleek glass and steel frame of a newer, smaller structure, half hidden by sycamore trees. This was it, the FBI's TID Lab. She knew enough about Total Immersive Displacement to understand that it was still a highly experimental technology. But it was her only chance.

She could tell Zak was nervous, but hoped he was smart

enough to understand the ramifying consequences of not helping her. At first, he had tried to argue that *he* should be the one
to displace. But she had persuaded him that it had to be her –
because if anything went wrong she would need him to bring
her back.

Total Immersive Displacement had been feasible for many
years, ever since the early days of virtual reality. Shireen
remembered her father talking to her about it when she was
younger. She had grown up in a world where virtual reality
was a given, but it had been mainly used in the entertainment
industry, first for fully immersive gaming experiences and then,
with widespread use of 360-degree stereoscopic cameras and
binaural audio, in movie-making.

TID was very different. Full displacement technology, whereby
one could, in the most real sense imaginable, experience being in
a different physical location, remained a tightly controlled technology because of its security and ethical implications. Yet, it
was an open secret that many countries' militaries had perfected
true TID some years ago.

Zak hadn't said a word as they had made their way to the
laboratory building. Now he presented his eyes and palm to the
scanner and the doors slid open. As they entered the deserted
building, the lights flicked on. Shireen hoped that their presence
wouldn't attract attention. They walked along the corridor
towards the lab, accompanied by the echo of their footsteps; as
they went Zak outlined what the procedure involved. 'The subject is injected with nanobots directly into their bloodstream,
which navigate their way to the brain.' Shireen felt him look
at her as he continued. 'There they take over control of the
neurons responsible for visual, auditory and other senses.'

Even though he wasn't telling her anything she didn't
know already, she let him talk as it seemed to relax him. TID
had been something of an obsession of hers ever since she'd
heard about it. But she never imagined she would be able to
experience it herself, and certainly not when the stakes were so
high.

The idea itself was, she thought, technologically beautiful.

The nanobots received their data from the remote location, transferring it directly to the subject and so giving him – or her – a total immersive experience: seeing, hearing, feeling, even smelling the location they were 'transported to' as though they were physically there. She felt her heartbeat quicken at the enormity of what she was about to do.

They reached the lab and, again, Zak had to be biometrically scanned in order to gain access. Shireen followed him into a large, brightly lit research lab. Everything looked pristine, as though no human had ever set foot in the place. One wall was covered with a bank of electronic instrumentation on which a few multi-coloured LED lights were blinking. The rest of the windowless lab was bare, gleaming white plastic. The only piece of furniture seemed to be a black leather reclining seat in the centre. It reminded Shireen of a dentist's chair.

She started to walk towards it when she noticed that Zak wasn't following her. She turned. He stood there, hovering just inside the lab entrance and looking more nervous than ever. She tried to control her frustration and smiled at him. 'Look, I know what I'm getting into here.'

He didn't reply but moved slowly to the bank of electronics and began switching on the instruments.

As the lab's background hum grew noticeably louder, Shireen suddenly acknowledged just what she was asking of the FBI agent. She went over to him and reached out to rest a hand on his arm. 'Look, Zak, I know this is mad. And I know it's dangerous. And the best we can hope for is that my worries are unfounded, the Project will go smoothly, and we'll both be arrested. But then if I don't—'

Zak's eyes suddenly flashed in anger. 'Don't you think I know that? Would you have got this far if I didn't?' He turned back to the instruments.

'I'm sorry.' Her voice was barely a whisper. She walked back to the chair in the middle of the room. Of course, there was every good reason to be nervous. What she was planning on doing had never been done before.

She ran her fingers along the smooth leather of the TID

chair. It had a certain hypnotic quality about it, beautiful, yet terrifying in equal measure. She had dreamed of a moment like this. But now that it was a reality, all the excitement and romance had vanished. All that was left was a sense of foreboding.

The low electronic hum rose in pitch as the system booted up. Zak walked over to her. He was carrying a metal tray on which there was a very ordinary-looking syringe. 'Look, Shireen, TID technology is perfectly safe as long as you displace somewhere alone. But you want to put yourself *inside* the Mag-8 facility. That's sheer lunacy.' Damn it, he was still trying to talk her out of this. 'There's a Mind in there that is on high alert for *anything* out of the ordinary . . . anything at all.'

'I know that, Zak, and I know the risk I'm taking, but I need to do this. Whatever the Purifiers *may* have planned, I think it will only become evident *after* Lockdown. If I displace too early, then I'll be detected and kicked out by the human controllers. But it's crucial I'm inside when Lockdown happens. I just hope that the Mind gives me a chance to explain.'

She hoped she sounded more confident than she felt. Zak looked far from convinced, trying to appeal to her common sense. 'Listen, you know as well as I do that a Mind can assimilate new information and learn new tricks a million times faster than any human. So don't tell me you can outwit it.'

'I'm not. And I don't want to get into a pointless argument about machine consciousness.' She paused and looked at him. 'It's just that I don't think an AI Mind is capable of recognizing a *psychopathic* human mind, one willing to destroy the world. Which is why I have to help it.'

Without waiting for his response, Shireen eased herself into the chair. It felt cold where it met her skin. 'Can we just get on with this please, Zak? We don't have long and have to time this just right.'

He nodded, reached around to the back of the chair and produced a jet black, full head-and-face helmet. 'Put this on. It has several thousand sensors and probes on the inside that pick up your brain's activity and transmit your thoughts to the remote location. At the same time, it'll be sending data back in the opposite direction.' He paused, as though he was worried he'd spooked her too much, before adding, 'But it should feel quite comfortable.'

Shireen gingerly pulled the helmet over her head and let out a gasp of surprise. The front visor, which had looked black from the outside, projected bright, pale blue light on the inside. She felt as if she was staring up into a clear summer sky.

She could hear Zak hooking her up to various machines – monitors that would record her vital signs and allow him to instantly kill the power to the nanobots and bring her back. She felt her nervousness rise a notch. She thought about her parents at home in Tehran. She knew they'd be worrying whether the world would be around for them to ever see her again. She thought about Majid. She missed him more than ever. And she wondered what Sarah must be going through right now, imprisoned and helpless.

Zak snapped her out of her reverie. 'OK, Shireen. Are you ready?'

Her mouth felt dry. The Sentinels protecting the Mag-8 Mind, and even the Mind itself, would fry her brain if they saw her as a hostile presence and rejected the merge.

'OK, let's get on with this,' she whispered, almost to herself.

'Right, relax your arm. I hope this doesn't hurt too much. I've never done it before.' Then there was a sharp sensation of pressure in her forearm. She sucked in a deep breath. So, this was it. No turning back now. Zak had injected her with the nanobots. Suddenly this didn't seem like such a great idea. Within seconds she was floating, her body no longer belonging to her. She experienced a brief sense of panic. As a child, she had suffered from sleep paralysis: being fully awake and yet unable to move or speak. This felt like that – and then the sensation fell away . . .

Slowly the monochromatic blue light changed, and Shireen

could pick out features. As her surroundings swam into focus
she saw that she was standing in a garden, a place she guessed
was a virtual-reality holding area for her to become familiar
with the sensation of controlling her avatar body before she
was displaced. She looked down to see that she was standing
barefooted on a manicured lawn. All around her were thick bushes
rich in colourful flowers. She could 'feel' the grass beneath her
feet and smell the sweet scent of jasmines and roses. She tried
lifting her hand up to her face and found it very easy. She told
herself that what she was looking at was a computer-generated
hand. It wasn't hers. She knew that back in the lab her own
hand would not be moving. Her brain had sent a signal to the
muscles to raise an arm, but the nanobots had intercepted it and
translated it into the sensation of lifting the imaginary avatar
limb.

Shireen had spent her life playing immersive VR games and
was perfectly at ease experiencing the sensation of moving
around and interacting in a computer-generated world. Wearing her gaming helmet, haptic suit and gloves, it was easy to
fool the brain into believing you were in some fantasy world of
aliens and monsters – but you still had to swivel your head to
look around you, and you still had to physically move your
arms, or manipulate your fingers, for your actions to be translated into the virtual world.

This was different. Every one of her senses was confirming
to her that she was physically standing in the garden and the
illusion was utterly impossible to shake, however hard she
tried to convince herself otherwise. She fought back her panic
and forced herself to relax, to accept it.

And when Zak spoke softly to her, she realized that
it was a subtly different experience from the usual sensation
of hearing, as though his voice was being generated inside
her head: *OK, Shireen, listen to me because this is very
important: there isn't any way the outside world can make
contact with the Mag-8 Mind once Lockdown has been initiated, so it'll be up to the Mind to find you, not the other way
round.*

*I'm ready.* Shireen could hear her own voice 'in her head' but wasn't sure if her lips had moved in the lab. However, her thought had clearly been transmitted to Zak because he immediately responded. *Good. Everything seems in order from this end. Now we just wait.*

# 42

SARAH COULDN'T JUST GIVE UP NOW. SHE MIGHT BE LOCKED in with this monster, but she was still recording his confession. She needed to know what he had planned. *I have to play for time. Keep him talking. Let him think he's won.*

'So, tell me, Senator. Make me understand. What would motivate you to want to do this?'

'There's that amateur psychologist again,' laughed Hogan. He seemed to relax a little and stepped back from her, as though he felt he had all the time in the world and was having second thoughts about terminating their conversation just yet. 'Maybe I need to lie down on a couch if we're going to do this properly. OK then, Dr Maitlin, it's only a few hours till the end of the world, so why not? In any case, I don't plan for you personally to even live *that* long. Let's see if you have the intellectual capacity to understand.'

*Jesus, he's going to confess his entire warped ideology to me. Then he's going to kill me.* Her back was pressed hard against the electron beam pipe. The metal felt cold. She stole a quick glance behind her to see if there was anything she could use as a weapon, hoping he hadn't noticed. *What if he does? He must know I'm not going down without a fight.* There was nothing. But she needed to keep him talking, get him to reveal something.

'Any evolutionary psychologist will tell you that your feelings of altruism – your empathy and compassion towards fellow human beings – is an evolved trait. You're not nice because you choose to be – it was in our ancestors' interests, going back a hundred thousand years, to show kindness, to cooperate. Or maybe you try to be good because some holy book says you had better be, otherwise you'll incur the displeasure of some Divine Creator. But on an individual basis, what use do we have for altruism other than to make us feel better about ourselves? What if you could turn off that switch? You would be liberated. Free from the desire – the need – to make others happy.'

'And you feel liberated, do you, Hogan? Is that it? But that's not enough for you, is it? Being ambivalent towards fellow humans is one thing, but your empty, psychopathic antipathy . . . I mean, that takes a special kind of insanity.'

Hogan didn't look remotely unsettled.

'The truth is I can't really remember when my feelings towards my fellow man . . . and, ah, woman . . . sorry . . . actually began. Did you know I read the work of Immanuel Kant as a student? Back then I thought I understood who I was – what I was – no different from a million other young men. A misanthrope. Only the more I read, the more I came to realize that men like Kant, or writers like Gustave Flaubert, or even geniuses like Michelangelo and Newton, all supposedly famous misanthropes, were just loners who didn't like being around other people – nothing more than a social phobia that led them to dislike everyone around them. They were weak, pathetic sociopaths, Sarah, and I grew to despise them even more than the rest of humanity.' He smiled that smile again. The dead smile that made her want to retch.

'You know, I really did try to rationalize my feelings, to understand my nihilism. And I think I did, in the end.' He paused, and looked away, as though trying to invoke human emotions. But he quickly snapped his attention back to Sarah and the cold sharp focus was back in his eyes.

'You do know we've brought this all on ourselves, don't

you?' His voice was suddenly louder. 'How long have we been destroying our planet? And how long did you think it would be before the planet fought back? We changed its climate, we plundered its resources, we poisoned the land, the oceans and the atmosphere. Finally, Mother Earth has had enough. Is that so difficult to comprehend?' Flecks of spittle had appeared around the corners of his mouth.

*My God, he really is totally, utterly mad.* She tried to keep her face expressionless. In this new spirit of openness, would he finally reveal what she needed?

'It wasn't so difficult to take on the persona of Maksoob, either. People find the notion of a respected US senator leading such a double life so unlikely as to be laughable. And Maksoob is such a comic-book villain, isn't he? In my late twenties—' He paused, tilting his head to one side. 'By the way, you don't mind me telling you all this, do you? I mean, I hope you didn't have anywhere else you needed to be? Any other "pressing" engagements? Only, it's so lovely to be able to chat so candidly. And so close to the end of days. Anyway, as I was saying, in my late twenties, I was spending a lot of time in the Arabian Gulf advising governments on a proposed new clean energy programme. One day, I was driven out to the Eastern Desert, where I met with disaffected Bedouin tribesmen. Many of them had grown up in the wealthiest countries in the world, with every conceivable luxury at their disposal. But with the oil crash of '28 coinciding with the new breakthroughs in solar energy tech it became clear that the world had lost its appetite for fossil fuels. Almost overnight, once-rich Gulf nations were plunged into deep poverty. It's not surprising they became bitter and angry.

'Easy pickings. I began recruiting on the dark web, first from the Middle East and gradually from every corner of the globe. But I was given an Arabic name, Maksoob, which I believe means "Recruited One". Bless them for thinking *they* had recruited *me* to their cause. I *gave* them the cause.'

He sighed. 'And there you have it, Sarah, now you know me. But I still don't suppose you can see why this is all necessary, can you?'

There was a madness in his eyes now that she hadn't seen before. As though he'd spent his life suppressing it in order to appear normal, to appear human. And now he could afford to let the mask slip, to reveal the monster beneath.

'Why *what* is necessary, Hogan?'

'Oh, I'm quite enjoying this. You want me to tell you what I have planned. Well, let's just say that it is deliciously simple – a basic oversight that everyone will be kicking themselves for missing, for the entire remainder of their lives, which I believe will be around ten minutes after Ignition.'

The table next to him was littered with an array of electronic detritus – discarded tools, components and dust-covered display pads. Hogan looked down and selected an ugly-looking spanner, testing its heft by moving it from one hand to the other and back again.

*Shit.* Was this it? Sarah felt a chill ripple through her. Hogan was bigger and physically stronger, and he was about to bludgeon her to death as if this was a nightmarish game of Cluedo. A whimper of fear escaped her lips and he grinned. It seemed to please him. He stepped towards her. Incredibly, she heard him humming to himself.

His sheer arrogance and over-confidence meant that he was still looking down at the spanner when she struck. With a war cry of rage, she leapt at him, channelling all her fear, her rage into her right arm. She punched forward, locking it just before impact. '*FUCK YOU, HOGAN,*' she screamed as the palm of her hand connected hard with his nose. She heard the crunch of breaking cartilage and the look of surprise on his face became a rictus of pain as his nose exploded in a fountain of blood. He was thrown backwards, tripping over thick cables, arms scrabbling to find a handhold as his head thudded against the edge of a steel casing protruding from the side of the booster ring.

He was unconscious before he hit the ground.

Adrenalin pumping, Sarah turned and ran back towards the winding corridor that led to the exit. She had no idea how she would get out. Hogan had said he'd locked the door remotely from within so presumably it could be opened from the inside.

Reaching the steel door, she slammed her hand against the large EXIT button on the wall. Nothing happened.

Letting out a feral scream of frustration and rage that echoed around her, Sarah began hammering on the door. She had the proof that they so desperately needed that the Purifiers were planning something, but couldn't do anything with it. What were Marc and Shireen doing? Less than two hours till Lockdown and she had no connection with the outside world.

Pushing back a growing panic, Sarah wondered whether there was another way out, then remembered the e-pad that Hogan had been looking at when he'd stepped out of the shadows. Of course, that had to be how he had locked the door remotely.

She retraced her steps to the accelerator hall.

A streak of blood glittered wetly on the floor, but Hogan was nowhere to be seen. And neither was the e-pad he'd left on the table.

# 43

MARC SPRINTED BACK TO THE MAIN MAG-8 BUILDING. No time to formulate a plan. If Aguda had locked Sarah inside the electron booster hall then surely that was evidence not only of his guilt, but that he was planning something and wanted her out of the way. But would he be stupid enough to think that she was working alone? This wasn't a scenario they had contemplated.

All he knew was that he had no choice now but to confront the geologist.

Shireen had said that Gabriel Aguda was somewhere in the main building, but he wasn't among the rest of the dignitaries in the main viewing gallery. Trying to appear calm and not draw attention to himself, Marc ran through his options. He didn't have many. Well, this was it, no more cloak and dagger heroics. He needed to alert security.

Marc couldn't claim to know General Hussain Hassan, a retired army general, well but he knew enough to suggest that Hassan was the sort of man used to dishing out orders, not taking them. And Marc had no reason not to trust him.

He took the stairs down to the ground floor three at a time. Outside the general's office, he flashed his ID at the two guards who moved to block him. Too late: the door was open and the general waved him in.

The head of security at Mag-8 sat behind a large mahogany desk and in front of an even larger framed photograph of the King of Jordan. There were several others present, including a couple of UN officials Marc recognized, all engaged in an animated conversation.

Marc didn't have time for pleasantries and launched straight in.

'General, apologies for interrupting things but what I am about to tell you is critical, and you must believe me because we don't have much time.'

The general stared at him, his face unreadable.

'I have reason to believe that Dr Aguda is a dangerous man,' Marc continued, 'and we need to speak with him urgently.'

'Why do you say that, Professor?' The general's voice betrayed no emotion and, Marc thought, he didn't look particularly surprised. Did he already know about Aguda? If so, why wasn't Ignition being aborted?

Hassan didn't wait for a response from Marc. Instead he continued, 'You're late to the party, Professor Bruckner. We have this in hand.'

Marc was stunned. What the fuck was going on?

'Listen to me, goddammit, the Project itself is in jeopardy.' He slammed his fist on the desk and leaned towards the general. 'Gabriel Aguda is not who you think he is. He's plotting something, and we need to find him pretty damn quickly.'

'And I just told you,' Hassan said, his voice measured, 'that we have it under control.'

Kicking back his chair, the general stood and walked round from behind his desk. He nodded at the others in the room. 'Excuse me, everyone. Come with me, Professor.'

Baffled, Marc was led out of the office and down the corridor to the far end of the building. A pair of Jordanian soldiers stood guard outside what Marc assumed must have been one of the many administrative offices. He could hear murmured conversation coming from within.

The soldiers jumped to attention, one opening the door.

Whatever it was that Marc expected to see, it wasn't this. A group of men and women parted to let the general and Marc through. That's when Marc saw Gabriel Aguda. In the far corner of the room, he sat at a terminal table, his head thrown forward and resting in a pool of slowly congealing blood. His glassy stare seemed to be directed straight at Marc. In his hand, hanging limply to one side, was a gun. He looked quite dead.

As he approached, Marc could see a neat hole above Aguda's ear where the bullet must have entered.

He felt bile rise up in his gorge. The general was speaking, and he forced himself to look away, to focus.

'We found out about Dr Aguda's involvement in a plot here at Mag-8 just under an hour ago. Within minutes, we found him here. We were warned that he would try something. The man was clearly unhinged and desperate to sabotage the Project.'

'But . . . what happened here?' muttered Marc, gesturing in the direction of the geologist's corpse. 'This looks like a suicide.'

'It would indeed appear so. Especially since he has conveniently left us a message.' The general raised a bushy eyebrow.

Was this Aguda's parting shot? Set whatever plan he had in motion, then, because he knew his cover had been blown, take his own life to keep it secret?

'So why have you not stopped Ignition?' Marc shouted.

'As I said, Professor, we have it in hand. Aguda was planning to set off an explosive device timed for the moment of Ignition. It would have destroyed Mag-8 just as the dark-matter beam arrived from CERN.'

Marc stared at the general. 'And how do you know all this?'

'Because, Professor Bruckner, we were tipped off, by the same source who alerted us to Aguda. The information was indeed reliable. We found the device hidden in the basement, just where we were told it would be, and defused it.'

Marc's mind was reeling. There was something not quite right here.

'But . . . How? . . . I thought security around all the sites was meant to be so tight you couldn't smuggle in a cheese sandwich without it raising the threat level. So, who . . . who told you all this?'

'If you must know, it came from the very top. Senator Hogan himself had been alerted and he informed me. Now if you'll excuse me, Professor, I need to find the Senator, who also seems to have gone missing.'

The general turned to leave the conference room, then slowed down and turned back to Marc.

'Actually, Professor Bruckner, I meant to ask you, how did *you* come by this information? Have you spoken to the Senator today?'

'What?' Marc tried to make sense of all this. Somehow Hogan must have received his own intelligence at the same time as Shireen. Was that coincidence? He doubted it.

'I'll explain in a few minutes. But if you're sure the danger is over, I need a few of your men to come with me to help open the locked door of the booster hall. Aguda has locked Dr Maitlin in there.'

The general stared at Marc for a few seconds, then signalled to the two armed guards to go with him.

As Marc hurried across the compound flanked by the two silent soldiers, he tried to piece things together. Something was bugging him. The timing was all wrong. He checked the time as he ran. It had been forty-five minutes since he'd lost contact with Sarah. She'd been locked inside just after that. But if Hassan was right and Aguda had shot himself an hour ago, then he couldn't have been the one who had locked Sarah in.

It took just a few minutes for the soldiers to deactivate the electronic locking device hidden behind a wall panel and pull the large steel door open manually. As soon as there was enough of a gap, Marc pushed past them before they could stop him. As his eyes adjusted to the dim light inside he saw Sarah running towards him, shielding her eyes from the harsh glare of sunlight as she did so. He threw his arms around her. She was shaking.

'Marc, thank God,' she sobbed, but then suddenly pushed herself away from him. 'We don't have much time left.'

'It's OK, Sarah. They've found a device. And Aguda's dead. Shot himself.'

'Aguda's dead? Yes, that figures. Marc, it's not Aguda. It never was. It's Hogan. He's Maksoob. And he's completely crazy.' Then she added, 'And it's not over. Not by a long shot.'

Everything suddenly dropped into place. Of course it was Hogan. How could he have been so slow? This whole charade was set up by Hogan. Did he have Aguda killed? Did he do it himself?

'Marc, Hogan's in there somewhere.' Sarah turned and pointed back into the darkness. 'He was going to—' Her voice cracked and she paused, composing herself. 'He's hurt. I hit him and he fell but now I can't find him. We need to get to the control room and abort Ignition, now!'

Seeing the look of desperation in her face, he didn't ask any more questions.

'OK, we need to go. Tell me what you know on the way.'

But as he turned to go, he came face to face with the two soldiers, weapons aimed straight at him and Sarah.

'We are sorry, Professor,' said one. He looked almost apologetic. They were the first words he'd spoken. 'But General Hassan has ordered us to keep you and Dr Maitlin here until Lockdown.'

'What the fuck?' Sarah moved towards the door. 'This is insane. Did you not just hear us? Senator Hogan is the one you should be worried about, and he's somewhere in there and planning something that will kill you and everyone you love.'

The other, older soldier stepped forward and shoved Sarah back. Marc tensed, and grabbed Sarah's hand before she could retaliate. The younger man continued: 'General Hassan said you would accuse the American, Hogan. Now please, step back from this entrance. We have orders to shoot if you do not comply.'

As if to emphasize his point, he moved his gun from Sarah to Marc. For a brief second, Marc contemplated rushing them, but this wasn't a fight he could win.

Holding their guns level, the two guards backed out into the

sunlight. As the doors began to slide shut, the younger soldier repeated, 'We are sorry. We will be outside. You will be
released as soon as Lockdown has been safely initiated.'

The doors closed and Marc heard the click of the electronic
lock.

# 44

A DIGITAL CLOCK HOVERED IN THE TOP LEFT OF SHIREEN'S field of vision. Zak had set it to countdown and she had been watching it for over an hour. With minimal sensory inputs for so long, she was beginning to hallucinate – drifting in and out of a vivid dream world so that she was finding it hard to remember where she was and what she was about to do. Once again, she forced herself to focus. She was still standing in the garden, and while she could move her arms and head, she seemed unable to move her feet away from the spot.

At last, she heard Zak's voice in her head. It sounded clear, but faint, as though coming to her from a great distance. *OK, Shireen. The countdown to Lockdown has begun and I'm sending you in.* Eight seconds to go and the garden began to dissolve away. A sudden bolt of excitement surged through her. It was working. She was inside the Mag-8 facility.

Her first sensation was that of a hundred different sounds. After the quiet of the TID Lab and then the peacefulness of the garden, now a cacophony of hums and drones of machines and electronics greeted her. It all sounded so real; and the illusion that she was physically inside Mag-8 was remarkable. There above her head were the huge black superconducting magnets fixed in place on vast steel and graphene girders, with a multitude of cables, instruments and multi-coloured lights everywhere.

The air against her skin felt warm and dry. She could almost taste the dust of the desert.

And her hunch had been correct: Lockdown hadn't severed the link. It was supposed to mean that all communication between the Mind and the outside world was now blocked, and yet the nanobots in her body were still receiving data from within Mag-8 and feeding it to her brain. Would she be able to send her thoughts back, through the mouth of her avatar standing in Mag-8, to communicate with the Mind?

Now that Lockdown was in place, the link made just moments earlier between her body in Washington and the Mag-8 Mind ten thousand kilometres away wasn't via the Cloud at all. It couldn't be. That was the point of Lockdown. Instead, the information exchange seemed to be being maintained purely by long-range quantum correlations. The nanobots were sufficiently quantum entangled with the molecules of air inside Mag-8 for quantum information to be exchanged. This TID technology was almost like magic, and it seemed – incredibly – to be working. Shireen felt a surge of pure elation.

*This is the ultimate out-of-body experience. Einstein hated the idea of quantum entanglement, calling it 'spooky action at a distance', and yet here I am, my thoughts teleported halfway across the world from my physical body.*

She was standing on a gantry high above the ground within a large enclosure. Looking about her she noted that she was close to one of the huge bending magnets. It hummed as though it were a living thing. In front of her was a waist-high safety bar. She reached a hand towards it. It felt cold and solid to the touch, pushing back against her fingers. How could that be when none of this was real? *No, wait, that's wrong. All of this . . . it is real. I'm the one who's not real. I'm actually still in Washington, DC. What's being reconstructed in my brain is whatever is being recorded by all the cameras and sensors inside the facility.*

Shireen's avatar peered down over the railings. The gantry she was on was about ten metres above the ground. The magnet closest to her was the uppermost one of the first level.

Down on the ground directly below was a cubic structure, which she guessed housed the focusing magnet – the place where the dark-matter beams would come together and head vertically down. Shireen leaned out further still and looked up. The other two levels of magnets towered majestically and vertiginously far above her.

She now needed to make contact with the Mind and to persuade it to look for something, anything, that was out of the ordinary – something that would have become apparent only *after* Lockdown.

And first she had to earn its trust.

The dilemma she was acutely aware of was that her own presence here wasn't physical. In fact, she was no more 'real' than the Mind itself. They were both mere data. And to communicate and cooperate they would need to merge into one – a unique combination, a human–AI consciousness.

Shireen didn't have long to wait. Without warning she was plunged into blackness. Was this the work of the Sentinels protecting the Mag-8 Mind? They were less powerful AIs than the Mind itself, but their role was a simple one: to ensure that no alien software could penetrate and infect the Mind. That had to be it: they would have detected data flowing from the lab in Washington and were attempting to block it.

No, please don't let this be the end of it – that all this was for nothing. Shireen felt time running away from her. She had to reach out.

*My name is Shireen Darvish and I am using TID to communicate with you. I am not a threat. I want to help.*

Nothing. Sentinels would have figured this out anyway, but she wasn't sure what else to say. Suddenly the enormity of what had happened to her over the past few months crowded into her consciousness and for the first time in her life Shireen Darvish began to understand the true meaning of despair.

And it was then that she received a reply. She couldn't describe it. It wasn't a response transmitted in words as such but more of a feeling, a sense of meaning. Yes, that was it! And it was neither friendly nor aggressive, simply a statement of fact.

Shireen Darvish. You are not permitted to interact.
Lockdown has been initiated.

A wave of relief crashed through her. Any communication suggested that they didn't see her as an immediate threat and that meant there was still hope.

*I understand. But you require my help. Ignition may have been compromised. Give me access to the Mind.*

The Mind cannot be accessed. No compromise has been detected. Lockdown is in place.

OK, maybe a different tack was needed. These guardian AIs were simply doing what they were programmed to do. Hell, *they* were no more than sophisticated software programs. Now was probably a good time for her to stop thinking of them as living entities.

She felt a buzzing sensation in her head, which grew louder and more urgent, only it wasn't a sound – more like a vibration inside her skull, a hundred billion neurons trying to break free of their moorings. She was suddenly overcome by an indescribable giddiness, as though she were tumbling through space. The spinning sensation was horrible. There was no up or down, no anchor. She was lost in the void and her head was about to explode.

*Let me off this ride. It's scary. Mama, can you tell them to stop? I don't like it . . . It's going too fast. I'm going to fall off . . .*

A presence.

*Get out. Get out of my head. I don't want you here.*

Then . . . Empty. Silence. Nothingness.

She floated and observed and waited . . . and existed, without any feeling, purpose or sense of self. She couldn't think, or rationalize, had just a dim awareness that she had lost her mind.

Then, just as quickly as it had started, it was over, and she was back in control of her own thoughts. *What the hell had just happened?* She'd felt a dislocation, as though she were nothing more than a detached presence observing the functioning of her mind from afar. It felt as if her corporeal self had been pushed aside while her thoughts, dreams and memories were ransacked.

Could that be the Mind? Yes, it had to be.

Rather than observe the exchange between her and the Sentinels, it had decided to find out who the intruder was for itself and had merged with the intruder's thoughts! Shireen tried to rationalize how it could have done this. It must have sent sophisticated spyware into her head via the nanobots in order to read her thoughts. She felt as though she had been violated, exposed, laid bare.

More importantly, though, contact had been made. She tried again.

*I hope you now believe me when I say I wish no malice.*

Suddenly, the lights came back on inside the facility and she heard a deep, rich, soft, unmistakably female voice.

You are Shireen Darvish. You believe Mag-8 to be compromised. Yet I do not detect any anomalies. I do not understand the nature of the possible attack. Your thoughts are confused. Please explain.

*There are those who do not wish for the Odin Project to succeed. They want Mag-8 to fail.*

Many do not want the Odin Project to go ahead. I understand this. They calculate the risks to be too high. But you are speaking of those who suffer from a corruption of human reasoning. Those who wish Ignition to go ahead, but for it to fail.

*That's right. And I believe they've planted something inside Mag-8. Something you have not, and would not detect, unless you knew what to look for.*

Had her hunch been correct? A nanoswarm could indeed be lurking inside Mag-8. Each bot would have specialized pincers to destroy almost anything in its path. A swarm could slice through matter like a knife through butter, dissolve reinforced armour, or get inside secure buildings through the tiniest of cracks.

She shuddered as she thought about it, or rather she would have done if she'd had control of her physical body. She was jerked back from her thoughts by the voice in her head.

> You believe a swarm may have infiltrated the facility. You believe that if it is running autonomous software off-grid then I would only be aware of its presence if it interacted physically with anything within the facility. This is correct.

This wasn't proof that there really was a swarm floating somewhere in here, waiting, biding its time until the last moment to attack, but if it *were* present then the Mind would not necessarily know about it. A swarm could hover indefinitely like an invisible cloud, powered by artificial photosynthesis from surrounding electromagnetic radiation. The Mind could only see and feel what the sensors and cameras built into the facility could detect.

*Is there a way to expose it if it is in here somewhere?*

> Yes.

The next second everything went completely dark. Had the Mind just turned off all the lights? Why? Before she could puzzle over it any further, the facility was suddenly bathed in a low-level blue-violet colour that gave the place a dreamlike quality. At the bottom of her field of vision Shireen saw the words:

*MONOCHROMATIC UV LIGHT. 280 nm. 4.43 eV.*

The interior of Mag-8 was being bathed in ultraviolet light. The Mind had squeezed the wavelength of the light produced by all the facility's LEDs down to 280 nanometres.

While she waited, it occurred to her that had she been truly physically present here, she would have remained in total darkness. Pure, monochromatic UV light is invisible to the human eye. But she wasn't looking through her physical eyes. The nanobots floating inside her body back in Washington had received the data and helpfully rendered it as visible violet light for her benefit.

Then, without the colour of the light she was seeing changing much, the numbers on her AR display altered. The light's wavelength had become shorter, while the second number, which she guessed was the corresponding energy of the light, had increased:

*HIGH ENERGY UVC LIGHT. 100 nm. 12.4 eV.*

What did this mean? She cursed as she struggled to remember her first-year introductory physics course on quantum theory. Something about the energy of light connected to its wavelength . . . What was it? Come on, think. OK, high-energy radiation, like X-rays and gamma rays, had very short wavelength. That meant the shorter the wavelength the more energy the light carried. So, the Mind had just turned up the energy dial on the light. Had she been physically inside the facility at this moment, not only would she not see anything, but she would have been killed by the ionizing radiation too. What was the Mind up to? As though reading her thoughts, it spoke again.

If a nanobot swarm is present, it will react to high-energy ultraviolet light. Damaging to all life forms.

*But nanobots are not living things.*

You are correct. Living biomolecules are damaged by ultraviolet light. But although nanobots contain biological components, DNA building blocks, this UV frequency will not harm them. They have more rigid molecular bonds than living biological matter, which vibrate in the extreme UV range. Shining light of

the correct colour on them pumps these bonds full of energy
and they vibrate, emitting the energy as light again. Look below
you.

Then it hit her what the Mind was doing. It was tuning the
frequency of the light in Mag-8 until the swarm became visible. She leaned over the gantry railings and peered down at
the ground beneath her.

What she saw made her gasp – or at least the sensation in
her chest was as if she had taken a sharp intake of breath.
Hovering in the air close to the large apparatus was a swirling
cloud of bright sparkling lights that surrounded the focusing
magnet near the entrance point in the ground where the dark-
matter beam would disappear. It was hypnotically beautiful – like
the twilight bioluminescence of a swarm of fireflies, only here
she could not quite make out individual dots of light, but rather
smeared-out clumps. The cloud was changing shape slowly
and hovering in the same location.

The swarm is re-emitting the UV light that it is absorbing,
betraying its presence. This will make it angry.

Shireen found that a very strange way to describe unthink-
ing machines. What did the Mind mean? The swarm could not
show emotions such as anger, but if it was programmed to remain
hidden and then it was threatened . . .
*This UV light is not destroying them, is it?*

No. I cannot increase the energy of the light any higher or it
will damage the instruments.

As if to confirm that the swarm now knew it had been
exposed, it suddenly changed shape from a nebulous cloud into
a concentrated snake-like formation that circled around a few
times, sparkling as it did so. Then, without warning, it darted
upwards, almost too fast for Shireen's avatar eyes to follow, sli-
cing through one of the graphene girders supporting the magnet

structure. It did this several times, back and forth, until Shireen felt a jolt as the platform she was standing on moved slightly.

Had it detected her presence? Was this an attack on her? And if so, how? She wasn't physically there. Could it be somehow sensing her as mere information? Something alien within Mag-8? Maybe cutting through the girder had nothing to do with her. Maybe once it was exposed, its task was to create havoc.

But the swarm now regrouped and was hovering, still sparkling, almost at eye level with where Shireen was standing. It seemed to be waiting for something. Maybe the brief act of destruction was a warning. Maybe it was being petulant, like an indignant toddler.

But she was wrong.

The swarm started to move slowly towards her. *Oh, no. This is crazy. The swarm can't 'see' me.*

And still the swarm came closer. The shimmering lights of the nanobots were now blocking her entire field of vision as it loomed in front of her. Shireen felt terrified. *I'm not really here. I'm not really here.* To prove to herself that it couldn't physically harm her, she slowly reached out her hand to touch the front edge of the swarm. A searing pain shot through her fingers and up her arm, jerking her backwards.

Of course. For the same reason she could feel the solidity of the metal gantry beneath her feet, or the cold metal barrier in front of her, she could touch the nanobots. And if they were able to do to her what they did to that graphene girder . . . *But I'm not even here! The pain I felt is just an illusion. They can't physically harm me. It's all in my head.* And yet her hand and arm were now throbbing with pain. She backed away from the swarm, panic rising, until she came up against the cold metal casing of the magnet wall behind her. She had nowhere else to go.

And still the swarm approached her. It was as though it was contemplating how best to deal with this annoying presence.

*Zak, Zak, pull me back! I don't think I can take the pain if they attack my face!* Where the hell was he?

She felt as though she was experiencing a dreadful nightmare, while knowing it was only a dream. No, this was worse than that. The whole point of total immersive displacement was that the pain she would feel would be as real as anything her physical body could experience. The swarm was now centimetres from her face. It was then that Shireen knew she was going to die. She closed her eyes and waited.

The cold, when it came, penetrated her inner core. She gasped and froze for a few seconds, feeling icier than she had ever felt before, but just as quickly the sensation was gone. She opened her eyes. The swarm was still there, writhing in front of her, but it didn't seem as bright. At first, she didn't understand. It looked almost as though it was evaporating. Then, suddenly, without warning, the entire swarm snapped out of existence. Shireen hardly dared breathe. She waited, trying to make sense of what she had just witnessed.

*Mind, what just happened there? Where's it gone?*

The swarm has been neutralized. The danger is gone, Shireen Darvish.

Around her, the blue light gently returned to the normal LED white.

She remembered the display on her AR. It had changed. It now just read:

TEMPERATURE: 210 KELVIN.

She stared at the words. 210 Kelvin translated to a chilly 63 degrees Celsius below zero. No wonder she had felt cold. The nanobots in her brain must have readjusted the temperature just as they had changed the wavelength of the light. Would they also have protected her from the pain of the swarm if it had attacked? Shireen gave an involuntary shudder.

*Mind. Please explain. Have you just done what I think you've done and frozen the swarm? How could it be that easy? Help me to understand.*

The soothing, almost maternal voice replied.

The bio-molecular building blocks of the nanobots cannot function below 230 Kelvin. All other instrumentation and electronics in the facility is able to operate at optimum levels down to 200 Kelvin. I will maintain this temperature until after Ignition. I have run full diagnostics checks again. All systems and instruments are operational. Damaged graphene girder will complete self-healing in twelve minutes. Misaligned magnet now back in position.

The run will proceed.

Thank you, Shireen Darvish. This has been an interesting experience.

And with a jolt, Shireen was back in the VR garden. The Mind had said its piece and simply ejected her. The transition was so abrupt that for a moment she felt confused. She couldn't make sense of the sudden tranquillity of the garden after the noise inside Mag-8. The near-omniscient presence of the Mind, along with the threat of the swarm, had gone. She felt strangely alone.

*Bring me back please, Zak.*

Gradually, she became aware of a different sensation, one not of standing up, but of lying horizontally. And there was Zak, gently removing her helmet with a worried look on his face. 'Shireen? Shireen. You're back now.' His voice sounded distant, as if he was at the other end of a long tunnel.

Shireen knew she should smile but suddenly felt her stomach heave. Pushing herself up and away from the FBI man, she was violently sick.

She felt his hand on her shoulder. 'I'm so sorry, Zak,' she slurred. She was shivering uncontrollably, and she noticed that she was drenched in sweat. Every inch of her body ached. It felt as though she was one big bruise and her head pounded with a sickly headache.

She could see the concern in Zak's eyes but didn't yet have the strength to stay sitting up and instead flopped back on the chair. Then she looked at him and mumbled, her voice a croak, 'I was right, Zak, there was a swarm inside Mag-8. It . . . it . . .

it was horrible. It would have destroyed everything.' She shud-dered and wiped her mouth with the back of her hand.

The look of horror on Zak's face impelled her to continue quickly. 'But I think it's OK now. The Mind . . . it spoke to me, Zak . . . and it neutralized the swarm . . . Ignition will go ahead.'

Again she tried to smile, because she felt the situation war-ranted it. She couldn't believe she had done it. Or rather, the Mind had done it.

And she couldn't stop shivering.

It was one hundred and sixty minutes to Ignition.

# 45

MARC AND SARAH WERE RELEASED FROM THE BOOSTER HALL a few minutes after Lockdown. They persuaded the younger of the two soldiers guarding the block to lock the door behind them and to remain stationed outside. They had tried and failed to find Hogan inside the labyrinthine building – there were just too many places he could hide – but they were certain he was going nowhere.

It was too late to stop Ignition now, but they still hurried back to the Mag-8 building. Marc attempted to contact Shireen. She wasn't responding.

Inside the facility it was a hive of frantic activity. With a brusque 'C'mon, we need to find Hassan', Marc grabbed Sarah's hand and headed for the control room. They pushed their way through the milling scientists, technicians and officials, but there was no sign of the security chief. Marc recognized one of the younger accelerator physicists and stopped him as he was dashing past. 'Wait. You. What the hell is going on in there?'

'We don't know for sure. No one can make sense of it,' he replied breathlessly. 'The Mind is behaving irrationally. First it went completely dark in there, then the temperature suddenly dropped to colder than a deep-freeze. We've no idea what it's up to.'

'And the Mind hasn't told you anything?'

'No, we're in Lockdown. All we can do is guess at what the issue has been.'

Everything seemed to be falling apart. This was the nightmare scenario. 'So, has it aborted Ignition?'

'No, it seems it's still going ahead. But something is very wrong.' The young man was close to tears. The dismaying conclusion had to be that after everything they had gone through, a Mind had been hacked, again. This was the end of the road.

Qiang now appeared by Marc's side. 'Where've you been? Have you heard? The order has just been given to evacuate both CERN and J-PARC.' He had a wild pleading look in his eyes, as though sure his older colleague could figure out a way to make things right. 'Marc, they say that's all we can do now. That if we can't abort and have to assume Mag-8 has failed then we have to destroy two of the dark-matter labs before Ignition.'

Marc just stared at Qiang. If those labs were destroyed that would knock out six of the eight beams. Yes, they would avert an immediate catastrophe, but it would signal the end of the Odin Project. He was turning to Sarah when his wristpad pinged. Shireen. He didn't really want to talk to the young cyb, but there was an urgency in her voice that focused his mind. She breathlessly recounted what she'd experienced with the Mind.

'Hold on, Shireen, I need to stop you there. I'm going to patch you through to everyone here. They need to hear this from you.' He jabbed at his wristpad, patching her in to the main control-room network. Her face suddenly appeared, multiple times, on the screens in both the control room and the viewing gallery. There were gasps as the young Iranian told her story. Beside him Sarah mouthed, 'Oh, my God,' and held her hands to her mouth. Disbelief quickly turned to amazement and awe as Shireen's account was corroborated by the young FBI cybersecurity officer who stood at her side.

Shireen appeared dazed by what she'd been through. Dark bags shrouded her eyes, her normally olive-coloured skin looked pale and sickly. And yet at that moment, for Marc at least, she was the most beautiful person in the world. It seemed she had just, single-handedly, averted the destruction of all life on Earth.

A tide of relief and excitement was quickly spreading through Mag-8. Surely, thought Marc, the order to destroy those two labs would be rescinded once these new revelations were communicated.

He was snapped out of his reverie by the sudden arrival of General Hassan, who pulled him and Sarah to one side.

'These are extraordinary times, so I will dispense with any apologies for what occurred earlier.'

He didn't look like a man expressing regret and Marc studied him dispassionately. Would he listen to them now?

The officer continued: 'And I admit that I appear not to have had it "all in hand" as I indicated earlier. Your friends in Washington have done something that I do not fully understand, but my scientists inform me that it was both foolish and brave and may indeed have just saved the Project.'

'So, has the order been given to stand down those missiles aimed at CERN and J-PARC?' Marc glanced at Sarah.

'Not yet. That would be foolish. But all the labs around the world have just watched that extraordinary message from Washington. So, the fingers are, shall we say, no longer hovering over the buttons.' He let out a snort that Marc assumed was meant to indicate amusement.

'Good. Because Dr Maitlin has something she needs to tell you.'

Marc nodded to Sarah and then left her to bring the general up to speed on what she had learned from Hogan. He checked the time. 15:05. T-minus 40 minutes. He turned back to Qiang, who appeared to be in a daze.

'How are you holding up, mate?' he asked.

'I'm not sure. I don't think I can cope with much more of this. Anyway, you look pretty terrible yourself.'

'Thanks,' Marc grunted. 'Listen, can we just run through what we know?' Qiang nodded. 'OK . . . So, as far as we can tell, the swarm hasn't caused any irreparable damage, right?

But is there any way that it, or something else, could have infected the Mind itself?'

'I doubt it. I think we just have to trust the Mind now.' Qiang neither sounded nor looked in the least bit reassuring.

'So, tell me, why do I still have this nagging feeling we're missing something?'

Just then Sarah touched him gently on the shoulder. He turned to her.

'A security team have been dispatched to the booster hall to find Hogan,' Sarah said with grim satisfaction.

The general nodded. 'If he's in there, we'll find him. We have to get some answers out of him and we don't have much more time. Now, will you please excuse me?'

Sarah said, 'Marc, Shireen wants to connect up with you, and Qiang too. She can't do much more from her end, but we could use her brain on this.'

'Sure,' said Marc. Everyone else seemed to think that they now had a clear run to Ignition. A bomb had been defused and the swarm had been neutralized. So, why was he still feeling so uneasy? It didn't help that both Qiang and Sarah seemed similarly anxious.

Shireen's voice popped into Marc's ear. She sounded nearly back to her old self. Good. 'Actually, Marc, though of course I'll do anything to help, I really think you and Qiang are best placed to know what could possibly still go wrong. Hopefully nothing, of course. But you two understand the science better than anyone.' Marc looked at Qiang. He couldn't think of anything to contribute.

'Maybe this will help.' Sarah frowned. 'When he thought he'd trapped me, Hogan boasted it would be something *simple*, something that could be easily overlooked. That doesn't sound like he was referring to the nanoswarm. But if not, what could he mean?'

Marc shook his head slowly. 'The Mind should be able to check every tiny component, and if it finds anything wrong it can either correct it or abort Ignition.'

'But what if the swarm has indeed been successful?' suggested Qiang.

Marc and Sarah looked at him. It was Sarah who completed his train of logic. 'Jesus. You mean, when it attacked and sliced through those girders, that was just a distraction? We were meant to think that it had been caught *before* it could carry out its plan—'

'—when in fact, it had already caused the damage it was meant to,' finished Qiang.

The enormity – and implications – of Qiang's suggestion was beginning to sink in when they were distracted by a sudden commotion. Several soldiers had entered and with them a restrained Senator Peter Hogan. Dried blood covered his face and the front of his shirt. He didn't seem to be resisting.

General Hassan turned and screamed at his men. 'Get him out of here! Now!'

One of the soldiers blurted out, 'But, sir, you said to bring him to you as soon as—'

'NOW! *Ibnil kelb!* Take him down to my office.' With that, Hassan marched off behind them out of the control room.

As he was being led away Hogan pulled back for a second and turned to look at Marc and Sarah. And he winked.

Could he sense their worry? Did he know they had thwarted the nanoswarm? And if he did, was there something else? Something so simple that it had occurred to no one?

Marc rubbed his eyes – God, he was tired – and turned to the others. He wasn't an experimentalist. He dealt with equations and lines of computer code, not real magnets and electronic instruments. But it was Shireen he addressed. 'Shireen, are you still hearing all this? OK, you said you first saw the swarm down by the focusing magnet, just above the vertical shaft where the beam disappears. What could—?'

Then it hit him. 'Of course. The shutter! We need to check the shutter,' he shouted. Qiang and Sarah, along with many of the technicians in the room, just stared at him.

'What do you mean?' said Qiang. 'What about the shutter?'

'Think about it. What's the simplest component that could go wrong? I mean, short of flicking a switch that turns off the electricity to the superconducting magnets. Isn't it the shutter that blocks off the beam path?'

'But why would the beam path ever need to be blocked off?' Sarah jumped in. 'That doesn't make sense, Marc.'

But he was no longer listening. He could feel the adrenalin beginning to kick in as he looked around the control room. 'Where's Maher? I need to see Maher.' He hurried to the nearest Mag-8 technician, a young woman sitting at a terminal desk. 'Where is Maher?'

'Who?' she blurted, looking nervous.

'Maher bloody Haydar. Your boss! The chief fucking accelerator engineer. Where is he?'

'Oh, I . . . I—'

'Never mind. I'll find him.' Marc knew he should stop and explain, but never had time been more precious.

'Wait there,' he yelled over his shoulder at Sarah and Qiang as he barged out of the control room. 'I'll be back in a minute.'

He ran down the metal steps to ground level. The Project's engineer was talking to a couple of technicians by one of the giant steel doors that secured the interior of the Mag-8 hall from the outside world.

'Haydar!' Marc yelled. The man looked up, a concerned expression on his face.

'What is it, Professor Bruckner? You look like you've seen a jinn.'

'The shutter on the focusing magnet,' Marc began. 'You told me it was both the simplest and the most important component in the whole place, correct?'

'It is, yes.' The engineer smiled. 'If that shutter is closed when the chargino pulse reaches the quadrupole, then it will be blocked entirely.' He paused, a frown crossing his face. 'Why do you ask?'

'And you'd know if it was closed, right?'

Maher Haydar, a man fiercely proud of SESAME and what had been achieved with Mag-8, looked at him as if he had lost his mind. 'But *of course* it is open. We made sure it's open and the Mind will have done so too.'

'Yes, yes, but is there a way of checking now?'

Haydar looked bewildered, then relaxed a little. 'Professor, of all the things we have to be concerned with, believe me, the focusing-magnet shutter is not one of them. Even if it, somehow, got closed again – say from a sudden wind blowing off the desert, through some foul miraculous trickery of Iblis himself – then it would trigger a warning and the Mind would know about it.'

Out of the corner of his eye, Marc noticed that the two engineers Maher had been talking to were shaking their heads as though he were a fool. He ignored them.

'Damn it, tell me if I'm wrong—' He paused, to gather his thoughts. He had to get this right. No room for any mistakes now. 'Every one of the thousands of components within the Mag-8 facility has a multitude of instruments and sensors, monitoring and calibrating constantly, making sure everything is running smoothly, and ready to warn the Mind about any anomaly, yes?'

'That is correct.'

'Everything, apart from the shutter in the beam line just below the quadrupole magnet. That's the one component that relies on old technology. We joked about this a couple of days ago. It's so that it can be operated manually. It has a safety override that allows human intervention.'

'Again, correct, Professor. I don't understand where—'

'So how does the Mind know if it is open or closed?'

'Well, of course there is a sensor there that tells it—'

'—but just the one sensor, right? Not like every other component in Mag-8.'

'Just the one, yes. We build in redundancies, but in some cases that really isn't necessary.'

Marc grabbed the Jordanian by the shoulders. 'And what if that were damaged somehow – say its electronics had been fried, so the Mind still thought it was open when it wasn't?'

Maher stared at him in stunned silence for a couple of seconds, then he looked down at the pad he was holding and tapped it. As he did so he said, 'There is a camera inside the magnet casing pointing directly at the shutter, that is not currently in use. It is not linked to the main network controlled by the Mind, so I may be able to turn it on remotely.'

Suddenly, the engineer let out a horrified whimper. He looked up at Marc and turned the pad towards him so he could see the screen. Marc felt a chill run through him. There was the shutter – a ten-centimetre-thick lead disc the diameter of a dinner plate – and it was sitting across the opening through which the chargino beam was due to pass in a few minutes' time.

He looked up at the engineer. 'Is there any way of getting inside Mag-8 and manually opening that shutter?'

Haydar had a glazed look on his face. The man was in complete shock. 'Maher!' Marc shouted. 'Please!'

The Jordanian's eyes refocused. 'There is a way, yes. But to use it . . . it would be suicide.'

Marc checked the time: five minutes to Ignition. 'Where? How? Talk to me, damn it.'

Haydar's eyes brimmed with tears. He nodded. 'Follow me,' he said, his voice no more than a whisper. He turned, his colleagues seemingly forgotten, and walked quickly away, with Marc at his shoulder.

'There's a way in around the other side. Few people know about it. The Mind certainly doesn't. There are no sensors there and the entrance is made entirely from basic non-smart materials, so it's totally off-grid.'

As they made their way round the building, Marc went over what he knew. If the shutter was closed, all the charginos would be stopped before they transformed back into neutralinos. There would be no contribution from Mag-8 to provide the precise balance required in the core when the other seven beams met, and that would be that. He cursed under his breath. He couldn't believe it, after all these months. This was the nightmare scenario everyone had worked so hard to avoid. They had to open that shutter, and they had less than five minutes to do it. They were now in a quiet corridor that skirted the concrete shielding dome that housed the giant bending magnets. On the far side of Mag-8, Haydar stopped at a large, nondescript grey metal door. He stared at it for a moment as though he'd forgotten why he was there.

'Maher. Now open it, please!'

Haydar turned to him, an expression of desperate sadness on his face. 'But, Professor Bruckner, it won't do any good. We've got no time to send a bot in there. And even if we did, the Mind wouldn't let it get very far.'

Marc paused and took a deep breath. 'I know,' he said. 'We're not sending a bot in. *I'm* going in. Now open the goddam door!'

'It's four minutes to Ignition, Professor. You don't have time. And if you are in there when the beam arrives . . . the radiation burst . . . Also, it's sixty degrees below zero in there at the moment. You won't last four minutes without proper—'

Marc sighed. 'Just open the door, Maher. What other choice do we have?'

Haydar must have sensed something in his voice, because he turned and punched a multiple-digit number into a keypad by the door, and it clicked open. Marc pushed past him.

And he was running – running through a narrow alleyway that zigzagged between concrete shielding walls that towered like smooth white cliffs metres above him. He could feel the air getting colder. It was beginning to hurt his chest, so he tried to take shorter breaths. It occurred to him that he hadn't got around to calling Evie. Damn it. She'd be so cross with him. And now he was letting her down again. He thought about Sarah and Qiang. He didn't think they could see him from the control room. Just as well. He knew he had to do this. It was the only way. The Odin Project was his greatest achievement and he wasn't prepared for it to fail now. Not when they were so close. The earlier panic and stress seemed to fall away. He had a job to do.

He emerged in the large open chamber. Above him rose the array of giant magnets, their superconducting coils humming a deep monotonous tone that he could feel in his bones. Ahead, at the very centre of the hall, was the quadrupole magnet itself, suspended above the borehole down which the dark-matter beam would travel to the Earth's core. If it could.

As he hurried towards it, he was stopped in his tracks by a sound that reverberated around the dome. It was the Mind, and it sounded like the voice of God.

> Marc Bruckner. You should not be here. I cannot allow you to compromise the run.

Even though he had been expecting it, and knew it was nothing more than a synthetic voice generated by an artificial intelligence, it still filled him with awe. Yet he couldn't allow it to distract him. As he ran, he shouted out, 'Listen to me. I have been speaking with Shireen Darvish. The swarm you destroyed has already compromised the run. The shutter on the quadrupole magnet is closed.'

> This cannot be so. My diagnostics would have alerted me.

He stopped briefly. The cold felt like sandpaper on the back of his throat. Where was the entrance to the central chamber? He looked up. 'The shutter sensor was destroyed by the swarm. You can't rely on what it's telling you. You must be able to check a different way. I mean, you're a fucking Mind.'

The cold was seeping through to his core and every breath he took in was like a sharp knife in his chest.

There was the briefest of pauses before the Mind responded.

> You are correct. The shutter is closed. I am unable to open it.

'Then abort the run. Now.'

> I can do that. But there is a risk.

'Oh, my God. Why?'

It is T-minus one hundred and twenty seconds. All three accelerators now have their proton-beam energies ramped up. The
only way to abort now is to close six of the other seven shutters too and block the beams.

Marc tried to understand what he was hearing, but the cold
seemed to be seeping into his brain, slowing it down. Why six
shutters? Why not all seven? Yes, because they could afford to
have one beam pass through, because it would simply carry on
uninterrupted through the Earth and out the other side.
    The Mind was still talking.

I have just communicated with the other Minds and determined
that there is a non-negligible probability that one or more of
them will not comply with my decision to close their shutters.
They estimate there is a twenty per cent probability that the
swarm has compromised me too and therefore cannot trust
that I am being truthful.
    If three or more Minds do not close their shutters, it will
lead to catastrophic failure of the Project. I calculate a 42.32
per cent probability for this outcome.

He'd heard enough. *What's the point of entrusting so much
to artificial intelligences if they are just as bloody unreason-
able as humans?* If he left now the Mind would order the other
shutters to be closed. A forty-two per cent chance of disaster
was too high. Too terrible to contemplate.
    *Fuck it. So, this was it, then. He'd have to do it manually.*
    Hoping that the Mind would understand what he was about to
do, Marc Bruckner ran towards the quadrupole casing, searching
for the way in. He was shivering uncontrollably now, and his
breath came out in great white plumes. There! A gap between
two three-metre-high metal towers packed with electronic
instruments. He squeezed in between them and there it was. The
magnet sat inside its chamber, large enough for a man to fit inside
when not operational but it was now under high vacuum.

And the shutter was somewhere inside.

The small porthole in the side wall of the chamber had frosted over, which meant he couldn't see inside.

How much time did he have left? His AR contacts had frozen and were useless now. He knew it couldn't be very long.

Everything was covered in a white frost. At first, he didn't know where to start, but then, as though the gods were finally taking pity on him, he spotted a lever. A good old-fashioned lever. The edge of a metal panel was just visible through the frost beneath it. Using his sleeve to wipe the panel clear, he saw what he was looking for. Bold red letters declared: **SHUTTER MANUAL OVERRIDE**.

Of course, something as important as a beam shutter would always have a mechanical lever for an operator to control during construction and testing. He grabbed hold of the metal bar with both hands. The searing pain of the cold metal scalding his palms and fingers shot up his arms. He tried to pull the lever downwards, but it wouldn't move. He realized that his hands had now frozen to the lever too. He felt himself smile. He wasn't quite sure why but a strange thought ran through his head. *I am one with my experiment. I am now physically part of the Odin Project.* He knew he was becoming weaker – his breathing shallower. Was hypothermia setting in? Probably. He thought of Evie. He could see her. She was admonishing him for taking such a stupid risk. But Evie, and Sarah and Qiang and everyone else he'd ever known, wouldn't be around anyway to know that he'd tried. And with that realization came a renewed sense of urgency.

He leaned his entire weight on the lever and, without warning, it swivelled downwards.

Had he done it? Had he made it in time?

He managed somehow to pull his hands from the lever, ripping away layers of skin but feeling nothing. A voice from somewhere deep in his mind was telling him it wasn't such a great idea to hang around here. But he was feeling so sleepy now. And it didn't seem nearly as cold any more. The Mind – the other one – was saying something too, but he was no longer listening.

His vision was blurring and he tried to rub his eyes with his ruined hands. As his lungs began to freeze, his shallow breath was no longer creating a white fog in front of his face. His mind felt heavy and slow. He tried to recall what he was doing here. Then from deep within his barely conscious self, he remembered. He'd done it. He'd cleared the path to the Earth's core. Come on through, little neutralinos. I've opened the gate for you. The thought gave him the beginnings of a smile on his frozen lips just as he felt a mild tingling sensation followed by a sour taste in his mouth. Then, just as quickly, it was gone.

He had a brief moment of clarity. He *had* made it in time after all. The pulse of dark matter had just passed through Mag-8 and was on its way down to the core, leaving in its wake a burst of high-energy x-rays, and good ol' Marc Bruckner had just received a lethal fifty Sievert dose, equivalent to several thousand CT scans all at once.

His legs gave way beneath him and he slowly folded to the ground. The lyrics of an old song came into his head: *Que será, será*. He began to hum tunelessly.

*I'm so sorry, Evie. I love you so much.*

And then . . . nothing.

# 46

*Tuesday, 17 September – 15:47, Mag-8, Amman*

EVERYONE WAS RUNNING. AS SOON AS IGNITION HAD TAKEN place, the Mind had raised the temperature inside the Mag-8 and ended the Lockdown. Sarah reached Marc a few paces ahead of Qiang. Maher Haydar, the Mag-8 chief engineer, had been alongside her, going on and on about how Professor Bruckner had saved the world. But Sarah didn't need to be told what had happened. All she knew was that Marc had been inside during Ignition.

She pushed aside two paramedic bots that had arrived at the scene quickest and dropped down beside Marc's prone figure. She lifted his head gently off the ground and cradled it in her lap.

His eyelids slowly opened and he looked up at her. 'Sarah? Sorry, I can't see very well,' he said, his voice a hoarse whisper.

She didn't know what to say and couldn't stop the tears rolling down her cheeks.

'The shutter was closed, Sarah. I had to open it.' His voice was so faint now, she had to bend down to hear him.

'I know it was. You did a very brave thing. Very stupid, but brave.' She didn't need to tell him that he'd just received a fatal dose of radiation.

His breathing was shallow now and he was shivering

uncontrollably. She looked down at his ravaged hands. The skin hung off them in long red shreds. As she stroked his head, she could feel the cold seeping from him.

'Sarah, have you heard from the other facilities? Did they all work?'

'I guess we'll know soon enough.' She smiled down at him. If any of the eight beams had failed or missed the central collision spot, a seismic wave could come up anywhere on the Earth's surface, but satellites would tell them instantly if it did. Maybe this was the time for loved ones to hold each other tight as they awaited their fate. All she could do now was to sit with Marc and cradle him in her arms, talk to him. Reassure him.

Marc smiled back weakly. 'I expect they'll put up statues of us in years to come. Make sure mine is huge, won't you?'

Sarah laughed shakily through her tears. 'I'm sure it will be. It has to match your ego, after all.'

She felt she should keep talking to him but wasn't sure he was still listening. He seemed to be drifting in and out of consciousness.

Only vaguely aware of the minutes passing by, she tried to care about whether the Project had been successful or not, but found she couldn't. If they'd failed then everything would be over in a few minutes anyway. It was right that she and Marc were together at the end.

It was then that Sarah became aware of a growing and palpable sense of elation and relief around her. People had started clapping and cheering. Dared she hope that the Odin Project had worked? It certainly sounded as if it hadn't failed – not in the way Peter Hogan had planned. She leaned closer to the man she realized she loved. 'Hey, Professor Marc Bruckner. You did it. We did it. I have a feeling it will work, too.'

Marc's eyes fluttered briefly. 'Ah, I hope so . . . Make sure Qiang gets most of the credit . . . He was always the smarter one, you know. And if it doesn't work . . . blame Qiang. It was his stupid idea.' He let out a breath and closed his eyes. His shivering had stopped.

She thought he'd lost consciousness again, but he now whispered so quietly she could barely hear him: 'And Sarah . . . um, thank you. Thank you . . . for making me . . . the man I never . . . I never knew I could be.'

They were his last words.

# 47

*Friday, 22 November – Southsea, England*

SARAH'S FEET CRUNCHED ON THE SHINGLE AS SHE WALKED. The Southsea beach was deserted, which she found surprising considering what a beautiful day it was on the English south coast. There was a chill in the air and she was glad of her thick jacket, but the sun was bright and the sky a clear blue. She looked out to sea; across the Solent, the Isle of Wight seemed a lot closer than usual. Often, she could barely make out its tree-lined hills through the mist and sea fog. Today, its water-front buildings glittered as their windows reflected the afternoon sun.

The days were getting a little easier now, even though her sense of loss was still so palpable. Wasn't it strange that Marc had now been gone for longer than the length of time she'd loved him when he was alive? She'd wondered whether her feelings for him had been magnified by the extraordinary circumstances in which they'd found themselves – not only because so much responsibility had rested on their shoulders, but because of a sense that they might have so little time together. That last bit at least had been true. She'd wondered too how much what she felt now was guilt – that she and the world had survived thanks to him – or gratitude for his selfless act.

No, this gaping emptiness inside her was real.

But yes, it was getting easier. Now, she did all her crying as

she walked along Southsea beach. Marc used to hum one particular tune all the time. It drove her mad: a song by his
favourite band, the Killers, called 'Mr Brightside'. So, every
day, she walked along the beach, playing 'Mr Brightside' as
loudly as she could, over and over again. And the tears would
flow freely. Her parents had of course been supportive, but she
still preferred to spend most of her time alone, even away from
the beach, unable to share in the feelings of hope that so many
people desperately clung to.

Two months had passed since Ignition, and the world was getting used to the reality that it still had to deal with the same old
problems facing humanity, even if the immediate threat from the
Purifiers had now receded. Although there had been plenty of
false dawns, with many people claiming they had detected a
strengthening in the magnetic field, the official line maintained
that these were just isolated remnants that had been there before
Ignition. A dying magnetic field wouldn't fail uniformly around
the globe – there would be pockets of it that survived for longer.

The fact was, no one had a clue how a planet-sized
defibrillator – essentially what the Odin Project had been –
might work in reality; how long it would take for the energy
from the dark-matter collision to turn the chaotic, turbulent
eddies of the molten iron and nickel core into a regular flow
that would kick-start and sustain a magnetic field again. But
there was undoubtedly a general hope that the darkest days
just might be over.

Sarah left the beach and climbed up to the footpath that
skirted around the sea-facing battlements of Southsea Castle.
The sixteenth-century artillery fort built for Henry VIII offered
a stark reminder of permanence and nostalgia. She still recalled
long summer days playing here with her brother, racing him to
be the first to climb up and sit astride one of its huge, now
ornamental, cannons outside the gates.

For a few weeks after Ignition she'd just felt numb. Returning to England, she had tried, mostly successfully, to avoid the
media circus. After her testimony in court and her recorded
conversation with Hogan had been released, she had insisted

on being left alone, hiding away from the spotlight. Many were desperate for her to tell her story, so she felt grateful that there were people around her to shield her from the frenzy.

The hardest thing she'd had to do was travel to New York to meet Evie and Charlotte. At Evie's request, they'd met in Bryant Park. She had wanted to know every detail about what her father had done, and why it had to be him.

It had felt awkward initially with Charlotte being there too and Sarah was grateful to her when she said she would leave them alone for a while. They had sat together on a park bench and talked. After a while, the words dried up, so they sat and held hands in silence.

She'd met up with Qiang on that trip too. He'd been giving evidence to the UN before his return to China. He said he was being hailed as a national hero back home even though there was no indication at all that the Project had succeeded in its mission.

She hadn't heard from Shireen for a few weeks now, but the young woman continued to impress her with her maturity. Despite all the media attention and the lucrative job offers, all the Iranian cyb had wanted to do was to get back home to her parents and to finish her studies.

Now, over the last couple of weeks, the number of reports of a strengthening field had seemed to be growing. Sarah had ignored them all. She could, if she'd wanted, have very easily checked the overall status of the magnetosphere from the hundreds of measurements and simulations being carried out. But that wasn't the way she wanted to do this.

Every day for the past six weeks, come rain or shine, she had come out for her walk along the seafront. And every day she would stop at the same spot, at the base of Southsea Castle below the black and white striped lighthouse, and take out the little compass that had been a gift from her grandfather. He had given it to her when she was eight. They had stood in this very spot, and he'd shown her how its needle always pointed due north, away from the water, past the lighthouse and across the Common, towards the city of Portsmouth.

Today, she stopped as usual and reached into her pocket. She had taken to going through the motions so absent-mindedly these days that the mere act of holding the compass flat on the palm of her hand had in itself become a ritual. She would watch the needle spin around aimlessly for a few seconds and then place it back in her pocket, never truly allowing herself to believe. Today, however, something about the little instrument from a long-forgotten era dragged her gaze back down to it. She twisted and wobbled it between her thumb and forefinger. The needle no longer moved around freely beneath its glass casing. Instead it behaved in a way it hadn't done for a long time. It remained resolutely fixed. But now it pointed across the Solent – not due north as it used to, but due south. The Earth's magnetic field had flipped, and it had recovered suffi-cient strength to grip and align the tiny magnetic needle.

The Killers played in her ears. Destiny was calling to Mr Brightside to open up his eager eyes.

She felt the familiar warm tears rolling down her cheeks. But this time they weren't just tears of sadness. She looked out to sea, then back at the compass, afraid that, like a holographic projection, it might just fade away.

The needle was holding firm. And it was the most beautiful thing she had ever seen.

# Technical Note on Dark Matter

THE CENTRAL PREMISE OF THE ODIN PROJECT RESTS ON THE behaviour of dark matter. But how accurate is this scientifically? Well, let me make a couple of things clear. Firstly, dark matter is real. It is what holds galaxies together. In fact, there is five times more dark matter in the universe than normal matter. The problem is that, as of the time of writing in December 2018, we still don't know what dark matter is made of. Whatever its constituent particles are, they are nothing we currently know of. Physicists refer to it as 'non-baryonic matter'. We know dark matter feels the force of gravity but not the electromagnetic force (which is what allows it to pass through normal matter as though it weren't there). The second point is that it is indeed the case that one of the potential candidates for dark matter is called the neutralino, a hypothetical particle predicted by a still speculative theory called Supersymmetry. My concern in using the neutralino in *Sunfall* was that it would either be discovered before the book came out or, even worse, ruled out entirely by some new experimental result; and that another particle would be discovered to be what dark matter is really made of. But, so far, so good. Neutralinos are still in the running.

As for dark-matter beams self-interacting, well that is sort of correct, as far as we currently know. However, I have taken some liberty here in the sense that self-interaction of dark matter is likely to be rather weak, otherwise we would see evidence of it in astronomy. But then if the beams are intense and energetic enough when they collide . . .

The other business of decay of heavy neutralinos into charginos and back again to light neutralinos – all that stuff necessary for the bending magnets to work – is, well, not wrong, just oversimplified. Theoretical physicists around the world are currently working on speculative mathematical models with such technical names as the Minimal Supersymmetric Standard Model with complex parameters (or cMSSM) and the cosmological concordance model, $\Lambda$CDM, which is read 'Lambda-CDM', standing for Cold Dark Matter plus the Cosmological constant. Well, you did ask! What's that? You didn't? Oh, OK.

# Acknowledgements

WELL, THAT WAS AN ADVENTURE! OVER THE PAST THREE years, whenever I was able to prise open a sufficient block of free time – a day here, a weekend there, evenings and long journeys – I would immerse myself in an exciting world of my own creation. Escaping from my familiar, solid reality of academic teaching and research, broadcasting and, crucially, *non-fiction* writing, I would shut myself away in my study at home in Southsea, shake off the deterministic shackles of having to understand the real world and soar over a universe where I got to play God, proactively deciding for myself where the dice would fall.

Don't get me wrong – imagination and creativity are just as important in my scientific research as they are in storytelling, so it's not as though I had to flick a switch in my brain every time I sat down and teleported myself into this new reality I was building. It's just that, well, I'd not been used to such freedom.

As an academic scientist, I have always been at ease with facts and mathematical truths, with theories and hypotheses that describe some aspect or mechanism in the natural world, tested and checked against empirical data and observation. I am also an *explainer* – what I have understood about the nature and workings of the physical universe, I have endeavoured to transmit and describe as best as I can through my broadcasting work and non-fiction writing over the past twenty years.

So, making stuff up? Really? Was I allowed to do that? Would I be thrown out of the Royal Society of London for besmirching the good names of Newton, Darwin and Faraday? Would my students believe anything I tell them ever again?

Well, to hell with it. I have discovered that writing fiction is just as exhilarating as scientific research. And by freeing myself from the fetters of describing the world 'as it is', I can take the smallest of sideways steps into a world that 'could be'; one, by the way, in which no laws of physics are violated – I could never bring myself to invent bad science – and one that our own world could easily become in the near future. Indeed, *Sunfall* is our world. Of course, I have speculated – here and there I have pushed what we currently know a little beyond the comfort zone of established science – but I reckon I can still look my colleagues in solar physics, particle physics, dark-matter physics, computer science and nanotechnology (it's a long list) directly in the eye. And I am indebted to all those who have reassured me that everything I describe in the book is utterly plausible. I am also grateful to the nearly two hundred remarkable scientists and engineers that I have had the privilege of interviewing over the past seven years on my BBC Radio programme, *The Life Scientific*. These men and women have not made me a polymath – my brain couldn't possibly retain all the information that I have picked up – but they have opened my eyes to the vast range of exciting science across so many different fields being carried out at the moment, and I have tried to include as much of it as I can in this book.

As for my leap into fiction writing itself, with all the aplomb and subtlety of a swimming-pool dive bomb, well, it turns out there's more to the craft than mere storytelling. And so, for all his patient guidance, advice and tutelage, I have to thank, first and foremost, my editor at Transworld, Simon Taylor. When I first started the book, I came clean with Simon that I had never even taken a basic creative-writing course. He reassured me that he was prepared to roll up his sleeves and guide me throughout the process. He has been true to his word. So, thank you Simon; I am sure that the word count of all your notes and comments that have helped me shape *Sunfall* over many drafts must come close to that of the book itself.

As always, and as I have done repeatedly over the almost two decades we have worked together, I would like to thank my literary agent, Patrick Walsh. As all those many authors under Patrick's wing will attest, he is far more than just an agent. His encouragement, advice, comments, suggestions and amendments to the story meant that I actually had two excellent editors to guide me.

I owe a huge debt of gratitude to both Charlotte Van Wijk and Julie Crisp who went through early drafts of the manuscript so carefully and offered so many brilliant suggestions that have vastly improved and tightened the storyline and plot.

Among friends and colleagues who also read early drafts and offered suggestions and advice, the two that stand out are Richard Millington and Mark Richardson. Thank you both for indulging me, and I hope you enjoy reading the final product. I must also thank my Surrey University colleagues, Justin Read for his advice on dark matter, and Alan Woodward for his words of wisdom on cybersecurity.

I am indebted to Elizabeth Dobson, a wonderful (and incredibly thorough) copy-editor, for all her corrections and suggestions for tightening up, smoothing over and making the various plotlines consistent. Thank you also to Vivien Thompson at Transworld who looked after the copy-editing and proofreading stages of the book.

I am immensely grateful to, and hopefully forgiven by, the many people I know – friends, colleagues and family members – from whom I have stolen names, identities and personality traits. Particular thanks to my sister, Shireen Al-Khalili (here it really was just your name that I borrowed), to my friend, solar physicist Lucie Green, to my ex-postdoc, particle physicist Qiang Zhao, and of course to CERN director-general, Fabiola Gianotti.

Last but not least, of course, I must thank my wife, Julie, who, as ever, is always there to steady the ship. Her calm, organized mind compliments my chaotic, flitting one. Whenever I'm asked how I have managed to fit writing a novel into my schedule, I always say that I have Julie to thank for maintaining order and sanity in my life and for helping me slot the different pieces neatly together. She's always been good at jigsaw puzzles.

## ABOUT THE AUTHOR

JIM AL-KHALILI OBE, FRS IS A QUANTUM PHYSICIST, AUTHOR and broadcaster based at the University of Surrey, where he holds a joint chair in physics and the public engagement in science. He has written ten books, translated into over twenty languages. He is a regular presenter of TV science documentaries and also presents the long-running weekly BBC Radio 4 programme *The Life Scientific*. A recipient of the Royal Society Michael Faraday Medal, the Institute of Physics Kelvin Medal and the inaugural Stephen Hawking Medal for Science Communication, he is also the current president of the British Science Association. He was appointed OBE in 2007 for services to science and was elected a fellow of the Royal Society in 2018. *Sunfall* is his first novel.